To my wife Debbie,
because she knows where all
the skeletons are buried.

From the Private Patient Files
of Dr. Ford Freud

www.mascotbooks.com

Dr. Ford Freud: Skeletons Are Not Scary

For more information, please contact:
Mascot Books
620 Herndon Parkway, Suite 320
Herndon, VA 20170
info@mascotbooks.com

Library of Congress Control Number: 2021912304

CPSIA Code: PRV1021A
ISBN-13: 978-1-64543-803-8

Printed in the United States

Dr. Ford Freud:

SKELETONS
ARE NOT SCARY

J. A. Ford

Book Three of the Fordian Trilogy

CONTENTS

University City Sentinel

April 16, 1978

LOCAL PHYSICIAN HAS BECOME A HOUSEHOLD NAME, BUT HE'S NOT HAPPY ABOUT IT!

By Willy Woodward
(on assignment with United Press International)

One of University City's greatest scholars has recently become a household name . . . but he's *not at all* pleased about the notoriety!

Dr. Ford Freud is a physician, psychologist, psychiatrist, and modern art enthusiast who was featured in recently published books that bear his name. *Dr. Ford Freud: A Cure for Nightmares* and *Dr. Ford Freud: Proving Monsters Don't Exist* focus on two children who received psychiatric assessment and treatment from him. These books have shown a broad appeal to young and adult readers alike and have made Dr. Freud a celebrity not only in University City, but nationwide.

"It is appalling to me that despite all of my important scholarly writings and compelling research into the human mind, it is the garbage written by Mr. Ford that has made me famous, or shall I say, infamous," Dr. Freud scoffed during a recent interview. "People should recognize me because of my groundbreaking work studying the human mind, not the unsubstantiated tripe published by the *alleged* author Mr. Ford."

To publicize his ongoing research at the University, the world-renowned physician granted this journalist the opportunity to discuss the areas of human behavior he is studying.

He also advised me he wanted to set the record straight about the two books that have been written about him. The longer Dr. Freud spoke about the books, the redder his face became. Dr. Freud is infuriated by the author's failure to stick to the facts surrounding his analysis and treatment of difficult patients.

"At the conclusion of the first book, my patient becomes some kind of ethereal being who weaves complex dreams for sleeping children. This was followed by a book wherein my young patient was allegedly stolen from his family by a tentacled monster living under his bed. These books were supposed to be in-depth investigations into some of my most challenging patient files, but they are actually nothing more than preposterous musings of an ex-lawyer."

Despite the fact Dr. Freud is thoroughly displeased with these two books and does not want to have any further contact with the author, he's been advised by his legal team he's contractually obligated to do so. "My attorneys have concluded I am required to finish the trilogy," Dr. Freud bemoaned, shaking his head. "I must tell you I find it suspicious that my attorneys and Mr. Ford are all of the same profession. There is apparently no honor among thieves!"

Even though Dr. Freud is required to provide additional patient files to Mr. Ford for the third book, he refuses to further interact with the author. "Instead of spending time with attorneys or ex-attorneys, one would be better off with pursuits of a similar quality, such as bathing in liquid sewage."

A TROPHY CASE BEFITTING A LIVING LEGEND

Dr. Freud showed me his impressive display case, which is chock full of impressive awards. It's Dr. Freud's hope that the public will ignore the characterizations penned by Mr. Ford, and instead recognize him for his many professional citations.

"For example, I am particularly proud of the most recent accolade bestowed upon me by the Occupational and Observational Psychiatry Society," the professor declared, tapping the glass of his trophy case. He pointed to a large gleaming award depicting two open hands reaching towards an overturned can of paint. Engraved on the statue were the words, "In recognition for a lifetime of scholarly work: Dr. Ford Freud, honorary member of O.O.P.S."

"I was elected the Chair of the Psychology Department more than twenty years ago," Dr. Freud stated. "After that I was elected the Sofa of the Sociology Department, then most recently I was chosen to be the Ottoman of the Occupational Psychology Department."

"I have been honored to consult with law enforcement on several interesting cases." Dr. Freud pointed to another award: a brass sculpture of Lady Liberty holding the scales of justice, with the engraving, "To Dr. Ford Freud: with thanks from the State Police."

"This statue was bestowed upon me by a group of police detectives who were wise enough to seek me out to evaluate their case. Much like Lady Liberty, I can see all truths. I have interviewed hundreds of these criminals, in part because I can see through deception as if it was nothing but a window. If you lie to me, I will detect it."

"Isn't Lady Liberty blindfolded? How can she see any-thing?" I asked Dr. Freud.

"Because she is merely wearing the Blindfold of Justice."

"Okay, but it's still a blindfold, right?"

"Yes, but it's imbued with justice." Dr. Freud explained, once again tapping on the glass of his trophy case. "I have provided services to law enforcement in several states, as well as the Federal Bureau of Investigation in the developing field of forensic psychology. Law enforcement has gradually realized that a learned professor such as myself can be of great value in criminal investigations."

I asked the doctor to provide an example of what he does for law enforcement.

"Of course, I am bound by a code of ethics and cannot provide specific details that would prejudice any ongoing cases. However, I am sure you will find it interesting how an expert such as myself can forward the interests of public safety and justice through the application of modern behavioral science.

"The vast majority of criminal cases do not require my services. Usually either the motive and/or circumstances of violent crimes are established through police investigation. A significant number of criminals confess to the crimes, especially when law enforcement confronts them with the physical evidence. Crimes often arise because of drugs or alcohol. Still others are simply crimes of passion, committed when a criminal cannot control his impulses.

"The cases in which I am consulted fall outside these typical circumstances. In particular, I have developed an expertise in dealing with a certain kind of criminal: those who claim they had no control over their body when they committed their crime. These cretins claim they have no recollection whatsoever of committing the act, or testify their minds and bodies were somehow hijacked by an unknown force during the crime."

Dr. Freud couldn't help but chuckle at the preposterous claim.

"Despite the fact they have no history of psychosis, drug abuse, or alcohol abuse, these patients will nevertheless swear they had absolutely no control over their bodies. Sometimes they postulate that some unknown force usurped their will-power, causing them to commit unspeakable acts despite their unwillingness to do so. I have been asked to examine and inter-view such persons, for the purpose of determining the validity of such claims. Over the years, I have travelled throughout the country, as well as overseas to evaluate such patients."

I asked the doctor if this was similar to the patient described in the 1973 book *Sybil*, which tells of a woman's harrowing episodes of not being able to remember what she did.

"That person alleged there were times her conscious mind 'turned itself off.' She further claimed to have no recollection of her actions committed during these episodes. As I recall from my quick perusal of that over-hyped popular book, she stated at times she felt she was there, but simultaneously *not* there. This kind of 'out of body' experience coupled with amnesia is referred to by some psychologists as a fugue state." Dr. Freud shook his head in disgust. "What I have discovered through my research is that there is no such thing as a fugue state. The of-ficial diagnosis of 'Fugue Dissociative Disorder' should have been removed from the scholarly literature years ago. In my lifetime, I hope that it will be expunged from our books.

"The truth of the matter is patients who claim not to realize that they are committing a crime, or who allege they have experienced fugue episodes, are simply trying to avoid the consequences of their inappropriate behavior. These patients concoct these stories out of thin air in order to avoid prosecution. Their stories are as ridiculous and unfounded as the two books written about me by Mr. Ford."

If what the doctor says is true, I asked him why many of

these people have been able to pass lie detector tests.

"Because they manage to convince themselves their fictional stories are indeed true. Remember: denial is not just a river in Egypt. Due to my insight and expert testimony at trial, the vast majority of these charlatans have been convicted and incarcerated."

Readers will no doubt recall the case of Richard Bogart, who in 1968 brutally beat his brother to death in University City. Mr. Bogart vehemently pled his innocence, claiming he had absolutely no recollection of the event. Confronted with the fact two witnesses watched him commit the crime, Mr. Bogart provided a bizarre explanation. At trial, he testified his body had been somehow hijacked by someone else, and it was this person or entity who committed the crime. Dr. Freud testified in that criminal trial on behalf of the prosecution, explaining that Mr. Bogart was of sound mind, and that a guilty conscience had the ability to forcibly eliminate unpleasant memories. Thanks in part to Dr. Freud's expert testimony, Mr. Bogart was found guilty by the jury.

DR. FREUD'S RESEARCH ON COMMON CHILDHOOD FEARS AND FANTASIES

Without a doubt, Dr. Freud is a workaholic. As soon as he completes a research study, he quickly moves on to another project. This work ethic explains why Professor Freud's name appears on such a diverse collection of research papers.

"Currently I am exploring the fascinating arena of common childhood fantasies," he explained. "Your readers will no doubt find it interesting to learn that some childhood fantasies exist in nearly all cultures. For example, a fascinating belief a child may develop is a concern he is not being raised by his true parents. A little boy may convince himself he is actually a prince.

Once the error is recognized and his royal parents rescue him, he fantasizes becoming king. Girls, naturally, believe that they are princesses and that someday they will be lucky enough to sit beside a king.

"These children envision being liberated from the doldrums of everyday life and rewarded with the royal title and esteemed status that is rightfully theirs. Psychologists have coined this the 'Foundling Fantasy Syndrome.' What is amusing is children always fantasize that their true parents are people of power and integrity: noble kings, skilled professional athletes, intelligent physicians, and the like. Children never believe that they are actually the offspring of undesirable people such as day laborers, convicted felons, or trial attorneys."

Dr. Freud tapped his temple with his index finger and continued, "What I am researching is why a child's brain concocts such a ridiculous fantasy. Why does this abnormal thought pattern develop in otherwise normal children, and how do we stop it?"

Dr. Freud explained that this research is an offshoot of his groundbreaking discovery that certain childhood fears are seen in youngsters across socio-economic classes and cultures. "I discovered that children in vastly different societies share a number of common fears. To wit, we see the fear of being taken from their parents in all cultures. Being afraid of the dark, monsters, and skeletons are other common childhood fears existing across the globe. This led me to investigate why children develop such similar fears. What is the psychological abnormality which causes a child in Africa to be just as afraid of a human skeleton as an American child?"

These fears can develop even prior to the child's mastery of language, according to Dr. Freud. "If you place an infant on a transparent plastic platform which is elevated off the ground, the infant will cry and show signs of being afraid. Even though the infant is not yet able to understand language, he has some- how developed a fear of heights. How can this be so?"

"Another well-known psychologist, Dr. Alfred Jung, has suggested that this may be as a result of a cosmic unconsciousness, wherein our species are born with certain innate fears, beliefs, and behaviors. This is, of course, nonsense, and I am in the process of proving that the reason children have similar fantasies and fears is because they are willfully rejecting authority."

DR. FREUD ALLEGES LAWYERS ARE THE SCOURGE OF HUMANITY

Does Dr. Freud have any faith that the third book in the tril- ogy will be more to his liking? Before answering this question, the learned physician loudly guffawed.

"While I certainly would appreciate a well-written, factual account of my diagnosis and treatment of patients, I will employ the old proverb of 'Hope for the best but prepare for the worst.' Since the book is being researched and written by a law school graduate, we have to resign ourselves to the inevitable conclusion that the final book in this sordid trilogy will be just as twisted and sick as the first two. I fear for the psychological health of anybody foolhardy enough to read Mr. Ford's books. My only hope is the good people of this world are wise enough to join my crusade to destroy any and all books written by this so-called author."

CHAPTER ONE

Rodney's Way-Outs

Most comic book heroes go through a similar two-step process regarding their special abilities. First, they must somehow become aware they have an ability others don't. This initial step can be deceptively difficult. If your special talent involves being able to leap tall buildings or burst into flame on a whim, then you're likely to recognize your abilities fairly easily. But what if your special ability involves something less apparent? How would you know that you had such a gift and who might guide you regarding the use of the power? Without a teacher or coach, how are you going to understand this rare talent and refine it?

Step two is deciding how you will use these powers. Will the world know of the hero's powers, or will things just magically happen without explanation? Will the hero become so afraid of the special gift that he/she refuses to use it under any circumstances?

If the comic book hero in question is a little boy, how could he possibly be able to traverse this complicated process of exploration?

Shortly after he started first grade, Rodney Barstow's unique ability started to declare itself. The first indication of this fledgling aptitude was when vivid nightmares began to interrupt his sleep. Prior to this, the little boy had little to no recollection of his dreams but now he remembered every detail. These nocturnal adventures ran the gamut from thrilling to terrifying. Sometimes he awoke in a cold sweat, the bedsheet sticking to his damp body. Other nights his limbs flew haphazardly as he dreamt, sometimes striking his headboard, and causing him to suddenly awaken in an ill-tempered confusion. After several weeks, Rodney's experiences while immersed in these curious dreams began to change.

While he dreamt, Rodney at times felt himself lift out of his body. His essence was free to observe the dream unfold as a detached third party. In this unattached state, he anxiously watched himself get chased by bloodthirsty creatures. On another night, he nervously held his breath as he witnessed himself falling from a tall building, waking up just as he was about to hit the ground. Over time, he became confident he was existing safely outside his body. Eventually, he was able to watch a dream or nightmare unfold as if it was nothing more than a movie. Some of the movies were nevertheless terrifying to watch, as it's always scary to see yourself in danger of being devoured by a monster.

It was entertaining to watch these events unfold in the dream-movies. At times he never saw himself in the dream and those were the best ones. Instead of watching himself be chased by a monster, Rodney could safely hover over the scene as a ghostly apparition and watch other children frantically run as long purple tentacles reached out to grab them.

Rodney developed a curious taste for watching others who were under duress. He enjoyed watching the story unfold, especially when they were peppered with unique characters and weird events which made no sense at all. In his article, "Fear Without Consequences: The Hidden Horror," Dr. Ford Freud explained that experiencing fear without truly being in danger is an abnormal personality trait which can lead a person down the cold and dark tunnel to psychosis. The learned physician listed several activities in which a demented mind may exalt in pleasurable fear without risk such as watching horror movies, attending demolition derbies, and going into a carnival's haunted house. Dr. Freud opined that the popularity of gladiatorial battles, where life and death struggles took place as people watched from the safety of their seats, caused widespread psychosis and was a major reason for the downfall of the Roman Empire.

Initially, young Rodney figured his dreams were no different than his friends.

"I had a nightmare last night," Rodney's best friend told him in the school lunchroom. "Dracula was coming after me. I tried to run but my feet felt heavy, like they had weights tied to them. The harder I tried to run, the slower I moved. It was really scary!"

In a matter-of-fact tone, Rodney replied, "But all you had to do was float up out of your body, and then you could just watch what happens. No big deal."

"What're you talking about? You can't leave your body! It felt like I was really there! He was gonna get me! I wasn't safe until I woke up."

Conversations of this sort led Rodney to conclude his dreams were extraordinary and unique to him. Comments by his parents strengthened this belief.

"Do you ever have a dream where you're being chased by something scary?" Rodney asked his parents one night at the supper table.

"Of course, honey," his mother said. "Everyone has nightmares from time to time."

"Did you have a bad dream last night, buckaroo?" his father asked. "Something scary?"

Rodney didn't respond to his father's question. Instead, he asked, "When you have a nightmare, do you think something's gonna happen to you? Like, are you scared that a monster is *really* gonna get you and hurt you?"

"Sure. Even I have those dreams," his father replied. "I've been chased by lots of things over the years. Lions. Big snarling tigers. Monsters. All kinds of things have tried to get me in my sleep. When you're dreaming, it feels very real, even though it isn't. How about you, dear?"

Rodney's mother thought for a moment, then said, "Ghosts. I remember an awful dream when I was a little girl where my teacher turned into a mummy and tried to grab me!" This memory caused her to shiver. "Even after I woke up, I was so scared! I just stayed completely still, waiting for the mummy to appear in my bedroom! But dreams are just make-believe. Having nightmares is just a normal part of growing up. It's just your mind playing tricks on you. You may think you're being chased by a monster, but you're not."

"When you're in a dream, though," Rodney continued, "you think you're really truly in danger? You're not there just watching like it's a movie: you think you're *really there*? Is that what you're saying happens to you?"

"Sure, that happens to everybody. It'd sure be nice if you knew it was all make-believe!"

After talking to his friends and family about their dreams, two things became clear to six-year-old Rodney. First, he concluded he was experiencing something special, and second, he needed to keep this secret. In Rodney's limited experience, it seemed that any time something special or unique came around, people tried to ruin it. If you had a neato baseball card, the rest of the world became fixed on getting it away from you. Even your friends. He decided it was in his best interest to keep his dreams private and not share them with anyone. Even his parents.

Something else that set Rodney apart from his peers was his struggle with debilitating headaches. The possibility of a headache flaring up was always present, stalking the boy. When one of them struck, he felt the sides of his head squeezed together in a vise. The insistent pressure swelling up behind his eyes made him sensitive to even the slightest amount of light. Rodney lost his ability to control

SKELETONS ARE NOT SCARY

his body temperature when a severe headache struck, causing him to go through alternating episodes of sweating, then shivering. Several doctors examined the boy, but none of their remedies provided any relief. A specialist at the university advised Rodney's parents he had "atypical migraine headaches with associated cluster headache features." This meant there was no way to know the cause of the headaches, nor when the next one might occur. The doctor lamented there wasn't much he could offer, so Rodney lived in a perpetual state of waiting for the next debilitating headache to descend upon him.

In all other respects, Rodney was a typical little boy. Each school year he missed a handful of days because of intense headaches. About twice a month, one of these headaches would strike, forcing him to spend the better part of an entire day in a dark, cool, and quiet room with a damp washcloth draped over his forehead and eyes.

Each night, he watched as a detailed dream played out for him. Although passively observing others run for their lives was entertaining for a time, young Rodney Barstow's interest began to wane as he got older. By the time he reached third grade, watching the nightly stories was becoming old hat, unless something really entertaining occurred, like when he got to watch a steamroller run down Howdy Doody.

"Help me, kids!" the freckled puppet cried as the huge drum rolled ever closer to him.

That was the exception, not the rule, however. Watching the dreams became mundane. To liven the experience, Rodney started urging the participants to do things. When a tiger was chasing his cousin in the jungle, Rodney encouraged him to confront the ravenous beast.

"Don't run away from the tiger," his detached spirit shouted as it floated above his annoying cousin. "Fight it!"

At first these commands had no effect, leaving Rodney disappointed as he watched the events unfold without his input. Occasionally, however, one of the people in his dreams paused, as if they heard Rodney's suggestion from afar. Through trial and error, Rodney learned it wasn't the volume of his voice that mattered: it was how hard he concentrated. If Rodney could establish a mental connection with the performer, he could hear their thoughts.

One night in a dream, Rodney visited a girl just a little older than himself. She was standing in her bedroom, trembling with fear as she looked warily at the closet door in her bedroom. There was growling coming from behind the closet door.

"Don't be afraid," Rodney thought. "Go ahead. Look in the closet. There's nothing bad behind the door. Don't be such a scaredy-cat!"

"But I don't want to!" the little girl whimpered.

"Come on, you know you want to see what's in that closet." Rodney said in a smooth voice. "Don't you want to see if there's a pony in there?"

When the girl tentatively opened the door and found Frankenstein in her closet, Rodney laughed at the girl's shrill screams. These instances when he was able to assert his will and control the performers were more thrilling than anything he'd ever experienced. When a dream began, he didn't know if he'd be able to tap into that special wavelength and link the two. The ability to exert control only came about once every other month but when it did, it was glorious.

The day after another particularly satisfying dream, Rodney was careless and mentioned it to one of his friends.

"Last night I dreamt about the Lone Ranger. There was a big pit of rattlesnakes, and even though he thought it was too big a hole for Silver to jump over, I talked him into doing it," Rodney reported, thinking fondly about the conversation that transpired between him and the masked cowboy. "It was so neat when he did it! I'm glad I talked him into doing it!"

His friend was incredulous. "You did *what* in your dream?"

"You know, when you take control of people in your dream and you make them . . ."

Rodney abruptly stopped talking when he saw his friend was looking at him with a combination of disbelief and horror.

"I sometimes talk in my dreams, but I can't make them do things. Are you saying you can make people *do* things in your dreams?" his friend asked.

"Naw, of course not. I was just joshing you," Rodney said, trying to sound nonchalant. He wanted to quickly change the subject. "Did you see Chuck's new yo-yo? He can do tricks!"

His friend took the bait and told Rodney about how he'd seen Chuck do a yo-yo trick called around-the-world. As his friend blathered on, Rodney thought about how he needed to be more careful with what he said about his dreams. Better yet, he decided to make doubly sure he didn't talk to *anyone* about his dreams or nightmares ever again.

Rodney experienced all the typical joys and disappointments of childhood, just like his peers. Five to six times a year, though, Rodney had a nighttime experience that none of the other children could ever conceive.

During the summer when he turned twelve, Rodney's voice began to crack. "You're becoming a man," his father pronounced. After his voice changed, Rodney stopped having the nightly dreams he'd experienced for half a dozen years. No longer were there movies to watch, or opportunities to direct the action. He didn't awake with a vivid and detailed recollection of the previous night's dream. He often couldn't remember if he dreamt at all. Rodney's body was going through a lot of changes, and he wondered if "becoming a man" meant he'd lost his ability to have special dreams.

His mother was fond of saying, "All good things must come to an end." While this might be true, Rodney couldn't help but feel disappointed when his special ability went away.

Rodney's parents went out to dinner one night, leaving their fourteen-year-old son at home. He was relieved to be left alone in the quiet house. For the past hour, he'd felt one of his headaches coming to a boil. He'd become adept at recognizing the subtle tell-tale signs of a headache preparing to strike. After coming home from school, he started seeing sparkling lights in his peripheral vision. This was usually Rodney's initial warning that an excruciating headache was just around the corner. Once his parents left the house, the young man retreated to his bedroom. The lights were off, and the curtains were drawn.

"Won't be long now," he murmured, opening his bedroom window just a bit so some chilly November air could waft in.

One of the many doctors he'd seen recommended that Rodney engage in deep breathing exercises and a type of meditation whenever a headache started. Rodney was surprised to find this unusual activity could sometimes take a little edge off the really bad ones. Through practice he'd become skilled at relaxing both body and mind, which provide some relief.

Sitting on his bed with crisscrossed legs, Rodney breathed deeply and closed his eyes. Just as he'd done so many times, he slowed his breathing. While pain and pressure built up behind his eyes, Rodney inhaled deeply, then exhaled slowly. He responded to the headache's wrath by focusing his thoughts on relaxing his muscles. As he slowly filled then emptied his lungs, Rodney let his mind drift aimlessly. Whatever thought popped into his head was acceptable, as long as it distracted him from the searing pain that was flaring up behind his eyes. His conscious mind was a butterfly, softly landing on one thought, then fluttering to another.

Rodney pictured himself walking on a deserted beach. The only sound was made by small gentle waves. By concentrating very hard, he could just barely feel the warm water rushing over his feet. As the waves retreated, he focused on the sensation of wet sand between his toes. A severe lightning bolt of pain dispatched him back into his bedroom. Rodney gathered himself and again tried to divert his thoughts away from the pain.

Despite the headache becoming more intense, he filled his lungs to capacity, then let the air out slowly as his thoughts wandered. Were his Christmas gifts this year going to be sparse or bountiful? He thought about a girl in his math class who he thought was cute. Would she consider going to the Winter Dance with him? He wondered what job he'd have when he grew up. Memory of the years of vibrant dreams popped into his head. Would he ever again experience the special dreams he'd had when younger . . . the ones when he could control people?

Rodney became so lost in his thoughts, the headache was almost non-existent. As he thought about the unique dreams he'd had as a child, he felt a short burst of cold air on his face. Although he wasn't asleep and certainly wasn't dreaming, he felt himself rising up from his body. Slowly he floated upward until he was hovering near the ceiling, looking down on himself seated on the bed. After lingering there for a few seconds, Rodney's essence flew up through the ceiling into the night sky. Just as he had in dreams as a little boy, Rodney was calm and felt no fear. He sensed this spectral version of him was both real and not real. He was in no danger.

While enjoying his view of the city, Rodney suddenly felt himself yanked across the sky. Suddenly he found himself floating in a tavern, just below its ceiling. There was a great deal of yelling inside the bar, and Rodney saw two men poised to fight. Other barflies had gathered and were shouting encouragement. In the stark and colorful light provided by neon beer signs, both men circled to their right with their fists raised.

"This is a mismatch," Rodney thought. "That big guy is gonna murderate that shrimp."

Although Rodney didn't recognize either man, he somehow felt a connection with the smaller one. When Rodney focused his eyes on the smaller man's face, he could just barely hear him thinking, "I'll show him! The big gorilla can't do that to me!"

"I'm gonna mess you up!" the larger of the two men thundered.

Rodney sent mental encouragement to the smaller man. "Fight! Do it! Let's see some action!"

There was a barely noticeable twitch in the smaller man's cheek, so he yelled again, "Do it! Let's see some action!"

At Rodney's bidding, the smaller man sneered at his opponent. "You're nothing! I'm gonna wipe up the floor with you!" the small man shouted.

The face of the larger man became beet red with anger, and it was clear the fight was about to erupt. Just as the bigger man cocked his arm to unleash the first punch, another man moved between them, holding out his arms to keep the would-be fighters apart. "That's enough! We're not gonna have that stuff in my place! I'll call the cops and have you both hauled away!"

Rodney felt the smaller man's raw emotion start to diminish. "No, don't stop now!" Rodney pleaded, concentrating harder. "You can't let him win! Go after him!"

Despite Rodney's war cry, both fighters slowly lowered their fists, while still watching the other warily.

"That's it," the third man soothed. "Put down your dukes and I'll get each of you a free beer. On the house! That's much better than spending the night in the clink!"

Even though the men began backing away from each other, Rodney tried to incite the small man. "He's a crumb bum! Go after him! Punch him while his guard is down!" For a few fleeting moments, Rodney thought he might be regaining some control.

"Yeah, he is a crumb bum," Rodney heard the man think.

Whatever control Rodney might have regained quickly slipped away. The men retreated to opposite ends of the bar with a fresh mug of beer in hand. Rodney couldn't hear the smaller man's thoughts anymore. Just as quickly as he'd been drawn into the bar, Rodney was roughly sucked out of the building. Ethereal Rodney zipped back to the house and into his body.

It took a minute for Rodney to regain his bearings. His first conscious thought was he felt ants crawling all over his body. Rodney opened his eyes and started frantically brushing his arm with his hand, only to quickly realize there was nothing crawling on him. As his right hand stopped brushing his left arm, Rodney noticed it looked strange. Initially, it looked like his hand was nothing but bones; it was a skeleton's hand. The hand quickly returned to normal, and the sensation of crawling bugs vanished.

Rodney sat perfectly still, wondering if anything else strange was in store for him. After nothing happened for several minutes, Rodney thought about what he'd just seen. Since he knew he couldn't turn into a skeleton and there were no bugs crawling on him, Rodney concluded that these had just been remnants of his imagination.

"That was way out there!" he said aloud to himself. "I just had a Way-Out!"

Nearly a year passed before Rodney experienced another Way-Out.

Just a few weeks after his fifteenth birthday, Rodney experienced several *firsts*. That afternoon, his heart was broken by a girl for the very first time.

Rodney was madly in love with Sallie Ketchum, the pretty girl with strawberry blonde hair in his science class. The teenage boy's emotions were volatile, apt to abruptly swing from the highest of highs to the lowest of lows. Nervously wringing his hands as he approached her, Rodney tried to sound confident.

"Um, hi Sallie," Rodney said, looking at the floor. "Homecoming is coming up and I was wonderin' if maybe you'd like to go . . ."

Rodney took such a long time to get the words out of his mouth, Sallie couldn't help but interrupt him. "I'm already going with Todd."

Standing in front of Sallie Ketchum's locker, Rodney felt as though he'd been stabbed in the belly with a butcher knife. Feeling unsteady, as though he was trying to walk on a sheet of ice, Rodney retreated down the hall, certain the mortal wound inflicted by Sallie was on display for all to see. He was sure everyone in the hallway was watching him—and laughing at him.

Sitting on his bedroom floor later that afternoon, Rodney looked at the doodles he'd drawn on his notebook earlier that week. "Sallie" had been written a dozen times. He used a black pen to obliterate the name. Ever since walking from her locker, his stomach had been painfully churning. He felt like he needed to vomit but couldn't seem to bring himself to do it.

"This has got to be what it feels like to be poisoned," he thought woefully.

Rocking back and forth with a stomach full of poison and a heart torn to shreds, it occurred to Rodney he was in danger of developing one of his bad headaches. As if his body heard these concerns, he began seeing the flashing lights.

"No, not today. Please." Rodney begged.

Behind closed eyes, Rodney watched the colorful explosions of light intensify. The bright fireworks soon caused pain to pulse behind his eyes. Usually he had a little time between the appearance of the flashing lights and the onset of the excruciating pain, but this was a day of firsts. It didn't take long before he was in the throes of a full-blown headache.

He focused his thoughts, trying to transport himself to the quiet sandy beach that existed in his imagination. Despite his best efforts to escape the torment, Rodney couldn't visualize himself being anywhere except sitting on his bedroom floor, suffering through an intense headache. Desperate for relief, he changed tactics. Instead of trying to escape his pain, he tried to defeat it. He thought of his headache as a raging fire, then tried to douse the flames with a steady stream of water from a fire hose. Rodney was encouraged when the pain seemed to lessen just a bit. Abruptly, however, the pain flared up. As if the blazing inferno of pain was furious at being momentarily weakened, it raged even fiercer.

Searing pain spread throughout his head like a wildfire. Soon he was a fireman in danger of being engulfed in the blaze he'd been battling. Rodney panicked. He needed to escape! He imagined himself changing from a firefighter to a ghostly apparition. Before the flames consumed him, he gently floated out of the fireman's body. He escaped the raging forest fire and was once again in his bedroom, looking at himself seated on the floor. In this vaporous form, he looked like a skeleton surrounded by a dense fog. He held out his hand, watching as his bones appeared, then were obscured in the dark gray fog that was swirling around him. Floating above his body, Rodney discovered he only felt a fraction of the excruciating headache.

He looked down at the teenager sitting on the floor next to his bed, and it was obvious the boy was suffering. Rodney wanted the physical version of himself to somehow feel the relief he was enjoying. Reaching his ghostly fingers into the skull of the teenager sitting on the floor, Rodney tried to massage the inflamed nerves causing his headache. After a few moments, the flesh and bone version of Rodney breathed a sigh of relief. When the gaseous hand pulled away, the pain wasn't quite as intense for the corporal version of Rodney sitting on the floor. Ethereal Rodney reached into his stomach, trying to open a drain and allow the acid to empty out of his body. Before he could find the drain, his gaseous form was drawn upward.

As if filled with helium, his ghostly self became buoyant, slowly rising out of the house. Looking down on the roof of his house, he inhaled the unmistakable sweet smell of burning autumn leaves. Rodney wasn't afraid as he continued to float upward, so high he was able to see the entire neighborhood. For some reason he felt assured there was no possibility of him suddenly falling out of the sky and plummeting to his death. The wind carried him where it liked, as he had no control.

The course of his flight was erratic. He flew several blocks away, only to quickly double-back, and return to his neighborhood. At times he just hovered in one place. After a while, Rodney noticed he could hear bits and pieces of conversations. It was as if he had a transistor radio inside his head, the dial being twisted as it tried to latch onto a strongly broadcasted signal through a blizzard of static. When a station was tuned in and the conversation was clearer, he began moving. If the transmission suddenly turned to static, he stopped and circled, as if trying to recapture the radio signal.

Rodney did his best to decipher what was being said on the radio stations, but he couldn't make sense of much of the conversations. Each snippet sounded like part of a heated argument. One side of the dispute was broadcast through the air, but Rodney couldn't hear the adversary's response. Suddenly, a clear resounding voice arose from the background noise.

SKELETONS ARE NOT SCARY

"I hate him! He's always ruining my fun!" the angry voice hissed. It sounded like the rant of a young boy.

When his internal radio dial latched onto the boy's voice, Rodney was spirited away. Rodney shot through the sky, the boy's voice becoming louder and clearer as he did so. In his mind, Rodney saw a radar screen with a bright blinking light on its perimeter. Rodney picked up speed until the flashing point of light was near the middle of the radar screen. As he moved in a direct path towards an unfamiliar house in an unknown neighborhood, Rodney noticed it was dark and raining. When he'd left his body and floated above his house, it was a clear autumn afternoon.

One moment he was floating in the sky and the next he found himself in a small bedroom hovering over a sleeping boy. The boy's legs were moving, as if he were trying to run while he slept. The sheet covering the boy was wrapped around one of his gyrating feet. Floating just above the boy, Rodney waited for the boy to say something. The boy's lips quivered, but what he said was so soft Rodney couldn't make it out. Rodney willed himself to float down closer to the boy and was pleasantly surprised when he was successful. Leaning his head close to the boy's mouth, Rodney tried to figure out what he was saying. Rodney smelled the boy's foul breath and heard a rattle in the back of his throat as he breathed, but Rodney couldn't understand what the boy was mumbling.

Instead of listening with his ears, Rodney tried to pick up on the radio transmission he'd followed. Rodney jumped when the radio receiver in his head snapped to life once again.

"Why does he keep doing this to me? I wish he'd just go away!"

Rodney realized he was listening to the boy's thoughts. When the little boy didn't say anything for a few minutes, Rodney became peevish and wondered if he could use his ghostly fingers to flick the boy's ear. He reached towards the boy and was surprised to witness his skeleton fingers pass through the ear and disappear. Rodney let out a yelp and immediately pulled his hand back. Summoning his courage, he once again reached towards the boy. His fingers, hand, forearm, and then entire arm were swallowed up. When he was elbow-deep in the boy's head, Rodney suddenly felt his entire body roughly sucked into the boy's head.

Startled to find himself plunged into pitch darkness, Rodney heard what sounded like the boy's voice being played on a hundred record players at the same time. Hearing a loud cacophony of voices saying a hundred different things was unpleasant. In frustration, Rodney yelled, "I need light! I can't see anything! I want to see what's going on!"

As if obeying Rodney's command, the boy's eyes fluttered open. Rodney was astonished to find himself looking through the young boy's eyes. In the moonlight he could make out the pajamas the boy was wearing. In addition to seeing through the boy's eyes, Rodney could feel the bed supporting his body, as well as the scratchy new pajamas irritating his skin. He tasted what the boy had for supper and he knew the boy hadn't brushed his teeth before going to bed. Despite the clamor of a hundred voices, the deep, slow respirations of the sleeping boy seemed to have a calming effect on Rodney. The two boys were sharing the same body.

After the boy closed his eyes, Rodney sternly ordered, "Open them back up! Open your eyes!" This time there was no response from the little boy, leaving Rodney once again swallowed in darkness amidst the many voices.

Bearing down, Rodney focused his thoughts on opening the boy's eyes. Gradually the eyes once again opened. Rodney couldn't be sure if the boy was responding to his commands, so he decided to conduct a test by willing the boy to stretch out his arm and open his hand. When this command was obeyed, Rodney felt the muscles of the boy's arm become taut as the opened hand slowly twisted to the left, then to the right. Yes, it appeared the little boy was responding to his directives. An ornery idea flashed in Rodney's mind. He pictured in his mind the boy's hand slapping his own face. The hand obeyed but Rodney felt the smack of the hand on his own cheek.

"Ouch!" Rodney thought. He was startled when the boy's dreamy, detached voice said, "Ouch!"

Rodney commanded the boy to stand, but nothing happened. He concentrated harder, visualizing the boy rising from his bed but the boy didn't respond. What Rodney pictured in his mind was the boy swinging his legs over the bed then standing, but no matter how many times he ordered this to occur, there was nothing but a slight twitch of the boy's leg muscles. The boy closed his eyes again, plunging Rodney back into darkness. Multiple times Rodney ordered the eyes to reopen but there was no response. When the boy refused command after command, Rodney became concerned he'd lost all control over the boy, and he began to panic.

"What if I can't get out? What if I'm trapped in here forever?"

In Rodney's mind, he saw a Venus Fly Trap. "Am I a fly that's been caught? Have I been lured here and now the jaws are closing over me?"

Desperately, he pictured himself floating out of the boy, but nothing happened. Like a goldfish bumping repeatedly against its glass bowl, Rodney felt as though he was bouncing against the boy's skull. Amidst the dissonant voices still echoing around him in the darkness, Rodney bore down, imagining himself escaping the boy's body as easily as it had entered. It felt as though he was buried alive, and he could sense the weight pinning him down. For a moment he started to rise out of the boy, only to be pulled back. For some reason Rodney was still moored to the sleeping boy and he couldn't tear himself free.

"Come on! Let me out! I want out!"

During these struggles, Rodney had a sobering thought: was there a deadline for escaping the boy? Was the clock running? If he didn't extricate himself from the boy what would happen to him? Concentrating as hard as he could, he was relieved when he began to steadily rise out of the boy. Still not safely free of the boy, Rodney was surprised to hear his mother's voice.

"Honey! Rodney, I'm back from the market," his mother called out. "I'm going out to the garden to pick some tomatoes."

Hearing his mother instantly broke the connection with the boy. Rodney was spirited quickly across the sky and back into his bedroom. Roughly dumped back into his own body, it felt as if he'd been body-slammed by a professional wrestler. Every muscle in his body went through a series of violent spasms, making Rodney look like a fish flopping on the shore. Bleary-eyed, confused, and his entire body throbbing with pain, he commanded his muscles to relax. His body didn't obey.

After several minutes suffering, his muscles' painful contractions abated, leaving the exhausted teenager splayed on the bedroom floor.

"I did it. I'm back," Rodney thought with a comforting sense of relief.

Many of the nerves in his body were still periodically firing, causing uncomfortable pin-prick sensations. The notebook that had been on his lap was on the other side of the room. When he reached out to grab it, he froze. His hand was nothing but bones. The foggy haze which surrounded him when he lifted up from his body was gone. All that was left were bones.

"No, no, no!" the teenager moaned in disbelief.

He'd been able to return to the real world: everything should be normal! Something bad must have happened in the process! He was shocked to see his clothes drooped over his bones. He was in over his head and desperately needed help. When Rodney tried to cry for help, nothing happened. It felt like there was something in his throat blocking air from entering or exiting his lungs.

SKELETONS ARE NOT SCARY

"I can't live if I can't breathe!" he thought with increasing terror.

Unable to scream, Rodney stared blankly at one of his skeleton hands. He then watched in amazement as his blood vessels, nerves, and organs slowly began to appear. In short order, the muscles and soft tissue materialized. By the time Rodney heard his mother come back into the house, he was back to normal. Rodney patted various parts of body to assure himself everything was as it should be.

Eventually he got up from the floor, walking towards his dresser mirror. He closed his eyes and stood in front of the mirror, afraid of what he might see. When he managed to open his eyes, he was relieved to see he looked normal. He was soaked in a cold sweat and his clothes were stuck to him. It appeared as if a bucket of ice-cold water had been dumped over him. Wiping his forehead with the back of his hand, Rodney managed to flash a smile.

"Time for you to set the table," Mrs. Barstow announced as she walked into the bedroom. Her son was standing in front of his dresser in drenched clothes. All color was gone from his face, leaving him pasty and gaunt. "Rodney! What's the matter?" She ran to him and touched his arm, finding his skin wet and clammy. "My word, do you have a fever?" Without waiting for a reply, she placed the back of her hand to his forehead. "How long have you been like this? Your skin is ice cold, but you're sweaty!"

Rodney remained focused on the mirror, concerned his body would suddenly turn into nothing but a collection of bones in front of his mother. Luckily, this didn't happen. Once the bones had been covered by muscles, soft tissue, and skin, they remained safely hidden away.

Immediate bedrest was ordered by his mother and there he remained for two days. As he lounged in bed, Rodney tried to remember every detail of his remarkable journey. After much thought, he concluded this was all tied to the strange dreams he'd experienced when younger. Apparently, his unique ability had changed since he was just a little boy. No longer did he need to be asleep to take one of his Way-Outs. He wasn't relegated to just shouting suggestions from the balcony. His ability had matured to the point where he could inhabit his subjects, controlling their actions from inside. He didn't have complete control yet, but he was confident his skills would improve with practice.

The prospect of exercising such power over others was thrilling. He imagined detailed fantasies wherein he punished those who'd wronged him by taking control of their thoughts and actions. No one would ever cross him again. Or refuse to go to the dance with him.

During the weeks leading up to his ill-fated invitation to Sallie, Rodney stared lovingly at the back of her head during class. From his desk two rows behind and to the left of her, he could at times get just a glimpse of her gorgeous profile. Now he stared at her with eyes full of scorn. In Rodney's mind, it'd be only fair if something happened to her to cause an equal amount of embarrassment he'd endured. Shouldn't she be laughed at, too? He imagined the teacher scolding Sallie for standing up in class and dancing. Rodney giggled quietly to himself as he envisioned Sallie being ushered to the principal's office for punishment. That'd be justice.

Blocking out the drone of the teacher's voice, Rodney focused all his thoughts on Sallie. He imagined parting her hair, then opening her skull so he could go inside. He tried to picture himself inside her head, looking at the teacher through her eyes. Nothing happened, even when he focused solely on just causing Sallie's hand to twitch a little.

As he laid in his bed that night, Rodney thought about his failed attempt to take control of Sallie. Chalking up this failure to the fact he was in a noisy classroom, Rodney tried to once again rise out of his body from the comfort of his own home. After going through his breathing exercises, he pictured himself in gaseous form, but he wasn't able to leave his body. He imagined floating through the sky, trying to find Sallie's radio frequency but this was nothing more than a jilted teenager's hopeless daydream.

Not once over the following weeks was Rodney able to leave his body. Neither in the waking world, nor in his sleep, did Rodney possess even a hint of the power he'd wielded on the afternoon he'd been turned down by Sallie. Frustrated at his inability to invoke this special ability, the teen over time was concerned it had just been a one-time event. Eventually he resigned himself to the fact his special ability had simply vanished, just like his unusual dreams.

Even after losing his exciting new talent, Rodney's life was full. He wasn't the most talented player on his baseball team, but he was the most dedicated. What he lacked in natural ability he made up for with sheer desire. For the most part, he thought school was okay. Although he didn't take a shine to English literature, Rodney excelled in history and science. In biology class, he was fascinated with how traits could be passed from one generation to the next.

"Could the next generation have traits stronger than the parents?" he asked his teacher.

"Sure. For example, if you splice the DNA of two types of corn, the outcome can be corn that is larger and tastier than either of its parents. When dominant genes are combined with recessive genes, the outcome can be a superior hybrid."

Stronger genes overwhelming weaker ones was a concept Rodney found very intriguing.

Six months later, Rodney was playing baseball when an opposing player threw a pitch directly at him in retaliation for Rodney hitting a home run the previous inning. Not able to duck soon enough, the baseball smashed into his upper arm with a loud *thud*. Rodney collapsed into the dirt. Almost immediately, Rodney felt a baseball sized welt swelling up on his arm. When Rodney caught a glimpse of the pitcher from the corner of his eye, he saw a broad smile on his face. Rage erupted inside Rodney. Disregarding his painful arm, he sprinted towards the pitcher, intent on evening the score with his fists. Before Rodney got a chance to throw a punch, the catcher tackled him from behind, holding him down until the coaches arrived.

After he got home, Rodney was still seething with anger. He kept replaying the scene in his mind. In these versions, however, the catcher failed to restrain Rodney and he was able to reach the pitcher's mound. In his fantasy, he punched the other boy while the other players and spectators cheered. No one came to the pitcher's aid while Rodney evened the score. As he daydreamed about the pitcher getting his just desserts, the muscles in his arm twitched.

While he was fantasizing, the flashes of light appeared. If the baseball had struck his head, he would've experienced less pain than the headache dished out. Later that night, Rodney experienced a Way-Out. He wasn't sure if it took place before or after he fell asleep. For a short time, Rodney inhabited a woman and convinced her to physically lash out at her unsuspecting husband. Although he couldn't punish the pitcher who plunked him, inciting the woman's altercation satisfied the angry teenager's need for revenge. An additional perk was if he had a headache, there was something about going on a Way-Out which ended it. He always awoke from Way-Outs pain free and wonderfully refreshed.

"Rodney is such a good boy," his mother often gushed.

By all appearances, she was right. He didn't have to be told twice to do his chores and consistently earned good grades. Rodney Barstow was the type of boy everyone seemed to like: the proverbial good egg. If one of his friends was in a quandary, Rodney was the first person they turned to for guidance because he was considered a "deep thinker." He had a knack for figuring things out and providing insightful advice. In a crisis, other boys his age tended to be impulsive, while Rodney seemed to always be in control of his emotions. Was this due in part because every once in a while, he was able to vent his negativity in a manner no one could see, let alone imagine?

CHAPTER TWO

Chrissy's White Knight

Most everyone has heard of the term *white knight*. Despite what many people might think, a white knight isn't just a character in an ancient story filled with damsels in distress and dungeons. A white knight can simply be someone who arrives in the midst of misfortune, using his skills to save the day. For Chrissy Sagen, her white knight was Rodney Barstow.

Chrissy was the youngest of three children. She didn't speak her first word until she was five years old. Because of this, she was labeled by both children and adults as "slow." Her language skills never caught up to the level of her peers. Without the ability to fire off a snappy retort, she was vulnerable to unkind teasing. Up until her very last day of high school, Chrissy was still tainted by the harsh labels which had been pinned on her by elementary school classmates. No matter what she did, Chrissy was always seen as the stupid, heavyset girl who rarely spoke and when she did, mumbled under her breath in an embarrassed voice.

By the time Chrissy was born, it was if her family's entire supply of intelligence, physical prowess, and good looks had been used up by her dashing brother and elegant sister, leaving Chrissy with nothing but dregs. She was a plain-Jane girl with a full moon face who wore dowdy, unflattering clothes. Even though a lack of social life left her with plenty of time to study, she at best was a C minus student. On those few occasions when she tried something new, she failed. Although she longed to discover a talent, skill, or sport that would set her apart from the crowd, Chrissy was never able to find it.

As a teenager, her ability to fail became a hobby of sorts. Never shying away from an opportunity to try something new, Chrissy jumped into it with both feet. When she failed and then abandoned her efforts altogether, she experienced a twisted sense of accomplishment. Her inability to succeed became a reward in and of itself. In the dour downpour of failure, Chrissy Sagen felt stability. The world was as it should be: she was destined to fail, and when she did, the world was in perfect order.

Homely and uninteresting, Chrissy never had a boyfriend in high school until her white knight swept her off her feet. Sure, she'd admired and pined over good-looking boys she passed in the hallway, but she never dared to even talk to them. Even when in the company of boys who were likewise plain and socially awkward, Chrissy was afraid. She'd built a sturdy wall to keep herself emotionally detached and thereby safe from others. It was acceptable to her that she'd failed at sports, academics, and the arts, but she drew the line at failing at love. That was a defeat she simply didn't think she'd ever be able to survive.

Stirring the punch bowl and ladling cups full of bright red fruit punch was her sole reason for attending the spring dance her senior year. Chrissy learned to experience a type of vicarious happiness from watching other couples dance. She wasn't jealous of the happy couples. Chrissy knew with certainty she wasn't destined to become a girlfriend, fiancé, wife, or mother. It was obvious she'd always just be plain old Chrissy and she'd reconciled herself to this fact. She wasn't wearing a party dress because she didn't own one. No one ever asked her to dance, so she had no reason to ask her parents to buy one. The night of the spring dance Chrissy was wearing the same old dress she'd worn to school. Nothing exciting. Just plain old Chrissy.

Rodney appeared from the other side of the dimly lit gym. In the years that followed, Chrissy took every opportunity to share her recollections of that magical moment.

"I was arranging some of the cups around the punch bowl, so they looked nice. I happened to look up and our eyes met. I'd never seen him before and had no idea who he was. The first thing I felt when I saw him was fear because, well, he was a boy. He had a James Dean devil-may-care smile that made me feel funny inside. He kept looking in my direction. Naturally, I turned around to see who he was looking at, but there was nobody behind me. That's when I realized he was looking at *me*!"

Although she'd tell others it was love at first sight, that wasn't how it actually happened. Chrissy's first thought was she was about to be victim of another cruel prank. The wry expression on the boy's face certainly supported this concern. Had this boy been brought in from another town to make fun of her in front of everyone at the dance? As he started walking across the gym towards her, Chrissy averted her eyes, looking nervously at the cups and needlessly rearranging them. When she dared to glance up and saw he'd nearly reached the table, her hands started to tremble with fear.

The list of things which Chrissy was afraid of was an exceptionally long one. Near the top of this list was meeting new people. Awkward Chrissy never knew what to say to strangers. When she tried to engage in conversation, she thought she always sounded like a dummy. Strangers who also happened to be teenage boys were even more frightening. Boys rarely talked to her and when they did, they were rarely kind. Sometimes they'd approach her wearing a kind, smiling face. They'd politely talk to her and just as she was about to let her guard down, they'd spring a cruel practical joke on her.

When it came to boys, she was caught in the middle of a vicious struggle between her brain and her heart. If she listened to her head, Chrissy wished all boys would just leave her alone altogether. If she didn't have any contact with boys, then she couldn't be the victim of their derision, and her heart would never be broken.

Other times her teenage heart managed to rise above logic, reason, and her prior bad experiences. Occasionally she couldn't help but becoming enamored with a boy, but nothing came from these schoolgirl crushes except disappointment. Despite knowing her social status, she still felt a little excited if a boy happened to look at her, or better yet talk to her. After all, her heart insisted there was always a remote chance the next boy who talked to her could be the one who was actually interested in what she had to say. At some point in her life, wouldn't there be a boy who talked to her for some reason other than to set the stage for a mean joke about her round, acne-covered face, or the plain clothes she wore? Math wasn't her best subject in school, but didn't the law of averages establish that *some* boy out there would be interested in Chrissy? Even though it hadn't happened yet, her heart professed there was always a remote possibility the stars could align in her favor.

To both her delight and horror, the boy was standing in front of the table. Chrissy's brain warned her that another mean boy was preparing to belittle her, while her heart held out hope that this time would be different. As this internal conflict was taking place, Chrissy's feet were waiting for the command to run from the danger. Her fear intensified when the boy smiled sweetly at her, but so did her excitement. Chrissy's logical, rational brain became increasingly concerned her emotions were strengthening and might gain control. It appeared the soft lighting and beautiful music her classmates were slow dancing to were teaming up to invigorate her emotions, causing her to forget about all the times she'd been ridiculed and embarrassed. Her brain urged Chrissy to sprint from the gym so that the bright light in the girl's bathroom could clear her mind and hopefully subdue her unrealistic teenage emotions. Paralyzed by conflicting desires to both flee and stay, Chrissy couldn't do anything but awkwardly gawk at the boy.

With the confidence of a young man who knows what he wants and knows how to get it, Rodney held out his hand with an exaggerated flourish, and asked, "May I have this dance?"

Words failed Chrissy. She was frozen in fear, unable to speak. All she could manage was to quickly shake her head. When she did so, her head didn't move very much from side to side, making it appear as though she was shivering.

"Come on," Rodney cooed with a smooth voice, "I won't bite."

Every muscle in her body was trembling as she slowly raised her hand towards the boy.

"What are you doing?!" her rational brain screamed. "Run!"

When he grasped her hand, she felt a surge of warmth spread throughout her body. She'd overheard girls gush about the wonderful tingle that travelled through their body when they held hands with their boyfriends, but Chrissy assumed this was just a silly exaggeration. It wasn't an exaggeration at all.

Rodney led her around the table and onto the dance floor. More than a few of her classmates were shocked to see Chrissy Sagen being escorted by a young man. Swaying on the gym floor with her hands on the boy's shoulders and his on her waist was nearly an out-of-body experience for Chrissy. She felt lighter than air and wondered if she'd start floating up to the ceiling if he let go of her.

"My name's Rodney. I'm a senior at Roosevelt," he said, moving slowly from side-to-side somewhat in rhythm with the music. "What's yours?"

Chrissy still hadn't regained full use of her voice, but she managed to squeak her name.

"I didn't hear you." Rodney said, leaning his head closer to her. Just a little louder than before, she said, "Chrissy."

"That's a pretty name. Do you go to school here?"

She nodded her head nervously, again looking as if she was shivering.

"One of my buddies wanted to come," Rodney explained, never taking his eyes from hers. "I don't much like dancing, but I came anyway."

The boy smiled at Chrissy with the confidence of someone who's been provided all the correct answers for the upcoming final exam. He wasn't the most handsome boy in the gym, but Chrissy surmised he was the most confident. Rodney had an air about him that suggested he had everything under control. Even though she was still apprehensive, his confidence had a calming effect on Chrissy. It was as if her abiding fear declared, "This boy seems to have everything under control, so I can take the night off."

The slow dance ended too soon for Chrissy. The PA system belted out The Beatles' "Love Me Do." Chrissy was looking down because she was afraid she'd trip over her own feet. She concentrated on recreating the steps she'd performed while dancing by herself in her bedroom on countless evenings. The longer she moved in time with the music, the more her inhibitions faded. It took a lot of courage, but she was eventually able to lift her eyes from her feet to the boy dancing across from her. When she saw he was looking at her with a sweet smile, she quickly looked back down at her feet. Chrissy felt a smile coming on. Her lips and cheeks were twitching, as if her face wasn't quite sure what was happening.

When they sat down on the bleachers to take a break, Rodney brought her a glass of punch. Of course, Chrissy had drunk fruit punch many times, but it'd never tasted as wonderful and sweet as it did that night.

"Are you graduating?" he asked, his knee just a few inches from the hem of her skirt. "I mean, are you graduating in May?"

Chrissy wanted to say something that sounded both confident and cute, but nothing that fit the bill came to mind. Even if she'd thought of something clever to say, her tongue for some reason felt swollen, so she wasn't confident she'd be able to speak. Concerned she wouldn't be able to say anything intelligible, she just smiled and nodded.

"Me, too. I'll be glad when high school's over and I can start earning some real money. I'm tired of being poor. I'm thinking about moving to University City 'cuz it's got lots of businesses where you can get a job. Have you ever thought of moving away from here?"

Living a hundred miles away in University City was something she'd never desired to do. She always envisioned living with her parents until they passed, then spending the remainder of her days in her childhood home. There was nothing for her in the big city. It was teeming with hundreds of thousands of people, none of whom she knew. Plenty of kids in her class said they were going to leave their small town and seek their fortunes in big cities, but Chrissy always maintained she was content to live her entire life within a ten-mile radius of her birthplace.

Chrissy heard a girl's voice say, "Yes, I've thought of moving there, too." She was surprised when she realized it was *her* voice.

Rodney and Chrissy saw each other nearly every day after that. Rodney's car wasn't flashy, but it was reliable, and he took her to places she'd never visited. She surmised she logged more miles in a car during the time they were dating than she had in all her previous seventeen years combined. Sometimes they just sat in his car and talked about what they thought the future had in store for them.

The details of their first kiss were indelibly burned into her memory. He'd walked her to her front door after they'd gone to see a movie in an adjoining town. For the past week, Rodney had taken her out five times. That night during the movie he'd ventured his hand close to hers and she let him hold it for a while. Chrissy broke the embrace when she became aware her hand was sweating a great deal; she didn't want Rodney to be appalled by her wet, clammy hand.

The two held hands as they walked from Rodney's car to her house. Chrissy wished the trip to the front door would have taken them longer. Her father had left the porch light on and a few insects were bumping against the bare bulb.

"Can I kiss you, Chrissy?" he asked, giving her hand a little squeeze.

When she tried to respond, she discovered that her lungs had no air in them. She tried to say "Yes," but what came out was more of a hissing sound: "Sss." Before she had a chance to second guess herself or worry she'd do it incorrectly, he leaned towards her. When their lips touched, it was the most amazing feeling she'd ever experienced. When he pulled away, he was smiling, so Chrissy figured she'd done it right. She'd heard of girls getting weak in the knees, but Chrissy's legs were so rubbery she was truly concerned she might collapse right there on the porch.

"I'll see you Friday night, kiddo?" he asked, still holding her hand.

Once again, her reply sounded like "Sss." He flashed his trademark confident smile, where the right side of his mouth turned up a little higher than the left side. As he walked back to his car, her inner voice was screaming, "Please come back! Kiss me again!" When his car pulled away, she waved at him and he waved back. Despite being in her pajamas and in bed by 11:00, Chrissy couldn't fall asleep until long past midnight. Over and over again, she replayed everything that occurred that evening, and in particular, her first kiss.

Six months later, Chrissy married the dashing white knight who'd swept her off her feet and they moved to Camelot. Pursuant to the typical white knight storyline, they were allegedly destined to live happily ever after.

CHAPTER THREE

A Quite Memorable Evening

Conventional wisdom is something that's been around so long, it's accepted as fact. Chrissy knew conventional wisdom dictated it was bad luck to announce a pregnancy prior to the third month, but she couldn't help it. As soon as she believed there was even a possibility she was pregnant, she wanted to share the exciting news with her husband. The prospect of adding to their family was simply too wonderful to keep to herself.

After Rodney got home from work, she tried her best to hide her excitement and act as if everything was normal. At supper while he droned on about work while she nodded politely, waiting for just the right opportunity to spring the happy news. While she looked like a demure housewife on the outside, she felt that at any moment she might burst open and spill the news.

"Are you okay?" Rodney asked. "You're pretty quiet tonight." When she looked up, he was surprised at her beaming smile. "What? What's so funny? Did I say something?" Chrissy shook her head, her broad grin still displayed. "What is it, then? What're you laughing at?"

She felt a little short of breath when she finally spoke. "I think I'm pregnant," she said softly, in a voice just above a whisper.

Chrissy was surprised at her husband's reaction. Even years later when she thought about that night, she was still shocked at what happened next. Rodney jumped up from the supper table, causing his steaming bowl of tomato soup to turn over. He paid absolutely no attention to the mess he'd caused. He jumped again. And then again. In fast succession, he jumped around their kitchen as his young wife held her hand to her mouth in astonishment.

"Yes! Yes!" Rodney trumpeted at the top of his lungs. "I can't believe it! Yeah!"

Rodney repeatedly pumped his fist into the air, hopping around the room in a chaotic victory dance. Chrissy giggled as she watched her husband act like a little boy who'd just hit the game-winning home run. After he finished his antics, Rodney knelt beside Chrissy's chair, peppering her with questions. "How far along are you? Does it feel like a boy or a girl? Can you tell? When's the baby going to be born? Does it feel like a boy?"

Through tears of happiness and joy, Chrissy shared with Rodney everything she knew, which was very little. Rodney enveloped her in a bear hug, squeezing her so hard that she felt a twinge of pain in her shoulder. "Ow, that's too tight!" she squawked.

Rodney released his wife and patted her arms softly. "I'm sorry, Chrissy, I didn't mean to . . . I mean . . . are you okay?" Once he saw his wife was still smiling, he leapt into the air again. "This is so great!"

Throughout that night, Chrissy never saw the elated smile fade from her husband's face. Rodney was typically a quiet man, not prone to overt displays of emotion, so his bubbly excitement was quite a pleasant surprise for Chrissy.

As she got ready for bed, she looked carefully at her midsection, even though she knew it was much too soon for her body to start changing shape. Rodney glanced up from his magazine and smiled when she came to bed. Chrissy noticed Rodney's left eye was twitching.

"Are you okay?" she asked. "Your eye looks kinda funny."

Rodney massaged his left temple with his fingers in a circular motion. "It's nothing. Might be a headache coming on. I'm hoping it's not one of the bad ones and it'll just pass. I'm too happy for one of the bad ones to come. If it does, it's probably because I got so excited and worked up tonight. I wonder what could have caused that?"

She giggled, then asked, "Do you need anything?" Rodney shook his head, still massaging the sides of his head. She kissed him on the cheek and said, "Good night, dear."

"I'm gonna try to read for just a little while longer before going to sleep," her husband replied. "If I keep my mind off the headache, hopefully it'll just stay away."

"Whatcha reading?"

He closed the magazine and showed her the cover of *True*. "It's an article about Marco Polo. He explored Asia before anyone else had. No one knew what was in Asia until he went there and explored," he explained with admiration in his voice.

"Ooh, that sounds scary. Going somewhere new where you don't know what to expect?" she said with a tinge of disdain. "No, thank you!"

"Yeah, it probably was kinda scary. If you're the first person to try something, or go somewhere new, I'll bet you end up flying by the seat of your pants lots of times. All the great explorers did this. They went into unknown territory trying to figure it all out on their own. There was a lot of trial and error, but the good ones kept trying."

"Well, you enjoy your story," she said, laying on her side with her hand resting on his shoulder. The light from the lamp on her husband's nightstand was a little bright, but Chrissy didn't let it bother her. This had been one of the most wonderful nights of her life and nothing could diminish her joy. Nothing.

A few hours later, Chrissy was roused by Rodney's voice. Slowly she began to emerge from her slumber. As her eyelids fluttered open, she heard him say, "It's what you want to do. Go ahead." He spoke in an emotionless monotone. His words sounded hollow, resonating almost like the vibration of a distant drum.

She couldn't remember hearing Rodney talk in his sleep prior to that night, but she knew people did. As she understood it, people could not only talk but also walk around while still in a deep sleep. From somewhere deep in her memory, she recalled that you weren't supposed to wake up someone who was sleepwalking, but she couldn't remember what to do if the sleeping person was just talking.

Chrissy couldn't see anything in the pitch-black bedroom as her husband's unusual conversation continued. "Come on, you know you want to do it. It'll be so simple. Here, I'll help you do it." She remained still, peering towards where she knew her husband was lying. A cold shiver ran down her spine, then back up again. Her mother's claim that you got a shiver when someone walked over the ground that would one day be your grave popped into her head. This caused another shiver to rattle down her back.

"I'm going to show you what you need to do," Rodney said.

"He must be dreaming," she thought. "It sounds like he's teaching someone how to do their job." Chrissy was proud that even in Rodney's dreams, he was willing to help others.

Curiosity changed to fear when Chrissy heard Rodney grumble, "If you can't do it yourself, I'll have to come into your head and do it for you." His voice still sounded distant, but it was tinctured with something unpleasant.

Once again, she tried to remember if she'd heard or read anything about what to do when someone is talking in their sleep, but nothing came to mind. "Do I just let him keep on going?" she asked herself in a trembling inner voice.

"That's it. Let me take control. I'm making all the decisions, *not* you. Now you can get revenge! Hit him. Hit him hard!" Her husband's increasingly baleful voice chilled Chrissy. She'd never heard Rodney use such a menacing tone, even on the few occasions when he was very angry. Chrissy remained still, wondering what happened if you *did* awaken a sleepwalker. Or a sleeptalker? Could someone die just because you woke them up while sleepwalking?

"Surely not," she thought, but she wasn't sure at all. "Maybe he's just having a bad nightmare. Could anything bad happen if you woke someone up from a bad dream?" Chrissy considered this possibility, then thought, "Certainly that would be okay, right? People wake up in the middle of nightmares all the time, don't they?" Chrissy's inner voice was trying to sound resolute, but the young wife wasn't certain what to do.

Chrissy's decision was made when Rodney shouted, "Hit him! Hit him!"

Her hand shook as she reached through the darkness towards her husband. "Rodney, honey, you need to wake up," she said softly, pushing her fingertips lightly against his upper arm. As far as she could tell, Rodney didn't respond, other than to grunt a couple of unintelligible words. Pushing just a little bit firmer this time, she said, "Come on, Rodney. You're having a bad dream. Wake up."

Chrissy felt his body abruptly jerk as if he'd been electrocuted. She let out a surprised yelp and quickly pulled her hand away. She continued unsuccessfully to try to see the outline of her husband in the darkness. Rodney didn't say anything further, although she could just barely hear him groan a few times. When Rodney let out a long groan, she worried there might be something wrong with Rodney. Was he sick? Did he need to go to the hospital? Chrissy knew she had to act. The only way to find out if he was okay was to turn on the lights.

After rolling to her left side, Chrissy reached towards her nightstand lamp. She pulled the small chain and was momentarily blinded by the light. When she turned back towards her husband, she let out a shrill *yip*. Looking as if he'd just been pulled from a frozen lake, Rodney's entire body was quivering. His arms were shivering so severely that his hands were bouncing off the bed. Although Chrissy had never seen someone have a seizure, she wondered if Rodney was in the midst of some kind of epileptic attack.

She put both of her hands on him while begging, "Wake up! Please, honey! Wake up!"

Despite her pleas, his eyes remained closed. His violent shaking raised a concern he might fall off the bed. Chrissy grabbed his arm with both hands, pushing him down onto the bed as best she could. While she was trying to hold him, she kept pleading, "Wake up! Wake up!"

Both of Rodney's eyes simultaneously shot open and he stared upward while he let out a long, labored groan. It sounded as though Rodney picked up something very heavy and was struggling to carry the weight.

"It's okay, I'm here. Settle down. It's okay," Chrissy repeated as calmly as she could. Patting his arm reassuringly she tried to reassure him. "I'm here. Everything's okay."

With Rodney's eyes remaining open and expressionless, Chrissy watched his skin quickly become very pale. While it was true Rodney was a pale man, Chrissy was quite troubled when he rapidly became bleached of any color whatsoever. Within a few seconds his skin was almost transparent. It was soon thereafter Chrissy became certain she could see *through* his skin.

She raised her hand to her mouth in shock, a high-pitched whimper escaping from between her lips. In rapid succession, she could see first his blood vessels, then his muscles, and finally his bones. Terror froze her in place as she watched his internal organs appear then disappear, fading in and out of sight each time he took a breath. For a few seconds he looked normal, but then Chrissy could see all the way through to his bones. Her high school science teacher kept a plastic transparent model of the human body on his desk. The memory of this see-through body flashed into her consciousness. There was an indentation in the mattress of Rodney's entire body, even when he was nothing but a skeleton.

She managed to slowly slide off the bed, then backpedaled until she bumped against the wall, all the while unable to take her eyes away from her husband's metamorphosis. Pressed against the bedroom wall, Chrissy felt her entire body shuddering. A part of her wanted to turn her head away from the spectacle, but for some reason she couldn't look away. She watched as the body of her white knight pulsed with differing views of the inside of his body. When his muscles and organs faded, she was looking at just a skeleton, its wide bony grin appearing to mock her terror.

"Am I having a nightmare?" she thought. Sometimes in bad dreams her legs felt heavy and immovable, just as they did now. She pinched herself. "Wake up, Chrissy! Wake up!" she screamed inside her head, but nothing happened.

A timid voice from deep inside Chrissy pleaded with her legs to run, but they refused to respond. That same meek voice urged her to close her eyes so she couldn't see the ghastly scene any longer, but this command was likewise ignored. Try as she might, something inside her *demanded* that she watch her husband's body fluctuate between transparent and normal.

Chrissy stood against the wall for less than a minute before his body became normal and blessedly stayed that way. Chrissy held her breath, fearing that the pulsing changes in Rodney's body would return. She stared at her husband as he lay quietly in bed for an entire minute, then two. His breathing returned to a regular, measured rate. If Chrissy had walked into the bedroom at that moment, she'd never have known that anything had been amiss.

Watching Rodney rest peacefully broke her paralysis. No longer cemented in place, Chrissy darted around the foot of the bed. She ran so fast she slammed into the bedroom door before her hands could open it. Fumbling with the doorknob, she pushed frantically on the door for a few seconds before successfully pulling it open. Staggering down the hallway in long, uncoordinated strides, Chrissy managed to get to the harvest gold phone sitting on the edge of the kitchen counter.

Hands still shaking, she fumbled to take the receiver off its cradle.

"Who can I call?" Chrissy wondered aloud. After a brief delay, she said, "911!"

It took a lot of concentration on Chrissy's part to successfully insert her trembling index finger into the rotary dial on the phone's face. With some difficulty, she dialed 911. Holding the phone to her ear with both of her unsteady hands, she waited anxiously. She heard nothing: no one answered, there was no busy signal, nor was there any kind of recorded message. After waiting a few moments, she hung up the phone, then redialed. It took an eternity to dial "9." She put her finger in the dial and moved it all the way around until it stopped. Once she took her finger out, she had to wait until the dial slowly rotated back into place before she could dial "1" twice. When she still heard nothing, she again entertained the possibility this was all a nightmare. Her thoughts were interrupted by the phone's loud three tone alert, followed by a woman's recorded voice: "If you wish to make a call, please hang up, and try again."

The phone company's loud recording jostled a recollection out of Chrissy's memory. University City hadn't yet adopted the new 911 system that was spreading throughout the country. A new emergency telephone system had been promised by the local government, but it wasn't yet in service.

"I need help!" she thought. Chrissy was flustered and scared, causing her to momentarily forget she could reach a friendly operator simply by dialing "0."

"Yes! The operator!" she exclaimed.

After putting her finger in the last hole of the dial, she moved it in a large arc around the dial. While watching the dial move back to its original position, Rodney emerged from the hallway and stepped into the kitchen.

"Put the phone down, Chrissy," he said in a sleepy, quiet voice.

Chrissy startled and dropped the receiver. It clattered on the tile floor, then yo-yoed in the air from its coiled cord. After letting out a brief surprised yelp, she put both her trembling hands to her mouth.

"It's okay. I'm fine," Rodney said, slowly shuffling towards her as if he was a frail old man. "Everything will be okay," he reassured her in his dreamy voice.

"Rodney . . . I . . . I . . ."

"Shhh." As he was shushing her, he continued to approach her with open hands. With his palms facing Chrissy, he motioned as if he was slowly fanning a fire. "Shhh."

"Operator: how can I help you?" came a woman's voice from the phone. Rodney picked up the receiver and softly settled it back down onto its cradle.

The young husband and wife stood a few feet from each other. Chrissy had no idea what to do. Run? Scream? She couldn't take her eyes off Rodney, the love of her life, who now appeared entirely normal. He was no longer skinned down to his muscles, nor was he a skeleton. It was her white knight, sporting just a hint of his trademark devil-may-care smile.

"It's okay. Everything's gonna be alright," he said in a soothing voice. "Shhh."

Despite Rodney's reassurances, Chrissy was still very afraid. Graphic memories of the grinning skeleton lying in their bed flashed into her conscious mind. Once again, she had the urge to run, but she had no idea where she'd run to.

"I'm sorry you're scared, but it's all over now."

His soft, sleepy voice soothed her, helping to calm her frayed nerves. Unable to move, all she could do was look at him with her quivering hands still covering her mouth. When he lovingly touched her hands with his, she twitched, as if she was expecting his hands to carry a painful electrical shock.

"That's it. Shhh," he cooed. He slowly enveloped her in his arms, and she buried her face into his chest. Long, deep sobs began to flow out of her. It sounded as if she spoke a few words while sobbing, but Rodney couldn't understand what she said. He was still recovering, so he was supporting himself against Chrissy just as much as she was holding onto him. He kept shushing her quietly and gently rocking back and forth, as if she was a crying baby who'd awakened with a start in the middle of the night. They remained in this embrace for several minutes, shifting their weight from left to the right in a slow moonlight dance unaccompanied by music.

Chrissy wanted to put her hands on his temples and kiss him, but she hesitated. She was afraid of what she'd see if she pulled away and looked into her husband's face. Would a skull suddenly be grinning menacingly back at her? As they swayed, Rodney squeezed his eyes shut periodically, trying to regain all his faculties. How long was he going to feel this dizzy?

Finally, Chrissy summoned the courage to lean back from her husband enough so she could see his face. In the faint glow provided by streetlights, she was relieved to see the face of the man she'd fallen in love with. The man whose baby she was carrying. She was full of so many questions, but all she managed to say aloud was, "What . . .?"

Their slow dance in the kitchen had given Rodney the time he needed to collect himself. Mercifully, by the time Chrissy looked up at Rodney, the room wasn't spinning as much as it had minutes earlier, and his legs didn't feel as weak as they had when he stumbled out of the bedroom. He spoke to her firmly, but still gently, "Let's sit down and talk about this."

Rodney turned on the kitchen light and they sat down at their small Formica kitchen table. Both of them were relieved to be off their feet, as neither felt completely sturdy. With his wife's hands sandwiched between his, Rodney took a few additional moments to collect his thoughts. When they'd first got married, he'd foreseen the possibility he might have one of his spells in the presence of his wife, so he'd prepared a story for her benefit. It was now time to find out how good of an actor he was. There was a bead of nervous sweat rolling down the back of his neck, as he recognized his performance needed to be flawless and convincing.

"First, tell me what you think you saw and what you heard," Rodney said, making sure to sound very calm. He needed to gently coax information from his young wife, hopefully without causing her to become distraught.

Because she was still scared, Chrissy's voice was higher pitched than usual. She nervously recounted what she saw in one long, uninterrupted sentence. "I woke up 'cuz you were talking in your sleep, and you kept talking, so I turned on the light, and I could see inside your body all the way down to your bones, and it would fade then come back, and I got really scared . . ."

"Okay, okay," Rodney said softly, giving his wife's hands a little squeeze. Looking comfortingly into her eyes, he waited a moment until her face relaxed just a hint. Speaking as he would to a frightened child, he said, "That must have been very frightening to you." Chrissy nodded in response. "I'm so sorry I scared you: I didn't mean to. I know how much you hate to be scared." Again, Chrissy nodded, looking at her husband in desperate hope that he was somehow going to make this all better. "Most important, what you need to know is that everything is fine. I'm going to tell you some things, but in the end, the story ends happily, okay? Everyone likes a story to end happy, right?" She managed to smile just a bit and nodded. "Good. The ending of this story goes like this: everyone is okay, and they lived happily ever after, understand?"

Rodney held her hands lovingly as he told the story he'd concocted. To his credit, he gave a very convincing performance that night.

"Since I was a teenager, I've sometimes had an unusual type of seizure." Rodney did his best to sound a tad embarrassed as he began his story. "It's kind of like an epileptic attack. I talk and may say some crazy things. Whatever I say is just nonsense and doesn't mean anything. When one of these seizures happens, I say weird things and I look really pale."

"Yes, you *were* pale," Chrissy interrupted. "White as a ghost."

"Doesn't surprise me at all. Doctors have told me that's because all the blood is being sent to my brain as my body tries to fix itself. I become so pale you might think you're seeing through me." Chrissy let out a little gasp, bringing her hand to her mouth as she nodded eagerly. "If someone sees me, they become understandably scared. They struggle to make sense of this very strange thing they're seeing. Then that person's imagination can kick in."

Chrissy's eyes started to well up with tears, so Rodney paused to let her swell of emotions subside a bit before asking, "Did I wake you up while I was talking during my seizure?"

"Yeah, that's why I woke up, because I heard you saying some things."

Outwardly, Rodney's facial expression didn't change but inside he was smiling. Chrissy was already adopting the story as her own. "It sounds like you were just waking up when this seizure was going on?" Chrissy nodded. "So, you've woken up from a sound sleep because you heard me saying some kind of nonsense. Did you then turn on the lights to see what was the matter with me?"

"Not at first but I turned on the lamp a little later."

"Okay, so you're half asleep, then you turn on the lights." Once again, his wife nodded her head. "You're still half asleep, feeling groggy, and confused as to what's going on in the middle of your good night's sleep." Chrissy kept nodding her head, a clear indication to Rodney she was thus far willingly accepting his suggestions. "You see me like you've never seen me before, with absolutely no color in my skin. I'll betcha I looked like a corpse. Or you saw through me? Maybe you even thought you could see what's inside my body?"

"Yeah, like muscles."

"Sure, and it must have been terrifying when you thought you saw that. You must've been very afraid. I don't get scared very easily, but I know it'd shock the dickens out of me if I saw something like that." Rodney smiled just a little and his wife managed to return that smile. "The good news is there's nothing wrong with me, other than I occasionally have these strange seizures. I've already been seen by lots of doctors, who say it's not dangerous to me or anybody else. You're totally safe, hon. I don't need to take any medicines and the doctors say these spells won't shorten my life. It's a very rare condition that maybe happens once in every billion people. It's not dangerous, it's just scary if you happen to see it."

"What's going on with you when it's happening? Do you know what's happening?"

Under his breath, Rodney let out a little chuckle and smiled, hoping this would help put his wife at ease. What he was about to say was patently false. "Truth is, I have no idea the seizure is happening. I just think I'm sleeping. I wake up like nothing ever happened. I might be dreaming during the seizure, so sometimes I talk while it's happening. But everybody knows dreams are just little plays put on by the brain for our entertainment." Chrissy nodded, as she'd heard that same thing somewhere. "The seizure passes and everything's back to normal. My mother saw me have one of these and it nearly sent her to an early grave. Can you imagine?"

Chrissy thought of her mother-in-law and how special of a person she was. She was a gentle woman who'd passed away a month after their wedding. Chrissy shuddered to think of how shocking this must have been for Rodney's poor mother. "How often does this kind of thing happen to you?"

"Not very often at all. I can go five or ten years without an episode," he lied.

"Why didn't you tell me this before, so . . . so I knew?"

Rodney shifted his acting skills into high gear, trying to look and sound wounded. "It's . . . very embarrassing. I have this awful condition that no one has ever heard of, except for a few special doctors. Sometimes I babble on and on, which can terrify anyone who happens to see me." Rodney sucked in a deep breath, as if he was going to confess a dark personal secret. "I don't want anybody to know because if they did, they'd look at me like a freak. Or like I'm some kind of psycho. I'd be cast out. I probably wouldn't be able to get a job or get a pretty girl to marry me."

Chrissy reached over the table and squeezed Rodney's hands. "That wouldn't have stopped me from marrying you!" she assured him. Chrissy knew all too well what it was like to be an outcast. When you're not accepted by others, you're left with nothing but your lonely thoughts to keep you company. Sometimes those thoughts can turn ugly, and you doubt you'll ever be accepted by anyone ever in your life.

"That's why we must keep this between us and never talk to anyone about it. Even your parents can't be told about this, do you understand why?" Chrissy now had a smile on her face when she nodded. "This will just have to be our little secret between husband and wife. And remember what I told you before: everyone lives happily ever after."

For quite some time, they remained seated at the kitchen table holding hands. Rodney told Chrissy everything he figured she needed to hear in order to buy into the story. As Rodney hoped, the tale of being a lonely outcast resonated with Chrissy. Just like her, she understood that Rodney was different from the rest of the herd, and through no fault of his own, he was in danger of being victimized by others.

"Do you think you can still love me even with my faults?" he asked.

Leaving Rodney was the last thing on her mind. Chrissy felt her stomach drop at the mere thought of losing the only man she'd ever loved. She longed to start a family with Rodney, and she was willing to do whatever it took to make that dream come true. His detailed, heart-felt explanation checked all the boxes on her wish list: he was born like this; doctors have been consulted; he's in no danger; she's in no danger; their baby won't be in danger; Rodney is going to live a long, full life as a husband and soon-to-be father.

Sometimes it's difficult for third parties to fully grasp why someone accepts their spouse's faults and blemishes. When you're starving, though, and have been starving for most of your life, even rancid lunchmeat can taste like filet mignon.

When they returned to bed, she slept with her head resting on Rodney's chest. Although she knew it was much too soon for it to occur, Chrissy thought she felt a little tickle in her stomach as if the baby kicked. Although Chrissy unquestionably accepted Rodney's story, it was nevertheless difficult for her to fall asleep. Every time she closed her eyes, she saw a skeleton's grinning skull.

CHAPTER FOUR

The Librarian

For several weeks, Chrissy kept a watchful eye on her husband. In particular, she was on high alert each night they went to bed. Although she didn't see anything out of the ordinary throughout the remainder of her pregnancy, she couldn't help but feel edgy. She was always waiting for something unexpected and possibly terrifying to rise out of nowhere.

Rodney was a perfect husband, just like always. He gushed with excitement whenever talking about adding to their family. In stark contrast to some men, Rodney actively participated in the joyous preparations for their baby. On one occasion he was able to leave work early so he could attend one of Chrissy's pre-natal office visits.

"I'm surprised to see you here," the doctor remarked as he entered the examination room. "I usually don't meet fathers until the day of the delivery."

"I pulled some strings so I could be here with my Chrissy," Rodney beamed.

After the doctor examined Chrissy and announced that everything was proceeding as planned, Rodney asked, "Can I be there in the room? You know, when our baby is born?"

The doctor pulled his head back with a mixed expression of shock and disdain. "Of course not, Mr. Barstow! I wouldn't have you in the delivery room any more than a surgeon would let you stand in his operating room during your wife's appendectomy. Don't be absurd! A delivery room is a place of medicine, not a pool hall for husbands to hang around. There will be plenty of other men in the waiting room you can kibitz with while I'm delivering your baby."

"I'll be fine, dear," Chrissy reassured her husband, patting his hand.

"Okay, I just thought I'd ask," Rodney replied with disappointment. "I just get worried about the baby and you being alright."

"You just stay in the waiting room and get ready to pass out cigars!" she said.

After witnessing her husband's horrifying transformation, Chrissy had difficulty completely relaxing when she went to bed. Even on those nights when she was very tired, a part of her wary brain wouldn't shut down. A sliver of Chrissy's mind refused to sleep, perpetually concerned that Rodney would again change into something horrible. She lived in fear she'd awake to find a skeleton lying next to her. Sometimes she'd wake up in the middle of the night and look at the other side of the bed for any telltale sign her husband had become . . . something else. Every morning after she woke up, she immediately looked towards her husband to make sure he hadn't changed.

This apprehension gradually faded when months passed without any further incidents. Chrissy was well into the second trimester before she could once again enjoy a full night of blissful sleep. Preparing for the upcoming birth also helped Chrissy forget the awful skeleton. Even so, there remained a voice inside her that periodically asked questions about Rodney's seizures. Her mother was Chrissy's only friend and the only person she'd even consider confiding in, but she couldn't even tell her mother about her husband's transformation; she promised Rodney she'd keep his secret safe. Keeping this information confidential made sense to Chrissy. She knew firsthand how people could be cruel when they discovered that you weren't like everyone else. Still, it was hard to keep this from her mother.

"Even though I can't talk about what happened, it wouldn't hurt to do a little research on my own," she concluded.

After Rodney left for work, she walked eight blocks to the nearest school. It was a junior high school her child would someday attend. The office receptionist invited Chrissy to use the school's modest library for her research. She didn't find any information about Rodney's type of disorder in three different sets of encyclopedias. Chrissy checked under "sleep," "dreams," "nightmares," and "human behavior," but found no helpful information. She got excited when she found a book cited in the card catalog that had "nightmares" in the title. Although the book's title claimed it was a cure for nightmares, it was nothing but a stupid, scary make-believe story.

An elderly librarian who was anxious to have a conversation with someone over the age of thirteen asked if she could help Chrissy. Careful not to divulge too much information, Chrissy inquired about any books which might help her understand Rodney's condition.

"I'm looking for a book that talks about a person who sleeps . . . and then kind of changes," Chrissy explained.

"Like sleepwalking?" the librarian asked.

"Even more of a change. Something like a change of the person itself."

"I think you're going to have to go to a bigger library, maybe at the university, to research something like that. The best you're going to get here is maybe a book that teaches kids not to be afraid of their bad dreams," the librarian lamented.

Chrissy always thought of librarians as the smartest person in the school. As she was growing up, it seemed that whenever a teacher didn't know the answer to a student's question, they were sent to the librarian. She figured that in order to become a librarian, you had to possess an encyclopedic knowledge of nearly everything.

Since a book on the subject wasn't available, Chrissy thought she'd explore the librarian's personal knowledge on the subject.

"Have *you* ever heard of anything like that? I mean, someone actually changing during their sleep?"

The librarian's eyes turned upward as she searched her memory. After a few moments, she looked at Chrissy and replied, "Not exactly. I know there are people who talk in their sleep and there are of course those who walk in their sleep. Some people can even do things while sleepwalking, like open the refrigerator and pour themselves a glass of milk just as if they were awake." When Chrissy shook her head, the librarian added, "Some people can have seizures, like an epileptic seizure."

"Yes! What happens during those kinds of things?" Chrissy asked eagerly.

"I'm not an expert on that subject but if you look in one of the encyclopedias under epilepsy, I'm sure you'll find at least some basic information."

Chrissy followed the librarian's advice, reading the encyclopedias' description of epilepsy and seizures. Again, however, the information in the books didn't come at all close to describing the odd transformation of Rodney's body. While hunkered over an encyclopedia, Chrissy was startled when the librarian placed her hand on Chrissy's shoulder.

"Any luck finding something, dear?" the librarian asked.

"No, nothing. What I'm really looking for is . . . well, it's hard to explain. Kind of where a person's body changes, you know, to something different."

The librarian scrunched up her face. "You mean . . . like a werewolf, or something like that?"

Chrissy felt like she was a child once again, trying to describe something to an adult that she simply wasn't able to adequately put into words. "No, more like someone who is completely normal ninety-nine percent of the time, but sometimes he turns into something else."

The librarian thought for a moment, then said, "I'm still not sure I know what you're driving at, dear. That almost sounds like Dr. Jekyll and Mr. Hyde."

"I don't know who those two people are," Chrissy was embarrassed to admit.

In a good-hearted way, the librarian chuckled a little. "They're not real people. I'm talking about the characters in the story *Dr. Jekyll and Mr. Hyde*. Have you heard of it?" Chrissy shook her head. "I think it was written by Edgar Allan Poe. It's a really strange and creepy story, so it must be Poe."

Chrissy was intrigued. "What happened in the story?"

"Well, Dr. Jekyll drinks a potion and turns into Mr. Hyde, who is a very evil man. Eventually Dr. Jekyll is concerned he'll turn into Mr. Hyde and stay that way. It's scary!"

Chrissy, of course, hated scary stories, so she'd never encountered such an awful tale. The librarian's description was alarming, causing Chrissy's imagination to run wild. What if Rodney lost control and he became a skeleton forever?

The librarian spotted the terror awash on Chrissy's face. She touched Chrissy's arm and tried to reassure her. "But that's just an old horror tale, dear. Things in scary stories aren't real. Kids might get scared, but we adults know they're just nonsense stories some demented author thought up."

Chrissy looked a little relieved and asked hesitatingly, "So, that doctor never really had that happen to him?"

"No, dear, it's just make-believe."

"So, no one before or after that story really had that kind of thing happen to them? You know, where their body is taken over?"

Once again, the librarian chuckled a little, but remained supportive of her frightened patron. "No, dear, it's never happened. You can relax. No one has ever changed into Mr. Hyde, and the Grinch never tried to steal Christmas! There's nothing to be afraid of!"

The librarian's wide, friendly smile made Chrissy feel much better.

"Just make-believe," Chrissy said, returning the smile.

"That's right, dear," the librarian said happily.

Chrissy shook the librarian's hand said, "Thank you, I really appreciate it."

"I don't think I did much, but you're welcome."

Chrissy's walk back home was pleasant. The fact that a demented writer came up with the fictional Jekyll and Hyde story made her feel a little more at ease. How Rodney explained his occasional seizures made a lot more sense than Poe's spooky story about Dr. Jekyll. Besides, Rodney didn't drink a potion: he was just born with his affliction. The encyclopedia listed all kinds of things that could happen to someone who had a seizure. While it didn't say that people could become so pale you could look through them, she figured the encyclopedia couldn't list *everything* that could happen.

The conversation with the librarian was the closest she'd come in confiding to someone her abiding uneasiness. Even though she'd kept her promise and not given up any secrets, just talking in general terms with the librarian made Chrissy feel somewhat better. This experience gave her the confidence to embark on a similar conversation with her mother. Although she knew she couldn't come right out and tell her mother what happened, Chrissy wanted her input.

As long as she wasn't travelling, her mother drove into University City on Thursdays to have coffee at Chrissy's house. After chatting about soap operas and gardening, Chrissy moved the conversation to a more important matter.

"I need to ask you something about Rodney," she said, trying to disguise the depth of her concern.

"Sure, darling, what is it?"

Earlier that afternoon, she'd practiced in her head what she was going to say. When it came to actually saying the words aloud, though, she spoke hesitatingly. "When it comes to Rodney, you see . . . I feel like something bad could happen at any second. You know the old saying: waiting for the other shoe to fall? That's kind of how I feel sometimes. Things have . . . happened with Rodney, and I'm afraid of what might happen next."

Because she couldn't tell her mother the entire truth, this description didn't sound quite right to Chrissy. It was the best she could do without giving up secrets, though.

Chrissy's mother looked at her with concern. "Isn't Rodney happy about the baby? Do you think he's getting cold feet?"

"No, he's excited and he tells me almost every day how he can't wait for the baby to come," Chrissy reassured, absently rubbing her protruding belly. "It's just . . . well . . . how can I say it? He's . . . he's not the man I thought I married. He's different now."

Patting her daughter's hand as she sported a wide smile, her mother replied, "Darling, that's what men do! Men change! Every time you think you've got a handle on them, they change on you! You're just going through what all young wives experience from time to time." Her mother winked at her and added, "Keep in mind your body is going through a lot of changes right now. That baby is causing everything in your body to go crazy. Just because the morning sickness has gone away, doesn't mean your hormones are back to normal. That rollercoaster of emotions you're feeling is something every expectant woman has gone through. When I was pregnant, I'd start bawling my eyes out for no good reason whatsoever. Even after the baby is born, you can still have strong emotions rise up out of nowhere. That's all normal. It's the burden we women endure."

"It's just that I get a little scared what might happen next . . ."

"Of course you do! You've never had a baby before, and it can be frightening to say the least. What's important, though, is for you to keep those crazy emotions under control. Push those feelings down and keep them locked in the cellar. Remember, Rodney is going through a lot as a first-time father. You need to make sure you're supportive of him. He needs you to be a sturdy rock, not an emotional wreck."

Chrissy tried again to explain her concern without telling her mother too much. "But, what if . . . what if you thought your husband was becoming something totally unexpected? What if you knew he was . . . starting to change into something else?"

Her mother nodded, confident she knew precisely what her daughter was driving at. "I understand," she said. Even though they were alone in the house, she leaned across the kitchen table and lowered her voice to just above a whisper. "All men from time to time are going to develop a bad case of a wandering eye: that's just their nature. What you need to do is be a loving, doting wife who makes sure he's happy at home." When her daughter looked less than convinced, she added, "Remember what Tammy Wynette told us ladies? Do you?"

Chrissy lowered her head and mumbled, "Yes, mother."

"Anytime you're not sure what to do, just sing "Stand By Your Man." If you follow Tammy Wynette's advice, then everything'll be just fine." Chrissy's face showed she wasn't entirely convinced. Normally her daughter unquestionably accepted her mother's advice, but today she was resistant. "Darling, when it comes right down to it, there's a lot of truth behind the old saying 'a good man is hard to find'."

Chrissy nodded. She knew she wasn't the belle of the ball, but she'd somehow stumbled upon a good man. She had a man who loved her and provided for her. At times when she was feeling down, Chrissy heard an accusatory voice in her head proclaim,

"You're lucky to have such a man! You don't deserve him!" That voice in her head sounded a lot like her mother.

Her mother realized Chrissy's misgivings were tied to being afraid. She'd seen her daughter spooked innumerable times. Being a short, overweight, plain girl with few social skills made Chrissy an easy target for teasing and bullying. It wasn't surprising when Chrissy developed into a young lady who was afraid of most things. Her mother figured anybody would become this way under the circumstances. Mrs. Sagen realized quite some time ago that her daughter's abiding fear was an effective way to protect herself from a world that could be quite cruel. She rarely felt it was healthy for her daughter to be confronted with the fact that most of her fears were baseless. To do so would take away her daughter's primary way to defend herself. Today, though, she decided tough love was needed for her daughter to sober up to the realities of married life.

"Look, hon, this isn't the old fashioned 1950's. I realize it's 1968 and the whole country has kind of gone off the tracks," she said in a firm voice. "Despite all this talk of Women's Lib, you need to realize it's still a man's world. A woman on her own these days is just as powerless in your generation as they were in mine. All big businesses are run by men, not women. Colleges and universities are filled with men. Everyone knows the only two reasons for a woman to go to college are to become a nurse or a teacher. Before you start letting your imagination get out of hand, you need to recognize the harsh reality of the world. If you were out there on your own with a baby, you'd find that just getting by would be a steep hill to climb."

After pausing a moment so her daughter could absorb this wisdom, she continued, "Don't forget the proverb about the grass being greener on the other side of the fence." Chrissy nodded silently: she'd heard that adage many times. "You've got a man. Do you understand that? You've got a husband! Soon you'll have a family. Those are the most important things in the world, and you need to do everything possible to keep it that way." Once again Chrissy nodded.

Finally, it appeared her daughter was coming around. "Here's the secret all the men in suits in their big fancy offices don't know: women are actually stronger than men!"

Chrissy looked at her mother with a mixture of confusion and hope. "Why do you say that? You said *they* have all the power."

"There's a difference between having power and being strong. Us women have had to keep the household running and families together for centuries. What's the old saying: behind every great man is a great woman? The men may have all the high paying jobs but it's women who have the most important job in the whole wide world: to keep the family together.

"While men are at work or bowling with their buddies, it's us women who have to make sure that the family is fed, clothed, and loved. We have to do these things even in the face of adversity. So, it's up to us to make sure the family stays together even in those times that the husband is weak. Keeping the marriage and the family in one piece is the most important job a woman has. Think about the great Abraham Lincoln for a second. President Lincoln knew that he had to keep the country together even though some of its people left the union. No matter what the Southerners did, he was determined to make sure the marriage of the states survived. That's what *you* need to do: make sure that regardless of everything else, your family remains together."

Under her breath, Chrissy mumbled, "Yeah, that makes sense."

"Before you start letting your imagination get the best of you and you start thinking crazy thoughts, you better understand the entire situation," her mother said sternly. "Do you remember me telling you about my Grandpa Mike?" Chrissy nodded. "Grandpa Mike had a very loud, booming voice, so whenever he spoke, we all paid attention. He used to say, better the devil you know than the devil you don't. That's good advice for us all, don't you think?"

Chrissy replied, "Yes. That's true." What her mother said made sense.

Her mother smiled and said, "Good. Good. So, let's talk about happy things like me going to Yellowstone next week and bury all of this negative talk deep underground."

Chrissy was confident she could follow her mother's advice. She figured she could bury her feelings, but she had no idea what kind of plants would spring out of that ground, nor what kind of bitter fruit they might bear.

CHAPTER FIVE

April 1969

Jered Barstow was born on a brisk and rainy April evening in 1969. At times the rain struck the hospital so hard it sounded like ice was pelting the windows.

"Is every pregnant woman in the city trying to give birth to-night?" Nurse Madeline Stokes asked while surveying University Hospital's nursery. Her lament was drowned out by the discord of newborns wailing.

Working in L&D (labor and delivery) typically wasn't too bad of an assignment and not nearly as hectic as a shift in the emergency room. A night shift in the labor and delivery unit normally meant Nurse Stokes had to care for one, possibly two women at a time. Over the course of this crazy night, though, seven women waddled into the hospital in the throes of labor. When added to the three car-ryover women who'd been hospitalized earlier that day, the nurse's patient load was a nightmare. Two nurses called in sick, leaving Nurse Stokes on her own. Scurrying between the nursery and L&D, she was hopelessly overwhelmed. Telephone calls for PRN help (potentially reliable nurses) went unanswered, leaving Madeline the star of a Lucille Ball comedy skit wherein the chocolates on the conveyor belt just kept stacking up.

Since L&D only had six beds, some of the laboring women were put in rooms on the surgical floor located two levels down. Since she didn't have the luxury to wait for elevators, Nurse Stokes ran up and down the stairs multiple times that night. A surgical floor nurse pitched in to help, but the situation was still chaotic. The two nurses were perpetually crisscrossing each other, trying to handle L&D, the maternity ward, and the women on the surgical floor.

To make matters worse for Nurse Stokes, most of the women who presented to L&D that night were first-time mothers. Doctors and nurses know all too well that first-time mothers were like a high school fire alarm: annoyingly loud and usually going off for no good reason.

"Why am I feeling this pain right over here?"

"How much longer will my labor last?"

"When is the doctor going to be here?"

Luckily for Nurse Stokes, once the contractions started in earnest, the doctors typically ordered enough pain medication to keep the women in a semi-comatose state. L&D was much quieter and easier to manage once the women had been loaded up with narcotics.

In the midst of her drug induced stupor, one of the laboring women had a lucid moment. Although very weak, she managed to push the button that summoned a nurse. In a soft, feeble voice, she asked Nurse Stokes, "Is the baby here yet?"

"Not yet, Mrs. Barstow," Madeline replied curtly. "Once the baby is delivered and you're good and awake, your baby will be brought to you."

"Okaaay . . ." Chrissy replied in a sing-song voice as she slowly drifted back into the dreamy realm her doctor had prepared for her.

In addition to all these tasks, Nurse Stokes had to call the OB-GYN doctors from time to time to give updates. It seemed the goal of the doctors was to not show up in person until mere minutes before the baby was delivered. When the delivery was imminent, the doctor swooped in and delivered the baby. It was the doctor who was the recipient of all the accolades and hugs, while the nurse was busy dealing with the somewhat gruesome bodily fluids which are part of every delivery.

During the time Madeline was managing the laboring women, fathers paced in the bottom floor waiting room. Nervous men waited anxiously for updates, filling the room with thick clouds of cigarette and cigar smoke. Sometimes Madeline fantasized that having the fathers at the bedside (possibly sharing a smoke with their wives), might soothe *everyone's* nerves, and take some of the burden off her shoulders. This was an absurd thought, as everyone knew L&D was certainly no place for a man. Unless the man was a doctor, of course.

That night ten expectant fathers were crammed into a waiting room designed to comfortably accommodate five. While a couple of the men had been through this process before, most of them were first timers. The veteran fathers were able to sit and quietly watch the black and white television, whereas the rookie fathers were prone to nervously pacing. When the door to the waiting room opened, their heads snapped to attention, hopeful for news.

The small waiting room was filled with so much cigarette smoke it looked as though the men were in a deep London fog. Rodney didn't smoke and became annoyed when the acrid haze started to cause his eyes to burn. When he left to use the restroom, he noticed he was followed by a gray cloud of tobacco smoke. He tried to be patient. Shortly after they arrived at the hospital, Chrissy had been whisked away in a wheelchair, at which time a nurse warned Rodney that labor could take anywhere from a few hours to more than a day.

Despite being subjected to the waiting room's foul smoky air, Rodney remained in high spirits. As the other men in the congested room blabbered about sports or work, Rodney stared at the wall with a satisfied smile. This was the culmination of something he'd envisioned while still in high school. He was certain his child would inherit his special abilities and that under his careful tutelage, his child's powers could become more powerful than his own. Unlike

Rodney, the child wouldn't have to hide the unusual abilities he'd eventually develop. His child wouldn't have to figure out the limits of these unique skills on his own, because Rodney would be there to groom and foster them. Like many fathers, Rodney believed his duty was to make sure his child became something greater than himself.

While Rodney was contemplating what his child was destined to achieve, the activity in L&D peaked. "Yes, I'll be right back Mrs. Thompson, I've just got to go to take Mrs. Stewart's baby to the nursery," Madeline said as she was walking out of the room. She ran to the nursery, carrying the newborn safely in both hands.

Whenever she brought a baby to the nursery that busy night, she was greeted with a choir of wailing. Each of the newborns wanted it made clear to the world that he or she wasn't particularly pleased with their overall experiences outside the womb. Madeline had no choice but to do multiple things at the same time. She lifted a baby out of a clear plastic basinet, trying to calm him, while simultaneously rubbing the belly of another child with her free hand. Eventually she was holding a newborn in each arm while singing soothing lullabies.

"Go to sleep . . . go to sleep . . ." she sang softly, "go to sleep my darling babies . . . go to sleep or you're going to rupture a blood vessel in my brain . . . go to sleep . . ."

While the babies cried, Madeline had a sudden moment of panic. She was holding three babies in her arms, each of them wrapped in a pale green hospital blanket and unrecognizable from the others. Three babies who hadn't gone through the process of hand and foot printing because there simply hadn't been anyone who could spare the time. She checked under the blankets of each of the babies. Three boys with similar skin color, eyes, and hair.

"I can figure this out," she said aloud, attempting to calm her frayed nerves and reassure herself. "I picked this baby up first and then . . ."

Amidst all the newborn bawling, she placed the babies back into their basinets. She took a moment to assess, then reassured herself she'd returned the newborns to their proper cribs.

"Whew, that could've been a disaster with a capital D," she remarked with relief.

Jered was nearly two hours old before his mother was alert enough to see and hold her

newborn son. Even though her head was still very foggy, Chrissy knew for certain this was the most wonderful night of her life. The magical evening she met Rodney and the afternoon of their fairy tale wedding were now relegated as the second and third greatest experiences of her life. She smiled lovingly at Jered as she made nonsensical cooing noises. Shortly after her baby was brought to her, Rodney was allowed into the room. Reeking of cigarette smoke, her delighted husband bent over to kiss her forehead. During the adoration of their newborn, the parents couldn't help but notice that his right ear was an unusual shape. The upper portion of the ear was folded over, as if it had been stapled to itself.

"Probably just as a result of the birthing process," the doctor reassured. "It'll straighten out as he gets older. I'll have the pediatrician come by first thing tomorrow morning to talk to the you about immunizations and well-baby checkups, if that works for the two of you."

"I'll make sure I'm here bright and early," Rodney replied.

Once visiting hours were over and he kissed Chrissy goodnight, Rodney realized how wrung-out he was. Driving home it felt as though every ounce of energy had been drained out of him. He didn't realize how nervous he'd been about the birth until it was over. It was an effort just to walk across the parking lot to his car.

On the drive home, he became quite sleepy. Trying to keep his mind alert, he thought about what additional abilities his son might possess. Would he be able to select who he visited, as opposed to being randomly linked to someone who was emotionally vulnerable? Instead of being limited to just a few trips a year, might his son be able to do it more often? He also had to consider the possibility the special power would be the same as Rodney's, or only inch forward slightly on the evolutionary scale. That would be fine with Rodney as well. Even if Mother Nature and the ghost of Charles Darwin only bestowed upon the child the same abilities as Rodney, it would still be glorious. A father and son who both possessed the special gift could join forces, making them even stronger.

Turning his car into the neighborhood, a bright burst of light flashed in Rodney's peripheral vision. "No! Not now! I'm so happy. Please stay away."

He went straight to bed after he got home, not bothering to even change out of his clothes. If he went to sleep right away, he hoped the brunt of the headache might be avoided. Since he was so exhausted, he figured he had a shot at falling asleep even though the pain was beginning to declare itself.

Later that night, Rodney was floating through the night sky. He felt like a virulent bacterium, searching for a host he could latch onto. The subject he was eventually paired with was particularly strong, able to resist Rodney's efforts for quite some time. Eventually the defenses were breached, allowing Rodney to dictate the host's actions.

"Hit him!" Rodney ordered.

In a weak voice that was barely audible, the host objected. "But he's my brother!"

"Never mind that. Do it now!"

SKELETONS ARE NOT SCARY

"The pediatrician should be here in a few minutes," a nurse informed Chrissy.

Despite his promise to be present, Rodney wasn't at the hospital. She asked the nurse to call their house, but the nurse reported there was no answer. While their home phone was ringing, Rodney was lying on his back, his body spread out on the bed in the shape of a large "X." As the echo of the telephone's final ring was fading away, the bones in Rodney's arms and legs were clearly visible.

She was still feeling the aftereffects of the anesthesia. Since waking up after the delivery, she had to contend with a thousand emotions racing through her mind. All these emotions seemed to be ganging up to overwhelm her.

"I feel really funny," she told a nurse.

"It's normal to be a little loopy for a day or two after being put to sleep," the nurse assured her. "It'll pass."

The nurse ended up being right and by the time she was discharged two days later, these odd sensations had faded away. On the morning after her baby's birth, though, she was still trying to make sense of it all. While she waited for Rodney and the pediatrician to arrive, the new mother started having some stark realizations. Because she now had a beautiful baby, she knew something bad was about to happen. Chrissy had been on a winning streak but now it was certainly time for reality to cruelly strike back. She convinced herself it was time to pay the proverbial piper for having a loving man and healthy son in her life.

When Rodney didn't show, Chrissy had to meet with the pediatrician by herself. Despite knowing the doctor was providing important information, Chrissy was having trouble paying attention. While the doctor was talking about common childhood illnesses, Chrissy was thinking about all the ghastly things that could be wrong.

When Rodney first saw the baby, did she notice just a hint of disappointment? As they were gushing about the baby the previous night, did he spend too much time looking at the baby's misshapen ear? Sure, he was smiling and chatting happily, but the new mother wondered if she might have been able to detect something deeper. When he didn't show up that morning, Chrissy contemplated whether Rodney was upset his son wasn't perfect.

"I'll see you and your son in a few weeks," the pediatrician said, reaching for the door.

Chrissy nodded vacantly, still awash in her thoughts. When she made a list of all the reasons why Rodney wasn't at the hospital, they were all bad. In her imagination she saw Rodney's car engulfed in flames. Then she saw him packing his car with his possessions, preparing to escape to a new life. Speeding down a deserted highway, she clearly saw the resolute expression etched into his face as he sped away. Chrissy was lost in this unsettling vision when Rodney burst into the hospital room.

Rodney flung the door open and rushed to his wife's bed. Panting, he apologized profusely. "I'm so sorry, honey. I overslept. Am I too late? Has the doctor come yet?"

Rodney's forehead glinted with sweat, and his hair hadn't been combed. One side of his shirt was tucked in but the other wasn't. He could have been mistaken for a hung-over alcoholic or bum. To Chrissy, he looked like the most handsome, wonderful man on earth.

"Rodney!" she squealed in delight, pulling him to her so she could wrap her arms around his neck. In her head she kept joyously repeating, "He didn't leave us! He didn't leave us!"

She covered his face with kisses as he continued to apologize for his tardiness.

"I wish my wife was that understanding when *I* was late!" the pediatrician mused, smiling at the affectionate new parents.

"I'm so sorry," he whispered into her ear. "I want to be with you every step of the way."

Chrissy was so relieved that she started to cry.

As he was hugging his wife, Rodney thought, "You bet I want to be there. I want to train and mold my son into something great. Something the world has never seen before. Who knows what the world will look like after my son is taught about the power he has?"

CHAPTER SIX

Eight Years Later: September 1977

In a magazine interview promoting his book, *Fairy Tales: The Intense Emotional Response of Children to the Senseless Slaughter of the Big Bad Wolf, and Other Disturbing Fairy Tales*, Dr. Ford Freud commented on how something as innocent as a beloved Christmas story can have elements of profound psychological phenomena woven into the plot.

"Take for example the story of Rudolph the Red-Nosed Reindeer," Dr. Freud explained. "In this story children are warned anything that sets them apart from the rest of the herd will become a platform for recrimination. Rudolph has a trait which none of his peers possess and it is this trait that leads the other reindeer to exclude him from the herd. Social psychologists have noted this kind of exclusionary behavior in all species of animals. The unconscious goal is to keep the herd as healthy and perfect as possible, thus any member who does not live up to this notion of perfection is ostracized. In the wild, unprotected outcasts become prime targets for predators. Therefore, through this cautionary Christmas tale, society warns children that if they are unique, they run the risk of being excluded from all 'reindeer games,' and they will likely die."

So it was in Jered Barstow's formative years. Even before he started kindergarten, other children exhibited an innate uneasiness around him because of his misshapen ear. Something in their genetic make-up compelled the children to avoid someone who looked different than every other child they'd ever seen. The stark title of Dr. Freud's 1974 article published in the *Journal of Education,*

Rearing, and Emotional Development (*JERED*) summed up the situation: "Children and the Development of the Social Structure: Why Children are Horrible Monsters Set Loose to Create Chaos."

From the day he was born, Jered was destined to remain outside the protective confines of the herd. Whereas his peers had two perfectly formed ears, Jered had but one. He entered this world with a physical abnormality that was easily seen and incapable of being hidden. Because of the application of the old proverb, "birds of a feather flock together," Jered was never permitted to roost with his peers, because none had the bent feathers he had. As if they had a preternatural urge to avoid anything unusual or abnormal, his peers avoided Jered at a very early age. Even before they'd fully developed language skills, other children somehow knew they needed to stay away from anything that didn't fall safely within the spectrum of "normal." The rules established by his peers clearly dictated that he wasn't a bird of the same feather, and therefore Jered shouldn't try to join their flock.

Contrary to his physician's initial prognosis, the appearance of Jered's right ear didn't improve with time, and he was never able to hear much through it. This reduced ability to hear slowed his early speech development. Jered heard a constant whooshing sound in his right ear, as if he was standing on a beach listening to the crash of ocean waves. As children with disabilities often do, Jered became accustomed to the white noise and did his best to adapt. Even though he couldn't hear sounds coming from his right side, he was able to function fairly well. The constant roar in his right ear was at times beneficial. He found the background noise soothing. The constant *whoosh* was always there, like a faithful best friend. In addition to providing a soothing soundtrack to his life, the sound of the roaring surf also covered up some of the unkind things other children said behind his back.

Despite these challenges, Jered was a pretty happy boy who found enjoyment in solitary activities. By far his favorite was drawing. At every opportunity he drew, be it on a restaurant napkin or in his mother's magazines. If he was idle for more than a minute, he usually began searching for something to write with and to draw on. Everything from the phone book in the kitchen to the owner's manual of his dad's car were adorned with Jered's sketches. With the sound of the crashing ocean as a soundtrack, Jered lost himself in the pictures he drew.

Even before he started kindergarten, it was evident to everyone the little boy had talent. When he started school and was introduced to new tools such as bright Tempera paints and bold magic markers, his artistic skills bloomed. While Jered's reading and language skills were below average, his artistic skills far exceeded his peers. Eventually the other children began noticing his talent, but this skill unfortunately didn't gain him acceptance into the herd. Teachers labeled him "the strange, quiet, but creative boy who could draw."

Making friends was quite difficult for Jered. In addition to his physical deformity and hearing loss, his mother instilled in him a strong distrust of others. Young Chrissy had been subjected to unrelenting teasing and she wanted Jered to somehow avoid this same ordeal. This caused Jered to become a timid little boy. Like all children his age, Jered's primary desire was to be accepted by his peers and permitted to join in their reindeer games. Some children, however, are never able to seamlessly mesh with the rest of the herd and they become outcasts. This difficult process of socialization is addressed in Dr. Ford Freud's 1971 paper, "Pack Mentality: Why Children Are Nothing More Than Crazed Wild Animals."

Much as his mother had done when she was young, Jered eventually abandoned all efforts to be accepted by his peers. Being in the company of other children made him nervous, so Jered sought the comfort of his own world. When he was alone, he could relax, not concerned that a cutting remark was about to be made about him. Jered's vivid imagination made the time spent alone enjoyable. With the whooshing sound as background music, Jered enjoyed the solitary world he'd created.

Jered was the proverbial apple of his parents' eyes. Rodney told anyone and everyone how there were *big* things on his son's horizon. "The sky's the limit for my boy!" he'd say. Chrissy didn't like it when her husband boasted about Jered, as she was concerned that a parent's lofty expectations could be a heavy yoke for a child to carry. She also was concerned that lauding their son's bright future could tempt Fate. She didn't care if Jered went to college or chose manual labor as his occupation, as long as her son was healthy and happy.

Although she presented herself as the model of a doting, loving wife and mother, Chrissy was actually a nervous wreck most of the time. Her lack of self-confidence caused her to be in a state of perpetual foreboding. Because of what she considered a stroke of amazingly good luck, she'd achieved things she'd thought would always be beyond her reach: a loving husband, a beautiful son, and a tidy little house of their own. Now that she'd arrived at Shangri-La, Chrissy couldn't help but feel the cruel world would at any moment rip these gifts from her. Deep down she believed she didn't deserve to be this happy, thus she lived in perpetual fear of the day her wonderful life would come crashing down upon her. She did her best not to tempt Fate, steering clear of anything she sensed was the least bit dangerous or scary. If something eventually tore her happy life apart, it would certainly come in the form of something scary.

Since Chrissy was afraid of so many things, it's of little surprise her son adopted many of her fears and phobias as his own. Jered wasn't fond of the scary aspects of Halloween and wouldn't even watch Scooby Doo on television because there were monsters in nearly every episode. Rodney was annoyed of his son's timidity, and he knew his wife stoked these fears.

"When he develops his gift," Rodney mused to himself, "he won't have to be afraid of anything. Or anyone! Someday he'll come out of his shell." Comforted by this belief, he did his best not to be overly concerned about his wife's continual babying of Jered.

For as long as he could remember, Jered questioned whether he was being raised by someone other than his true parents. Since neither of his parents were psychologists, it's of little surprise that the label "Foundling Fantasy Syndrome" was never mentioned in their household. There wasn't a single event or observation that triggered Jered's suspicion. It was just a gut feeling. Although he looked a little like his mother, Jered didn't think he resembled his father at all. They were nice people and good parents, but Jered thought their relationship was not quite right. He'd seen other kids showered with public displays of parental affection he'd never received. While it was true his mother doted on him and his father was always interested in hearing of Jered's accomplishments, there was rarely the gush of emotion he'd seen other parents exhibit. In Jered's mind, this was due to the fact they might not be his real parents.

It didn't seem farfetched to Jered that somehow he'd been placed in the wrong family.

His parents told him tales which recounted instances of babies and young children being taken away from their mothers to be raised by strangers. Rapunzel was taken from her real mother by an enchantress and sequestered in a tower. Moses was discovered floating in a basket and was raised by a queen.

Children are told to make a wish before blowing out the candles on their birthday cake. It's been suggested parents instituted this tradition to encourage children to look to the future, thereby taking the child's mind off the inadequate birthday gifts the parents purchased. While a child may be disappointed his birthday present from his parents was a new shirt, he'd nevertheless be upbeat because of the possibility that his birthday wish would come true. Some of the darker, more suspicious critics in our society have opined this is yet another circumstance where adults expect children to carry the emotional baggage created by the adults' parenting shortfalls.

Like every child, Jered had the thrilling belief he had the power once a year to dictate his future. Each spring as his April birthday approached, Jered hoped this would be the year his birthday wish would be granted. On his fifth, sixth, seventh, and eighth birthdays, Jered blew out the candles after silently making the same wish: that his real parents would arrive and sweep him off to his *true* home.

If he indeed was being raised by two strangers, he didn't know if it was due to mistake or some kind of devious plot. He fantasized about the day he'd be reunited with his real parents. When his birthday wishes didn't come true, Jered concluded that the grand scale of what he was requesting required more than just one or two attempts. Jered recognized this was a lot bigger than wishing for a new Evel Knievel action figure. Although he didn't know what the actual cost would be, he estimated it might take up to ten birthday wishes before his true parents came for him.

Young children rarely exhibit patience, but Jered figured he could wait a little longer for that wondrous day to arrive. Until then, he was being cared for by two loving people. In particular, Jered was very fond of his "mother." Jered loved her almost as much as if she'd been his real mother. Whoever his real mother was and wherever she might be, Jered hoped she'd be as sweet as this woman.

Jered idolized the man playing the part of his "father." To Jered it appeared his father had accomplished a great deal. His job must have been particularly important because he was always talking about it. Jered surmised that part of the reason his father didn't shower him with attention was because of the strain caused by his important job. It was when Jered accomplished something at

SKELETONS ARE NOT SCARY

school or drew something particularly well that his father became emotionally engaged. After praising the boy, he'd always encourage him to "take it to the next level." It disappointed Jered that there never seemed to be time for he and his dad to celebrate Jered's accomplishments. Jered sensed his father just looked upon it as another step towards a future undefined goal.

Third grade was shaping up to be the best school year ever, in Jered's opinion. From kindergarten through second grade, Jered earned below average grades. Between his failed attempts to gain acceptance from his peers and his diminished language skills brought about by his partial deafness, school was a challenge. Teachers focused their time and attention on outgoing children, as well as kids who created problems, leaving the quiet introverted students to fade into the background. Reticent children such as Jered learned that elementary school is often a direct application of the proverb, "the squeaky wheel gets the grease." Why would a teacher pay attention to a child who quietly keeps to himself?

Fairly soon after starting third grade, however, there were indications this year was going to be different. His third-grade teacher, Miss Moran, was by far the best teacher Jered ever had. The young teacher's vivacious energy intoxicated Jered. Teacher and student bonded on the afternoon she first saw one of Jered's drawings. She showed a genuine interest in his drawings and encouraged him to explore the entire range of his artistic abilities. She taught him how a drawing could come to life with modest shading and the use of perspective. Jered was awestruck when Miss Moran demonstrated these advanced drawing techniques to him. Suddenly he was no longer just the quiet, introverted boy everyone ignored.

"When you're drawing eyes, you want to make sure to leave a small area of reflected light in them," she demonstrated to Jered. "You see? Now the eyes are fuller and reveal life in them, instead of just being flat."

Never before had Jered felt so special and he glowed proudly when she complimented his artwork. She sometimes asked Jered to stand in front of the class to display his drawings. The first few times he'd done so were terrifying and his hands were shaking as he held up his drawing for the class to see. Over time, however, he got to the point where he'd confidently stride to the chalkboard and display what he'd created. Out of the corner of his eye, Jered could usually see Miss Moran's admiring smile as he explained his drawing to the class.

Miss Moran's spirit also encouraged Jered to work harder on all his studies. His goal was to please her. Although he knew he'd never be at the top of the class, Jered wanted to do well enough in math, spelling, and social studies to make Miss Moran happy and proud.

"This must be the way it works," Jered thought one night as he was lying in bed. "The further I go in school, the better the teachers become. The worst teachers are at the bottom, in kindergarten, and the teachers keep getting better as you move up grades." This reasoning made sense, but he couldn't imagine how magnificent his teachers would be by the time he got to high school. Miss Moran was ten times better than his second-grade teacher. If his fourth-grade teacher was ten times better than Miss Moran, well, the outlook would make your head spin!

Over time, Chrissy's concern she'd awake to find her husband so pale he was almost transparent faded. As far as Chrissy knew, Rodney hadn't had any more of the bizarre seizures. Years passed with neither one of them even mentioning the frightening events of that night. It was too scary for Chrissy to raise the issue, and Rodney was hoping it would become erased by the passage of time.

When Jered was about three years old, she asked Rodney about the episode as they ate supper. "Have you had any other times that you've, you know, had another seizure thing like you did that one night?"

Rodney was blindsided and choked on the piece of Swiss steak he was chewing. Doing his best to sound nonchalant, he replied, "Nope. None at all. Hopefully, I've just grown out of it." Rodney tapped his knuckles on the kitchen table. "Knock on wood. I think it's best if we never talk about it, though. I don't want to jinx myself."

Chrissy made a gesture as if she were locking her mouth shut. This made good sense to her: no reason to tempt Fate.

In truth, Rodney had experienced a handful of Way-Outs since that night. A pattern started to form, which helped him predict when one was likely to occur. If Rodney was experiencing strong emotions, whether terribly angry or filled with joy, it might trigger an episode. When strong emotions were paired with one of his crippling headaches, the likelihood increased even further. If he was in a foul mood because of a particularly bad day at work or was celebrating a promotion, Rodney made an excuse to sleep on the old basement sofa.

"I'm not feeling very well," he'd tell Chrissy. "Could be the flu. I'll sleep downstairs tonight, so I don't give it to you." If a Way-Out occurred, he was safely hidden from his wife.

It seemed Rodney's unique talent had become a bit stronger since his son was born. After Jered's birth, Rodney went on his special excursions two or three times a year. He wondered if Jered's slowly developing ability was somehow accentuating his own abilities. Rodney thought of a formidable thunderstorm being bolstered by a smaller, less powerful squall.

One of the Way-Outs was particularly vivid. And particularly satisfying. Rodney was floating on the cool night wind when he was abruptly drawn into a man who was watching television while seated in an overstuffed chair. The man was watching the local news and Rodney noticed the people on TV had unusual accents.

"I wonder where I'm at?" Rodney thought.

On this occasion Rodney didn't just hear his host's thoughts: he also felt them. His host's anger burned inside Rodney. The man was angrier than he could ever remember being. Rodney's pulse increased as he experienced the man's rage. The man was nauseous, and Rodney felt stomach acid gurgle up into the back of his throat. He tasted outrage. Resentment.

Rodney hollered a question into the vast chasm of his host's mind and listened to it echo several times before it faded away: "Who's to blame?"

After a few moments of silence, a response echoed from afar. "Her!"

When he was younger, Rodney was a clumsy hack, yelling orders at his hosts, demanding they obey. Experience honed his skills to the point he could usually persuade the host to do his bidding instead of simply mandating blind compliance. Sure, it was fine to order people to obey under threat of punishment. It was far more satisfying, though, to convince the host into believing the act was his own idea all along.

"How could she have done this to us?" Rodney whispered to his host. Their thoughts became joined, sharing a single mind. "How often are we expected to endure this?"

"Yes! I've suffered so much!" the man replied. "How much can a man take?"

"If only there was some solution to the problem," Rodney mused. When there wasn't a response, Rodney added, "Is there some way I can fix this situation?"

"I've always been able to fix things," the host said in a dreamy, detached voice. "I'm good at fixing things with my hands."

"That's true," Rodney soothed. "Things become broken: that's what they do. Then my hands fix the problem: that's what they do."

"I can fix anything that's broken," the host said.

"Is that true? Can I truly fix anything?" After a brief silence, Rodney asked, "Or am I something less than a man? Am I stuck being surrounded by broken things?"

The angry voice quickly returned. "I'm a man! I can fix this!"

Slyly, Rodney asked again, "Can I?"

With long, loping strides, the host marched resolutely to the bedroom door. Curled up under the comforter was the cause of his rage.

"She's broken," the host stated.

"And it appears she wants to take us down with her," Rodney added. "If there was only something I could do to fix this problem. Fix it, once and for all."

These words were fuel being thrown on the proverbial fire. Although he was only a passenger, Rodney felt the woman's pulse through the hands wrapped tightly around her neck. Once the deed was done, there was typically a very sudden change in the host's emotions. The realization as to what just occurred turned the host's tenacity to panic. This mood swing was Rodney's cue to depart. A skydiver must recognize when the experience is over and pull the rip cord so he can do it again another day. Rodney pulled the rip cord, floating away on the same breeze that delivered him.

Driving to work the next morning, Rodney became lost in thought about his latest Way-Out. Was his power becoming stronger so he'd be better able to guide his son?

CHAPTER SEVEN

Miss Kerri Moran

Kerri Moran didn't even consider becoming an elementary school teacher until after finishing her sophomore year in college. Prior to changing her major from fine arts to elementary education, she was destined to become the next great painter, whose art would adorn the walls of the biggest and best museums. Her name would be included with the grandmasters of fine art: Michelangelo; DaVinci; Van Gogh; Moran. Soon after starting college, however, she was faced with the sobering realization she could draw a few things very well but struggled mightily with most other subjects.

In high school she'd received accolades for her drawings, which consisted primarily of dogs, cats, and a few other small animals in various poses. The animals were lifelike and elicited a warm, fuzzy feeling when you looked at them. When the art instructors in college forced her to branch away from drawing animals, the result wasn't very promising. Encouraged to practice and then practice some more, Kerri drew hundreds of hands, fingers, and faces but none of them looked very realistic. When she saw the detailed, expressive pieces her classmates were creating, she realized her talent wasn't as impressive as her high school friends led her to believe.

"It's better I figure this out now, I guess, as opposed to years down the road," she mumbled to herself as she contemplated her options. "I don't want to end up drawing cheesy caricatures of people with huge heads holding tennis rackets at the county fair." She'd reached the unpleasant conclusion she probably couldn't even do that, since she'd failed to grasp the skill of drawing lifelike faces. Or hands. Or feet.

"You can still draw even when you're a teacher," her mother encouraged. "You'll have your entire summer vacation every year to work on your art."

Kerri changed her major to elementary education, hoping to become an art teacher. Although her talent was limited, she figured she had enough skills to teach kids how to draw. With her four-year teaching degree in hand, she discovered the need for art teachers was extremely low, maybe even lower than the need for grand-master artists. At 22, she was facing the unfortunate reality that neither her chosen field, nor her back-up job were viable options. She accepted an offer to teach a third grade class. Kerri hoped this would lead to a position as a full-time art teacher if, and when, one became available.

The young teacher loved teaching that initial class more than she could've ever imagined. Being with the same group of children every day gave Kerri the opportunity to emotionally bond with them in a way that wasn't possible when she was a part-time student teacher. Each child had his or her own unique personality and learning skills, and Kerri found the challenge of reaching each of them very rewarding. Experiencing firsthand the moment when a child finally understands a difficult topic was exhilarating.

Jered Barstow was Kerri's diamond in the rough. During the first few weeks of school, Jered kept to himself and rarely spoke to anyone. Kerri asked Jered's second grade teacher about her experiences with the boy the previous year. Mrs. Lowery was a fifteen-year veteran who spoke in a gravelly voice exacerbated by cigarettes.

"He's not a difficult child to deal with. Not the brightest bulb on the string but not an out-and-out dummy," Mrs. Lowery explained. "It's hard to get his attention: he seems to live in his own little world. You won't be able to connect with him, but he's harmless. Just leave him be. He won't cause you any problems."

Kerri had no intention of letting Jered or any of her twenty-three students, simply fade into the background. She pledged to discover what Jered had to offer and what brought him joy. Before the second week of school was over, she'd found it.

One afternoon she asked her students to draw a picture about what autumn looked like. While the children drew, she played a Mozart record so the soothing music could nourish their creativity. The results of the exercise disappointed Kerri. There was rancorous complaining about the classical music from several students: it was too old-fashioned. When she saw what they'd drawn, Kerri thought this assignment might have been too advanced for her third graders. Many of the boys resorted to drawing football scenes. Although she never mentioned fall foliage when she gave the assignment, most of the girls for some reason drew similar pictures of trees with dark yellow and red leaves. How had they all chosen the same uninspired subjects? As Kerri walked around the room inspecting her students' unimaginative creations, she'd pretty much chalked up the activity as a failure. And then she saw Jered's picture.

Jered used crayons and colored pencils to create a vast and detailed masterpiece. The perspective was that of looking down from a bluff, with a golden field of wheat stretching into the distance. A small red schoolhouse was on the edge of these proverbial amber waves of grain, and children were dutifully walking towards it. An adjacent field was peppered with bright orange pumpkins, guarded by a one-armed scarecrow. Kerri was both amazed and enchanted with the drawing. It was a complicated, insightful creation. The quiet little boy created the detailed scene in a very short time.

"Everyone, can I have your attention please? Jered, could you hold up your paper and tell us all what you've drawn?"

When she saw the abject terror in Jered's eyes, she immediately felt bad for the boy. It certainly wasn't her intention to throw the introverted boy into the deep end; she'd just got so excited when she saw his picture, she wanted to celebrate it.

"Tell you what," she said, "I'll hold it up and you just remain seated at your desk. Tell us what you've drawn."

Kerri hoped this would reduce her student's anxiety. Even with this assistance, Jered's description was barely audible. He spoke with his chin tucked down to his chest, as if he was disclosing something that embarrassed him. The shy and scared boy didn't look up once while he mumbled a few unintelligible words about his picture.

"What did he say?" a few of his classmates squawked.

Pretending she'd understood what Jered had said, Kerri announced, "Yes, I can see that! Well, I think it's just grand! I hope Jered will draw more pictures like this as we go through the year!" When she returned the artwork to Jered, he was blushing so vividly one might have mistaken it for a terrible sunburn. As soon as the paper was back on his desk, he quickly lowered his head to his desk and returned to drawing. Kerri noticed Jered usually had a bland, unemotional facial expression. Throughout the remainder of that afternoon, however, she saw a hint of a smile on his face.

In the days and weeks that followed, Kerri devised ways to nurture her shy artist. She inserted opportunities for her students to give impromptu presentations into her lesson plan.

"Eddie, would you stand at your desk and tell us about the best food you've ever eaten?"

"Julie, tell us about your favorite toy when you were growing up."

Kerri knew all her students would benefit from honing their public speaking skills. She'd been taught in college that this was the basic purpose of having children participate in show-and- tell.

In particular, she wanted to coax Jered out of his shell. Since his primary interest was drawing, she used this as a springboard for his presentations to the class.

"Jered, would you hold up your drawing and tell us about it." Jered was slow to respond to these entreaties, and Kerri often had to egg him on. "We can see it's a picture of a bear trying to get honey out of jar. Please tell us how you thought of it."

Without lifting his eyes from the floor, Jered said in a monotone voice, "It's a bear trying to get honey out of a jar."

"And what else can you tell us about this very nice drawing?"

After a long silence, the shy boy offered, "Kind of like the Winnie-the-Pooh story, I guess, but I tried to make him to look different than Winnie-the-Pooh."

"Why does he only have one eye?" one of the girls asked.

Jered shrugged his shoulders. "No reason. He was just born that way."

Very gradually, Jered began to open up, to the point he no longer looked mortified when his teacher called upon him. Kerri also encouraged Jered to explore the limits of his artistic skills, challenging him to draw things he claimed were beyond his abilities. She enjoyed seeing his creations. He exhibited a degree of imagination and artistic ability Kerri recognized from her own childhood. He was obviously a gifted artist, but she was the first person who'd ever urged him to draw things outside of his comfort zone. She figured the last thing he needed to do was become another Kerri Moran who was an expert at drawing a handful of things, but unable to expand beyond that.

Kerri searched for opportunities for Jered to draw. When the cafeteria was looking to spruce up its pale green walls, Kerri suggested that Jered draw pictures on thick poster board. Instead of shyly avoiding this task, the new, more confident Jered gladly accepted this undertaking. Studying one of the pictures Jered had drawn,

Miss Moran asked him, "It looks like this deer is missing part of his antler: it doesn't look like the other one."

In a matter-of-fact tone, Jered replied, "Yeah, he was just born that way."

Watching Jered slowly emerge from his shell invigorated the young teacher. With a little prodding, Jered was increasingly comfortable when talking about his artwork. To the young teacher, knowing she was having a direct positive impact on her students was the best part of teaching.

Conversely, one of the worst parts of teaching was being subjected to the sour dispositions of the veteran teachers. It appeared to Kerri they were generally uninterested and not at all vested in their pupils. Whereas Kerri joined in the celebration of her students' achievements and endured with them every defeat, the rest of the faculty appeared to simply clock-in each morning and clock-out at quitting time.

"Don't you just love it when you can see in their eyes that they've finally figured something out?" she said excitedly to one of her colleagues in the teachers' lounge.

"That feeling will pass," the other teacher grumbled. "It gets old real fast. You'll get jaded over time, to the point that it's just a job."

Kerri swore to herself that she'd never become that kind of teacher. She was determined to be different. To be better.

Before and after school, teachers chatted in small groups in the teachers' lounge. When Kerri managed to join these conversations, she was disappointed when there wasn't any sharing of teaching techniques. Instead, they talked about TV, other teachers, and fashion.

"Can you recommend ways to encourage shy, quiet students to become more involved?" she asked a small group of her colleagues.

"Why would you ever want to do that? If none of my class said a single word all day, I'd be a happy camper!" one of the teachers guffawed, causing the other teachers to laugh.

Undeterred, Kerri followed up with another question. "How can you draw out the best of what the quiet, withdrawn kids have to offer?"

One of the other teachers asked curtly, "So, I just have to ask you this: why do you insist on wearing gypsy skirts?"

Kerri looked down at her patchwork skirt that brushed the floor. "Huh?" she said, using her hands to nervously iron out the top of the skirt.

Another teacher piped in on the subject. "You look like a hippie. Are you a hippie, Kerri?" She then displayed peace signs on both hands and said in a stoner's voice, "Hey man, were you at Woodstock, man?"

Kerri was taken off guard by her colleagues' raucous laughter. They had to have known Kerri was attending her suburban high school when the Woodstock concert was held in 1969. This was the first time Kerri had ever been accused of being a hippy and she wasn't sure how to respond. Was this good-natured ribbing of the new teacher or something harsher?

Still nervously stroking the top of her skirt, Kerri managed to say, "I just like long skirts." What followed was an uncomfortable silence, which Kerri broke by clumsily adding, "They're sometimes called broomstick skirts or maxis."

"Whatever you call them, you look like a hippie, not a teacher. Do you see any of us wearing those things?"

Kerri noted they all wore polyester dresses carefully hemmed to four finger widths below the knee. Kerri hadn't considered the length of her skirt to be a political statement, but she started to think there was a uniform of sorts the veteran teachers expected all their colleagues to adopt. Not wanting to make any waves, Kerri hemmed her two long skirts so that they were the accepted length. She wasn't the world's greatest tailor, but she thought the skirts ended up looking pretty good. The following week, Kerri was proud to wear one of her newly hemmed skirts, which no longer came anywhere near the floor.

As she approached two of the teachers standing next to the coffee pot in the teachers' lounge, one of them said, "Is hippie girl now trying to be someone else? Your budget a little tight, so you couldn't buy some proper polyester teacher's clothes?" She laughed, then added, "I'm just kidding! If anybody can pull off that look, it'd be you, dear."

No more broomstick skirts of any length were ever worn again by Kerri Moran. She was disappointed she hadn't been able to seamlessly integrate with the rest of the teachers, but she hoped as she spent time with them, they'd eventually warm up to her. What was most important was she was teaching her own class of kids and enjoying it.

During those first few months, Kerri couldn't conceive of how teaching could ever become dull. There were all kinds of stars in her class and Kerri saw exciting opportunities for them. Claire was the best reader in the class. Kerri was surprised how quickly Claire could read while maintaining an impressive recollection of what she'd read. In Kerri's mind, the world was Claire's oyster, and she had unlimited possibilities. Vincent was her math whiz who wore thick black glasses, and it was easy to see him becoming an accountant. Susan was born to be a politician, who inserted herself into disputes so that everyone would "play nice." Johnny was an annoying little boy with a limited intellect, who managed to get his way by manipulating his classmates. If this behavior kept up, Kerri figured the boy was destined either to be a lawyer or felon. Possibly both.

By far the student she enjoyed working with the most was the class artist, Jered. As so many adults do, Kerri saw Jered's talent and success as a consolation prize for her own failure in the field. Kerri thought it would be a glorious experience if one of her students became the talk of the art community. Just like the many little league fathers and dance school mothers who came before her, Kerri hoped to experience the joy of success vicariously through her student.

Kerri asked her mother about the drawing skills she had when she was Jered's age.

"Why are you asking about that?" her mother asked.

"My artist is really talented, and I wanted to compare where he is in his development to my own." As she and her mother were rifling through a box of her elementary school papers, Kerri gushed, "It's not just my artist who gets me excited. My kids are so talented! You wouldn't believe all the things they know and everything that they can do. I think they're way beyond where I was at that age."

"Someday you'll settle down and have your own kids, then you'll think *they're* even smarter!" her mother mused.

"Someday, sure, but these are the only kids I need in my life right now."

Her mother dug out some of the drawings Kerri made when she was in grade school and Kerri analyzed the artwork. Clearly Jered was demonstrating a level of skill that was above hers at that age. In particular, Jered possessed exemplary skills in the areas of perspective and color. While his classmates were doing well if they drew something that an adult could readily identify, Jered was already able to pretty accurately transfer what he saw in the real world or in his imagination onto paper.

Looking over his shoulder as he drew two lions gallantly walking through a jungle, she asked Jered if he'd ever taken any art classes outside of school. Jered shook his head.

"Did one of your parents teach you to draw like this? Maybe another relative like an uncle or grandparent?"

Without looking up at his teacher, Jered mumbled, "I've just always been able to do it. I like to draw, so I guess I just do it all the time." Jered glanced up at Miss Moran and saw her sweet face smiling down at him with admiration.

"I can tell you draw a lot: you really have a talent." She pointed to an area of subtle shadow he'd drawn. "I like this part here. You've started to create a three-dimensional effect."

Jered's full moon face turned up towards his teacher with an expression of awe. She wasn't just praising his artwork: she clearly understood the process he went through to create his pictures. Miss Moran was the first adult who seemed to recognize what it took to draw something well. She was leaps and bounds beyond what Jered typically heard from adults, which usually consisted of the insightful observation, "You're a really good drawer."

She cocked her head to one side, continuing to carefully analyze the jungle scene. "I like your choice of colors. It's very . . . vivid, almost like it's a scene from a colorful dream. Tomorrow I'll bring a book from home and show you a painting by Rousseau."

"Who?"

"Henri Rousseau. He painted a famous picture of a woman sleeping next to a lion. I think you'll like it. I want to show you some of the pictures other artists have painted, so you can get even more ideas for your own drawings. Does that sound like fun?"

The boy's heart swelled and his face felt warm, as if he'd turned to face a blazing summer sun. He nodded his head and Miss Moran smiled.

If you ask a third-grade boy to define "love," you'd expect him to do poorly, and Jered was no exception to that rule. An eight-year-old boy's definition of the gossamer concept of love would likely be stilted and unimaginative. Despite this limited understanding, Jered knew at that moment with absolute certainty that he *loved* Miss Moran. Loved her with all his heart.

CHAPTER EIGHT

The Bestest Teacher in the World

Jered blossomed under the tutelage of his teacher. Kerri Moran was the first adult who wasn't related to Jered who showed any true interest in the boy. He was a small houseplant who'd been sequestered in the protected confines of a dark closet. When exposed to Miss Moran's brilliant sunlight, he rapidly grew and prospered, as if he was making up for lost time.

For her part, Miss Moran did her best not to shower *too* much attention on her fledgling star. During her training, she'd been taught not to become fixated on a favorite student, lest the remainder of the class feel slighted. She called Jered's mother to get permission to provide private art training after school a few days a week.

"It would only be for an hour or so on those days I don't have other commitments," Kerri explained. "I'd teach him drawing techniques that are beyond the skill level of his classmates."

Everyone was very pleased with the arrangement. Chrissy enjoyed the gleam in her son's eyes when he showed her what he'd learned during Miss Moran's art instruction. Fueled by her pupil's bounding excitement, Kerri considered her sessions with Jered to be a special reward after a hard day's work. Of course, Jered was on cloud nine. Some of the drawing techniques Miss Moran taught him were so amazing it was almost like magic. He learned how to draw things he was sure he'd never been able to figure out on his own. All the while, his private art teacher's dark brown eyes melted his heart.

While broadening her star pupil's artistic skills, Kerri decided this was also an opportunity to foster growth of his poorly developed sense of self-esteem and courage.

"Let's try a new medium today," she announced, opening a stained and battered box.

"Medium? Huh? Like small, medium, and large?"

"No, a new medium as in a different way to create art. These are pastels; they're a special kind of chalk." Jered picked up one of the rectangular sticks, eyeing it with uncertainty. "They are really good for drawing landscapes, nature scenes, and portraits. See how they leave a softer edge than pencils?"

"I don't know about this," Jered said, crinkling up his nose. "I don't think I like these. I never drew with anything like this."

"Just because you've never done it doesn't mean you *can't* do it," Miss Moran replied in an encouraging tone. "Give them a try before making up your mind. See how I can easily make a full, beautiful tree with a green pastel?"

At first Jered wasn't very impressed with the new tool Miss Moran introduced. After an hour of experimentation, though, he gradually got the hang of how to use brightly colored chalk.

"That's it," Miss Moran said, trying to tamp down her excitement at how quickly Jered became comfortable using pastels. "You'll see that simply by using a different media, you can create different emotions in your work."

Once he saw firsthand what Miss Moran said was true, Jered's full moon face beamed in adoration at the only woman (other than his mother and grandmother) he'd ever loved. He was constantly amazed at the seemingly endless amount of knowledge she had. Miss Moran was the smartest, most talented person Jered had ever met, and he was thrilled at every opportunity to draw from her fountain of wisdom. He considered her the *bestest* teacher in the world.

The lesson was interrupted by loud banging on the outside of the classroom window. Three boys rushed up to the window, beat their fists on it, then ran away yelling, "Stupid!" Although the disruption was brief, Miss Moran was concerned at how quickly Jered's expression changed from pride to embarrassment. Instinctively, his shoulders drooped with shame, pulling his head down. The young teacher recognized immediate remedial action was required.

"Jered," she said in a friendly but firm voice. When the boy's head remained bowed, she said his name again, this time even firmer. Hesitatingly, he looked up at her and she explained, "Sometimes those who don't have your same interests or talents will decide they need to make themselves feel better by criticizing you." Jered never considered that this was the reason he'd been incessantly teased over the years. Jered assumed that the barbs from others were well-founded and appropriate attacks on his many limitations. "Whenever someone tries to bring you down, it's important to reject their efforts. Don't let someone else dictate the way you feel. Your happiness is determined only by you: nobody else gets that power. Do you get what I'm saying?"

Jered nodded. He'd never thought of it that way but now that he'd heard Miss Moran's explanation, this made perfect sense. He was chagrined he hadn't figured this out on his own.

Miss Moran further explained, "When someone tries to use words to take power away from you, try turning it around and using those words right back at them. What's important is you believe they can't control your emotions unless you let them. Their jealousy shouldn't make you feel bad. Does that make sense?"

It certainly did and Jered had the opportunity to use this advice the following day. The three boys who'd interrupted the art lesson were still snickering about their grand display of derision towards Jered and Miss Moran. After the bell rang and everyone was seated at their desks, the three boys continued to celebrate their defiant act.

Perturbed at their incessant giggling, Miss Moran turned from the chalkboard. "Is there a problem, boys?"

This caused another eruption of snickering. One of them replied, "There's no problem, Miss Moran. We was just wonderin' if Jered is going to be doing some pretty drawings for us!" The three boys burst out laughing, which caused many of the other students to join in.

Before Miss Moran could rebuke, Jered spoke from the back row of the classroom. Initially his voice was quiet and mousy: "You know, Eddie, I . . ." Jered recognized his voice wasn't quite right, so he sat up tall in his seat and cleared his throat before continuing. When he spoke again, his voice was more confident. "You know, Eddie, if you'd like me to teach you how to draw, I will. I'm sorry you can't draw good like me but maybe with a lot of practice you could someday get to be as good as me."

Eddie and his two compatriots stopped giggling. They turned to look at Jered with expressions of shock and wonder, as if they'd just been unexpectantly slapped across the face. After several silent seconds, Eddie was able to come up with a witty retort. "Oh, yeah?"

Jered continued to press the advantage he'd gained. "Yeah. I'll try to teach you. It could take a while because right now you don't draw very good at all."

Eddie and the other boys were dumfounded and silent. Miss Moran wanted to jump in the air and pump her fist in victory but that would've been wholly inappropriate. Instead, the demure teacher did her best to keep her expression neutral, saying, "Okay, now that's all over, let's not have any more talking during class."

Jered didn't hear much of what the love of his life said during the following fifteen minutes. He sat at his desk with an amazed expression on his face as he relived the episode where he'd bested

Eddie in a battle of wits. This was the first time he'd ever stood up to a bully. Because he'd never been able to muster this amount of confidence and courage, Jered had to reassure himself that he had indeed done it, and it hadn't just been an elaborate daydream. When Eddie later shot Jered a menacing, disgusted look, Jered knew for sure that it really happened!

When she turned back to the chalkboard, Kerri let a huge smile of satisfaction spread across her face. She was still wearing that satisfied smile hours later when she walked into the teacher's lounge after the final bell.

"No after school lessons today?" one of the teachers asked in a snarky tone, followed by a derisive giggle.

Unfazed, Miss Moran replied, "Nope, not today. Tomorrow is the next lesson."

"You should charge his parents a fee for working with that kid so much."

"I wouldn't accept any money, even if they offered," she said matter-a-factly. "I enjoy watching his artistic skills develop. He really has talent."

Annoyed at not getting a rise out of the young woman, the other teacher marched to the door. As she left the room, she remarked, "Yeah, you'll get over it."

Kerri Moran was still smiling as she drove home. Shy, scared Jered held his ground and was able to put the bullies in their place. This was proof she was truly making a difference, and his success invigorated her. Jered's small victory was a small victory for Kerri as well.

"*This* is what teaching is all about!"

CHAPTER NINE

Halloween Decorations

As best he could, Rodney waited patiently for his son's special ability to develop and appear. When a payoff is destined to occur at some unknown time in the future, though, it's difficult *not* to become impatient at times. On a date known by no one, Rodney was going to be presented with a gift from his son that was so grand it was beyond comprehension. Right now, however, he'd just have to wait.

Before Jered started kindergarten, Rodney made a point to regularly spend time alone with his son. Since Rodney's special skill first manifested itself with graphic dreams, he often asked Jered during these private times to describe his dreams and nightmares. Jered hadn't described anything yet, but Rodney thought fondly about what that day would be like. "Dad, something strange has started happening when I'm dreaming," Jered would confide. "It's as if I'm flying and listening to what other people are thinking: especially angry people."

Since Jered's power would surely be greater than his own, Rodney figured his son's ability would develop earlier than his own. Rodney's burgeoning abilities began to form when he was six years old, so he was disappointed when Jered hadn't reported any change in his dreams prior to starting school. Through kindergarten, first grade, and second grade, Jered had yet to report experiencing any odd sensations of floating in the air or hearing hundreds of voices merged into one while he was dreaming.

As the years passed, a cruel voice began occasionally interrupting Rodney's thoughts. "You're wrong. Jered doesn't have the gift. He's just a half-deaf boy who'll become nobody special." Rodney did his best to ignore these awful doubts

"Jered is the first son, of a first son, of a first son: he has been chosen to take this next step," Rodney assured himself. "I know it's so, because it *must* be so."

Much like a seedling just about to push through the soil and expose itself to the outside world, Rodney knew his son's special ability was just below the surface. He wanted to somehow encourage the seedling to emerge, but he didn't know how.

On a Saturday afternoon in September, Rodney and Jered were at Grant's Discount Store, picking up a few items his son needed for a school project. Lost in his thoughts, Rodney again ruminated that Jered was eight years old and not an inkling of his unique gift had declared itself. While Jered searched through a bin of clearance school supplies, Rodney thought, "How much longer am I going to have to wait?"

"I found an eraser for only a dime!" Jered announced, holding aloft his discovery from the depths of the clearance bin.

"Good job!" Rodney replied, pleased at his son's resourcefulness.

Watching his son dig through the bargains, Rodney mused how his son had characteristics of both his parents. He'd inherited his mother's round, full moon face, making him appear as if he was always apprehensive. From Rodney, Jered would inherit . . .

"What if that's all your son inherited?" a cynical voice in Rodney's head interrupted. "What if the special ability to control people began and ended with you?" It wasn't the first time the unkind voice raised this kind of question. Rodney took a moment to silence the voice. Rodney reassured himself these periodic episodes of doubt were normal. Brave trailblazers like Marco Polo must have experienced similar episodes of self-doubt on their way to redefining the world as we knew it. True courage involved pushing these irksome negative thoughts aside, then continuing the journey to change the world.

"They got Halloween decorations!" Jered exclaimed, his loud, shrill voice yanking Rodney out of his fog. "Can we look at them, Dad? Can we?"

Jered's excitement while checking out the Halloween decorations was infectious. The young father watched his son's frenzied antics in the Halloween aisle and wished there was something in his mundane adult life that could elicit such joy.

"Look at this! Wow, look at this!"

"They have some pretty neat stuff this year," Rodney commented, admiring the wide range of colorful and sometimes stark depictions of various All Hallow's Eve fair.

"See this laughing pumpkin, Dad?" Rodney chuckled as Jered tried to contort his face to duplicate the pumpkin's expression. "I'll betcha I could draw this!"

Some of the decorations had been removed from their packages and displayed in the Halloween aisle so shoppers could appreciate their full impact. One of these caught Rodney's eye. Scotch-taped to a pillar was a paperboard cutout of a life-sized skeleton. Walking up to the pillar so he could inspect the skeleton, Rodney was impressed at its realistic detail. Typically, Halloween decorations were cartoony. Even the allegedly scary cutouts of witches and vampires looked unrealistic. The skeleton, however, appeared as if it came right out of a medical book.

"It's amazingly life-like," Rodney thought, "or death-like, or whatever it should be."

The wall hanging had metal rivets fastened at several of the skeleton's joints, which permitted its arms and legs to bend. A Grant's employee had positioned the skeleton so that its hands were sitting jauntily on his hip bones. One of its legs was raised, making it look as though the skeleton was performing a jig. Jered noticed his dad looking at one of the store's pillars. The boy approached his father and was taken aback by the large skeleton. He grabbed the back of his father's belt, making sure his dad stayed between him and the ghastly skeleton. Jered couldn't help but shudder just a little at the sight of the ghoulish dancing skeleton.

— Rodney felt his son's grip on his belt, and remarked, "Pretty neat, isn't it?"

"Um . . . kinda scary, Dad," Jered said in a barely audible voice.

"What? Aw, come on: you're a big boy! This is really out of sight!"

"Mom says stuff like skeletons are scary. I think she's right: it's a scary thing."

Rodney heard the trepidation in his young son's voice. His wife was doing a good job of filling Jered with her innumerable fears and phobias. Right there and then in the Halloween aisle of Grant's Discount Store, Rodney decided to provide his son with a life-lesson. There was no one else looking at Halloween decorations on the last Saturday of September, so they could have a private conversation. He knelt down, putting his arm around Jered's shoulders. Rodney drew his son firmly against him but not so tight that the boy felt trapped.

"You know, your mom is scared of a lot of things," Rodney confided, "but that doesn't mean *you* have to be afraid."

This was a concept Jered had never considered. His mother was the parent who participated the most in his development and he accepted most everything she said as the gospel truth. "I don't? Then why is Mom always telling me to be afraid of things?"

Rodney chose his words carefully. "Well, she just wants you to grow up and not get hurt. But that doesn't mean everything she is afraid of you also have to be scared of. Just because she hates the taste of tomatoes doesn't mean you can't eat them, right?"

"I love tomatoes! They're good!"

"That's what I'm talking about. You can do your own thing, buckaroo."

After thinking about this for a moment, Jered confided, "Did you know Mom's scared of just about *everything*? She's a real scaredy-cat!"

Rodney laughed, ruffling his son's hair with his hand. "That's true but let's just keep that our secret, okay? Best not ever say that to your mother's face!" With a wry smile, Jered nodded his head. "Remember: she loves you a lot and only wants to protect you. It's just she sometimes goes a little too far. Does that make any sense?" Jered nodded, which caused Rodney to swell with fatherly pride. Rodney pointed towards the skeleton, "What do you say we buy that big skeleton? Wouldn't that be a fun thing to put up in the house?"

Jered wasn't as concerned about the huge skeleton as he'd been earlier, but he still felt uneasy about it. "Um, well, there's these other pumpkins over here . . ."

The boy started to pull away from his father, but Rodney held him close. "Forget about the silly pumpkins: those are for little kids. Big boys go for stuff like that skeleton."

Jered didn't say anything, but Rodney could feel he was trembling a bit. Rodney realized just how much his wife's anxieties she'd passed along to their son. While he was at work providing for the family, she was apparently filling Jered's young brain with a long list of things to be afraid of.

"Look, son, remember how afraid of the dark you used to be?" Jered nodded. "I taught you that only little kids are afraid of the dark, right?"

"I don't get scared of the dark as much as I used to," Jered proudly stated.

"That's right! You used to be scared of monsters being under your bed until I told you monsters don't exist." Jered nodded. "You don't have to leap into your bed anymore, right?"

Jered nodded, even though this wasn't entirely true. For as long as Jered could remember, he'd launch himself onto his bed so nothing could reach out from under his bed and grab his ankle. One night this caused the box springs to slide out of its frame and crash to the floor.

"Don't be such a baby! There's nothing under your bed to be scared of!" his father railed. "What am I going to do with a boy who still acts like a baby?"

After that, whenever his father tucked him into bed, Jered made sure to walk deliberately to the bed, then calmly climb into it. However, when his father didn't tuck him in, he sometimes still leapt the final three feet to his bed. While soaring over this area of danger surrounding his bed, Jered made sure to watch the floor, waiting for a gnarled hand or slithering tentacle to reach out in a fruitless attempt to grab his ankles. To date, Jered's efforts had been a resounding success, as his legs had never once been gripped by a monster living under his bed.

A sobering thought gripped Rodney: a kid who was scared of his own shadow was unlikely to embrace a new and exciting talent. Rodney decided he needed to start chipping away at the notion that the world was filled with nothing but scary things. His son needed to be taught that life should consist of more than just avoiding anything that was potentially frightening.

There were long-term ramifications of Chrissy's fearmongering that could have a direct impact on the development of Jered's special abilities. What would happen if Jered was taught to be afraid of skeletons and he saw his own skeleton through his skin after a vivid dream? Rodney remembered the shock at seeing his own skeleton when he was a child. Because he hadn't been taught to be afraid of

SKELETONS ARE NOT SCARY

such things as skeletons, however, Rodney was able to overcome his fears and embrace his special ability. Jered needed encouragement to rise above the silly fears his mother had instilled in him in order to reach his full potential. Rodney couldn't just wave a magic wand to make these fears go away. What this situation called for was a more indirect, gradual indoctrination of his son.

What Rodney wanted to do was buy the skeleton wall hanging, so he and his son could triumphantly march into the house with it. Wouldn't Chrissy absolutely freak out?! This wasn't the course to take, though. Rodney sensed his son was still uneasy about the skeleton, so he led Jered out of the Halloween aisle. No reason to rush things: even a soufflé takes time to rise.

There were times when Rodney wondered if it would just be easier to tell his son about the wonderful ability he'd inherited. He concluded that trying to explain this unusual skill would likely just confuse or traumatize the boy. Jered's special ability needed to develop on its own, just as Rodney's had when he was young. When possible, Rodney could try to carefully foster this development. The first time he saw his own skeleton after a Way-out he thought he was dying. If Rodney could slowly introduce skeletons into Jered's world, he might not be as scared as Rodney was when this occurred.

Psychologists such as Dr. Ford Freud use the term "systematic desensitization" to describe the process by which someone gradually learns to accept a stimulus. Dr. Freud lectured at the recent annual meeting of O.O.P.S. about how a behavioral medicine can nurture this acceptance. "If a child has a heightened, unrealistic fear of snakes, one certainly wouldn't prescribe an initial treatment that involved throwing the child into a pit of snakes. Doing so would not diminish the patient's irrational fear and likely would strengthen the phobia. Instead, the child should undergo a gradual process whereby he is introduced to aspects of snakes over time. Photographs of snakes may be shown to the child until he becomes comfortable with the sight of the amphibian [sic]. The physician would then introduce a toy rubber snake, which has the look and feel of a snake. After this step, the child will be taken to a zoo, where he can look at real snakes sequestered safely behind glass. This leads to the child stroking a snake that is being held by a trusted third party. As the child progresses through these desensitizing steps, the irrational fear of snakes gradually subsides. It is only then that the child is ready for the final step of the therapy and can be safely thrown into a pit of snakes."

Rodney Barstow never heard of systematic desensitization, nor did he attend Dr. Ford Freud's O.O.P.S. lecture on this subject. However, he knew he wanted his son to become gradually comfortable around skeletons, so Jered learned they were nothing to be feared. In another time or another place, skeletons and skulls may have been as popular as the happy yellow "Have a Nice Day" face. At such time or place, skulls may have adorned everything from Christmas cartoons to children's clothing. In 1977, though, skeletons were strictly reserved for Halloween decorations, pirate flags, and the warning labels on poisonous chemicals. Rodney thus concluded that this year he needed to take an active role in the selection of their Halloween decorations.

After work the following Monday, Rodney made a stop at Grant's, purchasing several cutouts for Jered to tape to the inside of the windows. Whereas other houses had windows decorated with depictions of ghosts and Jack-o-lanterns, this year the Barstow house only displayed skulls and skeletons. Rodney picked the most realistic skeletons and skulls, which Jered happily taped to the inside of the windows. Much to the chagrin of his wife, the windows of their house were peppered with various types of skeletons by the first week of October. She felt the house had become spooky and unsavory.

The *coup de grace* (as a French boy might say), was Rodney's purchase of the life-sized skeleton. Printed on thick, sturdy paper nearly as thick as cardboard was the realistic skeleton that initially caused Jered to hide behind his father. Once Rodney thought his son became accustomed to the smaller skeleton decorations, he planned to unveil the large skeleton.

One evening while his wife and son were in the living room watching *The Tony Orlando and Dawn Rainbow Hour*, Rodney retrieved the skeleton from the trunk of his car. He attached the skeleton to the closet door in Jered's bedroom by pushing a thumbtack through the top of the skull. Rodney lifted the left arm, so the hand appeared to be waving and placed a thumbtack through it. What he wanted was to create a friendly skeleton who appeared to be waving his hand and saying, "Hi there, Jered! I'm a skeleton, and I'm your friend! Have you ever thought about becoming a skeleton like me? We can have so much fun! We can travel through the sky, looking for people who have angry thoughts in their head!"

"This looks great!" Rodney said to himself. He was confident that since Jered had been gradually introduced to skeletons over the past few weeks, he'd be less apprehensive when he saw it in his bedroom. In addition, Rodney reasoned the skeleton's grinning face and friendly wave would put the boy at ease. "And this isn't even the best part!" he mused.

"Jered, come to your bedroom," Rodney called out, "I've got something neat to show you!"

"Can't it wait until a commercial?" his wife replied from the living room.

What Rodney wanted to say was, "No, this is important in the development of my son!" but instead he said, "Sure." Rodney shut the closet door so there could be a big reveal of the skeleton when it was opened. He patiently sat on his son's bed, smiling at how thrilled his son would be. A few minutes later, Jered and his mother came to the doorway of the bedroom.

"What did ya want to show me, Dad?" Jered asked.

With all the excitement and splendor of an artist unveiling his latest work of art, Rodney strode to the closet and grasped the door-knob. "Take a look at this!" Rodney swung open the door, revealing the waving skeleton tacked to the inside of it.

Surprised at the sight of the life-sized skeleton, Jered leaned back, bumping into his mother. Much as he had when he first saw it in the department store, Jered felt an uncomfortable trembling sensation in his muscles. If Rodney had bothered to read Dr. Ford Freud's missive "The Pitfalls of Systematic Desensitization," he would have known that employing the element of surprise into the gradual presentation of scary stimuli is rarely a good idea. Springing something on the patient from out of nowhere, Dr. Freud warned, can cause an unintended *increase* in fear.

Whereas his father saw a skeleton wearing a friendly smile, Jered felt it was a sinister grin. It was the kind of mean leer he'd seen on the faces of children who made fun of him on the play-ground. Instinctively, his mother reached a protective arm over Jered's shoulder, putting a comforting hand on his chest. Even through his thick sweatshirt, she could feel the rapid thudding of his heart. Although the gentle pressure of his mother's hand on his chest was somewhat comforting, Jered was still scared.

"What . . . what's that?" Jered asked with an unsteady voice.

Still smiling, his father said, "It's that skeleton, buckaroo! You know, the one we saw at Grant's! I knew how much you liked it, so I went back to the store and bought it!" When Rodney saw the fear in his son's eyes, he was taken aback. His son's apprehension caused Rodney to quickly become frustrated. "Oh, come on! It's just a Halloween decoration! This *can't* scare you! For crying out loud, it's October! Aren't you in the Halloween spirit yet?" Even though his son still looked scared, Rodney decided to up the ante. "I haven't even shown you the best part yet! Turn off the light, Chrissy!"

She hesitated for a moment, then did as her husband suggested. Rodney had already drawn the curtains, so once the overhead light was off the small bedroom was quite dark. After his eyes adjusted to the darkness, Jered saw a glowing green outline of the skeleton's bones.

In an excited voice, Rodney said, "They used glow-in-the-dark ink! Isn't that a riot?"

Because all that could be seen was the skeleton's outline, it appeared as though it was levitating just above the floor. Jered held his breath, trying his best to steady himself. Memory of his heart-to-heart conversation with his dad in the department store flashed into his mind. His father wanted him to be braver and not be scared of so many things like his mother. The boy knew if he showed too much fear, his father would likely become cross with him. If his dad became angry enough to yell at him, Jered knew all too well not even the roaring ocean in his ear could drown out his dad's tirade.

Summoning his courage, Jered tried to say something that belied his fear. "Wow, Dad. It looks a lot different than it did in the store. That's really . . . neat. It's . . . it's glowing,"

"You betcha it is!" his dad replied, slapping a hand onto his thigh with satisfaction.

Chrissy didn't want to see the glowing skeleton any longer, so she flipped the light switch. Having the light back on made Jered feel a little better. Once the lights were turned off later that night, however, Jered knew that the eerie, glowing apparition would once again be in his bedroom.

"Are we going to put that downstairs somewhere?" Chrissy asked in a hopeful voice. "What, are you kidding? It looks great right here in Jered's bedroom! Right, buckaroo?"

His father looked down at Jered with an excited smile that was nearly as disconcerting to the boy as the skeleton's unnerving grin. Somehow, Jered managed to squeak, "Sure, Dad."

"That's my boy!" his dad trumpeted, slapping his thigh once again with the palm of his hand. "Dig it: this can stay up as long as you want. I'll bet once you get used to having a skeleton friend the in your bedroom, you won't ever want to take it down. It's so out of sight, I'll let you keep it up even after all your trick-or-treat candy is eaten!"

Chrissy was aghast, so she could only imagine how scared Jered must have been. She hated being scared: always had, always would. Why people exposed themselves to things that were creepy, macabre, or suspenseful was a mystery. Not once had she been inclined to watch disturbing television programs like *The Twilight Zone* or *Night Gallery*. When commercials for these types of programs came on, she often got up and changed the channel because seeing even a short snippet of those shows made her uncomfortable.

As one would expect, Chrissy was in particular not fond of Halloween. Sure, she enjoyed seeing the neighborhood children dressed up in their costumes. Watching little cowboys, superheroes, and princesses going house to house was cute. Decorating the porch with a smiling Jack-o-Lantern was inviting. Plastering the house with skulls and glow-in-the-dark skeletons was something else altogether, though. Chrissy was certain *she* couldn't have slept if she knew there was a glowing skeleton on the other side of her bedroom's closet door. Her motherly concern was Jered wouldn't be able to get the rest young children needed each night because of the ominous Halloween decoration his father had inexplicably placed in his bedroom.

If it'd been up to her, she'd have torn the skeleton into pieces and thrown them immediately into the metal trashcan on the patio. Chrissy knew, though, she needed to proceed with caution, as she'd

SKELETONS ARE NOT SCARY

seen the excitement and sense of purpose in her husband's eyes when he unveiled the skeleton. Unless she wanted to spark an unpleasant marital tiff, she needed to deal with this situation with the utmost diplomacy.

"Okay, we'll just see how things go *for now*," Chrissy said in a wary voice which subtly communicated her displeasure to her husband. Chrissy felt she'd adequately made her objection while also exhibiting enough deference to Rodney's authority to avoid igniting an ugly confrontation in front of their son.

"Better a skeleton *on* the closet than one *in* the closet!" Rodney joked.

Chrissy didn't laugh.

When she tucked Jered into bed later that night, Chrissy quietly closed the closet door. Jered was glad she'd done so. He was old enough to realize the green glowing skeleton was nothing more than a piece of paper, but he didn't like the idea of trying to fall asleep while the ghoulish skeleton watched him. Jered told himself he wasn't a scaredy-cat, but he also didn't see any reason to go out of his way to surround himself with scary things like a glowing life-sized skeleton. His mother turned off the light, softly closing his bedroom door.

Jered knelt on his bed and opened the curtains so the faint autumn moonlight made his bedroom not so dark. Lying in bed with a quilt pulled up to his chin, he gazed up at the ceiling, doing his best to ignore the sobering fact that there was a life-sized glow in the dark skeleton on the other side of his closet door. Instead of dwelling on the skeleton, he tried to occupy his mind with more pleasant thoughts, like what costume he could wear trick-or-treating.

In Dr. Ford Freud's textbook, *An Overview of Child Behavior: Making Sense of the Madness*, he warned readers about Halloween. "Many children spend unwarranted time making plans for this absurd autumnal event. Countless hours are wasted by children as they become fixated on choosing just the right costume, and the most efficient means of collecting free candy. In a literal sense, this lurid holiday is nothing more than a *time vampire* that sucks away a child's attention from more appropriate pursuits."

Dr. Freud explains in this missive how Halloween can damage the emotional development of children. "It is as if the child believes he can catapult himself forward in his developmental process and simply *become* that which he desires. He does not wish to go through the training necessary to become a fireman: he simply wants these skills magically bestowed upon him. In his young mind, all he needs to accomplish this is to wear the correct costume, or wear the hat, assuming he has the hat. It is therefore a shock to the child and a stressor to his psyche when he discovers he cannot become a certified cardiac surgeon simply by wearing a smock that says 'DOCTOR.' If it were that easy, our society would crumble, since it would be filled with nothing more than princesses, cowboys, astronauts, and ghosts!"

Prior to that night, Jered had already given some serious thought about his costume. Originally, he thought about making his own superhero costume. Instead of Batman or Spider-Man, though, he'd become his own special version of superhero: one who could hear through *both* ears. Jered sketched what this superhero would look like, but it didn't look very impressive. As best he could determine, such a superhero would be a muscle-bound man with a cape fluttering behind him and big elephant-sized ears, which gave him the ability to hear everything. That wasn't going to work. He couldn't figure out how to make big ears for the costume, and even if he did, Jered anticipated being laughed at by the other kids. They wouldn't understand this superhero because they could all hear just fine.

After giving up this idea, he'd narrowed it down to two costume possibilities. One option was to be a ghost like he was the previous Halloween. He learned from watching *It's the Great Pumpkin, Charlie Brown*, that cutting the eyeholes in the sheet required skill, lest you end up looking like a partially peeled potato. His mother agreed to cut the eye holes and the final product was impressive. While draped in an old white sheet, Jered liked it that no one could see his misshapen ear.

While most children travelled in roving packs, Jered had canvassed the neighborhood on his own. Disguised by the sheet, he wasn't the dumb little boy with a weird ear who couldn't hear very well. As an anonymous ghost, Jered was pleasantly surprised how free he felt. At times that night Jered was so happy he skipped from house to house. Normally, no boy would *ever* want to be caught skipping, as everyone knew skipping was only for girls. On that Halloween night, though, Jered could do whatever he wanted because he had a cloak of anonymity to protect him.

"Wouldn't it be boss if everyone wore a costume that hid their identity, not just on Halloween, but *every* day of the year?" Jered pondered.

If they did, there wouldn't be anyone who'd be picked on simply because of how they looked. He could live his life as a ghost nobody recognized: a ghost without a misshapen ear, because ghosts didn't have them.

Another costume possibility was dressing up like Steve Austin, the Six Million Dollar Man. Ever since he saw an episode of *The Six Million Dollar Man*, Jered often wondered how much money it would cost to fix the appearance and function of his right ear. If it took six million dollars to put astronaut Steve Austin back together after his horrific crash, Jered figured just fixing someone's hearing wouldn't cost nearly as much. Maybe a hundred and fifty dollars? Two hundred? If Jered dressed up in Steve Austin's red jumpsuit, he could pretend the government spent lots of money to fix the appearance and function of his ear. The problem with that costume, however, was it didn't provide the ghost costume's freedom of anonymity. Also, where was he going to find a red jumpsuit? He decided he needed to weigh the pros and cons of each costume a little more before making a final decision.

While Jered was thinking about his costume, he heard the door to his bedroom slowly open. The hallway light wasn't on, so Jered couldn't see who opened it. Clouds obscured what little light had spilled through the window, so his bedroom was very dark. From what he could see in the darkness, there was large figure standing in the doorway. When the figure gave a disgusted snort, Jered knew it was his father. In three large steps, his father marched to the closet door and opened it, exposing the glowing green skeleton.

"Is everything okay, Dad?" Jered asked meekly.

His father whispered, "I thought you were asleep, buckaroo. I was just checking on you and saw your closet door was closed. You'll want to keep it open."

"How come?"

"So you can see the skeleton, of course!"

"Why's that important?"

His father's dark silhouette moved across the room and knelt beside his bed. He straightened the quilt a little, then said, "You see, son, I want you to become something great. I know I push you to do well in school but the reason I do is because I want you to be a great, great man. I want you to be better than me. Does that make sense?"

"You mean, like the president?"

"Even bigger!" his father said, still whispering. "It's hard for me to explain everything to you until you get older. I wish I could tell you everything I know about you and what you're destined to become, but I think you're still a little too young to fully under-

SKELETONS ARE NOT SCARY

stand." There was a short pause while his father thought. "You see, son, you inherited things from both me and your mother. Your hair color, your eyes, how you look . . ."

"My ear?"

"I'm not sure where *that* came from. You inherited other things from me. Did you know I was a very good drawer when I was a boy?"

"Really? Like me?" Jered got a little excited when he heard this.

"Shhh, you're mother's sleeping. Yes, I really liked to draw when I was a boy, and I was pretty good. But let me tell you a little secret: you're much better than I *ever* was. You may have gotten your drawing skills from me, but your talent leaves mine in the dust."

"How come you don't draw anymore? I've never seen you draw nothing."

There was another silent pause before his father replied. "I got good at . . . other things. I learned I could do things that other kids couldn't do as well. Or things that other kids couldn't do at all. The same's gonna to happen to you. Drawing isn't the only thing that you'll be great at. Something else will come along and it'll be even more important than drawing."

"Like what, Dad?" Jered was very intrigued and sat up in bed. He reached out and grabbed his father's arm, shaking it a little to show his insistence. "Like what?"

"Let's just say you'll develop skills as you get a little older. You'll find out about them on your own, but I'm going to be here to help you along the way. With my help, you'll reach the top. But for now, you need to go back to sleep. Just remember: the skeleton is here to watch over you and protect you. You see, this skeleton is special. This skeleton is your friend."

Jered was incredulous. "How can a skeleton be your friend? Skeletons are supposed to be scary."

"Skeletons *aren't* scary, though. Even though most people are scared of skeletons, there are special people like you and me who know that skeletons are actually our friends."

Jered still wasn't grasping the concept of a friendly skeleton. "But . . . how can . . .?" he stammered.

"Let me try to explain it another way." His father took a few moments to collect his thoughts, then said, "You know there are lots of people, like your mother, who are afraid of snakes, right?"

"Yeah, she's *really* scared of them!"

"Remember how you used to be scared of them, too?" Jered nodded. "Are you afraid of them anymore?"

"No, Dad, because you caught that garter snake and let me touch it," Jered replied, thinking back to earlier that year. "You showed me that it doesn't even have any teeth. So now I don't care if I see a snake."

"Isn't it better not to be afraid of snakes now?"

"Yeah, because they can't scare me no more."

Rodney slapped his thigh with his hand. "That's my boy! Skeletons are just like snakes: even though other people are afraid of them, *you* don't have to be."

"Okay, I see kinda what you're saying," Jered said. "You don't want to be a sissy fraidy cat, do you?"

"That's right, Grasshopper."

"Why did you call me Grasshopper? What's that mean?"

Rodney chuckled and explained, "That's what the boy on the TV show *Kung Fu* is called by his master. It's one of those TV shows your mother won't let you watch because she says it's too scary for little boys. But that doesn't matter right now. Just get some sleep. There's no reason for you to be a scaredy-cat. Your friend the skeleton is here to protect you as you sleep."

Jered's father lightly kissed his forehead. Just as he was about to leave the room, a question popped into the young boy's head. "Protect me from what?"

"Huh?"

"You said the skeleton is going to protect me. What's he protecting me from?"

Rodney was momentarily stumped, then came up with an answer. "The skeleton keeps away bad dreams and nightmares. It's a cure for nightmares."

Jered thought this made sense. "Okay, Dad, see you in the morning."

After his dad closed the door, Jered didn't go back to thinking about his Halloween costume. Instead, he thought about the floating green skeleton that was watching him from just beyond the foot of his bed. The idea that the skeleton was protecting him was interesting. Jered had never heard of a skeleton being a good guy and none of the TV shows he'd seen ever had the hero be a skeleton. Jered wondered why this was so.

His father's vague claim that Jered was going to be something great was exciting. Jered thought the suggestion something fantastic was going to happen in the future might be a subtle hint that his real parents would eventually come for him.

Despite his father's assurances, the glowing skeleton was still a little scary, so Jered tried not to look in its direction. He eventually nodded off and dreamt of being chased by a bloodthirsty vampire who looked like a sinister version of Count Chocula. Usually the Count was seen during Saturday morning cartoons, hawking a delicious chocolate breakfast cereal. In Jered's dream, though, the vampire only wanted one thing.

"I waaant to suuuck your blood!" Count Chocula hissed.

Jered tried to run but couldn't move. Even if he could escape the vampire, he wondered if Frankenberry and Boo Berry had likewise turned to the dark side of breakfast cereal. The vampire was only a few feet from Jered when a glowing green skeleton appeared out of nowhere and tackled the vampire.

"Leave him alone!" the skeleton commanded, pointing a bony finger in Count Chocula's face. "I don't want to see you here again!"

The skeleton gave Jered a thumbs up, then dashed away as quickly as The Flash. When Jered awoke, there were no cereal characters in his bedroom, but the glowing green skeleton was still there keeping an eye on him.

CHAPTER TEN

Halloween 1977: The Bestest Trick-or-Treating Ever!

After a handful of restless nights, Jered gradually acclimated to having a glow in the dark skeleton in his bedroom. Each night for a week, his father repeated the story of how the skeleton was his protector. Jered warmed to the idea the cutout was a type of guardian angel. The fact that skeletons were generally considered scary made Jered's relationship with the Halloween decoration in his bedroom seem all the more special. Whereas the rest of the world cowered from skeletons, the one thumbtacked to the closet door became a welcoming sight to the boy.

"Are you sure you don't want me to take that thing down?" Jered's mother asked on more than one occasion. "Isn't it creepy to have that awful thing in your room?"

"No, it doesn't bother me, Mom. I'm not afraid of skeletons like I used to. It's just like I'm not scared of snakes anymore."

Chrissy shuddered at just the mention of snakes. She hated snakes so much she insisted Rodney change the radio station if Jim Stafford's song "Spiders and Snakes" was played.

"Aw, come on, honey," Rodney moaned, "it's just a silly little song."

Her hope was Jered would soon grow tired of the skeleton and decide to take it down on his own. Kids were fickle and she thought it was likely the skeleton would lose its allure once Halloween was over in a few weeks.

On a Tuesday morning in late September, Kerri noticed a little tickle in the back of her throat. She didn't think much of it since she usually fought with hay fever in the fall. By Friday of that week, she was sick with the flu. She was able to deduce the tickle in her throat earlier that week was the first symptom of a larger illness that was developing.

On a Thursday in the middle of October, Miss Moran noticed something about Jered. She didn't know at the time if it was nothing to be concerned about or the beginning of something much larger and disturbing.

When Miss Moran asked her class to draw a picture that represented friendship, the students created happy scenes of friends and family members enjoying each other's company. She usually looked at Jered's artwork last because it was always the best. Her first thought after looking at Jered's picture was he'd somehow misunderstood the assignment.

"What . . . what have you got here?" Miss Moran asked.

Jered knew by then that Miss Moran was his number one fan, so he answered honestly and with pride. "That's me and a skeleton."

"Jered, I didn't ask you to draw a Halloween picture."

"I know. You said to draw what we thought of when we heard the word 'friendship.'"

By now the other students were curious about what Jered had drawn and many had risen from their desks, craning their necks to get a glimpse at the picture. Miss Moran walked to the side of Jered's desk, so her body blocked the students' view of Jered's drawing. She couldn't imagine why her star art student decided to create such a macabre scene: it certainly wasn't a representation of friendship.

"What did he make?" one of the other boys asked.

"Never mind," Miss Moran replied curtly.

Jered's teacher taught him to be proud of his creations, so he announced, "I drew a picture of me and my friend the skeleton."

A few of the boys guffawed. "A skeleton? Who has a friend that's a skeleton?"

"I do. He watches over me while I sleep."

The young teacher was confused. "Are you talking about . . . a *real* skeleton?"

Jered giggled. "No, it's just a glow in the dark Halloween decoration my Dad put up on my closet door. My Dad told me that it looks after me while I'm sleeping."

She guessed this made at least a little sense, since Halloween was only a few weeks away. Nevertheless, it was an odd thing to draw. Kerri wasn't going to worry. At this point, she decided the odd drawing was nothing more than a hay fever tickle in her throat.

A few days before Halloween, Jered's father called him downstairs to his work bench. The unfinished basement's gray cement floor and cinder block walls made it the ideal place for his father to tinker. After stepping down the creaky wood steps, Jered saw his father working under his bench's florescent shop light.

"Did ya call me, Dad?"

"Come over here, buckaroo, I want to show you what I've made for you!" his father said with a voice teeming with pride and excitement.

Laid out carefully on his dad's workbench was a boy's black pair of pants and a black sweatshirt. His father was holding a small paint brush. He'd used white paint to draw bones on the black clothing. "What do ya think?"

"What is it? Whose clothes are these?" Jered knew he didn't own anything that looked like what was on the work bench.

"I got these old clothes from the Goodwill store. I painted on them so you can be a skeleton for Halloween. Isn't that cool?"

Jered was hesitant to respond. "But . . . but I was going to be a ghost."

The fact that some children take great delight in expressing their imagination during Halloween is well known. Dr. Ford Freud addressed the darker aspects of this phenomenon in his article, "Halloween Horrors: How Candy and Costumes Threaten Parental Authority." Dr. Freud explained that dressing up on Halloween is a passive-aggressive act through which the child disparages what has been provided to him by his parents. "Costume wearing is a means for the child communicating to his parents he is not satisfied with the clothing they have so thoughtfully provided. To show their displeasure, they dress up in bizarre costumes. This is obviously meant to be a slap in the face to the parents and rejection of parental authority."

His father's excitement was palpable. "You'll look just like a skeleton, see?" His dad had done a good job of painting white bones on the black clothes. Lying next to the clothing was a small skeleton cutout and Jered figured his dad used the window decoration as a basic guide.

"It's just . . . I thought I was going to go to Halloween as . . ."

"But this is so much better," his father interjected. "At night when you're roaming around the neighborhood, you're going to look just like a skeleton walking around the streets. Won't that be a gas?"

Jered was hesitant to say anything, since his father was clearly very proud of what he'd created. His father was rarely very demonstrative with his emotions and Jered didn't want to do or say anything that would diminish his father's good cheer.

"Yeah, this is great. It's just . . ." Jered was about to tell him he'd already picked his costume when he saw a black stocking cap sitting on the end of the bench. "What's that?"

"Oh, that's the best part," his father trumpeted while picking it up. "I got an extra big stocking cap that'll cover your entire head." Rodney pulled the stocking cap completely over his son's head and face. He lined up two eye holes he'd cut out so Jered could see. "Take a look at this!" his dad said, grabbing a hand mirror off the workbench.

What Jered saw in the mirror was stark. If he'd still been afraid of skeletons, Jered might have jumped right out of his clothes, but skeletons no longer frightened him. With great care, his father had painted a skull's face on the stocking cap. Jered tucked the end of the stocking cap into the front of his shirt so his neck was covered. In the dim light of the basement, it looked like Jered's head had been replaced by a skull. His misshapen ear couldn't be seen at all.

Thinking back to the previous Halloween, Jered remembered how he'd tripped over his bed sheet several times as he canvassed the neighborhood. Wearing pants would solve that problem and give Jered more freedom to move. The longer he thought about it, the more he thought the costume his dad made was a definite improvement from being a ghost.

Under the stocking cap Jered was smiling. "This is neat, Dad! Really boss!"

"Try on the rest of it," his father said. "Just be careful, the paint is still a little wet."

Once he'd removed his clothes and slipped on the costume, Jered was delighted at what he looked like. He looked completely different. The skeleton costume gave Jered the anonymity he wanted and was much more impressive looking than the white sheet.

"I love it! Thanks, Dad!"

When Jered paraded around the house later that night in his costume, Chrissy scowled at her husband. "First the skeleton on the closet door and now this!" she said to Rodney with an icy voice. Chrissy shot Rodney a scowl that clearly put him on notice this issue would be discussed further in private. Seeing her sweet little boy looking as though his body had been picked clean of its flesh was very unpleasant. She decided to appeal directly to her son. "Why do you have to be a skeleton? You can be anything else! Why not a cowboy or a ghost or . . . something else?"

"Don't you see, Mom? This is even better than those!"

As Rodney was brushing his teeth before bed that night, Chrissy couldn't keep her emotions bottled in. She was careful to use a quiet, almost hissing voice that wouldn't travel down the hall to their son's bedroom. "Why did you make that awful costume? It's horrible!"

With a mouthful of toothpaste, Rodney replied, "Kids like to dress-up to look scary on Halloween. He loves it."

"I just find it horrible that you want to dress him like he's dead and rotted away."

Once again, his wife was blowing things out of proportion. He was tired and not interested in a lengthy debate. "Give it a rest," he said as he spat out the toothpaste.

"But I think . . ."

Rodney brought a swift end to the conversation. Between gritted teeth he growled, "He likes it and that's all that matters. Done deal."

The sharp rebuke startled Chrissy. Although Rodney had never struck her, she thought his sharp words were just as hurtful as a slap across her face.

It didn't bother Jered in the least when he didn't win first prize at the school's costume contest. His skeleton disguise wasn't meant to impress other people: it was meant to give him a new identity. While trick or treating that night, he was so happy at times it felt like his heart was going to burst from his chest. The anonymity his costume provided imbued him with a sense of dynamic energy he'd couldn't remember ever experiencing. No one knew it was Jered at their door. All they knew was that a small skeleton was holding out a bag and waiting for candy.

Jered ran from house to house, eager to see the looks on the faces of the adults who opened the door. Did a few of them look a little scared? Could that be so? He was just a kid in a costume: did they really think he was a walking, talking skeleton? Jered hoped so.

His exhilarating joy was so great at times Jered felt almost as if he was gliding over the sidewalk. Two kindergartners dressed as cowboys saw a skeleton materialize from a dark yard and screamed. Jered let out an almost maniacal laugh as he ran past them. It was clear: Jered owned Halloween! During the school's costume parade held in the light of day, his alter-ego wasn't that scary. In the darkness of Halloween night, though, he was the king of the haunt.

Chrissy was concerned when it was 8:30 and Jered still hadn't returned. She was nervously standing at the front window peering down their street, waiting for a boy-sized skeleton to appear. Rodney was casually lounging in his chair watching television. Ever since he and Chrissy sent their son off into the night to demand candy from strangers, Rodney wore a self-satisfied grin. To Chrissy, the smile was a little creepy, reminding her of the drawing of the Cheshire Cat in Jered's *Alice in Wonderland* book. The broad smile seemed to say to her, "I know something you don't! I've got plans in the works you'd never understand!"

When the front door swung open, Chrissy let out a startled yipe.

From behind his stocking cap mask, Jered laughed, "Did I scare ya, Mom?" Chrissy put her hand to her chest and Jered pulled off the stocking cap. "It's me, Mom! Don't be such a scaredy-cat!"

"I'm not scared," she replied defensively. "I was thinking about something else, and you just caught me off guard."

Jered and his father laughed at Chrissy's awkward attempt to hide her fear.

"Let's pour it out and take a look at your haul," Rodney said excitedly, as if he, too, was eight years old. "Let's use the kitchen table." When the Halloween treats were laid out, there was a kaleidoscope of shapes and colors displayed. Rodney picked up a green popcorn ball that had been wrapped in cellophane. "I guess you won't mind if I eat this?"

"I've told you before, Dad, those things hurt the roof of my mouth! You can have it!"

Rodney bit into the popcorn ball. "Mmm, mmm, you don't know what you're missing!"

Without hesitation, Jered said, "Yes I do: a sore mouth!"

This caused his dad to laugh, and a little bit of popcorn flew out of his mouth. "Looks like you did a pretty good job relieving the neighborhood of its excess candy, my boy!"

A wet blanket was quickly thrown over their fun. "All right, pick out one piece of candy to eat and then it's off to bed. It's already past your bedtime and you've got school tomorrow, young man!" Chrissy pulled the large Dutch oven out from under the stove and started filling it up with candy she scooped from the table.

"Wait! Wait! I haven't picked out a piece yet!" Jered protested.

Without stopping, Chrissy warned, "Better choose quickly: the candy store is about to close."

The blue writing on a Three Musketeers chocolate bar caught the boy's eye and he snatched it before it was shoveled into the big metal pot. As Jered ate the candy bar, his mother finished clearing the table and put the treasure chest of candy in the cabinet above the stove.

"Ask your Dad or me to get that down if you want a piece, got it?"

Still chewing the sweet chocolate candy bar, Jered glanced toward his father. Rodney rolled his eyes, causing his son to let out a stifled laugh. Brown juice spilled down Jered's chin, which he wiped off with his sleeve. Chrissy hadn't seen his eyes roll, but she suspected her husband had said or done something that caused Jered to laugh.

"I mean it. Isn't that right, *Dad*?" Chrissy said in a strict, authoritative voice as she glared at her husband.

Rodney nodded. "Yes, that's right, buckaroo." When Chrissy turned around, he again rolled his eyes, which caused Jered to snicker.

"And now you get to brush your teeth. We'll see how that tastes smarty pants!" Chrissy said.

"Come on, let's do as your Mom says," Rodney instructed, gesturing towards the hallway bathroom. "Let's get you ready for bed."

While Jered brushed his teeth, Rodney stood in the doorway and asked him about his Halloween exploits. "How far did you get tonight?"

Jered answered while he was still brushing but his father was able to get the gist of what he was saying. When Jered spat out the toothpaste, the sink was splashed with brown mud. "Oooh, look at all that, Dad!"

Rodney laughed and said, "It looks like you ate a handful of dirt! Make sure you wash all that down the drain, otherwise your mother will skin us both!"

After tucking Jered in, his father sat on the edge of the bed in the dark room. "I hope you had a lot of fun tonight, son," Rodney said as he was about to get up and leave the bedroom.

"Yeah, it was great Dad," Jered replied, excitement still in his voice. "But there was something more than that. I felt something kinda weird. Cool, but weird."

Rodney didn't stand up. "What do you mean?"

Jered took a moment to find the right words. "I felt like I was special. I was the only one out there that looked like that. People didn't know what to think of me. There were some little kids I scared without even trying. It was like I was the strongest, bestest kid out there tonight."

The curtains were drawn, and the only light was what seeped from the hallway through the partially closed bedroom door. There wasn't enough light for Jered to see his father's eyes widen. As if Rodney was a trained psychotherapist, he encouraged his son to talk more about how he felt. "Tell me about feeling strong. What do you mean when you say that?"

It was a challenge for young Jered to adequately describe the surge of energy he'd felt flowing through his body. "It was just . . . weird, ya know? I felt tingly, like all the hairs on my arms were standing straight out. I don't know how to tell you."

"Sure," his dad replied as he remembered similar sensations he'd experienced when his special abilities began to surface. "Did you feel like you were powerful? Stronger than usual?"

"Kinda, yeah," Jered agreed. "I was so excited I almost felt like I could fly if I tried."

His dad gasped a little, but Jered didn't hear it. After taking a moment to collect himself, his dad asked, "Did you try, you know, to fly?"

Jered blurted out laughing. "No, Dad! Boys can't really fly! It just felt that way because I was so excited. I know I'm not a bird!"

Rodney pondered what his son said. He surmised Jered's unusual euphoria could have been just a product of trick-or-treating, especially if he'd eaten a few candy bars during his quest. But the more he thought about it, Rodney believed there was something more to it. This wasn't just an excited kid: something else was happening.

Rodney got up from the bed, quietly closed the door, then returned to his son's bedside. "I want you to try something for me."

"What is it, Dad?"

"It's . . . an exercise."

"Like jumping jacks?"

"No, it's a relaxation exercise. I was taught how to relax my mind when I was a little boy. A doctor taught me how to clear my mind when a headache came."

"But I don't have those kinds of bad headaches you have."

"Right, but you can use these exercises even when you don't have bad headaches. I want to see if you can make yourself feel the same way you did when you were out there tonight. Does that sound like fun?"

"You mean like I'm almost flying? Sure, Dad, let's try!"

"Lie back and put your head on the pillow. Close your eyes and take a deep breath," Rodney's instructions were in a quiet, soothing voice. "Think about relaxing every muscle in your body. Start at your toes, then let the relaxation slowly move up your body. Your legs are now floppy because the muscles are all relaxed. Now move to your stomach, then your chest. All the muscles are going limp. As you're relaxing, keep taking deep breaths. Your face and even your teeth are relaxed." After a few silent moments, Rodney asked, "How do you feel?"

"Sleepy," Jered replied in a quiet voice. "I feel like I can go to sleep."

"Can you feel the hairs on your arms standing up like earlier? Do you feel like you're almost flying?"

"No, just tired. Really tired."

"Think hard: are you sure you don't feel something strange?"

"Huh-uh: just relaxed and sleepy is all. Am I supposed to feel something else?"

"We'll try again tomorrow night, how's that sound?"

"Sure, Dad," the boy said sleepily. "What do you call this?"

Rodney smiled with satisfaction. "Ever since I was a little boy, I called it a Way-Out. When I was younger, it was the beatniks who'd say, 'Way out.'" He altered his voice so it was slow and drawn out. "Now I guess it's kinda like a hippie who says, 'Way out, man!'"

Jered laughed at his father's impression. "Say it again like that!" Rodney complied, which caused Jered to laugh even harder.

"I guess these are kind of like Way-Out exercises so you can get better."

"Better at what?"

"At going on a Way-Out, man!"

Rodney was a little disappointed he hadn't managed to recreate Jered's feelings from earlier. He knew, however, that this was just the first baby step in the development of his son's special ability. "It's getting late, and you're so tired, so go to sleep."

"Okay, Dad. These exercises were fun. A lot better than jumping jacks!"

"I'm glad you like them. We'll keep doing them, so you get even better." Rodney was about to stand up, then had a thought. "Could you do me a favor, son?"

"Sure, Dad."

"Remember how sometimes we talk about dreams you have at night?" Jered nodded. "If you start having any odd dreams or you ever feel kind of strange, make doubly sure you talk to me about it, okay?"

"I guess, but what do you mean feel strange?"

"You'll know it when it happens. Just make sure to tell me, though. It'll be our little secret. Alright?"

"Okay. I'm tired. I'll bet I fall asleep right away."

Just as he predicted, Jered had no problem falling asleep. His father, however, tossed and turned throughout the night as he contemplated the night's events. This surely was the breakthrough Rodney had been waiting for. Just an inkling his son's power was beginning to surface. Whether Jered would've experienced these feelings without having a glow in the dark skeleton in his bedroom or a skeleton costume, Rodney didn't know for sure. But Rodney went ahead and patted himself on the back for helping his son's special ability to at last manifest itself.

About the time that Halloween was becoming November 1st, Jered dreamt he was once again trick-or-treating in his skeleton costume. He was certain that he was in his neighborhood, even though none of the houses looked familiar. Oddly, there were no other kids trick-or- treating, although he thought he saw out of the corner of his eye a boy dressed in a tuxedo. When Jered turned his head to better see the boy, he'd vanished.

"Oh well, that means more candy for me!" he thought, walking to the nearest house.

When he arrived at the door, Jered couldn't find the doorbell, so he knocked on the door. No one answered immediately and Jered wondered why the porch light was on if the people weren't passing out candy. Just as he was about to leave, the door opened. In the doorway was a full-sized skeleton, holding a gift-wrapped box. It was the size of a shoebox and was decorated with a big red ribbon.

Startled by the sight of the skeleton, Jered tried to back away from the door, only to discover his feet were welded in place. Despite his attempts to yank his legs from their mooring, Jered couldn't move. Silently, the skeleton held the gift out to Jered. With hands that were trembling just a bit, Jered accepted the box, and the skeleton instantly disappeared. Jered wasn't sure what to do with the gift, since it was obvious it wouldn't fit into his treat bag. When he held the gift over the treat bag's opening, it magically shrank to the size of a pack of gum, then dropped effortlessly into the bag.

"Of course, they can do that," the boy thought. "I've always known that gifts can shrink if your hands are full." He wondered why he briefly doubted that the present would fit into the bag in the first place.

Suddenly a wind whipped up, so strong it picked up Jered. Without wings, Jered soared through the raw autumn air, causing every nerve in his body to tingle. He was carried to the next house, where he landed softly on the doorstep. Once again, a skeleton answered the door and Jered was given a wrapped present. By the time he'd visited the fourth house, Jered was no longer apprehensive when a skeleton answered the door. He visited several houses and was whisked from place to place by the unusually strong wind.

"What's in all of these boxes?" Jered wondered.

The young boy was disappointed when he awoke in bed and found he didn't have a bag full of wrapped presents given to him by skeletons.

CHAPTER ELEVEN

Día de Muertos

Every child learns about the dramatic transformation a caterpillar undergoes. It's common knowledge even amongst kindergartners that a caterpillar spins a cocoon and eventually emerges from this structure as a beautiful butterfly. Children are unaware, however, of the amazing transformation adults undergo when they become grandparents. Without the aid of a cocoon, many parents with questionable child rearing abilities and poor judgment magically transform into revered grandparents. Adults who were at best marginal parents, somehow become the paragon of childrearing the instant they become grandparents. They then enter into a rather bizarre symbiotic relationship with their grandchildren, wherein each of them believes the other is an absolute treasure.

It therefore comes as little surprise to learn that Jered was enthralled with his grandmother. Jered told anyone and everyone: "She's the bestest!" Although he knew deep down the people raising him might not be his true biologic parents and therefore his grandmother also wasn't a blood relative, he'd always had a very strong connection with her. While his mother did a pretty good job of filling in for Jered's true mother, he couldn't imagine his true grandmother could be any better.

"JoJo!" Jered exclaimed when his grandmother opened the front door.

The woman dropped her parcels, knelt, and stretched out her arms. "There's the most handsome boy in the world!"

For Jered time had moved very slowly the two hours since his mother told him his beloved grandmother was going to stop by for a visit. Most grandparents are put on a pedestal by their grandchildren, but JoJo's was especially lofty, in part because she was Jered's only grandparent. His parents told him that his other grandparents had gone to heaven either before he was born or when he was a baby. As much as Jered adored his grandmother, she cherished her only grandson even more.

Eight years earlier when she visited Chrissy and her newborn son in the hospital, Chrissy proudly announced, "Here comes Grandma Sagen! Say hello to Grandma Sagen, Jered!"

Something about the title "grandma" just didn't sound right to Jolene Sagen. In her mind, a grandma was someone who sat around doing needlepoint. Ever since her husband died a few years earlier, Jolene Sagen spent her days travelling the world and never once picked up a sewing needle. Instead of being called grandma, she came up with the name "JoJo." It was catchy and before her son could even speak, Chrissy was calling her mother JoJo. As far as Jered knew, everyone had always referred to his wonderful grandmother as JoJo.

JoJo was always eager to share tales of faraway places she'd visited. The young boy was rapt as she told him about visiting cathedrals, ancient castles, and majestic canyons. He'd never left the confines of University City, so her travel stories were spellbinding. If he had a million dollars and didn't have to go to school, he'd explore the world with his grandmother.

"I don't know how you can go to all of those places," Chrissy remarked after her mother regaled them about her trip to Mexico. "All those countries filled with strangers who all have their different rules? You never know if you're going to do something wrong." Chrissy shuddered at the thought of being in such a predicament.

"You just have to relax and take it as it comes," JoJo explained. "You're going to make some mistakes and stub your toes occasionally, but that doesn't mean you shouldn't take the journey."

"I guess, but I've got everything I need right here with my two strong men," Chrissy said, putting her arm around her son. She smiled and looked across the room at Rodney, who was reading the newspaper. He'd heard plenty of JoJo's travel stories and wasn't particularly interested in hearing another one. "You don't need to travel if you've already got everything you need at home."

"Oh pishaw!" JoJo replied, waving the back of her hand at her daughter. "What do *you* think, Jered? Do you want to go travelling like JoJo when you get older?"

"Sure do!" Jered said eagerly. Everything JoJo did and said was amazing. If JoJo said she'd wrestled Godzilla and asked Jered if he wanted to try it, he would've immediately agreed.

While Jered was in the bathroom and Rodney was in the kitchen pouring himself a cup of coffee, JoJo leaned in towards her daughter, and asked quietly under her breath, "Everything else okay?" JoJo made a small head gesture in Rodney's direction.

"Yes," an embarrassed Chrissy replied, "everything's just fine."

While it was generally true even the plainest of girls eventually snagged a husband, JoJo always harbored a nagging concern her daughter might end up a spinster. JoJo should have therefore celebrated Rodney as a white knight, but something held her back from wholeheartedly embracing him. Neither JoJo nor her husband could put their finger on the reason they didn't immediately warm up to Rodney. When it came down to it, Rodney simply wasn't blessed with all the qualities Chrissy's parents wanted her white knight to possess.

JoJo was a firm believer in romantic love, and she told her daughter many times she distinctly remembered hearing birds singing the summer afternoon she met her late husband. When JoJo looked into Rodney's gray eyes, she didn't see a raging brushfire of adoration for her daughter. She kept wondering if a disastrous character defect would eventually rise to Rodney's surface. Because the length of their courtship and engagement was short, JoJo was concerned not enough time had been allowed for any warts to show up. In the end, though, Chrissy was happy and that was all that really mattered. Mr. and Mrs. Sagen rejoiced in their daughter's marriage and accepted their son-in-law into the family.

"You said on the phone you're off to someplace else next week?" Chrissy asked.

"Yep. I've never been to Yellowstone, so that's my next stop."

"I'm so happy you're enjoying yourself. How did you ever get the travel bug in the first place?"

"As a girl I dreamed about travelling but I put that on hold to have a family. Your father planned ahead and made sure we had a lot of insurance. I thank him every time I set foot in a new place." JoJo smiled, but it was a sad smile, as she thought how her travels would be even better if she was accompanied by her husband. "I like to see you happy, too, Chrissy. Are *you* happy?"

Once again, Chrissy was embarrassed. "Yes, mother, I'm happy." After a few silent seconds, she added under her breath, "Happy enough."

JoJo lowered her voice and asked, "Have you been following Tammy Wynette's advice?'

Exasperated, Chrissy barked, "Yes!"

Jered ran into the living room and asked, "What did I miss? What did you tell Mom?"

JoJo kept her eyes on her daughter, trying to determine if her daughter was being entirely candid. Chrissy smiled and looked at her mother sternly. JoJo recognized Chrissy wasn't going to say anything further on the matter, at least for the time being.

JoJo reached for one of the three brightly colored paper bags she'd brought with her. "Well, I was just telling your mother that I got something for my best grandson while I was in Mexico," she said, handing the bag to Jered.

"What is it?" Jered asked eagerly.

"Open it and see! Be careful though, it's breakable."

Under a wad of tissue paper was something hard and round, the size of a softball. He carefully pulled the tissue paper away, exposing a colorfully painted skull.

"Wow! What is it?"

"Come over here and I'll tell you a story about it." As Jered sat on his grandmother's lap, he gingerly rotated the skull in his hands. "In Mexico they don't have Halloween. They have Día de Muertos, which means 'The Day of The Dead.' They say it's the night the souls of their dead relatives come back to earth. The people cook meals for the spirits and have picnics at cemeteries. I was walking down a dirt street on Día de Muertos, when I saw a man wearing a dusty, tattered tuxedo and a tall black top hat. He had a pushcart filled with candy skulls, and when I saw them, I knew you should have one. Then he told me he could write on the candy skull with frosting he squirted out of a tube. Can you see what's on the back?"

"Look, Mom, my name's written on the skull!" The man in the old tuxedo must have had a shaky hand, because the writing was uneven.

"Yep, I had him write your name on it."

All the color washed from Chrissy's face as she tried to hide her revulsion. She didn't like skeletons, particularly since witnessing Rodney's horrible seizure.

"Yeah, isn't that something," Chrissy said begrudgingly.

Rodney left the comfort of his easy chair to inspect the gift. "That's a really neat skull you got there!" Rodney said to his son cheerfully. "You know the skull is part of your skeleton, right?"

"Of course I know that, Dad," Jered replied dismissively. "Everyone knows that!"

Rodney was smiling broadly, and JoJo was pleased he chose to become engaged with the rest of the family. "That's a really thoughtful gift, JoJo," he said, turning to her. "Very unique. I've never seen anything like that.

"I'm glad you like it," she said, "because I got one for each of you."

Rodney seemed just as pleased as his son with the sugar skull. Chrissy unwrapped her skull but set it down quickly on the end table. Rodney asked, "Can you eat these? Are they really made out of sugar?"

"That's what the man in the tuxedo told me," JoJo replied. "I saw lots of kids walking around nibbling on sugar skulls and sugar tombstones, so that must be the thing to have instead of Halloween candy. It's a little creepy but I figure it's all in good fun. No different than some of our scary Halloween decorations, I guess."

"Are we scared of skeletons anymore?" Rodney asked his son.

Without hesitation, Jered proudly declared, "Nope!"

"Are you going to eat it or just look at it, buckaroo?"

Jered turned the skull around in his hands. "It looks really good, but I don't think I want to eat it right away. I want to just look at it for a while. Is that okay?"

"You betcha," JoJo replied. "It's just sugar and some food coloring, so it should last a long time. Just don't get it wet! If you do it will be *melting*!" JoJo cried "melting" as a ten-syllable word, like the Wicked Witch of the West in *The Wizard of Oz*.

JoJo and Jered's dad laughed but Chrissy remained reticent. "Well, I'm going to take a bite out of mine right now!" Rodney proclaimed. "Okay, here I go." There was a loud crunching sound as if he was biting into an apple. "It melts in your mouth! Here, son, have a bite of mine."

Jered took a bite and reported, "I guess it tastes sorta like a thicker, crunchy kind of cotton candy!"

JoJo was pleased Jered and Rodney were enjoying their gifts, but she was a little concerned Chrissy had become so quiet. "Are you alright, dear?"

Chrissy quickly came up with a little white lie and replied, "I'm fine. I started a new diet this week, so there'll be no sugar skull eating for me."

"You don't need to diet, dear," JoJo said, "Go ahead and enjoy life!"

"Maybe after I've gone a few more days without cheating, I'll reward myself." Chrissy was unnerved her son was so delighted with the macabre gift. The thought of him consuming the awful thing made her nauseous. "I don't think you should eat that. Sugar isn't good for your teeth. I think it's a good idea to just look at it for a while." In her mind, she added, "At least until something tragic happens and it ends up in the trash."

"That sounds good, Mom. I'm just gonna look at it."

Jered put his sugar skull on the nightstand next to his bed and right under the window. When his mother tucked him in that night, she made a mental of note of how close it was to the window, and how it might *accidentally* be ruined if the window was left open during a downpour. If the candy skull got wet, it would turn into mush and the food coloring could stain the nightstand and floor. She'd have no choice but to immediately throw it away if that happened.

Lying on his side, Jered looked at the skull sitting on the nightstand. He'd never seen anything like it and he'd never heard of "*El Dee Tortoise*," or whatever his grandmother called Mexican Halloween. Jered briefly considered bringing the skull to school. During show-and-tell, he'd listened to his peers tell the class about trophies, polished rocks, and vacation souvenirs. Wouldn't it be keen if he showed the sugar skull to the class and told them the story about the man wearing a tuxedo who sold it to JoJo? He smiled when he thought of his classmates' wide eyes of amazement. *Ooohs* and *ahhhs* would certainly fill the classroom as the other kids looked at the strange candy. He thought Miss Moran would enjoy it as well.

As he played out these events in his imagination, the scene started to take a sinister turn. Visions of the skull being dropped and shattering on the floor flashed in his mind. Other kids might try to take it away from him. After further thought, Jered decided to just keep the skull at home. His bedroom was the safest place for the skull to be.

During lunchtime the next day, Jered found a quiet corner in the playground where he could draw. As his classmates ran around and played, Jered tried to draw the candy skull from memory. It wasn't easy, especially getting the jawbone at just the right angle. When Miss Moran saw Jered was carrying a few sheets of paper, she asked to see what he'd drawn.

Kerri was taken off guard at the dark subject matter of the drawing. Much like Jered's mother, Kerri Moran wasn't fond of things that were scary. Setting these feelings aside, she thought he'd done a good job. Jered used shading techniques she'd taught him, which made the empty eye sockets particularly creepy.

"Did you draw these because last week was Halloween?" she asked.

Jered answered honestly, "No. I just felt like drawing a skull."

She looked into his eyes. There wasn't any cruelty or vindictiveness in Jered's expression, but she didn't like the idea of him getting fixated on something so gruesome.

"Do you understand that a skull means someone has died?"

"Sure, everyone knows that." Once again, Jered answered truthfully.

His response was so matter-of-fact Kerri felt an uncomfortable tingle down her spine. She knew from her college psychology courses that people who are fixated on images of death, cemeteries, and the like often don't think this is an unusual interest.

Kerri managed to control her anxiety and thought, "Come on, Kerri, settle down. Just because Jered drew a picture of a skull doesn't mean anything. Some of the houses he passes to and from school every day probably still have Halloween decorations up. Don't be like Chicken Little and think the sky is falling. Let the kid be a kid."

It was still just a hay fever tickle in the back of her throat. It was just a little stronger.

CHAPTER TWELVE

Skelly

It can be difficult to recognize when a change is taking place. Water in a pot over a stove burner looks the same whether it is tepid or hot. It isn't until bubbles start to form on the water's surface that the cook realizes the water has gone through an important change. Rodney hadn't noticed any indication that Jered was starting to undergo a change until Halloween. He was pleased at how his son had taken to the gradual presentation of skeleton imagery over the past month. What Jered said about his feelings while trick-or-treating, though, was extraordinary. His graphic account of feeling free from the bounds of the mundane world while he wore his skeleton costume thrilled Rodney. When Jered described the euphoria of trick-or-treating, Rodney knew his son was at last beginning to exhibit the first manifestations of his burgeoning ability.

Rodney tried to turn up the heat on the maturation of Jered's special abilities and it appeared he'd been successful. Quite by accident, Rodney's mother-in-law supplemented these efforts by gifting Jered a skull from Mexico. This was a welcome surprise! Rodney recognized Jered had a special connection with JoJo and anything she gave the boy would instantly be cherished. Rodney was pleased to see how much his son delighted in the skull.

"Just another connection," Rodney thought. "Just another link to what he will become."

Each night since Halloween, Rodney volunteered to tuck Jered into bed, and his exhausted wife was happy to oblige. Before turning down the comforter, Rodney sat on the floor with his son and guided him on relaxation exercises. Once Jered reached a nearly self-hypnotic state, Rodney encouraged his son to envision himself leaving the confines of his physical body.

"Can you feel yourself slowly drifting out of your body? Can you let yourself float towards the ceiling?"

His young son was eager to please his father, but he was having difficulty achieving the goals set by his father. If Jered concentrated really hard, he could briefly imagine himself being magically drawn from his body, but he was quickly pulled back to reality after just a second.

"I can do it for just a little bit but then it goes away," Jered lamented to his father. "It's like moving a piece of metal away from a magnet: I can pull away for just a sec, but then I snap right back."

"That's okay, son. This might take a little time. We'll just keep practicing and you'll get better over time. Does that sound like fun?"

"Sure, Dad. I like using my imagination."

After each failed session, Rodney reminded himself of the proverb his grandfather was fond of saying: "Slow and steady wins the race." Even though Rodney was anxious for his son to move ahead, there was no reason to rush things *too* much.

Jered enjoyed doing the exercises each night before bed. His dad's soothing voice during the exercises were hypnotic. After a couple nights of exercises, Jered noticed his dreams were more vivid and detailed, so he reported this to his father.

"Do you ever feel like you've left your body during the dream?" his father asked, to which Jered shook his head. "How about this: do you sometimes think you can control what happens in the dream?"

"No, I never felt nothing like that. It feels like I sleep better, and Mom says I'm peppier in the morning."

Once again, Rodney reminded himself of his grandfather's proverb.

Although he didn't know it, Rodney was teaching his son what healthcare professionals call emotive imagery. He was teaching his young son how to relax his mind and use vivid images from his imagination to evoke an emotional response. His goal was to help Jered break through the limitations of the physical world and enter the next stage of his development. After several sessions, Jered became adept at relaxing his mind and body.

Dr. Ford Freud discussed a novel use of emotive imagery in his 1972 article, "Should Naughty Children be Beaten? The Acceptable Answers are (a)Yes, and (b) Absolutely Yes!" In this scholarly publication, Dr. Freud explained that the use of emotive imagery can be employed to curtail future unwanted behavior. "At the time physical punishment is being administered, it is important for the parent to augment it by adding emotional trauma. It is not just the father's belt but the *thought of the belt* which will affect the subject's future behavior. By linking bad behavior with the image of the belt, when a child has an opportunity to misbehave, it should create a significant negative emotional response and the child will remain obedient."

Rodney was somewhat concerned Jered hadn't been able to duplicate the feelings he'd experienced while trick-or-treating. Setting aside this frustration, Rodney attempted to examine the situation as a scientist would. A *mad* scientist? On Halloween, Jered reported he'd felt powerful and free spirited but despite Rodney's nightly interventions, he hadn't been able to recreate those feelings. Rodney thought about his own episodes and how they were often triggered by strong emotions. Intense feelings ranging from joy to despondency often preceded a Way-Out. It was therefore possible Jered had a similar trigger. Because the boy had been so excited about Halloween, Jered may have been more likely to feel the effects of his special power. Just like his dad, Jered couldn't simply turn the tap on or off at will . . . at least, not at his current level of development. Hopefully at some point Jered would be able to use his power whenever he wanted, and when that occurred, Rodney mused the world would change forever.

Jered had always been good at transferring what he saw onto paper. Drawing skeletons was a challenge. Sometimes as he laid in bed, he studied the glowing bones of the skeleton grinning at him from the closet door. In the light of day, he examined his candy skull to see in three dimensions how the bones fit together. Once he figured out how to duplicate the angle of the jawbone and space the eyeholes just right, he was able to draw fairly realistic skulls.

This success caused Jered to draw skulls a lot over the following weeks. He tried to draw the rest of the skeleton but ran into problems. Even sitting on his bed and staring at the skeleton on his closet door, Jered's drawings of the ribcage were not particularly good. After trying to draw other portions of the skeleton and being disappointed, Jered returned to drawing skulls. At some point he wanted to draw an entire human skeleton, but he figured he'd have to wait until he got older. He adorned some of the skulls with flowers and bright colors in the same fashion as his *El Dee Tortoise* skull.

Drawing the same thing repeatedly was something Jered had done in the past. Earlier that autumn, Jered became fixated on drawing football helmets. One of his classmates drew a helmet but it looked flat and unrealistic. Jered decided he wanted to figure out how to draw a helmet so it was more three dimensional. Just like he did with his skulls, Jered had to practice before being able to freehand a helmet that didn't look flat. Once he figured it out, he drew football helmets whenever he had a chance. Decorating the helmets with unique mascots of teams he'd made up was fun. The ability to recreate the helmets repeatedly was very satisfying. What got Jered to stop drawing football helmets was when he taught himself to draw skulls.

With the four-day Thanksgiving holiday on the horizon, Kerri Moran was becoming increasingly concerned Jered appeared to be pre-occupied with Halloween. Far too many skulls and portions of skeletons were showing up in his art.

"For today's fun activity, I want you to draw a picture about the coming of winter," she announced. "Don't draw Christmas decorations, presents under the tree, or stuff like that. Instead, really use your imaginations to show the change from autumn to winter. Be creative!"

When Kerri looked over the shoulders of her students and saw what they were creating, she realized this assignment was too challenging for third graders. With typical winter images off limits, many were having trouble even getting started. Marty drew Santa Claus punching a pilgrim. "Ya see?" he explained to Miss Moran. "Winter is beating up fall so it can take over."

As usual, Jered came up with a unique twist on the theme. He drew a series of five images showing how the passage of time effected a tree. The tree began as bare, developed buds in the second stage, and was covered with thick leaves to represent summer. The foliage became red and yellow in the next image, and the last one showed the tree once again bare.

Kerri marveled at the detail he'd included. This wasn't a run-of-the-mill drawing of a tree: the long branches were expressive. One of the large branches was broken off. Kerri was confident if she asked him what happened to it, Jered would respond that this was just how it was born. She was at one moment pleased with the picture, then abruptly troubled at a small detail.

In addition to the foliage, Jered differentiated the trees. The summer tree had an American flag hanging from its lowest limb and near the trunk of the autumn tree was a pumpkin. The winter tree was bare, surrounded by large snow drifts. What concerned her was a grinning skull nestled amongst the branches. Kerri thought the malevolent skull appeared to be looking with satisfaction over the destruction it'd wrought.

"Why . . . why is there a skull in the tree?" she dared to ask.

In a matter-of-fact voice, Jered replied, "Death. Isn't that what winter is: death?"

Kerri was so taken aback she struggled to reply. "Well . . . I guess you could say . . . well . . . winter is full of life, too. Snowmen are made. Pine trees are covered with pretty snow." Kerri couldn't take her eyes from the unpleasant skull perched in the winter tree. Why couldn't he have hung candy canes from the branches? Or tinsel?

Jered gleaned his teacher was trying to make a point, but he was having difficulty figuring out what she was driving at. "But all the plants are dead. The fields are bare. All the insects froze to death, right?"

Her star student was right, but the grimness of his drawing made her uneasy. She tried her best to write it off as "kids being kids," but she couldn't shake the concern Jered might be straying down a dark path.

"Is there something here," she thought, "or am I chasing shadows?"

Kerri decided she needed input from someone else. Since the other teachers at school were unlikely to have anything insightful to share, she contacted one of her favorite professors at the College of Education. Kerri confided her concern that one of her students was preoccupied with dark subjects, especially skeletons.

"The more you try to prevent a child from showing interest in something," the professor mused, "the stronger the kid is pulled towards it. They're drawn to it like moths to a light bulb."

"But he's such a talent. I don't want him to get off track. He could really be something special, I think."

"Keep in mind, Kerri, you only have so much control over the child's development. You're just a teacher who sees him about six hours a day for one school year."

"What if I can be the springboard to this boy becoming . . ."

"Remember that no one's development follows a straight and linear path," the professor interrupted in a cautionary tone. "If you try to put limits on a child's creativity, you can end up impeding their growth. So what if he's been drawing skulls lately? If Halloween is his favorite holiday, so be it! A couple weeks from now, he'll likely be fixated on something else, and *that* will start showing up in all his drawings."

What the professor said made sense: she was probably making something out of nothing. "Do you think that's all it is: just the soup *du jour*?"

"No doubt. Remember: this is your first real teaching job. You're like a mother who's had her first baby. Every time the infant sneezes or coughs, you convince yourself that your kid is about to die of the plague. You run to the doctor and discover it's just a normal part of growing up. I've been there! We all have!" the professor chuckled. "This is your first classroom of kids, so you're hypersensitive. You're responding to anything and everything the kids do, because you haven't learned yet how to recognize things that are truly significant. Totally understandable. All teachers go through this phase. Relax, Kerri, it'll be okay. After you've done this job awhile, you'll look back and laugh at yourself!"

Kerri tried to take the advice from her former teacher to heart, doing her best not to dwell on Jered's drawings. She was going to ignore the skulls and parts of human skeletons that showed up in his drawings. Deep down, however, she couldn't shake the feeling that this was a symptom of a greater ill. A few days later, this vague uncomfortable feeling became a definite concern.

When Chrissy asked Jered if he was ready for the life-sized skeleton to be put away, she didn't expect to get any pushback. She wasn't really asking his permission: it was just a matter of courtesy to let her young son know it was time for the skeleton to be put away with the other Halloween decorations, which had been taken down weeks earlier. She was less than pleased with his reply.

"I want to keep him up, Mom," he replied. "Just like Dad said, he's my friend. I like seeing him glow in the dark when I go to bed every night."

"It needs to be put away until next Halloween, Jered," she insisted.

"Why, Mom? He's not hurting nobody. It's *my* bedroom. Why can't he stay?"

Chrissy didn't tell her son the truth. She didn't tell him every time she came into his bedroom to change the sheets, she had to avert her eyes from the closet door. Likewise, she didn't admit she kept his bedroom door closed because it seemed to be watching her. Sometimes it evoked memories of the night she saw her husband appear like a skeleton. It could cause her to relive the scariest night of her life, and for that reason alone it needed to go away.

"It's not Halloween anymore, and it needs to be out of the way," she replied.

Chrissy also didn't tell her son about a suspicion that had been brewing inside her. Something about Rodney's recent emphasis on Halloween skeletons didn't sit right with Chrissy. In previous years, her husband paid little attention to Halloween decorations, so why this year had he shown so much interest? Left alone during the day with her thoughts, she began to link concerns with questions. She wondered if Rodney's insistence that the skeleton be prominently placed in Jered's bedroom was somehow linked to Rodney's transformation. Although she had no earthly idea how the two could be related, this thought weighed heavily on her.

"Why?" Jered's voice took on a whiny tone, causing this single word to be drawn out.

Jered's question was the same one posed by children to harried parents since the dawn of time. Often that same question is asked again and again by the child. As if they were nothing more than a parrot with a vocabulary of a solitary word, children can prolong the conversation by merely repeating this three-letter inquiry.

"It's not normal to have Halloween decorations up in the middle of November," Chrissy responded, trying not to let her voice expose the level of her exasperation. "It's just not right!"

Jered whined his follow-up question before Chrissy's last word faded: "But, why?"

On the brink of losing her temper, Chrissy decided to walk away from the conversation. Before resorting to the rationale, "Because I'm the mommy, that's why!" she decided to just let the subject drop. Chrissy left Jered's bedroom, shaking her head. She was comforted by the knowledge she was going to take down the skeleton while Jered was at school the following day.

"I'm home, Mom," Jered announced, then waited for the reply his mother always gave.

"You're *not* a home: you're not even a house!"

For as long as Jered could remember, this same interchange occurred with his mother each time he came home from school. Although Jered knew the whole thing was corny, he sort of looked forward to this silly banter.

"What do you want for a snack?" his mother asked.

Jered plopped down on one of the kitchen chairs, making a face as though he was thinking intently. "Hmm. Let's see. Cake. Pie. Ice Cream. One of each!"

"In your dreams, buckaroo."

"Okay. Just one: cake."

"You got it: one apple coming right up!" Chrissy retrieved an apple from the refrigerator and tossed it underhand to her son.

"I said *cake,* not *apple.*"

"You're the one with the overactive imagination: pretend the apple is a kind of cake, smart guy!"

Jered bit into the apple, then groaned in fake ecstasy. "Oh, Mom, this piece of cake is soooo good! This is the best cake I've ever had!"

"There's four more pieces of that cake in the fridge if you're still hungry. You can have as many pieces as you like!"

With a mouth full of apple, Jered said, "I'm gonna change clothes."

It didn't take long for Jered to notice the skeleton was missing. His first thought was the thumbtacks had come loose, causing the skeleton to drop to the floor. Jered scanned the floor, then looked under his bed. At first, he didn't even consider the possibility his mother had taken it down. When it was nowhere to be found, he jumped to the conclusion that an intruder must have snuck into his bedroom, taken the skeleton, then run off with it. The thought of a burglar in his bedroom made him remember JoJo's candy skull. He snapped his head towards the nightstand and was relieved to see the skull had been left untouched by the burglar.

"Mom! Mom!"

From the tone of Jered's frantic voice, Chrissy knew her son had discovered the skeleton's absence. She'd already planned how she'd respond if Jered got angry. At first, she remained silent. Since his mother didn't respond, Jered rushed to the kitchen.

"Mom! The skeleton is gone! Someone took him!"

Without looking up from the carrots she was slicing, Chrissy replied, "I know. I took that horrible thing down and threw him away."

Suddenly Jered had a hot stinging sensation on his face, as if his mother's reply was a strong slap to his cheeks. At first, he spoke in disbelief. "Huh? You what? Why?"

She replied firmly, "Halloween is over. It looked horrible and I didn't like seeing the thing. The time for scary decorations is over until next year's Halloween."

Jered felt anger surge through him, causing his retort to be sharp and accusatory. "He was in *my* bedroom. It's *my* room to do what I want to do with it, *not* yours!"

Chrissy turned from the counter, glaring at her son. "Don't you *ever* yell at me, young man! You better watch what you say, or I'll tell your father about this when he gets home!"

"But Dad said I could keep him up! Dad said so!"

"Well, I'm the mom, and I said it had to go! It's gone now!"

Jered darted out the back door to the garbage can kept on the patio. "He's not in here!"

Chrissy didn't reply. Jered marched noisily back into the kitchen. In an accusatory tone that made him sound a lot like Rodney when he was angry, he asked, "Where is it? What did you do with it?"

Chrissy wasn't prepared for this ferocious of a response. Always the one to avoid conflict and act as the mediator in any family conflicts, she offered an olive branch to the indignant boy. "Look, you've still got JoJo's skull in your room: that's plenty enough skeletons!"

Jered ran downstairs and saw the folded-up skeleton lying on top of the cardboard box with the other Halloween decorations. He grabbed the skeleton and ran up the stairs. Chrissy's back was turned, so she didn't see what her son was carrying as he ran through the kitchen. When she heard his bedroom door slam, she yelled, "And don't come out until you settle down!"

Jered tacked the skeleton back up on his closet door, then sat on his bed sulking. Even though the skeleton was back where it belonged, he was still very angry at his mother's transgression. She'd come into his bedroom, or rather *invaded* it. This was his domain! His outrage felt like a swarm of angry bees buzzing around inside his head. The more he thought about this breach of trust, the more frenetic the bees became. Jered eventually had to squint his eyes while shading them with his hand. It was as though the outraged bees ricocheting off the back of his eyeballs was making him sensitive to the bright afternoon light streaming through his window. The light made his head hurt, so he closed his eyes and covered them with his hand.

A headache began throbbing behind his eyes. The pain peaked with every beat of his heart. Normally his mother handled all medical issues but there was no way Jered was going to ask for her assistance. Jered remembered the relaxation exercises his Dad taught him and how calm he felt after completing them. Anxious for relief, Jered sat cross legged on his bed and began to take deep breaths. He focused on the swarm of bees in his head, imagining the insects gradually becoming lethargic.

"Slow down," he said to the bees. "Relax." Although initially the irate insects didn't respond, over time their frenzy started to decrease. After a few minutes, they'd stopped bouncing around inside his head and eventually the bees fell asleep.

"You're pretty good at doing that," an unfamiliar voice said.

Jered startled and immediately opened his eyes. His head whipped around but he didn't see anyone in his bedroom. Everything looked normal, except the position of his sugar skull had shifted. The brightly colored sugar skull that was usually pointed towards the window was now looking directly at Jered with its empty eye sockets. The jawbone quivered and the skull asked, "How did you learn to do that?"

SKELETONS ARE NOT SCARY

Jered was shaken and his heart thumped quicker and harder. He closed his eyes and took a deep breath, trying to keep his fear at bay.

His father taught him, "When you're calm, it's harder to be afraid."

After a few moments, Jered's pulse returned to normal. He wasn't going to be a scaredy- cat. With his eyes still closed, he replied to the skull as calmly as if he was speaking to one of his classmates. "Thanks. My dad is teaching me how to control my thoughts."

"Did he now?" the skull said in almost accusatory tone. "I have a friend called Bob who wasn't a good swimmer, but he was excellent at treading water. Bob was fond of telling me, 'There's no such thing as a free lunch.'"

Jered opened his eyes. "Huh? What's that mean?"

The skull appeared to tilt slightly, as if it was looking down its nose. "It's a prōverb, my boy. Haven't you ever heard of a prōverb?"

"I don't think so. My mom sometimes tells me old fashioned sayings, but she calls them *praw-verbs*."

"Do you believe everything your parents tell you? Hm? Aren't these the same people who convinced you a fat man in a red suit delivered presents to you every December? I guess you'll have to decide who're you gonna believe pronounces the word correctly?"

Jered had to admit that this argument had some merit. It'd only been recently that Jered learned of the Santa Claus ruse.

"You don't have to just take my word for it," the skull said. "Think back to what you learned in school. All you have to do is break the word down and it'll tell you what it means. The first part of the word is *pro*. Everyone knows what a pro is: it's a professional. The second part of the word is *verb*: an action word. So, a prōverb is a professional verb, as opposed to an amateur verb." Despite the skull's carefully laid out analysis, Jered's expression revealed he wasn't quite following the logic. The skull explained further,

"Prōverbs are old sayings from way back that teach us truths about life. For example, I once knew a woman who was quite an aggressive trial lawyer. Sue was fond of using the old prōverb, 'A stitch in time saves nine.'"

Jered cocked his head a bit to the left and asked, "What's a *stitchin*?"

"It's a prōverb, my boy. It means that surgery can heal a cat, thus saving one of its nine lives. Do you understand?"

"Um, not really, I guess," Jered stammered, shaking his head.

"Hmmm, let me think of another one. My uncle Jim was a very strong man who lifted heavy weights, and he used to say to me, 'People who live in glass houses shouldn't throw stones.'"

Jered thought for a moment, then asked, "Why would anyone build a house out of glass?"

"Precisely!" the skull interjected. "This prōverb teaches us you should always hire a capable construction team, general contractor, and architect to build your house, otherwise you could end up with a worthless home made out of glass."

"That makes sense, I guess," Jered said, nodding a little.

"When it comes to your father, it's important to keep in mind that things aren't always as they seem," the skull said in a somewhat cautionary tone. "That isn't a prōverb: it's just something important for you to remember from this point on."

"What do you mean by that?"

"How can I explain this? Well, consider the humble tomato."

"What's a *Humbolt* tomato?"

"Did you know tomatoes are a member of a class of poisonous plants? It's actually a close relative of the beautiful but deadly nightshade flower."

"No, they're not! I've eaten tomatoes lots of times and I never got poisoned!"

"It's true. Even though tomatoes are cousins of dangerous nightshade, you can still eat them. In this situation, what looks like a poisonous plant is actually quite delicious. The flipside is also true. What looks like a harmless fruit could poison you, or even kill you if you're not careful. This is what I want you to remember about your father."

Jered's face was awash in a combination of confusion and skepticism. "What are you saying about my Dad? My Dad is a great man."

"Look, I've clearly said too much, too soon. Your dad is just fine. I just want you to be alert. You know who Spider-Man is, right?" Jered nodded. "And every little boy knows that Spider-Man feels a tingle in his Spider-senses when something's not quite right. I need you to use that same kind of thing and be aware of things that don't seem quite right," the skull explained.

"But Spider-Man was bitten by a *radiostatic* spider: that's why he has Spidey-senses. I was never bitten like that, so I don't have them powers."

"We don't need to be bitten by a glowing insect to have special abilities. Anyone can have certain . . . how shall I put it . . . qualities. Yes, that's it: qualities. The trick is to figure out what they are and how to use them. Often in times of great stress or impending danger, these qualities can rise to the surface. In your case, I see big things coming and you need to use every special quality you have to successfully deal with these events."

"Huh? I still don't get what you mean."

"Well, I don't want to talk out of turn, but it looks to me you need to get prepared for some important events that are appearing on the horizon." Jered shook his head a couple times, still not following what was being intimated. "Let's just say that there are things you might not see approaching, but I do."

"How can you see things I can't? What exactly *are* you?"

Indignantly, the skull responded, "I could ask you the same thing. What exactly are *you*?"

"I'm a boy. My name's Jered. I'm eight years old."

"Okay, I'm a sugar skull. My name is Skelly."

"Skelly? Like the Skelly gas station? My dad and me walk to the gas station sometimes, and sometimes he'll buy me candy, and this one time I got . . ."

As kids often do, Jered was starting to ramble, so Skelly cut the boy's story short. "I'm not a gas station, but I'm quite familiar with candy. I was created sixty-three days ago by a man in Mexico. Are you satisfied now?"

"Well, not really. How is it you can talk?"

"I might ask you the same thing: how is it that *you're* talking?"

"Um, well, I just can. I've always been able to talk."

"That's my response to you. I just can. Just like you, I've always been able to talk."

"I guess I still don't understand how you can talk."

"I guess I still don't understand how such a creative boy can have trouble accepting the fact I can talk."

There was a brief silence, then Jered asked in an accusatory voice, "Is this some kind of joke?"

"No, I think what you just said is a question. Were you joking with *me*? If what you just said was supposed to be some kind of joke, young man, it certainly wasn't very funny."

"I'm serious!"

"I thought you were Jered. Nice to meet you, Serious."

"No, my name is Jered."

"But you just said you're Serious."

"I'm both! My name is Jered, *and* I'm serious!"

"Ah, I misunderstood. You see, I don't have a last name, so what you said threw me for a loop. My apologies. It's indeed very nice to meet you Jered Serious."

SKELETONS ARE NOT SCARY

"*Ttt!* No, that's not what I'm saying!" an exasperated Jered said.

From the other room, Jered's mother called out to her son. "Honey, are you okay? Who are you talking to?"

In a mocking voice, Skelly asked, "Yeah, Jered, who *are* you talking to?"

Jered's young brain quickly played out a number of little movies in his imagination, each one based upon a different response he gave to his mother's query. All the scenarios wherein he told his mother he was talking to his candy skull didn't end very well.

A child's ability to weigh the pros and cons of telling the truth to a parent was discussed at length in Dr. Ford Freud's 1973 article, "Devious Secrets Hidden by Children: A Ticking Time Bomb." Dr. Freud explained a child's innate ability to determine whether to be truthful is an offshoot of the "fight or flight" instinct every animal has at birth. It is this skill of deception which leads to the development of several pathological personality traits, according to Dr. Freud. Children who are skilled in deceiving their parents often develop difficulties dealing with authority figures, experience night sweats, and are prone to fixate on cartoon animals who are peddling breakfast cereals of dubious nutritional value.

"Nobody, Mom," Jered called out. "Just . . . just talking to myself."

"Alright . . ." she replied in an uncertain voice.

Jered and the skull remained silent, listening for the sound of any footsteps approaching the bedroom. When it was clear that they weren't going to be interrupted by Jered's mother, the skull said, "That was some good, quick thinking on your feet, buckaroo. It's best we keep our relationship private and not share it with others."

After giving it some thought, Jered replied, "Yeah, that's probably right. I just kinda thought I maybe shouldn't let her know about . . . well . . . talking to my toys."

"This situation reminds me of something my uncle Frank used to say to me. Uncle Frank was always truthful and very forthright, and he said, 'necessity is the mother of invention.' That's what kind of happened just now with your mother." Jered furrowed his brow as he tried to make sense of what Skelly said, but he couldn't quite figure it out. The skull added, "There was a necessity to keep this relationship secret, so you invented something to fool your mother. You see, you've been following the lessons of prōverbs even when you didn't know it."

Jered was a little amazed he'd apparently been employing a skill he never knew he had. "Yeah, I guess you're right."

"Has your dad begun talking to you about skeletons yet?"

Jered was taken aback, and his eyes widened. "Yeah. How did ya know that?"

"Let's just say that sometimes I know things that were meant to be private."

"He keeps telling me about skeletons, and how they're not scary, and how skeletons are my friends, and . . ." He stopped talking when he had a sudden realization. "Wait a sec: a *skull* is part of the *skeleton*. Has he been talking about *you* all this time?"

The skull's reply started out light and happy. "No, your dad doesn't know anything about me. I'm just a skull, not a whole skeleton." His voice then switched to a more serious tone. "If he knew about me, I'm quite certain your dad would prefer that you *not* talk to me."

"How come?"

"Hmm, how can I put this delicately? My cousin Cliff was a mountain climber, and Cliff used to say, 'What a tangled web we weave when first we choose to deceive.'" The skull waited a few moments for the boy to grasp the meaning of the prōverb, then explained further, "The meaning being spiders are deceitful by nature, so you have to be careful not to get caught in their web. Got it?"

"Sure. Spiders. Webs." Taking a quick look around his room, he asked, "Is a spider going to come talk to me, too?"

"Not as far as I know. If a spider *does* show up, just walk away from it! Don't say *anything* to it! That's really important! Got it?"

"Okay, yeah, don't talk to any spiders," Jered agreed.

"And just generally, keep your eyes open. You can never be too careful. That's not a prōverb: it's more of just a good general rule to follow in life."

"What am I looking for when I'm keeping my eyes open?" The skull didn't move or speak for almost an entire minute, causing Jered to ask, "Are you still there?"

"Yeah, I was just thinking. You know, using my head!" This quip made Jered giggle. "I don't know how to tell you what to look for other than to say, you'll know it when you see it."

"Like . . . ?" Jered drew out the word so it was five syllables long, hoping to prompt Skelly into providing additional information. After a few moments of silence, Jered leaned towards the skull. "Are you still there? Skelly?"

His mother opened the bedroom door and asked, "Are you doing okay?"

Jered was so startled he let out a high-pitched *yip* and jumped to his feet. Jered's sudden movement caused his hip to bump the nightstand. The sugar skull slid across the nightstand, teetering on the edge. From the corner of his eye, Jered saw his sugar skull was about to fall. He gasped and thrust out his hands. Luckily, Skelly softly slid into his hands and was saved from what Jered was sure would have been a fatal fall to the hardwood floor.

"Got him!" Jered said with a relieved smile on his face. "Whew, that was a close one! That could've been a disaster with a capital 'D'!"

Jered's mother felt it would have been so much better if he hadn't been able to snare the skull out of the air. If the horrible skull was reduced to nothing more than shattered shards of sugar scattered all over the floor, she would have jumped for joy. She choked back her disappointment and said, "Yeah, that was a good catch. I just came to tell you as soon as you decide to be a good boy, you can come out and set the table." Chrissy's attention was so focused on the skull's near destruction, she failed to notice the green skeleton hanging on the closet door.

After Jered's mother left the room and he waited until he was sure she was gone, Skelly broke the silence. "Thanks for catching me! You're a good friend."

"Thanks. I . . . I don't got a lot of friends," Jered confided in an embarrassed voice.

"That doesn't matter. Haven't you ever heard that quality is more important than quantity?" Jered shook his head, but since the skull didn't have eyes, he didn't know if Skelly could see his head move. "Good friends help each other and that's what I'm gonna do for my good friend Jered!"

"Yeah?" Jered was curious and a little apprehensive as to what kind of assistance a sugar skull could possibly offer him.

"If your family goes to Uncle Ted's for a chili feast, I think it'd be best you didn't eat it."

"Huh? Why?"

"Just take the advice of your friend. Find some reason to eat other things but promise me you'll stay away from Uncle Ted's chili."

"I usually can't eat very much of his chili because it's spicy and burns my mouth."

"Well, don't eat *any* of it this time! None!"

"Okay, if you say so."

There was a pause, then Skelly thought aloud, "I wonder what kind of tomatoes he uses in his chili?"

"Whichever kind is spicy," Jered replied.

SKELETONS ARE NOT SCARY

"It doesn't matter. Whatever kind of tomatoes he uses, just stay clear of the chili. Period."

"Should I tell my Mom and Dad not to eat the chili, too?"

"No, this is just a secret between two dear friends. It's best to leave the adults to fend for themselves. Besides, grown-ups already think they know everything; it's hard to get them to listen, especially if it's a kid talking."

"Yeah!" Jered agreed in a voice that was a little too loud. He then added in a softer voice, "They don't ever believe it when a kid tells them something, even if it's *really* important."

Skelly remarked, "One of the things that happens to you when you get big is you think you're in control of everything, when really you ain't in control of nothing!" Jered grunted in agreement, then the skull added, "When it comes to your uncle's chili, you need to follow the advice of my Uncle Mike."

"What did your Uncle Mike say?"

"Mike always spoke in a very loud, amplified voice and he was fond of saying, 'When in Rome, do as the Romans do.'"

Jered shook his head a little and replied, "But I've never been to Rome. I don't even know where it's at. What's that mean?"

"It means eat the pasta and stay away from the chili. Promise to do that?"

Jered was about to agree with Skelly when the candy skull warned, "Shh! I think your mom is coming again."

A few seconds later, Jered's mother walked past his bedroom to the bathroom. After he heard the bathroom door close, Jered whispered, "Thanks for the warning."

"You betcha. That's what friends do."

CHAPTER THIRTEEN

Chili November

A few days after talking to Skelly for the first time, Jered was in for quite a surprise.

Surprises can take several forms and different kinds of surprises can evoke a wide range of emotions. Take for example the pleasant surprise of receiving a new baseball glove for your birthday. This un-expected gift can fill you with such joy that it causes you to practice harder, becoming a better athlete. The flipside is a disappointing surprise. Instead of a baseball glove, your birthday present might be an odd book about a boy who struggles unsuccessfully to convince adults there is a monster under his bed. Such an unwelcome gift can cause such a pervasive depression you may decide there is no inherent goodness of mankind and become a lonely misanthrope. Or a lawyer. Then there are surprises that are so unusual you're not sure *how* to respond.

While Jered was sitting at the kitchen table doing homework, his mother surprised him. Standing at the stove and stirring a sauce-pan of gravy, she said, "Oh, by the way, I wanted to tell you this weekend we're all going to Uncle Ted's house. He's practicing for a chili cook-off and wants us all to try his new recipe. Doesn't that sound like fun?"

When her son didn't respond, she asked, "Did you hear me? Won't that be fun?" Chrissy looked over her shoulder, surprised to see Jered looking as though he'd just seen a ghost. He was very pale, and his mouth was agape. "Are you okay? You don't look so good," she asked with motherly concern.

Jered was temporarily speechless. Skelly told him earlier that week this would happen! Questions were racing through his mind. How could Skelly have known?! Was Skelly a crystal ball? Or a Magic 8-Ball? Can he see everything in the future? Could Skelly tell him the next time there'd be a pop quiz?

"Jered? Jered?"

He barely heard his mother's voice through his internal dialog. "Um, yeah, Mom," he replied, his mind still reeling. "Sorry, I was just thinking about this question . . . this homework problem. I . . . I'm just not sure how to answer it."

She smiled with relief and turned back to the stove. "I'm glad you're thinking so hard about your homework. I shouldn't have interrupted you while you were deep in thought."

"No, it's alright, Mom," he replied, still thinking about the advice he'd received from Skelly. It wasn't as if he hadn't believed Skelly. Truth was, Jered hadn't thought about the strange warning over the past two days. "Um, is it okay if I take a little break?"

"Sure, honey. Get up and stretch your legs, then you can come back and tackle that hard question. Do you need some fresh air?"

As he pushed himself away from the kitchen table, he replied, "Naw, I thought I'd just go to my bedroom for a few minutes."

"Okay, but not for too long. Pretty soon it'll be time for you to set the table and you need to have all of your homework done before supper."

Jered silently closed his bedroom door behind him. Since his bedroom was very close to the kitchen, he spoke softly to the candy skull. "Skelly, you were right! Mom says we're going to Uncle Ted's for chili on Saturday!"

"That's what I thought," Skelly said. "Remember what I told you: don't eat the chili!"

"How did ya know we were going? How could ya know that?"

"I just knew. It's best if you just accept the information and don't worry yourself about how I know it. My old neighbor Curt always spoke in a very terse and abrupt way. He used to remind me, 'Don't look a gift horse in the mouth.'"

"I don't know what a *gifthearse* is."

"No, a gift horse. It means a horse you're given as a present."

"You mean people really give horses as presents? Like big, regular size horses?"

"You betcha, and if you're lucky enough to get one, don't look in its mouth, because horses bite."

"Honest?"

"Yeah. Cows do too. Haven't you ever seen them in the pasture chewing their cud? That's just the cow practicing in case it gets a chance to bite someone."

Jered had only seen these animals from afar, but he made a mental note to be cautious around cows and horses if he ever visited a farm in the future. "I gotta go back to the kitchen. I'm still not done with homework yet."

"Cool," Skelly remarked. When Jered stood up, Skelly added, "There's another thing I wanted to mention. You might see something troubling in the near future. I mean like kinda scary. If you do, make sure you come talk to me about what you saw, okay?"

Jered looked both suspicious and apprehensive. "What do you mean, scary?"

"I said just kinda scary. What's important is that we talk about it after it happens, got it?"

"Can't you just tell me what's gonna happen?" he asked hopefully.

"No, because I don't know for sure it'll happen in the first place," Skelly replied. This was stretching the truth: he was almost certain it would occur. "Promise you'll come to me right away and talk about anything like that?"

"Sure, you're my friend."

"That's my boy!"

As Skelly suggested, Jered told his parents he had a bad stomachache the afternoon they spent at Uncle Ted's house. His mother said he didn't have a fever but to be safe, she wanted Jered to not eat anything spicy, like the chili. She advised him to try to settle his stomach by having Zesta saltines and 7-UP for dinner. As Jered nibbled on crackers, he watched as Uncle Ted's friends and family ladled bowls full of chili. It smelled really good, and Jered was disappointed he was missing it. His resolve was further tested when everyone began raving about how good it tasted. Bowl after bowl was eagerly consumed.

"Maybe just a little chili would be okay," Jered thought. "Skelly could be wrong. Maybe he was playing a trick on me."

In the end, it was the solemnness of Skelly's warning that swayed the boy's final decision. Jered heeded the warning, even turning down a spoonful of chili his father offered him.

After eating, the grownups sat around the living room talking about stupid adult stuff, while most of the kids played outside. Jered stayed in the house where he could observe the adults. Jered didn't know why Skelly told him to avoid the chili, nor did he know what would happen to those who ate it. When nothing happened over the following hour, Jered again wondered if Skelly had played a joke on him. While they were in the car on the way home, his parents were talking pleasantly and neither one mentioned any concerns.

"Maybe that skull didn't really say nothing to me," Jered thought. "Skeletons don't talk. Probably just my imagination. I'm so stupid—I should've known . . ."

His father let out a long, thunderous burp.

"Rodney Barstow! That's awful!" Chrissy tittered.

"Excuse me. I'm sorry. I'm not sure where that came from! It snuck up on me." Rodney looked over his shoulder to the backseat and added, "Don't ever do that, son. That's not a nice thing to do. It just kind of caught me off guard."

While lying in bed that night, Jered heard his mother and father going in and out of the hallway bathroom several times. Jered couldn't help but giggle every time he heard one of them rush into the bathroom. He wasn't exactly relishing in their anguish: it was just kind of funny.

"Do you hear that?" Jered whispered to the skull, then let out another snicker.

"It's going to be a long night for everyone who ate that chili, my friend," Skelly said somberly. "Wouldn't want to be them right now."

While his parents were sick for the better part of the next two days, Jered felt just fine. He and his skull were wearing the same satisfied smile.

In a word, Rodney's job was crummy. As crummy as the warm lunchmeat sandwich he was joylessly eating in the break room. This day wasn't special: just another lackluster workday broken up by an equally bland lunch break. Not even a generous amount of mustard was able to pep up his bologna sandwich.

"Crummy," he thought each time his teeth came together to grind the tasteless wad of white sandwich bread and lunchmeat in his mouth. He worked in a crummy job, dealing with the constant barrage of crummy customers, all the while trying to placate his crummy boss. Dreary days like this tested his mettle. It took all his energy to keep from telling his boss where he could stuff his reports as he triumphantly marched out of the building.

"What happened?" Rodney asked himself from time to time. With a high school diploma in hand and a girlfriend who adored him, the world was his oyster. Somehow the mundane world had won and was now slowly chewing him up.

Sometimes he fantasized about wandering the world like David Carradine in the TV show *Kung Fu*. Without having any destination, Rodney would travel through the land, sharing his philosophical thoughts, and knocking the snot out of anyone who crossed him. Everyone would get what was coming to them and it would be Rodney who meted out this punishment. David Carradine didn't have a dull job, an oppressive mortgage, and mounds of responsibilities. His only duty each day was to enlighten people he encountered and punish those who didn't listen. Yes, that man had everything in his world under control.

Raucous laughter from some of his co-workers interrupted his daydream. Four men seated around an adjacent table were having a grand old time talking about . . . who knew? Most likely nothing important! Now that Rodney was back in the real world, he listened to the conversation, curious to know what was so funny.

"No kidding!" one of the men said in a voice that was too loud for the small room. "The ball went right over his head!" Once again, his lunch mates laughed. "My little Davey hit the ball over the left fielder's head and all the kid could do was throw his glove up into the air to try to knock it down! I'm not just blowing smoke here: Davey's turning out to be one heck of a baseball player."

"You're a little league dad, now!"

"Don't I know it! I've got to push that boy to make sure he practices. I was a pretty good ball player in my day, but I got lazy. I'm gonna make sure Davey works hard and turns out better than I was!"

One of the other men at the table suggested, "Maybe he'll get a baseball scholarship. Wouldn't that be a solid for you and the missus."

"Yahtzee! Goodbye college fund; hello ski boat!"

Initially Rodney scoffed at the thought of his co-worker doting over his son's athletic abilities. The more he thought about Jered's development, though, Rodney wondered if *he'd* become the ultimate little league dad. Just like little Davey's father, Rodney was doing everything possible to encourage the honing of his son's talents. Of course, the stakes for Rodney's son were much more than a Major League Baseball career.

"At least you got a kid who might get a sports scholarship," one of the others said. "I got me a clarinet player. Ain't any clarinet scholarships out there or people paying to see a clarinet player!" This remark caused the men to laugh once again. "How about you, George? Your boy gonna go to college, or will he have the good sense to save his dad some moola, and just get a job after high school graduation?"

George shook his head solemnly. "I don't know. At this point, I'm hoping he even makes it through high school. He's thirteen but hasn't got a lick of sense in him. He certainly wouldn't have survived if he was a kid living in the world *I* grew up in!"

"Ain't that the truth! Kids these days are lazy and don't know anything about anything."

"They know what's on the old boob tube!"

"Oh yeah, they know everything about TV shows! They just sit there like zombies. If they didn't have to go to school, they'd watch TV from the time it came on at 5:00 in the morning until it went off the air at midnight!"

"They'd hear the national anthem when the TV came on and then again when it goes off the air!"

This observation caused all four men to laugh. Rodney felt just a hint of pity for them.

"They have no idea what it's like to be raising a son who'll one day be the closest thing to a real superhero!" Rodney thought. He knew there'd be kids who were smarter and physically stronger than Jered, but their accomplishments would pale in comparison to what Jered would eventually accomplish.

What kept Rodney going was the reward he'd receive at some point in the future. He just had to accept that the dead-end job he endured five days a week was nothing more than a means for him to clothe, shelter, and feed his family. When Jered was able to spread his wings and gain control over his abilities, surely Rodney would be able to quit this awful job. His son could use his powers for a myriad of purposes, including providing for his father. When Jered sat on his throne, some of the power and riches he obtained would trickle down to his loyal father. Rodney would become the proverbial "man behind the man," who used his influence to sagely guide Jered. He chuckled at the thought he'd eventually become the world's greatest, most successful little league dad!

Until that time came, Rodney just needed to not let his job get him down. He needed to nudge his son forward without getting impatient. Chrissy already complained he was pushing Jered too hard at times. What was the problem with a father wanting his son to become great? The true sign of a father's love is how he helps his son become something better than himself. If a man didn't love his son, he'd pay no attention to his child's development. Rodney loved Jered so much that he'd long ago pledged he'd do whatever it took for Jered to eventually grab hold of his destiny.

CHAPTER FOURTEEN

The Straw that Broke the Proverbial Camel's Back

When you think about it, the old saying "the straw that broke the camel's back" is so bizarre and nonsensical, it should be banished from the English language. This phrase needs to be imprisoned on the island of unused sayings in the cell right next to calling a couch a chesterfield. It seeks to describe a situation that in no way deals with the number of drinking straws (elbow or straight) a typical camel would be able to carry before exposing itself to grave bodily damage. Nevertheless, adults insist on using this old saw to describe when someone is eventually pushed over the edge. Kerri Moran wasn't a camel, nor did she carry boxes of drinking straws on her back, but she did reach the point where she felt obligated to call Jered's mother regarding her concerns.

The straw that broke Kerri Moran's back was an assignment she gave her students the Monday before Thanksgiving. She showed a filmstrip titled *"Pilgrims, Indians, and the first Thanksgiving."* It ended up being a little too juvenile for third graders, but managed to communicate the concepts of brotherhood and working together to overcome adversity. After the filmstrip, she asked the students to draw a picture depicting the first Thanksgiving. With classical music playing in the background, her third-grade class worked on their creations. In just a few short months, even her less imaginative students had warmed up to these exercises and exhibited their creativity.

"Just a few more minutes," she announced. "Start getting finished up with your pieces. If you need some help, I'll be coming around. Remember, you're not trying to make it look perfect or like a photograph. Try to show emotions."

Almost all her kids drew variations of the same scene, which consisted of a table covered with food surrounded by happy Pilgrims and Indians partaking of the feast. A couple of children drew a Pilgrim and Indian reaching out to shake hands, which was pleasant. Kerri walked up and down the aisles, providing words of encouragement to her students as she looked over their shoulders.

"I like the way you drew the clothes on the Pilgrims, Jennifer. You've put the buckles exactly in the right place. Very nice. You've drawn a really fat turkey, Steve. They'll be eating *that* turkey for a long time!"

"He's fat because he's a jive turkey!" Steve responded. The boy had no idea what a *jive turkey* was, but he'd heard his father use it to describe the President, and Steve just thought it sounded funny. His classmates burst out in loud laughter.

"Okay, settle down," Kerri said, trying to sound serious while she was laughing inside.

She was brimming with satisfaction; her students responded well to the project and stretched their creative legs. As she walked behind the back row of desks, she got a good look at Jered's creation. Jered had drawn the same as most of his classmates: a feast attended by Pilgrims and Indians. His peers had all drawn happy, smiling faces on the attendees. In Jered's scene, skulls peered out from under large black Pilgrim hats. An Indian dressed in a brown vest with fringe was sporting a red headband, with a yellow feather tucked into it. The headband encircled a grinning skull. Maybe it was because she'd been feeling so good that she was unnerved by the drawing. Maybe it was because she'd eaten very little for lunch that she felt a little unsteady. The third graders were focused on their drawings, so none of them noticed their teacher put her hand up to her mouth.

Jered looked over his shoulder and asked, "What do you think, Miss Moran? Do you like it?"

Kerri Moran dropped the hand from her mouth, pretending she'd just yawned. "Mm," was her brief response.

She looked at Jered carefully, analyzing his face. There was no malice or evil in Jered's eyes. What Kerri saw in his expression was the same eagerness to please she'd seen ever since she first praised his artistic ability. He clearly wanted her approval and always tried to please her.

Trying her best not to betray her deep sense of concern, Kerri said, "Um, why don't we talk about it later? Maybe you could stay after school for a few minutes?"

Jered's face fell. The boy had become accustomed to Miss Moran's immediate praise for his artwork and when it didn't come, he felt as though he'd been punched hard in the stomach. It required extreme effort for Jered to reply breathlessly to his teacher, "Okay."

"Can we see it?" one of the children asked. All the kids knew Jered was by far the best artist in the entire third grade and some of them enjoyed seeing his creations.

"Not now," Miss Moran said hastily. "Put all of your crayons and drawings away quickly. I just remembered we need to finish another assignment before the end of the day."

Jered opened the top of his desk and quietly slid his drawing inside. As Miss Moran droned on about Plymouth Rock, the boy felt tears welling up in his eyes. Prior to that moment, the boy hadn't really experienced a broken heart. He was unsure why his stomach now felt so sour and his chest so heavy. The last thing a boy ever wanted to do was to shed a tear in front of his peers, so Jered fought hard to keep his eyes dry. This was a difficult task because he was ashamed: he'd failed Miss Moran. Luckily, no one saw the one time he surreptitiously wiped his eyes with the back of his hand.

While lecturing about Pilgrims, Kerri did her best to forget the awful drawing. With just over an hour left in the school day, Kerri's thoughts were more on the phone call she was going to make that afternoon than what she was saying to her class.

Although Jered dutifully kept his eyes on his teacher, he wasn't listening to her. Instead, he was focused on the fact he'd failed the love of his life. What had he done to fall so quickly from her grace? Would she ever talk to him again? Would she decide he wasn't worth her effort? An accusatory inner voice yelled, "You did something wrong! You're gonna get it now!" During this venomous rant, a pain began welling up from deep inside his head, slowly moving until it was wedged between his eyes. "She hates you! She hates what you drew! You never could draw good: people just said that because they felt sorry for the poor stupid deaf kid! Miss Moran never liked your drawings and she certainly never liked you!" His forehead gradually became uncomfortably warm, causing sweat to form above his eyebrows.

Once the bell rang and the students began filing out of the classroom, Kerri had a moment to collect her thoughts. While she lectured, she'd glanced in Jered's direction a few times and could see clearly the young man was upset. If Jered was a troublemaker who'd broken the rules, this counseling session would have been easy. If that were the case, she'd instill in the child a sense of fear that even more punitive measures would be taken if he didn't straighten up.

This student and this situation were much more difficult to address. As Kerri walked to the back row where Jered silently sat at his desk, he looked at her with eyes full of shame. Jered looked like an innocent man charged with murder who was waiting uncomfortably for a jury's verdict to be read aloud in court. As she made the long

SKELETONS ARE NOT SCARY

walk to Jered's desk, she noted how tense her neck and shoulders were. Kerri felt she was getting in over her head, but circumstances dictated she take action.

Seated at an adjacent desk, she did her best to use a measured, calm voice. "Thanks for staying after school for a few minutes. Your mother won't be worried if you're home a little late, will she?" The boy said nothing, sitting perfectly still as the jury foreman prepared to speak. "I'd like to talk to you a little about what you drew today. Actually, I wanted to talk to you about your artwork. It seems that you draw a lot of skeletons even though Thanksgiving is just a few days away. Why is that?" Jered didn't respond. "Is there something you want to talk to me about?"

Just like earlier that afternoon, Jered had to hold back the tears that wanted to be released. The skeleton tacked to his closet door wasn't at all scary to him, but this discussion with Miss Moran was terrifying. Not sure how to respond to his teacher, Jered fell back on the stock answer given by most children his age. "I don't know."

Kerri looked into the boy's eyes, searching for the truth behind them. She tried to prompt him into sharing what was on his mind. "Is there something you're trying to show me or tell me in your pictures? Something maybe you're afraid to tell me?"

After a lengthy pause, Jered repeated, "I don't know."

Kerri didn't get angry; she wanted him to open up to her. She managed to summon a smile, in an attempt to put the boy at ease. "You and I are friends, right?"

The way the word "friends" sounded to Jered, it should have been accompanied by trumpets. Prior to that moment, he'd never entertained the possibility their relationship was a two-way street. He'd known for quite some time he was in love with Miss Moran, but he was smart enough to understand he was just a boy and she was a beautiful genius. Hearing her say they were friends caused

Jered's heart to perform a happy somersault. Was she serious? Did she really consider Jered her friend?

"Sure, we are," Kerri smiled. "And friends can tell each other *anything*. Anything at all." When Jered didn't respond to these cues, Kerri continued to encourage the boy to confide in her. "Things like what's going on at home. Or at school. Or things you're scared about. Or mad at. Anything at all." There was another prolonged silence. "Is there *anything* you want to talk to me about?"

Although it was clear his teacher was trying to draw something out of him, Jered wasn't sure what Miss Moran wanted. He considered telling her the truth, which was he just liked to draw skeletons and bones, but it seemed she was expecting something much more than this. He certainly didn't want to disappoint her again. Jered became so conflicted as to how he should respond all he could do was fall back on an old standard. "I don't know," Jered shrugged.

In the boy's face Kerri saw the difficulty Jered was experiencing and it tugged at her heart. It seemed there was something going on and Jered was caught in the middle of it. She wanted to drill down for more answers, but she didn't want to damage the trust the shy boy had placed in her.

"Okay. That's all. I just wanted to talk to you a little bit by ourselves. If you ever want someone to talk to, will you promise me that you'll come see me? Would you do that?" Still unsure as to what Miss Moran was expecting him to confess, Jered gave a slight nod of his head. Trying to sound cheerful, she said, "Great! Have a good night, and I'll see you tomorrow, okay?"

While his teacher walked back to the front of the classroom, Jered opened the top of his desk, grabbed his drawing, and angrily stuffed it into his front pants pocket. He'd never wanted to get out of the school faster than he did that afternoon. Running in school was prohibited but he moved quickly across the classroom towards the exit while Miss Moran was wiping off the chalkboard. Just before Jered reached the doorway, Miss Moran had a final thought.

"Oh, and Jered?" she said, turning towards him. While the boy remained standing in the doorway, she added, "Let's not draw anymore skeletons for a while, okay?"

Jered looked at the floor, then bolted out before anything else could be said.

Earlier that day when Jered left for school, Chrissy made a beeline to his bedroom. She'd noticed Jered had once again tacked the skeleton to his closet door. Hoping to avoid a conflict with her son by letting his emotions simmer down, she allowed it to remain there for the past few days. Now, however, it was time to bring this unnerving episode to an end. As she pulled out the thumbtacks, Chrissy wouldn't even look at the awful thing. She'd considered throwing it in the trash but since Jered liked it so much, that seemed like a mean gesture. She carried it to the basement with two fingers and away from her face, as if it was a smelly diaper.

Chrissy walked downstairs and flipped the wall switch, illuminating two bare 60-watt light bulbs. There were no windows and as usual, it was cool and musty in the poorly lit basement. Sometimes when she went down there by herself, she got the uncomfortable sensation she was descending into a mausoleum. The cement floor, gray cinder block walls, and unfinished ceiling made this space only suitable for the laundry, Rodney's workbench, and stacks of cardboard boxes. Once the skeleton had been deposited in the box with the other Halloween decorations, her plan was to push the box to the back wall behind several other boxes.

She lifted the lid to cardboard box of Halloween decorations. Looking up at her from the box was the happy Jack-o-Lantern window decoration she'd bought at a craft fair. "Why couldn't my little boy like you, Mr. Jack-o-Lantern, and not *this* creepy thing?" she asked.

She laid the skeleton over the box opening, but it was too big fit. In the dim light, the skeleton's ghoulish green smile seemed to mock Chrissy's attempt to hide it. She unceremoniously folded the skeleton, closed the box, then buried it behind other boxes.

"With a little luck," Chrissy said to the empty kitchen, "he'll be so focused on Thanksgiving vacation he won't even notice it's gone."

"With a little luck," Jered thought as he was walking home from school, "I'll draw something that makes Miss Moran like me again. Like me in the way she did before."

As he passed a park, a trash can caught his attention. Jered removed the wadded picture from his pocket, squeezing it tighter and tighter like he was making a snowball. Each time he squeezed the wad of paper, he thought about how this drawing had somehow caused him to lose Miss Moran's affections. With a face full of disgust, Jered threw the wad of paper into the garbage can.

As he continued to walk home, Jered's mood was a small boat bobbing up and down huge waves of emotion. One minute he'd feel angry, but a few blocks later he was overwhelmed by grief. For a couple blocks he'd be teeming with energy, but then he'd feel all that energy escape, leaving him listless. He wasn't used to having a broken heart.

As soon as she saw Jered leave the building, Kerri went to the main office. She called Jered's mother, hoping to have a candid conversation with her prior to Jered arriving home.

"Is everything okay, Miss Moran?" Chrissy asked with obvious concern in her voice.

"Yes, nothing bad has happened: Jered is fine. It's just I wanted to talk to you a little bit about something I've noticed over the past few weeks."

"Oh? Has he been acting up?"

"No, no, nothing like that."

Chrissy let out a sigh of relief. "Thank heavens! He's never been a problem child, but you know how kids can change as they get older."

"He's one of my favorite students," Kerri said. "I enjoy looking at the pictures he draws. He's quite a talented artist."

"You know, even before kindergarten we were all surprised at how well he could stay in the lines in coloring books. Then he started drawing on his own. We're very proud of him."

"So, the reason for my call is I've been seeing certain things showing up in his artwork, and I'm a little concerned about it."

"Really? Like what?" Chrissy started to nervously chew on her thumbnail.

"I don't want to alarm you or make a mountain out of a mole hill, but he's been including a lot of skeletons in his pictures over the past month." Kerri couldn't see Chrissy's face suddenly fall. "Of course, during Halloween, kids draw all kinds of scary things like graveyards, tombstones, and monsters. That sort of thing isn't my cup of tea, but they get caught up in Halloween, so it's understandable."

"I don't like that stuff either," Chrissy said with her thumbnail clamped between her front teeth. She'd hadn't intended to share that piece of information; it just slipped out.

"Now that Thanksgiving is almost here, I don't expect kids to still be thinking about Halloween. Everyone knows that once November 1st comes along, Halloween is put on the shelf for another year. Jered is such an accomplished artist who can draw so many things, I was wondering if there's a reason he continues to draw skeletons?"

Chrissy's jaw muscles tightened, pressing her teeth even harder against her thumbnail. There was a long silence while Chrissy thought about the skeleton she'd boxed up that morning. She scowled at the thought of the eerie Halloween costume Rodney made, and the chilling souvenir her mother brought from Mexico. Truth was, Chrissy didn't want *any* of those horrible, scary things in her house, and certainly didn't want Jered exposed to them at such an impressionable age. What was happening? Why had her house become a denizen of scary skeletons against her will?

"Are you still there, Mrs. Barstow?"

Chrissy was jerked from her thoughts. "Yeah, yes, I'm sorry, I was just thinking."

"I learned during my training that sometimes the effects caused by a crisis can show up in activities such as how kids play or in their artwork. If there's some kind of change in the child's usual routine, it can manifest itself in a number of ways. I certainly don't want to pry, but I wanted to at least contact you to see if there is anything going on in Jered's home life that might explain this . . . this unusual fixation."

As best she could, Chrissy disguised her emotions, trying to sound nonchalant. "No, nothing I can think of. His father dressed him up like a skeleton for Halloween, so maybe he's just remembering how much fun he had trick-or-treating."

Kerri Moran wasn't a clinical psychologist, but she got the feeling Mrs. Barstow wasn't being entirely candid. "So, nothing else that you can think of?"

Chrissy was already formulating the words she was going to bombard Rodney with as soon as he got home from work. "No, nothing at all, but I'll talk to his father, and we'll fix this."

Kerri recognized Mrs. Barstow was getting angry, and the young teacher was concerned she may have accidentally caused Jered to be in trouble with his parents. "Keep in mind, he isn't in *any* trouble. Jered hasn't done anything wrong. I just wanted to make sure that there wasn't something going on at home I needed to be aware of."

"Nope, nothing." Chrissy said curtly.

It was clear to Kerri nothing was going to be gained from this conversation. "Well, I'm glad to hear that. If you ever want to talk to me about anything, I'm always available to you and Jered."

"Okay, thanks for calling," Chrissy said, which was followed immediately by the sound of the phone being hung up.

Kerri was still troubled by the notion there was a situation at home which was causing Jered to repeatedly draw skeletons. Deciding she needed expert advice, Kerri again called her favorite college professor. She tried to explain all the salient facts, without burdening the professor with too many details. Kerri described her concerns and that she'd talked to both Jered and his mother about these misgivings.

The professor started talking almost before Kerri could finish. "You're trying too hard," the professor counseled. "He's your student, but he's *not* your son."

"I know, but if he's suffering, I don't want it . . ."

"Listen, Kerri. It's your first teaching job and you're rip roaring ready to go. You've got to learn to back off. A garden doesn't grow better if you hover over it, staring at the seedlings."

"I don't want to become one of those teachers who doesn't care anymore," Kerri lamented. She was surprised at her favorite professor's reply.

"You've got to learn to pull back the throttle and not try so hard. If you don't let up a little, you're going to burn yourself out. They're just kids, and you're just an elementary school teacher. He's just one of hundreds and hundreds of kids you'll have contact with during your career."

The telephone conversation didn't last much longer. Kerri was very disappointed. Her favorite college professor sounded less like Kerri's mentor and more like the soured women in the teachers' lounge. The professor who'd encouraged her students to make the world better by educating the next generation just scolded her for caring too much about her student. It appeared the mentor Kerri sought for direction had soured, just like the other jaded veteran teachers.

"I'm home, Mom," Jered announced. He knew something was amiss when his mother didn't respond, "You're *not* a home: you're not even a house!" He felt a pall, as if the air in the living room was somehow heavy. "Mom?" he called out from the entryway, hesitant to venture further into the house.

His mother moved briskly from the kitchen to the living room. She wasn't running but she moved so fast it took Jered off guard. He took one wary step backwards towards the door before his mother enveloped him in her arms. Jered was pulled to his mother's chest, his head buried in her shoulder. He was so surprised he just stood stiffly while his mother hugged him.

Holding her son tightly, Chrissy asked, "Are you okay, Jered? Is everything okay?"

Since he didn't know of his teacher's phone call, Jered had no idea why he was being asked this question. His response therefore sounded more like a question: "Sure?"

Chrissy held her son at arm's length so she could look lovingly at his sweet, round face. Her precious little boy: full of wonder and life. Although she was smiling, his mother's face looked strained.

"Really?" she asked in a voice filled with hope. "You're really okay, honey?"

With more conviction, Jered replied, "Sure I am." When the tense smile remained on his mother's face, he asked, "What's the matter, Mom?"

Chrissy gave the one-word answer women have employed for millennia. It is the assurance that has bedeviled both children and husbands alike since the dawn of time. "Nothing."

She tried to widen her smile in order to reassure her son, but to Jered, she succeeded in only looking like a poorly drawn caricature of what a happy person is supposed to look like.

Jered's mother then abruptly reverted to what she normally talked about when he came home from school. "Are you hungry? Do you want a snack?"

Jered was profoundly confused. In just a few short moments, his mother had transformed from a frightened woman back to her typical self. Despite her assurance that nothing was wrong, the boy figured something wasn't right.

"Is everything okay, Mom? Did something happen?"

His mother responded in a fakey sing-song voice, "No problem at all. I was just happy to see my little boy, that's all. No problems. Let's go to the kitchen."

In high school, the introverted Chrissy Sagen never took a drama class, and it was just as well, since she was a very poor actress. Her son wasn't fooled by her crocodile smile, so he kept his probing eyes on her while she made him a peanut butter sandwich. As he ate, Jered scrutinized his mother's face, looking for any clue as to the cause of her unusual behavior. As she talked to Jered about what she planned to make for supper, her smile started looking more sincere and less forced. By the time he finished his snack, she looked like herself again.

"I'm gonna change clothes and go outside: is that okay?" Jered wondered if asking to leave the house on a blustery afternoon would cause the sudden reappearance of the stressed mother who'd enveloped him in the entryway.

Without hesitation, she replied, "Sure! Just make sure you wear something on your head; it's nippy out there."

As Jered walked into his bedroom, he was still struggling to sort out what occurred when he arrived home that afternoon. His brain churned through a myriad of thoughts regarding his mother's behavior. Since he'd never had a teacher call his parents, he didn't consider Miss Moran may have telephoned his mother as he was walking home. When he couldn't make heads or tails of it, he decided to just let it go.

"Sometimes parents do the strangest things," he thought.

"Yes, they do," a familiar voice piped in. "But keep in mind adults are typically rational creatures. For the most part, parents don't do things randomly."

Jered sat on his bed and addressed Skelly. "Then why did she act that way when I got home? She was being really weird at first."

"My step-uncle was a famous chef who tended to put too much seasoning on his dishes. Herb once told me, 'You can't judge a book by its cover.'"

After a few moments, Jered asked, "Are you telling me not to rely too much on what I saw?"

"No, I was suggesting that the Dewey Decimal System is a good way to find out what books are about." Jered looked quizzically at the talking skull. "Do you see?" Jered shook his head. "There are often better ways of determining what's going on than just relying on what you first see."

"What do you mean? Like what?"

"Has anything occurred recently which could explain your mother's odd behavior?"

"Not that I know of. Things have just been regular."

"Are you certain?" When the boy didn't respond, the skull added, "Didn't something happen today at school that was a little out of the ordinary?"

"What are you talking about? What do you know that I don't?!" he asked in a perturbed voice sharp with suspicion.

Responding to the boy's irritation with a calm, measured voice, Skelly said, "There are things I know and there are things I don't know. Conversely, there are things I know that I actually don't know. The things I know I don't know are not nearly as concerning as the things I don't know that I don't know. You know the answer to my question just as well as I do, so I'll ask it again. My question is simple and not intended to get a rise out of you. Didn't something out of the ordinary occur today at school?"

The boy's angry expression melted away, replaced by a look of realization. "You mean?" Being confronted at the front door by his mother had monopolized all his thoughts, causing him to momentarily forget about the dreadful mess with Miss Moran. "Do you think Miss Moran called my Mom, and told her . . ." The thought of the teacher he loved telling his mother that she was disappointed in him was almost too agonizing to consider. The mere thought this *might* have happened was crushing.

Skelly saw the shoulders of his young friend droop forward and a look of abject embarrassment spread across his face. The skull tried to reassure Jered. "This happens sometimes: teachers call parents to talk to them."

"It's never happened to me!" Jered sniped.

"How can you be so sure?"

"Huh?"

"How do you know it hasn't happened before?"

"Well, because my Mom never told me that she got a call from one of my teachers," Jered replied with certainty.

"For that matter, she hasn't told you that she spoke with Miss Moran this afternoon, either."

The two friends were silent as Jered considered what Skelly said. "So, what do I do?" Jered asked.

The skull thought for a moment, then said, "My young friend, it's important for you to remain *cooool* in the face of conflict. Sometimes I've noticed you can lose your head, letting frustration and anger overwhelm you."

"Not so much!" was Jered's retort.

"But sometimes you do. You can be very headstrong and determined, just like my old friend Will. It was Will who told me not to make mountains out of molehills. It's important you follow Will's advice. Whether it's the fact your teacher made a phone call or something else which might pop up very soon that makes you angry, you need to try your best to remain calm."

After considering Skelly's words for a moment, Jered asked, "You're saying don't make something bigger or more important than you need? Is that making a mountain out of a molehill?"

Skelly sounded excited. "Yes, you got it, *mi amigo*! One should call upon the serenity of moles, gophers, and voles, so that small problems don't get blown out of proportion. Do you think you can do that?"

"Sure, I guess."

"Even if something makes you *really* mad?"

There was something in Skelly's voice which suggested he was talking about something in particular. Jered looked at him warily. "What kind of thing are you talking about?"

Skelly didn't reply. The skull's empty eye sockets remained staring blankly across the bedroom. Jered watched his friend intently, but nothing happened. Something inside the boy suggested he follow the sightline of the skull. As far as Jered could tell, the skull had been looking at the closet door the entire time they'd been talking. When Jered realized there was no skeleton tacked to the closet door, he became instantly enraged. The promise he'd just made to his friend was quickly broken.

"Mom! Mom!" he yelled in an accusatory tone. "Mom!" The longer Jered stared at the closet door, the angrier he became. When his mother walked into the bedroom, he asked in the same accusatory voice, "Where is he?"

"What do you mean?" Chrissy asked coyly.

"You know what! Where's the skeleton?"

"You better watch your tongue!" Chrissy raised her voice; she didn't appreciate being yelled at. "That nasty thing's where it belongs!"

Jered wasn't sure if she meant in the trash or in the box with the rest of the Halloween decorations. Leaping from the bed to his feet, he declared, "I'm gonna go get it!"

Chrissy stood her ground, holding her palm out towards Jered. "No, you won't! In fact, you'll stay here in your bedroom until supper time because of your little temper tantrum! Wait 'til your father gets home!" She pointed towards his bed and he begrudgingly sat back down. "You better think about this long and hard! I will not have a little boy yelling at his mother!"

Chrissy felt assured she'd made her point, so she stormed out of the bedroom, loudly closing the bedroom door behind her. Jered couldn't remember ever causing such a response in his mother and it took him off guard. He looked across to the nightstand, but the skull was silent.

"Anything you want to add?" he asked, but there was no reply.

He followed his mother's command and thought long and hard about the situation. The more he thought about it, the more confident he became. It appeared his father would be the deciding vote on this issue and Jered was sure his mother would end up being outnumbered.

The oft-used threat "wait until your father gets home" creates a situation wherein it's typically the child who pensively watches the clock. On this occasion, though, it was Chrissy who was nervously checking the clock, wishing the hands would move slower. Chrissy knew Jered would tell his father about the skeleton and this would almost certainly lead to an argument between her and Rodney. She'd gambled that the absence of the skeleton would go unnoticed. She lost that wager and now it was going to be time to pay the proverbial piper.

Jered wasn't a tattle tale, but he couldn't wait until his dad got home so he could tell him what his mother had done. She knew Jered's bedroom was his private domain. He steadfastly believed the small room as well as its bed, chest of drawers, dresser, and toy box were a separate sovereign entity from the rest of the house. Jered was the sole ruler over this territory, and the rightful owner of everything contained therein. Everyone called it *Jered's Bedroom* because it belonged to him. What his mother had done was a breach of his personal space. An invasion.

The hollow, labored rumble from their car signaled Rodney had pulled into the driveway. Chrissy busied herself at the stove, acting as if she didn't have a care in the world. Just as she did every weeknight, she retrieved a can of beer from the refrigerator, placing it on the kitchen table. When Rodney came into the house, Chrissy was at the stove stirring a pot of boiling noodles. Sometimes people use the phrase "whistling through the graveyard." On this occasion Chrissy wasn't whistling, but she was quietly humming a tune in order to decrease her anxiety.

Rodney was grumbling under his breath about work as he entered through the front door and crossed the living room.

"Good evening, honey," Chrissy haled from the kitchen.

Rodney trudged into the kitchen. His face was drawn, making him look older than he really was. Banal pleasantries were exchanged between husband and wife, punctuated with Rodney placing an obligatory kiss on Chrissy's cheek. When Rodney grabbed the beer from the kitchen table, he grunted, which was his way of saying, "Thank you, dearest, for having a cold can of Olympia Beer ready for me to enjoy after a long day at work."

Chrissy heard Rodney turn on the TV then plunk himself heavily into his easy chair. A few seconds later, he let out a prolonged sigh.

"Supper will be ready in about fifteen minutes," Chrissy announced from the kitchen, trying to sound both upbeat and nonchalant.

Rodney grunted again, which was his way of saying, "I'm looking forward to the repast you have prepared for our evening meal."

Chrissy listened for any conversation, but Jered apparently remained in his bedroom and Rodney was glued to the TV. Minutes slowly dragged along, while Chrissy put the finishing touches on the meal. She set the table as quietly as possible, so she could hear what was occurring in the small house. All she heard was the droning voice of a TV newscaster touting the resounding success of the new two-dollar bill.

Still sitting on his bed and gazing angrily at the naked closet door, Jered became increasingly offended at his mother's actions. "It's *my* bedroom, not *hers*!" he griped.

"Ownership can be a rather fluid and ill-defined concept," Skelly piped in.

The skull had been silent for so long, Jered jerked with surprise. Being startled soured the boy's mood even more, so he responded to his friend in a bitter tone. "What's *that* supposed to mean, smart guy?"

"Whoa, whoa, whoa. Don't kill the messenger, as they say."

In the same sharp tone, Jered asked, "What are you talking about? Who says that?"

"Mainly messengers and the family of messengers, but it's an old saying applicable to a number of different situations," the skull replied in an analytical and unemotional voice. "Sometimes a friend, for your own good, will point out things you might not have noticed. That's what I'm talking about. Just because I tell you something you don't like, don't take it out on me. I'm just trying to be a good friend."

Candidly, Jered wasn't very experienced or knowledgeable in subject of the accepted parameters of friendship. Unlike most of his peers, he didn't have a long list of friends he confided in. Skelly hadn't told Jered how many friends the skull had, but it was pretty clear the skull had insights about friendship Jered simply didn't possess. "So, are you taking *her* side in all of this?" Jered tried to throttle down his anger, but his voice was still barbed.

"Not at all, my friend," Skelly responded in a voice that remained measured and thoughtful. "I'm just making you aware that the concept of property ownership is usually more complicated than we think it is at first blush."

"I don't care about that! She shouldn't have taken down the skeleton and I'm gonna tell Dad what she did. For sure, he'll put it back up. That'll show her not to come into my room and touch my stuff!"

"Or, you could just drop this unimportant issue and move on with your life without stirring up trouble between your folks. I served jury duty with a man who was the chairman of an international organization of people who were acutely afraid of deep water. During our deliberations, Wade told me that it was best to let sleeping dogs lie."

"What's a dog got to do with this?" Jered scoffed.

"It's a good lesson to remember: sleepy dogs don't get fixated on stuff that doesn't matter, like cardboard cutouts."

Jered glared unkindly at the skull. "I don't care about dogs! When I tell my Dad about this, he'll make it right!"

"You *could* do that, but you might want to be careful about the company you keep," the skull said in a cautionary voice.

"Huh? What kind of company are you talking about?"

"This situation reminds me of another thing I learned about dogs. For months I travelled through central Africa with a buddy I met in college. During our expedition, my dear friend Chad warned me that if you sleep with dogs, you'll wake up with fleas."

Even though Jered was still mad, he took a few moments to try to make sense of what Skelly said. "Is that the same guy who told you not to wake up your lying dogs?"

"Different friend. Different prōverb. Same four-legged animal." Skelly then barked like a dog, which caused Jered to laugh against his will. "Ruff! Ruff! Awooo!"

"Stop it! I don't want to laugh: I'm still mad!"

"And it's when we're sailing in the turbid waters of emotion that we often throw our anchor into dangerous places."

Jered voiced his frustration at Skelly. "Yeah, yeah. You say weird things like that all the time but what good are they to me?"

"Don't kill the messenger, my young friend. I'm just providing friendly advice; it's up to you to decide whether to take it. You're a big boy."

Jered thought about what Skelly told him and remembered how the sugar skull had previously provided sage advice. Now a bit calmer, Jered said, "So the dog, the fleas, and the anchor, what you're saying is . . ." Jered left the sentence open, wanting Skelly to finish it for him.

"In the end, when it comes to dogs, insects, boating, and all things nautical, you have to follow your heart," Skelly summarized for his friend.

The two were silent for a few minutes, as Jered kicked around thoughts in his head. He wasn't nearly as angry as he'd been earlier, but Jered was still perturbed at his mother's transgression. After thinking about the situation a little longer, he said in an uncertain voice, "I think I'm still gonna tell my Dad. I think. Well, maybe I might."

"If you do, you might want to invest in a decent flea collar."

When there was nothing brought up about the skeleton during supper, Chrissy started to believe the whole issue was going to pass without incident. While washing the dishes she was wearing a relieved smile, thankful there wasn't going to be any further conflict with her son or husband about the awful skeleton. As soon as she heard Rodney stomping angrily down the hall towards the kitchen, her smile dissipated. She understood her son must have spoken to his father about the skeleton's removal.

Rodney stormed into the kitchen, yanked open the cabinet under the sink, and started rifling noisily through the trash. Before she could ask him what he was looking for, Rodney barked, "Where is it? What did you do with it?"

She briefly considered playing dumb and asking what he was referring to. This was likely to further stoke his anger, so Chrissy replied in a voice that was as calm, and as matter-of-fact she could muster, "It's not Halloween anymore. That terrible thing needed to go away."

"Why did ya do that?" Rodney asked, still digging through the trash.

"Halloween is over," she bravely replied.

Once he'd gone through the garbage bin under the sink, Rodney marched to the backyard patio. It seemed to Chrissy that he was making more noise than was necessary as he rifled through the metal trash can. After not finding the skeleton, she heard him stamp down the steps into their basement. When he returned up the steps, the sound of his heavy footfalls reverberated throughout the entire two-bedroom bungalow. Chrissy envisioned the giant's thunderous gait as he pursued the child who'd stolen his golden goose in "Jack and the Beanstalk." All that was missing was for Rodney to bellow, "Fee! Fie! Foe! Fum!"

He confronted Chrissy, waggling the skeleton so close to her face the foul thing was nearly touching her. As it had before, the skeleton grinned at her, mocking her failure. It was almost as if the skeleton's grinning mouth was laughing, "You can't get rid of me!" Chrissy closed her eyes, turning her face away from its accusatory grin.

Rodney's voice was full of venom as he cross-examined his wife. "Why did you take it down? Hmm?"

Ever since her run-in with Jered that afternoon, Chrissy thought about this scenario. What was she going to say if confronted by Rodney? How could she maintain her composure when her husband and son joined forces against her? She decided her best tact would be to just stick to her guns, repeatedly stating the undisputed fact that Halloween was over. If she had to make this declaration a hundred times, she'd do it.

The problem with her plan was she hadn't anticipated her husband to be quite so impassioned. She also hadn't envisioned Rodney shaking the appalling life-sized skeleton just a breath away from her face. Chrissy had never been good at thinking on her feet and the degree of Rodney's anger further undermined her confidence. All she could manage was to open her eyes, try to look at her husband with conviction, and repeat what she'd told her son.

"It's not Halloween anymore," she replied with as much confidence she could muster, "it needs to be boxed up until next year!"

"Says who?" Rodney asked with an accusatory, sharp tongue. This, of course, was the adult version of a child's oft-whined lament, "But why, Mom?" Unfortunately, Chrissy couldn't use her trump card and say to her husband, "Because I'm the mommy, that's why!" The young mother once again turned her head, so she didn't have to look at the gruesome skeleton.

Chrissy considered what her mother would recommend in this situation. Wouldn't her mother suggest that telling the truth was the best way to calm these rough waters? Chrissy considered doing this and telling Rodney why she hated the skeleton. They'd been married nearly ten years and he certainly knew she didn't approve of anything that was scary. If she was going to be completely truthful with him, she'd confess she was scared of the horrendous skeleton. If she told Rodney about the sour feeling the skeleton caused in the pit of her stomach, he certainly couldn't be surprised.

Why not just admit to him that she didn't want a horrible monster looking down with a gruesome grin on their precious son? When she played this out in her imagination, though, things didn't go well. If she confessed that it made her uncomfortable, Chrissy was confident Rodney would make the point she was just having a silly reaction to a harmless Halloween decoration. While this might be somewhat true, it was nevertheless the way she felt. She was entitled to her own feelings, regardless of how everyone else felt.

While she was considering the best way to respond to her husband, a part of her brain continued to wonder why her husband was so infatuated with the wall hanging. Once again, Chrissy was concerned this was somehow linked to Rodney's horrible transformation years earlier. It continued to elude her as to how they could be linked, though. The more she examined these events, the less likely they seemed to be related to each other.

"Well? What do you have to say for yourself? Are you just going to give me the silent treatment?"

The prospect of telling Rodney about the phone call from Miss Moran wasn't very appealing. Chrissy was concerned how he might react to this news. Her husband could be very hard on their son, and he occasionally made offhand comments about Jered not maturing as quickly as other children. Rodney downplayed Jered's artistic skills, suggesting that this was just "kid's stuff" that he'd eventually grow out of. If Chrissy told her husband about Miss Moran's concerns, he might come down hard on the boy, maybe to the point of ordering his son to stop drawing altogether. Jered loved drawing and Chrissy was concerned at how he'd react if his primary means of expression was suddenly prohibited. Who knew what kinds of problems this could lead to?

"I'm waiting," Rodney said in a very impatient voice.

Every response she could think of appeared to have a significant risk of unpleasant ramifications. After careful consideration, she responded by silently shaking her head.

"Yeah, that's what I thought," Rodney announced triumphantly, at last pulling away the skeleton from her face. "It stays up! Don't you think I know what's best for my son?"

Even with his bedroom door closed, Jered clearly heard his father angrily stomping through the house. He also heard portions of the heated exchange taking place between his parents. When he reported his mother's act to his father, Jered let out all the anger which had been brewing inside of him. After hearing his father's exaggerated footfalls and the accusatory shouting directed at his mother, Jered felt increasingly guilty. He became embarrassed not only by what he revealed to his dad, but also the spiteful way he reported it. When Jered told his father about the skeleton being wrongfully removed, he did so with a thirst for revenge.

Once Jered heard his father's wrath raining down on his mother, however, his anger and desire for retribution made him feel small. He loved her, even if she was a scaredy-cat. Just as Skelly suggested, Jered could have just left the issue alone. Instead, he summoned a junk yard dog and ordered it to attack. When Jered pictured a junk yard dog loping towards his prey with fangs exposed, he felt the hair on the back of his neck tingle. When Jered absently scratched his neck, Skelly asked a one-word question: "Fleas?"

The boy was too focused on the heated debate occurring in the kitchen to respond to the skull's quip. Feeling a little shaky in the knees, Jered sat down on the side of his bed, his eyes glued to his closed door. Fidgeting uncomfortably, Jered didn't want to listen to the bickering, but he couldn't seem *not* to listen.

"Another messenger is here for you. Do you want to hear what he has to say, or are you going to kill the messenger?" the skull piped in.

Unsure what he should do, Jered said, "Tell me. Tell me what you have to say."

Skelly saw how shaken the boy had become and used his evenly measured voice to reach out to the boy. "My Uncle Matt always let people walk all over him and he used to tell me when the going gets tough, the tough get going."

Jered waited for Skelly to explain what he meant or at least provide an additional explanation, but he didn't. "Just tell me what to do, Skelly! Please!"

"Go outside! Now! The clouds are getting very dark, so you best go outside until this storm blows over! They aren't going to say anything you need to hear! Go!"

"But it's dark out. Mom says I'm not supposed to go outside if the streetlights are on," Jered moaned. "She says there are people who'll take away kids forever!"

"Sometimes the best path to take is the one that's the most frightening. Be brave, my friend! Do it!"

Without hesitation, Jered followed the skull's direction. He opened his bedroom door, ran through the living room, and was in the front yard in mere seconds. Once outside, he slowed to a walk, deciding to seek refuge from the loud conflict in the park a few blocks away.

Chrissy's bottom lip quivered, and it took all her self-control to keep from crying. She mumbled a few non-discernible words. Rodney stopped walking towards Jered's bedroom and spun around to face her.

"Hm? What was that? Do you have something to add?"

As she summoned her courage, she was vaguely aware of the sound made by the front door opening then closing. How she was feeling was important and she wasn't going to let Rodney bully her into being silent. She decided to follow her mother's advice and tell him the absolute truth. If this meant Rodney's ire came thundering down on her and Jered, then she'd repair the damage. At this moment, though, she resolved to stand up for herself.

"I never liked that awful thing! It's terrible!" she snapped in an emphatic voice. Since he thought the argument was already over and he was the victor, Rodney was taken aback. Chrissy glared at him with conviction. He wasn't sure what to say. When he hesitated to respond, Chrissy further pressed the issue. "It's not right to keep that thing in his bedroom!"

Telling the truth had changed the tide of the argument, so Chrissy charged forward. "On top of that, his teacher called me this afternoon." Rodney looked apprehensive. "Miss Moran told me she was concerned Jered was spending too much time thinking about skeletons and drawing them. So, I put my foot down and boxed up that horrible thing." Sensing she'd taken control of the situation, Chrissy added, "I should have burned it!"

Chrissy was very surprised at the bizarre way he responded. As if he'd just been handed a $500 year-end bonus check, a pleasant smile spread across his face. Gone from his face was any evidence of anger. Also gone was the haggardness he'd developed over the past few years. It was as if sunlight was bathing his face, and he had all the joy and innocence of the teenager who'd approached her in the school gym.

When Rodney spoke, his voice was no longer accusatory. "Oh, is *that* what this is all about?" He sounded both relieved and elated. Setting the skeleton down on the kitchen table, he enveloped his wife in his arms to comfort her. "It's okay. There's nothing to worry about. The teacher just doesn't understand our son is special."

While she was relieved to see her husband so happy, Chrissy was thrown off by his sudden change of demeanor. She was initially stiff and didn't hug him back. "What do you mean by that?" she asked hesitantly.

"There's no way a teacher could understand a complicated child such as Jered," Rodney explained. "She has no idea how to deal with a child who has special gifts, so she's left to grasp at straws." He pulled back and held his wife at arm's length, flashing her a satisfied smile. There's nothing to worry about. Nothing at all. Jered's just going through a bit of a transformation these days. It's all part of his development." When Rodney saw his wife's puzzled and concerned expression, he added, "He doesn't have a problem at all. You could say our little boy is beginning to . . . blossom."

Chrissy was hesitant to ask any follow-up questions, as doing so could potentially re-ignite their disagreement. Despite these misgivings, though, she couldn't help herself. "Blossoming into what? What on earth are you talking about?"

His wife's refusal to simply accept what he said caused Rodney's wide smile to shrink just a bit. He still looked happy; just a little less so. "Well, blossoming into . . . into a fine young man, of course!"

"How does drawing skeletons make him a fine young man?" When Rodney didn't immediately respond with one of his witty ripostes, she asked, "Don't you think it'd be a good idea to have him checked out by a doctor? Maybe even a psychiatrist? You know, just to make sure he's okay?"

The moment she said "psychiatrist," she saw Rodney's eyes widen in alarm. He nervously cleared his throat, then said, "Look, the simple fact is Jered is just a very, very creative boy. There are *no* problems. He doesn't need to see any kind of doctor. He isn't sick. His teacher doesn't know anything and now she's got you in a lather."

Chrissy couldn't dismiss Miss Moran's concerns so easily. She'd never received a phone call from a teacher, and she suspected such calls were only made once the teacher was convinced there was a problem. While the proverb discretion is the better part of valor is typically accurate, Chrissy decided to further press the issue. "Even if that's so, don't you think we'd better get him off this crazy obsession with skeletons? It just can't be good for a little boy to spend so much time thinking about such horrible things!"

Chrissy saw the frustration on Rodney's face. His lips were tightly pursed, and his jaw muscles were throbbing as he searched for a reply. Unlike Chrissy, Rodney was adept at thinking on his feet and it didn't take long for him to regain his composure.

"Don't waste money on doctors," he said firmly. "Our son is fine. The only thing those quacks can do is upset his progress."

"His progress to *what*?"

"To becoming something great." Rodney's proudly claimed. "Like a great artist. A master of creating . . . works of art."

"But to become a great artist he doesn't need to be fixated on *that*," she asserted while pointing an accusatory finger at the skeleton.

It had been a long day for Rodney. Most days at his crummy job were unpleasant, with some more unbearable than others. Today had been one of those particularly trying days. All he wanted to do was let his mind be wiped clean by the old boob tube. To his chagrin, he had to deal with yet more problems once he got home, and now he was strung out. Chrissy was doing an effective job of jousting with him and he was tired. This exhausting discussion simply needed to stop. Now.

"I've said what I need to say on this subject. We're done here." Rodney declared. Chrissy opened her mouth to object, but Rodney was already walking out of the kitchen. "I'm gonna watch some TV before going to bed early. This entire day needs to come to an end."

They hadn't argued very often but enough so Chrissy realized that Rodney had shut himself down to any further debate. She decided it was best to let things cool down, satisfied she'd made her position very clear. Once emotions had simmered down in a day or so, the issue could be raised once again if necessary.

His parents thought Jered was in his bedroom with the door shut until he walked through the front door a short time later. Jered's father wasn't concerned his son had been outside.

"There he is!" his father announced from his easy chair. "What did you find out there in the dark?" Jered shrugged his shoulders, walking towards his bedroom with his head bent forward. "You're a gloomy Gus. Did you get your heart broken, buckaroo?" his father asked.

Jered kept walking, thinking, "If you only knew how badly my heart was broken today."

His mother stopped drying the dishes, joining them in the living room. "Jered? Have you been outside this whole time?" his mother protested. "I thought you were in your room! It's dark outside! You shouldn't be out there when it's dark! Bad things can happen to you!"

Jered muttered "Okay," under his breath.

When their son retreated to his bedroom and quietly closed the door, the spouses looked at each other. They were both wondering if their loud argument caused Jered to flee the house. They dropped their eyes, faces tinctured with guilt. Chrissy decided to intervene right away.

"Knock, knock," she said in a sweet voice as she stood outside the bedroom door. "Can I come in?" Jered didn't respond but she slowly opened the door anyway. "You doing okay?" In response, Jered gave an unconvincing nod. He was sitting on his bed, looking out the window into the November darkness.

Chrissy sat next to her son and patted his knee. "You know, honey, sometimes people get into disagreements. Even moms and dads sometimes argue. Everyone does it. Does that make sense?" Eyes still focused on the November sky, Jered nodded. "Then they talk to each other some more and make up. I'll bet you've had arguments with friends at school, haven't you?"

Jered couldn't think of any, in part because he'd had so few friends over the years. Then he remembered he'd had some cross words with Skelly when Jered wanted to kill the messenger.

"Yeah, I have," he responded with no emotion in his voice.

"Sure, you have, but then you make up, and you're still friends, right?"

Jered didn't know the answer to this question because he hadn't talked to Skelly since their earlier dust up. He wanted to be alone in his room with his thoughts. If Skelly had some wisdom to share with him, he'd listen, but he really wasn't interested in what his mother had to say. He knew the best way to convince his mother to leave was to assure her everything was fine. Jered turned to his mother while trying to smile.

"Sure, Mom. We're taught in school that sometimes parents argue, but it's okay." When Jered saw his mother's face begin to light up, he continued the ruse. "I know that. It's okay. Everyone argues about stuff sometimes."

"So, you're okay?"

"Everything's cool," Jered responded with enough sincerity to fool his mother.

Chrissy was both relieved and pleased her son didn't require any further counseling regarding this incident. She stood up and kissed the top of her son's head. "Love you, honey."

Jered knew how to seal the deal. "Love you, too, Mom."

His mom left him alone, but Skelly wasn't talking. "What about you? You okay?" Jered asked the skull but there was no reply.

Shortly before Jered went to bed, his father tacked the paper skeleton once again to the closet door. "That's better, isn't it?" his father said with certainty in his voice.

Jered nodded his head, even though he couldn't bring himself to look at the skeleton. When he glanced in that direction, Jered felt shame. Instead of something that was watching over him as he slept, Jered felt the grinning skeleton was now a symbol of how his rash actions caused hurtful ramifications.

It was difficult for Jered to fall asleep. The air was still thick with strong emotions. Contrary to what he told his mother, he'd never been taught in school that parents fight. He couldn't remember hearing his father yell like he had that night. The more he thought about it, the more concerned he got that this could be the end of their family. Jered couldn't help but wonder if he'd be sent to some kind of orphanage if his parents decided they could no longer be a happy family. If he ended up being put in a home for wayward boys, or some kind of jail for kids, Jered reasoned he'd deserve it, since he was the one who ignited his parents' argument.

Lying on his side, looking towards his nightstand, he asked, "Am I going to be sent away somewhere? Maybe to a different mom and dad?"

"No, my friend," Skelly responded. "I know you feel bad right now, but it'll get better. I promise. My mother once told me the storm is always darkest before the dawn. The sun is going to rise in the morning, you just have to have the courage to wait for it."

Kerri tossed and turned in bed that night, the troubling conversation with the professor being replayed in a continuous loop in her mind. She eventually gave up trying to fall asleep, made herself a cup of hot tea, and sat on the couch. Her eyes drifted to the bookcase where she kept her college textbooks. The spine of the Child Psychology textbook stood out to her bloodshot eyes, emblazoned with bright red letters on a pale yellow background. She'd taken that class in her last year of college. Kerri smiled when she thought about the class.

Most of the lectures in child psychology were given by an unenthusiastic graduate student. Yawn. On a couple special occasions, though, the lecture was given by a man who was an icon in University City: Dr. Ford Freud. Kerri remembered being enthralled with the deep voiced professor as he pontificated on the finer points of psychology. She'd heard Dr. Freud referred to as a genius and after hearing his lectures, she was in complete agreement. If ever there was a doctor who might have insight into this conundrum, it was Dr. Freud.

After the heated run-in with Chrissy, Rodney wasn't surprised when a pain started pulsing behind his eyes, then gradually spread across his forehead. It was difficult for him to pay attention to the TV, due to his right eye twitching uncomfortably. To be safe, Rodney decided he'd sleep on the basement couch in case all of this triggered one of his Way-Outs. Since they hadn't spoken a word to each other since the argument, he figured it shouldn't raise Chrissy's suspicion if he slept downstairs. It had been a long day, punctuated by the unpleasant quarrel with Chrissy, so lying down in the cool, dark basement on a musty old couch was relaxing. With his head throbbing, he waited to see if he was about to go on a journey.

CHAPTER FIFTEEN

Why the Sky is Blue

Rodney was surprised as well as disappointed when he awoke on Tuesday morning after experiencing an uninterrupted night of sleep. Because of the argument, he figured a Way-Out was likely, but no such luck. If he'd gone on a Way-Out, he wouldn't still have the vestiges of his headache that morning. Some of the uncomfortable throbbing behind his eyes persisted, but he dared not call into work sick. His boss made it clear that anyone who called in sick during the short work week before Thanksgiving risked losing holiday pay. Despite struggling with light sensitivity and a band of pain stretched across his forehead, Rodney managed to make it to work on time Tuesday morning.

While at his desk, Rodney shielded his eyes with his hand. The fluorescent light directly above his desk was going bad. The periodic *tink* rattling inside the glass tube combined with the flickering light made him feel worse. By Tuesday afternoon many of Rodney's co-workers were already on cruise control, preoccupied with the impending four-day holiday. Rodney was preoccupied managing the lingering remnants of his headache.

On Tuesday morning while Rodney was driving to work and Jered was walking to school, Chrissy called Jered's pediatrician. She was pleasantly surprised when told that due to a recent cancellation Jered could be seen later that afternoon. Just a few minutes after hanging up with the doctor's office, JoJo called. "I'm leaving tonight," JoJo told Chrissy over the phone. "Can we move our regular Thursday lunch to today instead?"

"What? You're going to be gone for Thanksgiving?" Chrissy squawked.

"Yeah, one of my travelling buddies called me last night. There was a last second cancellation on a trip to Vegas, so a free ticket was available! Of course, I said yes!" When JoJo saw how crestfallen Chrissy looked, she added, "I didn't think you'd mind. This will give you some nice alone time with your family."

The dust hadn't yet settled from the previous night's argument, so Chrissy was hoping her mother's presence at Thursday's feast might help bring the family dynamic back to normal.

"Well, I guess," Chrissy said morosely, not making any attempt to hide her profound disappointment, "but I was kind of hoping that . . ."

"Marvelous! I'll be there at noon. How's that sound?"

"As long as we're done before Jered gets home. I need to take him to the doctor, and we're going to be on a tight schedule to get there."

"Is he sick?"

"No, just a checkup."

"That'll work just fine. I've got to be at the airport by late afternoon anyway, so I'll have to be on my way no later than 1:30. I'll see you at noon, hon."

Anyone who eavesdropped on one of these lunches would hear one long constant conversation taking place with few pauses. One or both women were always talking, as they addressed a whole host of subjects. JoJo recognized her daughter didn't have any friends to gossip with and confide in, so JoJo allowed Chrissy to inundate her with whatever she wanted to talk about. On this day, though, JoJo noticed Chrissy was uncharacteristically quiet.

"Are you okay, hon? You seem distant today," JoJo remarked. "What's eating you?"

"I'm sorry, Mom. I've just . . . I've just got a lot on my mind, I guess." What was primarily on Chrissy's mind was the previous night's squabble.

"Do you want to talk about it?"

Chrissy enjoyed dishing with her mother but this whole affair with the skeleton on the closet was something Chrissy thought best to keep to herself. She was little embarrassed by how much a Halloween decoration bothered her, and she wasn't in the mood to rehash the details of her argument with Rodney. "No, not really."

"Come on, what bee is in your bonnet?"

"Nothing big. Are you surprised we haven't gotten any snow yet this winter?" Chrissy asked, attempting to change the subject. She was relieved when JoJo willingly took the bait.

"Oh, it's early yet. No telling how much we'll get when it gets colder. That's one of the reasons I want to get out of town: I'm to the point in my life I can do without any more snow."

After they'd eaten lunch and were sipping coffee in the living room, JoJo regaled her daughter with the details of her upcoming trip. Chrissy was polite and did her best to appear interested, but she felt her mother's travels weren't nearly as important as what Chrissy was dealing with.

"I don't understand why so many people enjoy packing up everything and travelling to faraway places," Chrissy remarked.

"Someday you, Rodney, and Jered need to come with me. It would be good for you to see the world, hon."

"I've got everything I need right here," Chrissy replied, shaking her head. "I don't need to go where strangers live. My life is right here."

"Oh, *pishaw*! You grew up in this county, then you got married, and moved to another city in the same county! In your whole life you've barely left this zip code, right?" Chrissy shrugged. "You don't know what's out there! There are so many interesting things to see and experience."

"You and Daddy didn't travel. *You* didn't travel until after Daddy passed," Chrissy commented with a dash of peevishness.

"Exactly! And I didn't know what I was missing!" JoJo laughed.

Even though Chrissy refused to admit something was bothering her, JoJo could tell her daughter was struggling with some kind of burden. She could read her daughter like a book and it was clear Chrissy's thoughts had been elsewhere the entire time. JoJo didn't say anything for a while, hoping the silence would prompt Chrissy to finally open up. The only sound in the living room for a few minutes was the periodic *tinking* of the coffee cups as they were settled onto their saucers. "Did you and Rodney have a spat?"

Chrissy gave a barely noticeable nod of her head. The room was again silent. While looking towards the other side of the room, Chrissy admitted in an embarrassed voice, "I wish Rodney was a little more like Daddy. I'm not always sure our marriage is as strong as yours and Daddy's was." She couldn't look at her mother as she shared this revelation.

JoJo smiled, moving to the couch so she was seated next to her daughter. "Don't think for a minute that your father and I never had disagreements and fights. All husbands and wives bicker from time to time. I'll bet my bottom dollar your marriage is just as good as ours."

"Sometimes I just don't know . . . he's just . . ." Chrissy's voice trailed off as she continued to avoid eye contact.

"You're taking things too seriously. What you need is a nice vacation! What if the four of us made plans to go somewhere exotic?

Someplace Jered could play. A nice warm, relaxed place where you and Rodney could rekindle things."

A response popped into Chrissy's head, but she decided to keep it to herself. It was a question she'd asked herself many times but always been too scared to pose it to her mother.

JoJo could tell Chrissy wanted to say something but was for some reason holding her tongue. "What's the matter, hon? Spill the beans."

Despite the invitation, Chrissy remained hesitant to ask the question. With the possible exception of her son, she loved her mother more than any person in the world. The question that eventually came out of her mouth wasn't meant to be mean: it was something Chrissy had often considered in the years since her father's passing. When Chrissy spoke the words, though, Chrissy thought they sounded accusatory. "Mom, do you think you travel so much because you're lonely and you miss Daddy?"

It had been years since Chrissy referred to her as "Mom." JoJo figured her daughter had slipped into using the title because she was nervous. What Chrissy didn't realize was her mother had asked herself the same question from time to time since the sudden death of her husband. Sometimes her travels weren't exciting or fulfilling, leading her to wonder if she was trying too hard to compensate for her loss.

"I'm sorry, JoJo, I didn't mean to be . . ."

"Shhh, honey, it's okay," JoJo soothed, covering Chrissy's hand with her own. "You don't have to be embarrassed: it's a fair question. I've wondered about that, too."

With tears welling up in her eyes, Chrissy remained apologetic. "I didn't mean to sound like . . ."

In a firmer voice, JoJo said, "Chrissy Elaine, you didn't say anything that hurt my feelings. Really." After patting her daughter's hand, JoJo sat back in her chair and smiled. "Let me tell you what it's like to lose your husband. After that horrible accident took your father away from me, I didn't know what to do. I was empty and nothing seemed to relieve that hollow feeling. Up until then, my sole mission in life was to be a good wife and a good mother."

"You were both," Chrissy assured her mother. "You're still a great mother and grandmother."

"Thank you, hon, that means a lot to me. What I discovered, though, was all my friends and family couldn't truly fill the hole in my heart. A husband is more than just a partner: he becomes a part of you. If you lose him, you lose an important piece of yourself. To answer your question: I think you could be right. I try to fill that emptiness with the excitement of travel. It's the best way I've found to help me carry on. But I'll share a secret with you." JoJo leaned forward a bit. "It doesn't come anywhere near to taking his place. Not even close." JoJo leaned back in her chair when her daughter finally looked at her.

"If it doesn't, then why do you keep travelling?" Chrissy asked.

"Because it's the best alternative. You may be hungry, desperately craving a tasty hamburger smothered in onions, but if that's not available, you eat a cheese sandwich, and enjoy it as much as you can. In the end, it's better than nothing." Chrissy nodded, as that made sense. "That's why it's so important to keep a marriage going, even when there are bumps in the road. Nothing can replace your husband, the father of your son. Sure, there's people who get divorces then get remarried, but it'll never be the same as the first time you said, 'I do.' Don't you see how those people are just chasing their tails, trying to regain something that's been lost forever?"

"Some people say they're happier after they get divorced," Chrissy countered.

"People say lots of things but that doesn't mean it's true. I tell you how much I enjoy travelling, but I'd gladly trade all those wonderful experiences to be with your father. Heck, I'd be content to never step outside the house again if your father was still with me." JoJo's words got her a little choked up and she swallowed hard to push down her grief. "People might call me old fashioned, but I believe your greatest accomplishment is keeping your family together and happy. That's why I've always told you to do everything possible to keep your marriage and your family together. If worse comes to worst . . . if you're like me and Fate steps in to tear apart the family, then at least you have the peace of mind that this happened despite your best efforts."

JoJo lovingly squeezed her daughter's hand, then continued to counsel her daughter. "If a wife allows her marriage or her family to fall apart, then honey . . . she'll just be alone. By yourself. I love you and Jered dearly and I've come to accept Rodney, but none of you can replace your father. Once someone is alone, they're left doing things to try to lessen the sense of loss, just like I do. Don't pay attention to what movie stars say about divorce being the path to happiness. Your family is dependent on *you* to keep it together at all costs. If you let it fall apart, you might in time manage to get back on your feet, but it'll never be the same."

Information and advice you get from someone you revere can be a treasure, or it could be nothing but junk. Some of the nuggets of wisdom parents impart to their children are at best wild guesses or at worst just plain wrong. Even when they are old enough to know better, adults will sometimes remember things their parents told them decades earlier and accept them as the truth. As a little girl, Chrissy once asked her father why the sky was blue. "Because the sky is reflecting the water on the earth," he replied. From that point until the day she died, Chrissy believed the sky was nothing more than a reflection of the earth's oceans. She'd never had reason to question the veracity of this statement, because it was imparted to her from someone she adored.

Chrissy was instructed by her mother since she was a little girl in the skills which a good wife should possess. Her mother taught her all the manners and protocol a young woman should follow in order to maintain a happy marriage and a loving, cohesive family. Chrissy accepted this advice about marriage and family just as much as she accepted her father's explanation as to why the sky was blue.

During her lunch break, Kerri made a phone call from the office.

"Psychology Department. Dr. Freud's office. This is Madeline, how may I help you?"

"Hi, my name is Kerri Moran. I need to set up a meeting with Dr. Freud, please."

Madeline Stokes had only worked as Dr. Ford Freud's secretary for three days. Before accepting this position, Madeline was employed as a registered nurse. For over twenty years she worked in hospitals, primarily in the labor and delivery department, as well as newborn nurseries. Although she loved holding babies every day, she'd become sensitive to the fact her memory was not what it used to be. Getting sternly counseled by the head nurse for errors became a regular occurrence and she'd recently been terminated from a hospital for recording the incorrect dosage of a medication she'd given.

Nurse Stokes decided to step away from the hustle and bustle of patient care, choosing what she believed would be a less stressful secretarial position at the university. Unfortunately, she was provided very little guidance or training from the gruff old professor she worked for and was left for the most part to sink or swim on her own.

"Okay, Miss Moran," Madeline said, jotting the caller's name on a phone message slip. "What do you need to see Dr. Freud about, may I ask?"

"Well . . . I don't know if I want to . . . you know, go into details," Kerri Moran stumbled. "It's kind of secret, I guess you could say. Does that make sense?"

"Sure, dear, I'll just put down it's a secret matter. At what number can he reach you?"

"I don't really have access to a phone during the day, so I'm not sure what number I could give you. I thought maybe I could just make an appointment to see him."

"Oh, Dr. Freud made it clear to me I'm not supposed to put anything on his calendar without his prior approval. As you may know, he's a very important man, Miss Moran."

"Maybe if you'd just let him know I'm one of his colleagues," Kerri suggested. "I'll give you my home number, but I'm only there nights and weekends. I don't have a daytime number."

"That sounds fine, Miss Moran. Give me that number, and I'll pass along your message."

Kerri gave her the number, thanked the secretary, then hung up. Claiming she was a colleague of Dr. Freud was a bit of a stretch, but Kerri *had* taken one of his classes. Sometimes circumstances called upon you to swing for the proverbial fence. If Dr. Freud wouldn't agree to help her and Jered, Kerri wasn't sure where else she could turn.

CHAPTER SIXTEEN

Office Visit with Dr. Knowles

Chrissy kept very few secrets from her husband. She'd been taught in her high school home economics class it was important for a wife to treat her spouse as her most trusted confidant. The textbook for this class was printed in 1952 and was replete with several helpful rules of thumb for future wives and mothers. One of the maxims repeated multiple times in *A Young Woman's Practical Guide to Keeping a Happy Home* was she needed to always be frank and honest with her husband. "If your husband does not know about a problem, then he is not in a position to solve it for you," the insightful textbook explained.

Despite this sage advice, Chrissy decided *not* to tell Rodney she was going to make an appointment for Jered to see his pediatrician. If she had, it would have certainly led to another heated dispute. Rodney wasn't concerned at all about Miss Moran's phone call. Was Rodney's reaction linked in some way to the subtle changes in the family dynamic which had occurred over the past few months? Jered was becoming more confident, but in a negative way. For the first time, he was willing to challenge Chrissy to the point of outright defying her.

It was very unsettling to her that the two men in her life had become preoccupied with ghastly things such as skeletons. Was she somehow losing touch with her family? It was her duty to maintain a happy, healthy home, and she wasn't going to shirk that responsibility. Things at home were shifting and Chrissy wasn't sure how best to adapt.

Chrissy likewise kept very few secrets from her mother. Prior to that day, Chrissy told JoJo about nearly every event in her life (with the notable exception of witnessing Rodney's transformation). JoJo tried to get Chrissy to share more information, but Chrissy didn't tell JoJo about Miss Moran's phone call, or Rodney's nonplussed reaction. She worried JoJo might share Rodney's tepid response to the phone call. If *both* of them thought there was nothing to worry about, what did that say about Chrissy's state of mind?

"Once I get an answer to this problem," she said to herself as she stared blankly into her empty coffee cup, "I'll bring them both up to speed. Let me get it figured out first."

When Jered got home from school, she fed him a snack, then told him they needed to take the bus to the doctor's office.

"What for? I'm not sick."

"I know you're not, honey. It's just a check-up sort of thing."

Although Jered didn't have any idea why his mother was taking him to the doctor, he was almost certain his mother was lying when she claimed this was just a routine visit. As they rode the city bus into downtown University City, neither son nor mother said very much. The little boy's imagination was running rampant, coming up with all sorts of lurid reasons why he'd been hastily scheduled to see Dr. Knowles. His imagination ran wild, and he became concerned he'd somehow contracted an exotic life-threatening disease. The more he thought about it, the scratchier and drier the back of his throat felt. Were these the initial symptoms of the disease that would soon take his life? Or, worse yet, was the doctor going to give him a shot?

While Jered was self-diagnosing, Chrissy was trying to determine what she was going to tell the pediatrician. This wasn't a simple case of telling the doctor, "My son is coughing and running a fever." It was difficult for her to come up with a calm, rational explanation for her concerns. As they got closer to their stop, she felt her anxiety kicking in. She knew all too well she often became nervous and tongue-tied with authority figures. When smart people recognized she wasn't the sharpest knife in the drawer, it made her feel small. Chrissy needed to get answers, though, so she'd just have to do her best to explain her concerns to the doctor.

As they sat quietly in the examination room, Chrissy assured her son that everything was okay, and he needn't be afraid. "It's always good to get a clean bill of health from your doctor, right?" Even to her, the words sounded strained and fraudulent. "Getting a check-up is a good thing to do, don't ya think?"

"Mmm, hmm," Jered replied unenthusiastically as he sat on the end of the examination table, his shoes dangling in the air. The boy looked warily at the collection of shiny silver medical instruments that were laid out on the table just an arm's reach from where he sat.

Chrissy finally realized what she needed to say to ease her son's fear. "Don't worry, there aren't going to be any shots today."

Jered perked up instantly. He wanted a definitive assurance from his mother, since there was nothing as bad as getting a shot. "You promise? I mean *promise-promise*? No shots?"

She briefly hesitated, since she had absolutely no idea what the doctor was going to say or do. Wouldn't it be worse if she promised there'd be no shots and the doctor pulled out a syringe? Before she had to make a *promise-promise*, Chrissy was let off the hook by the doctor opening the door and walking into the room.

"Hello, Mrs. Barstow," he said with very little emotion.

Dr. Knowles had been Jered's pediatrician since the day he was born. Chrissy couldn't help but notice that Father Time wasn't being kind to Dr. Knowles; he looked exhausted and haggard. Everyone knew of the tragic car crash that took the lives of his wife and children in the spring of 1975 and it was obvious this calamity was taking a heavy toll on the young doctor. Dark puffy circles surrounded his eyes, making him look like a pummeled boxer. Chrissy detected a yellowish tint to his skin. His cheeks were sunken, making him appear gaunt. Dr. Knowles looked so poorly that Chrissy couldn't help but think his face had developed an almost *skeletal* appearance. When he shook her hand, his hand and fingers were ice cold, causing a shiver to run up Chrissy's arm.

"What seems to be the problem today?" Dr. Knowles asked in a perfunctory manner. The doctor said these words with all the enthusiasm of an elementary school student reciting the Pledge of Allegiance at the beginning of the school day.

Despite practicing her speech in her head on the bus, Chrissy's response was disjointed and hesitant. Doctors always made her nervous and whenever she spoke with one, she couldn't help feeling as though she was just wasting the doctor's valuable time. "Well, doctor, I've become concerned, I mean, both of us, both his father and I have noticed, Jered has been, well, recently has . . ."

Dr. Knowles didn't wait for Chrissy to finish her labored description before beginning to examine the child. While Chrissy was still talking, the physician asked Jered to open his mouth and stick out his tongue. After pressing a large popsicle stick down on Jered's tongue, Dr. Knowles said, "Throat looks good."

Jered was surprised to hear this given the fact his throat had become increasingly dry and scratchy during the trip to Dr. Knowles' office. Chrissy stopped talking when it was clear Jered's doctor wasn't listening to her.

The doctor placed his hands under Jered's ears and felt for swelling before declaring, "Lymph nodes are normal." Dr. Knowles took a step back from the examination table. After taking a few seconds to survey Jered's face and overall appearance, he said, "This boy looks healthy. Why is he here?"

"Well, um, like I was saying, his father and I have noticed he's been acting, well, a little unusual recently," Chrissy replied in a quiet, unsteady voice.

"How so?" the doctor asked, feeling the pulse in Jered's right wrist, then the left.

"Lately we've noticed he's spent a lot of time drawing skeletons, even though Halloween is over." When Chrissy heard her words, she was struck at how dumb they sounded. When she'd thought about what to say during the bus ride, these words sounded like a mother's reasonable request for assistance. That's not how they sounded coming out of her mouth, though.

Both doctor and patient turned their heads towards Chrissy and squawked, "What?"

For a few seconds the examination room was deathly quiet. Painfully aware of the two sets of eyes looking at her, Chrissy couldn't manage to say anything further. When Chrissy didn't respond in a timely manner to his inquiry, Dr. Knowles asked with disdain, "What on earth are you talking about?"

Chrissy cleared her throat, then did her best to speak with more authority. "Jered has been focused on things that are scary: like skeletons. He draws pictures of skeletons all the time. It's all he does anymore."

Jered was shocked at this allegation. That wasn't true at all! Where was she getting this information? He drew lots of things. Yes, he liked to draw bones, skulls, and skeletons, but those weren't the *only* things he drew. He opened his mouth and prepared to object but Dr. Knowles beat him to the punch.

"Is that it?" Dr. Knowles asked curtly. "You brought your boy to my office because of what he's been drawing in art class?"

She wanted to correct the doctor and advise him this was not just something that occurred during "art class." It was a fixation that was for some reason being encouraged by his father. Despite having much more to say, Chrissy just silently nodded her head, as she was too intimidated to speak. She felt her legs begin to tremble under the searing gaze of the man wearing a white lab coat. A familiar, bitter cocktail of fear, embarrassment, and helplessness coursed through her body. She hated feeling this way, and this was the main reason she avoided social gatherings, monster movies, and all things scary.

Dr. Knowles snapped his head back towards Jered, causing the boy to nearly jump out of his skin. "Skeletons are *not* funny," the doctor declared in a solemn tone to the frightened boy. "They're *not* some kind of toy. Skeletons are serious business! We all have them inside our bodies. When we die, that's all that remains of us! Just bones!" Dr. Knowles' face softened just a bit as he thought of the little skeletons inside children. "Just little bones. Tiny skeletons that will never get bigger."

Jered had never been as scared as he was sitting on the table with the doctor glaring down at him. All three of the people in the room felt their lower lips quiver involuntarily. An uncomfortable silence enveloped the room. None of them made a sound, nor did they move.

Jered's eyes darted from the doctor to his mother, and back again, trying to make sense of the strangest doctor's visit he'd ever had. The doctor's face had an almost confused expression. The frightened boy believed his doctor had somehow become what the older kids at school sometimes called *spaced out*. His mother looked scared, as if she was expecting the doctor to grab a syringe and give *her* a painful shot. Despite being taking off guard by the doctor's verbal assault, Jered figured he was the only normal person in the room. After several silent seconds, Dr. Knowles' expression changed once again. The doctor looked like a boy who'd just done something wrong and was just now realizing the potential consequences for his misdeed.

SKELETONS ARE NOT SCARY

"Um, yes, well, you're just fine," the doctor said to Jered in a voice containing no conviction. Dr. Knowles turned on his heels and moved swiftly towards the door. As he was exiting, he said, "If you're still concerned, just take him to a psychiatrist. This whole thing is outside my area: there's nothing here for me." The doctor closed the door behind him without looking back.

Neither mother nor son spoke immediately after the doctor left. A part of Jered wanted to lash out at his mother for what she'd told the doctor, but her pitifully embarrassed facial expression caused his anger to abate. Despite being upset with what she'd said to Dr. Knowles, he couldn't help feeling empathy. He'd been embarrassed plenty of times at school and knew how it made you feel empty and alone.

Chrissy's guilt spawned several frightening thoughts. Would her son ever trust her again? Would he still love her? She wanted to assure him she had the best intention for bringing this issue to Dr. Knowles, but she was finding it difficult to find the words. "I just wanted . . . to make sure, you know, that you . . . were okay," she tried to explain in a trembling voice. Chrissy was finally able to look at her son. She was afraid Jered would be glaring at her with the same anger she'd seen in Rodney's face the previous evening. Jered didn't look mad. If anything, she'd guess his expression was one of forgiveness.

Prior to that moment, young Jered Barstow had very few occasions to feel pity. Usually, pity is an emotion felt by those who are in a superior position than others. Jered rarely felt he was better off than another, so he simply wasn't in a position to experience much pity. Unless you're the prettiest, smartest, fastest, strongest, or most adept, pity is an emotion a child may not have much of an opportunity to experience. As he looked at his crestfallen mother, Jered understood she hadn't acted in malice. Jered saw in her eyes she was unsure of herself and had acted because of her concern and abiding fear. In addition, if she was acting only temporarily until his real parents arrived to claim him, her confusion as how best to raise Jered was understandable. It was pity that overwhelmed any of his remaining anger towards her. He wanted to alleviate her suffering.

"I'm okay," he told her, trying to provide a reassuring smile. "You shouldn't worry so much, ya know?"

It was difficult for Chrissy to hold back her tears. She thought, "Is there any more obvious proof that you've failed as a mother than your young son giving you advice? A child trying to impart wisdom to a parent is an absurd idea."

Jered slid off the table and tried to provide comfort to his mother. He took her hand and said, "A friend of mine told me you sometimes have to wait for the clouds . . . I mean, before the dark clouds can cover the sun you can . . ." Jered paused, trying to think of the right words and put them in the right order.

"Do you mean it's darkest right before the dawn?" Chrissy asked.

"I think maybe that's how it goes. Does that make sense to you?"

Her son's attempt to provide comfort caused Chrissy to smile just a bit. She might not be the best mother in the world, but her son was turning out to be a caring soul. When Jered saw the smile start to form on his mother's face, he responded with an even bigger smile. "That's it, Mom! It'll be okay!"

"Let's get to the bus stop. We might be able to get an earlier bus back home," Chrissy said, almost sounding like her normal self.

Mother and son held hands as they walked to the bus stop but very little was said. The adult was still trying to regain her composure after enduring the physician's odd tantrum. The child was still wondering why on earth his mother would bring him to the doctor simply because of what he'd been drawing. Each of them was trying to make sense of it all.

The bus was pulling up just as they reached the stop. The bus was full of riders, many of whom were returning home from work.

Jered and his mother walked to the back of the bus, then fell roughly into the last two seats when the bus abruptly pulled away. Jered noticed something and tugged his mother's sleeve to get her attention. Through the back window, they saw a man wearing a business suit running after the bus. They couldn't hear him over the sound of the bellowing bus engine, but it wasn't difficult to tell he was yelling, "Stop! Stop!"

"Bus driver?" Chrissy called out. "There's someone who wants to get on the bus!"

The bus driver asked "What?" Another rider repeated Chrissy's statement. Without taking his foot off the accelerator, he declared, "Should've got here sooner!"

The man's fervent chase of the city bus looked like a scene from an old silent movie. His arm movements became exaggerated as he lengthened his stride to cover as much ground as possible.

"He kind of looks like Gumby running," Jered said in a matter-of-fact voice. He wasn't trying to be funny: he was just describing the man's loping run. Mother and son looked at each other, then burst out laughing. The odd-looking man was the comic relief each of them needed. When the man finally stopped running, he took off one of his dress shoes and hurled it towards the bus. The riders seated in the last few rows cackled. Chrissy made a mental note she needed to tell Jered it wasn't polite to laugh at other people's misfortunes, but for the time being, she was laughing too hard to provide any wisdom to her son!

Even after the man had long been left behind, Jered and his mother were periodically giggling. Every time Jered thought about the man's exaggerated running and wildly waving arms, he laughed again. By the time they reached their stop, mother and child were both smiling. When they saw a kid holding a leash who was being pulled fiercely by a dog twice his size, the two started laughing once again.

Chrissy stifled her laugh, trying to sound serious. "Now, Jered, we shouldn't laugh at other people. It's just not a nice thing to do."

Jered looked up at his mother. "Okay. Mom. I won't laugh if you don't."

He looked at his mother, daring her to hold back her laughter. After just a few seconds, Chrissy burst out laughing again and he joined her.

"I've got to whip something up for supper," Chrissy said as she opened the front door. "Your Dad will be home pretty soon."

Jered watched from the kitchen table as his mother busily collected ingredients for their meal. He wasn't interested in watching his mother cook. He really wanted to say something to her. There were too many people on the bus to tell his mother what he wanted to say.

"Mom, I wanted to tell you something before you start cooking."

Chrissy didn't look at her son, as she had a lot to do and very little time to get it done. "What's that, honey?"

His mother had her back turned but Jered wanted to get her undivided attention. He walked to her, touching her arm. Chrissy was a little startled to feel her son's touch. She looked down at him. "What is it, Jered? Mommy has to get this done."

"Um, I just wanted . . . you know . . . please don't worry about me," he told her. "I'm okay. I'm sorry . . . sorry if I made you worry. I . . . I didn't mean nothin' by drawing stuff."

She smiled sweetly and knelt so she was at eye level with her son. "It's okay, hon, but I need to make sure everyone in my family is okay." Chrissy framed her son's concerned face with her hands. "Your father is under a lot of pressure at work, so let's just keep our visit today to ourselves, okay? We don't want to worry him too much about your check up with the doctor." Jered nodded. "Good. My job as the mommy is to take care of you and your father. It's up to me to make sure the family is chugging smoothly down the tracks. I'm sort of the mechanic who keeps this train running smoothly, so sometimes I'm going to worry about my little caboose!" She squeezed her son's nose between her fingers.

He felt his mother's train story, along with squeezing his nose, was something a mother would do to a kindergartner. Jered wasn't a little boy anymore. It'd been hard for him to confide to his mother, but she seemed to be playing it off as just childish blather. This was important! Jered was a little flustered, so what he said didn't come out of his mouth right. "I'm being *seriously*."

Chrissy giggled, and said, "What you are is seriously a goofus!" She laughed, then stood up to continue preparing their supper. Against his will, Jered started laughing along with her. Just as they had on the bus ride home, the laughter of one fueled the laughter of the other.

"You know what I meant, Mom!" Jered declared through his giggles.

Without looking away from her preparations, his mother chuckled, "And you know what *I* meant: that you are seriously the biggest goofus I've ever met! Now do me a favor and make sure you didn't leave any toys in the living room before your father gets home, okay?"

"Sure, Mom."

Just like on the bus ride home, their laughter provided a welcome relief from the tension. Before he'd left the kitchen, she asked "Do you want celery or beets with dinner?"

"Beets? *Blech!*" Jered was about to pontificate about the evils of beets but stopped himself when he thought of something else to say. "Are you *seriously* asking if I want beets?"

This started another episode of laughter. "Okay, that was a good one, but I need to *seriously* get to work." She looked at him with loving eyes, adding, "Your laugh always makes me feel better. I guess maybe the old proverb is right: laughter *is* the best medicine."

"Mom, it's called a prōverb, not a *praw-verb*."

Initially Chrissy thought Jered was still joking. "You're pulling my leg, right? You don't *really* think that's how you say proverb, do you?" When her son nodded his head, she asked, "Who told you to say it that way?"

"Well, um, a friend of mine." Jered said hesitatingly.

"Well, your friend, um, is *seriously* wrong. Look it up in the dictionary at school tomorrow: you'll see I'm right. Now run along Mr. Seriously Prōverb and let me get supper ready."

After performing a quick sweep for any toys in the living room, Jered went to his bedroom, eager to talk to his friend. "Skelly? Skelly, are you there?" he asked anxiously after plopping down on the bed.

"Sure I am."

"Guess what? My mom says you're wrong! She says those old sayings are called *praw-verbs*."

"She's entitled to her opinion, I guess, but I don't agree."

"She even told me a *praw-verb*, too. Do you wanna hear it?"

"Absolutely. Maybe it's one I've never heard before. What did she tell you?"

"Let me get it right," Jered said, pausing to make sure he got the words correct. "She said laughter is the best medicine." There was a prolonged silence, as Jered waited for Skelly's reply. When Skelly didn't say anything, Jered prompted him, "Well? What do ya think? Have you heard that one?"

Skelly sounded disgusted. "No, I've never heard that before, and I'm glad I haven't. That is the worst prōverb I've ever heard; it makes no sense whatsoever."

Jered was taken aback. The boy expected Skelly to tell him a story of how one of his friends or relatives explained the saying to him. "How come? What's wrong with it?"

"It's just wrong! First of all, laughter is *not* a medicine, and it's never better than such things as antibiotics or clean bandages. Also, you can take it from me that cancer has absolutely no sense of humor. None! Your mother is a nice lady, but she doesn't know what a good prōverb is, nor how to pronounce it, in my expert opinion."

Something his friend said struck Jered as odd. "Wait a minute. You just said my mother was nice: have you ever met her?"

"Sure, don't you remember when we were all in the living room: you, your dad, your mom, and your grandmother?"

"Yeah, but how could you tell from that she's nice?"

"Oh, I can tell, you'll just need to trust me on that. I know she's a nice lady just as much as I know your dad . . ." Skelly stopped talking in mid-sentence. The skull didn't have lips, but if he had, he would have been pressing them together to keep himself from saying anything further.

"What? What about my Dad?"

There was a prolonged pause as Skelly tried to find a way to cover his misstep. "Just as I know your dad is a *complex* man."

Although the sugar skull was incapable of exhibiting facial expressions, Jered nevertheless looked carefully at his friend, searching for any visible indication of emotion. When he couldn't detect any, Jered asked warily, "When you say *complex*, what do you mean?"

Skelly again took a little time to carefully select his words. "Over time you'll learn that kids see their parents as well-defined, black and white characters. Children perceive the people who are raising them as simple two-dimensional entities."

"Huh? Two-dimensional?"

"In other words, flat and well-defined: not having any gray areas. Either their parents are good or they're bad. Mean or nice. Happy or mad. Kids don't appreciate their parents have been living their lives for decades, and in the course of doing so, they've developed some qualities that are difficult for children to fully comprehend."

Jered wasn't following his friend's explanation. "I don't get it."

"Let me give you an example. How would you describe your mom?"

Jered thought for a moment, then said, "Really nice. Makes good pies and cakes. She can be funny every once in a while, like she was today. Um, let's see. Takes care of me when I'm sick. Oh, and she's a scaredy-cat."

"Let's address your comment that she's a scaredy-cat. Being afraid of something seems like a simple, straight forward emotion, but actually it's not. Fear is an emotion that can come about for any number of reasons. Fear serves many purposes, both normal and abnormal. It's also a tool one can use *too* often. Just because a wrench is an effective way to remove a nut from a bolt doesn't mean it makes a good hammer when you need to drive a nail."

Over the past few weeks, Jered was learning that talking to Skelly could be an exhausting exercise. The skull was always chock-full of information but getting a firm grasp on what was being said could be a challenge. Words weren't just words when Skelly started to pontificate. Every word Skelly said to Jered had to be carefully considered on its own, as well as in light of other things the skull said. It was a challenge for Jered to keep track of all the threads Skelly spun. Jered felt the effort was worthwhile, though, because Skelly was wise and the lessons he'd shared with him had been valuable. Jered considered what his friend said, then asked, "So what you're saying is that I have to look deeper and not just accept what's on the surface?"

"Wow! It sounds like you've talked to my old friend Gene!"

"No, I don't know anyone called Gene."

"Gene is a very opinionated person, who claims to have a blue-print for how everyone should live their lives." Skelly chuckled, then added, "When Gene was a little off kilter, things could really go off the tracks, I'll tell you that! Gene often told his friends that you should never judge a book by its cover."

After a moment, Jered offered, "There's more to a book than the cover: there's what's inside."

"Precisely! And people are a lot like books: there's much more to them than what you see on the outside."

"So, I should read every book to know how things really are?"

"That's an admirable undertaking but totally unrealistic I'm afraid. People are books with way, way too many pages for us to read. Even if you had the time and desire to try to get through the whole book, you'd find trying to discover what makes people tick is a fool's errand. It's kind of like analyzing your dreams: most of the time they simply don't make any sense."

"What are you saying I need to do then, Skelly?"

"What you need to do is remember what I told you. When something unusual happens, make sure you come to talk to me. Got it? Especially if it involves your dad, you need to let me know if something strange occurs."

"But I don't know what you mean by that." Jered asked sharply.

"Your father loves you very much, but you need to come to me if anything odd occurs with your dad."

"Like what?"

"Like, I'm not one hundred percent sure. I'm confident you'll know when it happens and when it does, make sure you come talk to me. Friends help friends, and hopefully I can help you with whatever it is. Okay?"

Jered smiled and said, "Okay, I promise to come tell my friend if something strange happens." He reached out to give Skelly a handshake, then lowered his empty hand.

Skelly laughed, "No handshake necessary, my friend! Your word is your bond!"

"My word is my bond? What's that supposed to mean?"

"It's an old saying that comes from the fact you can rearrange the letters in *word* and *bond,* so they spell the same word."

"Really?" Jered thought for a moment, then said, "No they don't!" Skelly laughed and Jered joined in, even though he didn't know why. When the laughter settled down, Jered lowered his voice to just above a whisper. "Mom took me to the doctor today."

"But you're not sick."

"I know! That's what I said!" Jered spoke a little too loudly, so he waited in silence in case one of his parents came to his bedroom. After waiting a minute, Jered continued, "She said it was for a check-up . . ."

"That's highly unlikely: it's not time for your annual check-up yet."

"How do you know that?" Jered asked incredulously.

"How do I know anything of things I know? The answer is unknowable, or what the French call *pour une raison inexplicable.*"

"Huh? I don't speak foreign languages."

"Nor do I. I learned that phrase from Pierre, a young friend of mine who is from France. Pierre was a reliable boy who'd hold your boat's rope when you came to shore. In any case, let's agree to continue speaking in English, shall we?"

"I want to tell you about my doctor's visit."

"Did he give you a shot?" Skelly asked with trepidation in his voice.

"No."

"Whew! That's good!"

"But my Mom told the doctor she was worried about me drawing too many skeletons. The doctor got in a huff and just left. Said I might need see some other kind of doctor."

"Your mother is very perceptive. I wonder . . ." Skelly said, his voice trailing off.

After waiting a few moments for Skelly to finish what he was saying, Jered prompted him. "You wonder what?"

"Let me think about this interesting development. In the meantime, you're going to let me know if anything odd happens, especially with your father, right?"

"Sure."

Supper that evening was uncomfortable. Jered sensed tension at the kitchen table, particularly between his parents. Not much was said during the meal or while the family was watching TV. He was a little relieved when it was time for him to turn in. Lying on his back, Jered stared blankly through the darkness up to the bedroom ceiling, still pondering the weird office visit with Dr. Knowles.

"I'm not sleepy," he said after quite a long time of tossing and turning. "Do you want to talk about something? Maybe about a prōverb one of your relatives told you?" There was no response from the skull. "Skelly? Skelly?" Jered didn't dare get out of bed and turn on the light. For as long as he could remember, he'd known the rule was once he was tucked in, the only reason to get out of bed was if he needed to use the bathroom.

Jered reached over to the nightstand, feeling around cautiously for his friend. He moved his hand slowly, so he didn't accidentally knock the candy skull to the floor. For what seemed to be the longest time, his blind attempts to locate the skull were fruitless. Eventually, though, his fingers touched the skull and Jered carefully grabbed it so he could examine the skull in the faint moonlight coming through the window. As far as he could tell, Skelly looked normal.

"Skelly?" he whispered to the area where ears would have been if it hadn't been a skull. "Are you there?" There was no reply. The boy cautiously eased his tongue towards the skull, letting just the tip of it touch the candy. He felt a little bit of the candy skull melt onto his tongue, which caused Jered to abruptly pull his tongue back. "I just wanted to make sure you're still here with me," Jered said apologetically, but the skull still didn't say anything. He placed the skull back on the nightstand.

Without Skelly to talk to, Jered should have gotten bored, then eventually dozed off. Jered just couldn't seem to settle his mind down or stop thinking about how his mother was so concerned about his drawings she arranged a doctor's appointment. He heard the door to his parent's bedroom close, which meant it was probably about 11:30.

It had to have been well after midnight when he decided to see if Skelly was talking yet. As before, the skull didn't respond, so Jered alternated staring into his dark bedroom and then through the bedroom window. From time to time his eyes landed on the green glowing skeleton hanging on the closet and each time they did, Jered had an unpleasant feeling. It wasn't fear he felt; it was guilt. He'd fought so hard for it, but now it had lost its appeal.

The more he thought about it, the more he felt the skeleton just wasn't worth the conflict it'd caused the whole family. He couldn't remember his parents ever arguing the way they did Monday night, and Jered carried the burden of knowing he'd singlehandedly caused it to happen. After thinking about it for quite some time, he decided he needed to start repairing the damage he'd caused. Since it was Jered's response to the skeleton's removal that caused the family discord, Jered decided he was going to take the skeleton down. Not only was he going to do it, he was going to do it right away. This would require him to break the rule about getting out of bed, but Jered felt he wasn't going to be able to sleep until he started the family's healing.

Jered pulled a chair up to the closet door so he could reach the thumbtack holding the skeleton in place. He carefully folded the arms and legs, so it looked just as it had lying on top of the Halloween decoration box a few days earlier. To really put an end to this dispute, Jered wanted to take the skeleton downstairs and put it away in the box of Halloween decorations. Wouldn't his mother be pleased that he'd done this all by himself? Hopefully, this would be the first step for the family's recovery and would relieve some of his guilt. Hopefully. Tonight, he was resolute in making the whole affair with the life-sized skeleton and with skeletons in general a distant memory.

That afternoon, Chrissy planned to start patching things up with Rodney as soon as he got home. Much like her son, she wanted things to return to normal. When he walked into the house, she noticed one of his eyes was periodically twitching. This was the telltale sign he was fighting a headache. Knowing that sound could trigger his headache pain to worsen, she asked him in a quiet voice, "Is it a bad one?"

"Started last night. Just can't seem to shake it," he lamented in his own quiet voice.

Rebuilding bridges would have to wait until another day. When Rodney was in the throes of one of his bad headaches, everyone in the house had one mission: make as little noise as possible. Chrissy was tasked with making sure the house was as quiet as a tomb so the headache would pass.

As Jered was lying in bed thinking about how he could fix the damage he'd caused, Rodney told Chrissy, "I'm going to go downstairs where it's dark and quiet."

"You can sleep in the bedroom. I'll go downstairs so I don't disturb you." she offered.

"No, it's better if I do it. Besides, I don't think you'd like how lumpy that old couch is."

Chrissy gave her husband a sweet smile and lightly kissed his forehead. Even while suffering through a headache, her husband was thinking about her comfort.

"I simply do not understand why it is so hard to find quality employees," Dr. Freud said to his colleague during a telephone conversation. As usual, the renowned professor was working on two tasks at once. While he was talking on the phone, he was filing through a large stack of messages left for him by his new executive assistant. "She is the eighth one I have hired this year alone. They appear to be fine during interviews but for some reason they become frazzled shortly after they begin working. For some reason they are able to hide their psychological problems from me until such time they begin employment."

"Perhaps you should require applicants to complete a battery of personality tests prior to hiring them. For that matter, maybe you should conduct a therapy session prior to hiring them," his colleague suggested. "Obviously troubled souls are managing to slip through your cipher."

"If I had the time to take those measures, I would," Dr. Freud lamented, "but I do not. Even if I instituted those precautions, I wonder if this inexplicable manifestation of their post-employment mental illness would persist. The new one is an experienced nurse, so I have high expectations she will not become a basket case simply because she is working at a renowned university."

"Perhaps that's a fertile area for a new research project: the sudden development of pathological mental phenomena after becoming employed at a learning institution."

Dr. Freud didn't respond, as all his attention was focused on deciphering a phone message written by his new assistant. He flipped

SKELETONS ARE NOT SCARY

the message over, hoping it would contain additional information, but it was blank.

"Are you still there?" his colleague inquired.

"I have to go," Dr. Freud stated, then hung up the phone. "Nurse Stokes! Come here presently!"

Dr. Freud continued to look curiously at the message. Stacks of papers and books littered his office floor, some taller than himself. While sitting at his huge mahogany desk, Professor Freud couldn't see the door to his office, so he listened for approaching footsteps. When he didn't hear any, he called out to her even louder. When the clacking of the assistant's high heels became louder, he knew she was making her way through the columns of papers towards his desk. Before she'd managed to arrive at his desk, Dr. Freud was firing off questions.

"What are you trying to tell me in this note? It makes no sense! Do you think you might in the future favor me with written messages that utilize the English language in an appropriate manner?"

One of the problems Dr. Freud encountered with assistants over the years was their inability to handle pointed, direct, and appropriate questions he asked them. Too many of them simply wilted under the heat of the doctor's inquisitive mind. Since Madeline Stokes worked as a registered nurse for decades, Professor Freud was confident he'd finally found an executive assistant who could adequately do her job.

"Which message is that?" Madeline asked, appearing from between two piles of books.

"First, you have written a message about someone by the name of Kerri Moran. I do not know this person. You were clearly taught by me during your orientation last week you should not accept messages from any person I do not already personally know. The reason is . . .?"

"Such people are undoubtedly trying to sell something." Madeline replied dutifully.

"Precisely. The next note says one of my colleagues is in desperate need of my assistance, but there is no name or number on it. All you have chosen to share with me is that it is of the utmost importance. Pray, how I am supposed to decipher this mess?"

Madeline's knees felt as though they might buckle. It was as though she was back at the hospital, being grilled by an angry physician about a notation error. Dr. Freud held two phone message slips out to her, which she accepted with a trembling hand. Looking at the message slips, she vaguely remembered the conversations, but not much of the substance.

"Well? What were you *trying* to tell me? Hm?"

Madeline knew she needed to respond quickly. With Dr. Freud's perturbed gaze burning into her, Madeline tried to make sense of the two cryptic notes she'd written. Or was it just one note? Yes! During this uncomfortable silence, the answer popped into Madeline's head.

"This is all one note: I just put it on two slips," Madeline replied. When she heard her explanation, its veracity became even more evident to her. "I was just writing on a second slip because I ran out of room on the first one, I think."

Not taking his probing eyes off Madeline, Professor Freud asked, "Are you saying, '*you think*,' or are you saying, '*you know*?'"

Looking again at the messages, her memory was even clearer. Her voice regained its confidence. "Yes, doctor, I'm sure. I should have stapled these two notes together for you. That was my mistake. I apologize for the misunderstanding I created."

Dr. Freud peered at Madeline while she tried to maintain a look of steely professionalism. She knew from decades of working for doctors that one of the challenges working for a genius was it was sometimes difficult to achieve the level of excellence he was entitled to. Despite the fact she'd made a mistake on this occasion, Dr. Freud still had a good feeling about his newest assistant. It appeared she understood her role, as well as how important such things as message slips were to a person of his stature.

"Yes, that is indeed what you should have done," Dr. Freud said as Madeline handed the messages back to him across his desk.

When he read the messages together as one, Dr. Freud instantly realized the gravity of the situation. His eyes widened. "Moran! Dr. Moran!" he uttered under his breath with excitement. "This is legendary!"

Madeline was confused. "What's that you say, Dr. Freud?"

"Call this Kerri Moran right away! She must not be kept waiting! This is obviously the learned Dr. Moran's daughter!" When Madeline didn't move, he added, "Go! I need to see her right away! Who knows what her father has asked her to present to me? Hurry!"

Madeline scurried out of the office while Dr. Freud put his feet up on his desk, leaning back in his overstuffed chair. The reclusive genius of emotional disorders had reached out to Dr. Freud for consultation regarding no doubt a difficult patient. How old was Dr. Moran? He was in his seventies when he dropped out of sight and that was over a decade ago. It caused quite a stir in the professional community when the illustrious Dr. Moran suddenly chose to live in seclusion like a medieval monk, eschewing almost all contact with the outside world. The only proof Dr. Moran was still alive were letters he periodically sent to professional journals for publication. To the uneducated, these letters were nothing more than rambling, nonsensical rants about human behavior. For experts such as Dr. Ford Freud, these letters were a clever puzzle Dr. Moran created to test the abilities of his colleagues. Only the gifted few who could unravel the meaning in these twisted missives would reap the harvest of his insights.

No one knew where Dr. Moran had sequestered himself, except for a few family members. Now the hermit psychological genius was asking . . . no, *imploring* Dr. Freud to consult with his daughter about a patient.

CHAPTER SEVENTEEN

Two Skeletons

Once he was confident the coast was clear, Jered tiptoed out of his bedroom and through the kitchen to the stairs leading to the basement. Jered stood on the landing while holding the handrail, wondering if he could successfully make his way down the stairs without turning on the light. He cautiously descended one step, then paused to reconsider his options. In his mind he saw himself falling down the stairs, spilling onto the hard concrete floor. Peering into the black void at the bottom of the stairs, he decided to flip the wall switch to turn on the basement lights.

Even with the lights on, the basement was still shadowy. Jered walked down two steps but when one of them let out a long, agonized creak, he froze. He didn't think the dim basement light would likely make to his parents' bedroom, but the groan from the wood steps definitely could. He listened for any indication his parents had been roused from their sleep. An uncomfortable bead of cool sweat formed on Jered's forehead, eventually rolling down to the bridge of his nose. He waited for what seemed like a long time but didn't hear anything.

Jered wiped the sweat off his face with the sleeve of his pajamas, then continued down the steps, this time being careful to shift his weight onto the edges of the steps in an effort to make as little sound as possible. Before he got to the last step, he could clearly see the big cardboard box marked "Halloween" in the corner of the room to his right. He made a beeline to the box, the concrete floor uncomfortably cold on his bare feet. Jered tossed the skeleton onto the box, then quickly retreated back onto the bottom step. The wood stairs felt a lot better than the cold floor.

Jered had a clear view of the stairs leading up to the kitchen. Now that his task was completed, he decided to turn off the lights. Although he didn't think the basement light could reach his parents' bedroom, it was best to be cautious. He flipped the light switch at the bottom of the stairs and the basement once again became dark.

Brightly sparkling ghosts danced in his eyes as soon as he turned off the lights. The little boy knew these would fade away once his eyes became accustomed to the dark, so he remained in place until they were gone. After a few seconds, he could see more clearly, so he started his slow, quiet climb back upstairs. He'd cautiously climbed four steps when he heard something that sounded like a quiet moan coming from the behind him. A part of Jered's brain ordered the boy to immediately sprint up the stairs as fast as he could while screaming for help. Jered managed not to panic and remained completely still. Despite a persistent urge to run up the stairs without any concern for waking his parents, he remained in place. With a heart that was thumping so hard Jered wondered if it could break, he listened intently.

"Probably just your ears playing tricks on you," a calmer voice inside his head suggested. "You probably didn't hear anything . . ."

Another slow, agonizing groan emanated from the dark basement. It was coming from the side opposite from where the boxes were stacked. There was something familiar about the sound. After he heard another moan, Jered asked under his breath, "Dad?" Since he was halfway up the stairs and both the wall switches were beyond his reach, Jered twisted his body and peered down into the basement. Jered remained in this position for quite some time but was unable to hear or see anything. When the silence was broken, it was clear his father was speaking.

"Yes. You can do it." His father spoke in a soothing voice.

From watching cartoons, Jered knew people sometimes sleep-walked with their arms stretched out in front of them. What he couldn't remember was whether any of these sleepwalking cartoon characters also spoke. He remembered Bugs Bunny saying, "Yes, Master," as he walked stiffly, but Jered couldn't recall if the rabbit was sleepwalking or hypnotized. Jered also learned from cartoons it was for some reason not a good idea to wake up a sleepwalker. What he couldn't remember was what would happen if you did. His father said a few more things in quick succession, but Jered couldn't make out what he said.

"Dad, are you okay?" Jered's meek voice barely registered in the large basement. "Do you need my help? Are you hurt?"

When his father didn't say anything for a few minutes, Jered became increasingly concerned his dad might have hurt himself while sleepwalking. Had he tripped down the basement stairs while in a trance? Was he lying on the floor with broken bones? These concerns caused Jered to take a few cautious steps back down the stairs as his eyes strained to locate his father in the dark. By the time he'd reached the bottom step, Jered would have bet a week's allowance his heart was beating at least a thousand times a minute. Through the darkness he thought he could see a faintly glowing horizontal line hovering just above the floor. It almost looked like a long tree branch was glowing in the dark as it floated sideways inches above the floor.

"Dad?" There was no reply, which led Jered to feel it was best to explain himself. "I know I'm not supposed to be out of bed . . . but . . . do you need help?"

The long stick faded back into the darkness, then a round, dark gray bowling ball began to materialize. Jered had been intently searching through the black obscurity for so long, his eyes started to ache. He could trace the sweat rolling down his back, making him feel cool and sticky. Jered didn't think to himself, "I think I'll turn on the lights." It just happened, as if his right hand flipped the switch on its own volition.

In the dim light, Jered saw his father lying on the old couch that abutted his work bench. At first Jered thought his dad was wearing pajamas with long gray stripes on them. Once his eyes had adjusted, though, he realized they weren't stripes. They were bones. He could see part of his dad's skeleton lying on their couch. Jered's right hand once again acted on its own, turning the lights off just a few seconds after it had turned them on.

Jered let out a long, quivering groan. All Jered could see were the white flashes caused by his eyes readjusting to the darkness. Before these bursts of light petered out, Jered was already questioning what he'd seen when the lights were briefly on. It certainly wasn't possible he'd just seen his father as part person, part skeleton. Jered's young brain worked feverishly to come up with a likely explanation as to what he'd just witnessed.

His father made a quiet sound as if he was trying to clear his throat. After a few silent seconds, his father murmured something under his breath, then said sleepily, "Jered?"

As soon as he heard his father call his name, Jered rushed up the stairs. Jered wasn't sure why he was running away. Normally he'd respond if his father called for him, but this was different. Although he still hadn't decided what he'd seen during the few seconds the lights were on, he knew with certainty he didn't want to be in the basement. After reaching the top of the stairs, he dashed through the kitchen, then down the hallway. Once inside his bedroom, he almost slammed the door in his haste, but managed to catch himself. Jered quietly closed his bedroom door behind him, took two steps, then vaulted himself through the air and onto his bed. He got on his side with his back facing the door and quickly covered himself with a quilt. The boy looked at the sugar skull sitting on his nightstand just a few inches away.

"Skelly? Are you there?" There was no response to Jered's whispered plea. The boy was becoming more frantic but managed not to raise his voice much. "Skelly? Where are you?"

The skull at last whispered, "What's the matter?"

"Something happened!"

"Like what?"

"Something strange: just like you said. I was . . ."

"Shhh, be quiet. Pretend you're sleeping. Someone's coming."

Jered stopped talking and tried to remain still, but he doubted it looked like he was sleeping. His heart was still beating very hard, and he was trembling.

"Close your mouth and breath only through your nose as slow as you can. It'll sound like someone deep in sleep," Skelly whispered.

Once again, the boy did as the skull ordered, the result being a soft rattling sound. After about a minute, Jered just barely heard someone open his bedroom door. He didn't hear anything else for quite some time, which meant either someone was observing him from the doorway or was stealthily crossing the room to his bed. In either case, he dared not move. All the while, Jered heard and felt a rattle of snot in the back of his throat as he breathed through his nose. He kept his eyes closed except for a small sliver of an opening so he could see Skelly's outline in the limited moonlight.

It'd been such a long time since he heard the door open, Jered wondered if the person had closed the door, but he'd just failed to hear it. Just before the boy was going to roll to his other side and face the door, he heard a soft snoring sound come from Skelly, as if he, too, was breathing through his nose. Jered recognized this was a subtle warning from his friend, so he didn't move. A few minutes later, he heard the bedroom door softly close.

Jered whispered, "Was my dad at the door?"

"Yeah, I saw him. He's gone."

"I'd hoped it might be my mom, but I knew it was gonna be my dad."

"Why's that?"

"Because of what I saw." In a hushed voice, Jered told Skelly about his trip downstairs. When it came to tell him the scary part, Jered felt a shiver down his back. "It kinda looked like my dad was part skeleton, but that can't be right. I guess I don't know what I really saw."

"Okay. I need to think about this. Give me a little time to sort all this out," Skelly said.

In the silent minutes that followed, Jered became increasingly tired. Once his adrenaline-fueled fear dissipated, he was wiped-out. Before long, Jered started drifting off.

"Before you go to sleep, I need you to promise me something again," Skelly said anxiously.

As he yawned, Jered asked, "What is it?"

"If your dad ever says anything particularly *odd* to you, come talk to me right away."

"What do you mean? Parents say weird stuff all the time."

"I mean something that when you hear it, you feel something in your guts."

"You mean like something gross that makes you scared or sick to your stomach?"

Skelly was frustrated he wasn't making himself understood to the fatigued boy. He thought for a moment, then asked, "How would you feel if your dad told you he was going to take you up in a hot air balloon?"

"Huh? Where did he get a hot air balloon? That doesn't make sense: he doesn't know how to fly one."

"Yes! As soon as you heard that, you knew it didn't quite make sense. If your dad says the two of you are going someplace you've never heard of, come talk to me right away. Okay?"

"Sure, I guess. I'm really tired now."

Skelly let his young friend drift off to asleep, unsure as to whether the boy understood the importance of his instructions.

As far as Way-Outs go, this one wasn't very spectacular. It was more of a thirty-minute sitcom, as opposed to a full-blown feature film. Rodney was relegated to watch events unfold without personally directing the action. The sense of achievement he had after operating the person's body as his own was missing, leaving Rodney feeling not quite satisfied.

When Rodney opened his eyes, he thought he got a glimpse of someone standing on the stairs. He was typically disoriented after returning from one of his Way-Outs, so he wasn't certain. After taking a few moments to get his bearings, Rodney looked back at the stairwell, but didn't see anyone. His first attempt to get to his feet was a failure, causing him to awkwardly slump backwards onto the couch. Eventually he was able to regain enough of his balance to shuffle slowly to the stairway, then up the steps into the kitchen.

He looked in on his son because it was the first doorway he reached. Jered was sleeping, his deep breaths whistling through his nose. While holding onto the doorframe for support, Rodney's head gradually cleared. After leaving Jered's room, he watched Chrissy from the doorway of the master bedroom. She, too, was sound asleep.

"Good," he thought. "My eyes were just playing tricks on me. I didn't see anything down there."

It would have been prudent for Rodney to go back downstairs in case another episode occurred that night, but he wasn't confident his shaky legs would carry him safely down the steps. Rodney collapsed into the living room easy chair, quickly falling asleep. Chrissy found him sprawled in the chair the following morning.

CHAPTER EIGHTEEN

Coast Day & Thanksgiving Morning

None of the teachers expected to get much accomplished the day before Thanksgiving. Everyone expected the Wednesday before Thanksgiving to be a coast day. Administrators, teachers, and pupils alike watched the clock as it slowly moved towards a four-day weekend. After getting a spelling test out of the way first thing in the morning, Miss Moran planned a day of easy activities that didn't require much thought.

"Until the bell rings, why don't you draw a picture about what you'll be doing tomorrow," she announced to her class late that afternoon. "You can draw your family eating Thanksgiving dinner, or travelling to see relatives, or whatever you want."

During the afternoon before a holiday, children tend to be a handful for their teachers. The anticipation of four days without school makes them fidgety, unfocused, and generally uninterested. Kerri's assignment, however, managed to keep the kids' attention away from just watching the clock.

Jered wasn't very interested in drawing for the first time in his life. The only thing he could think about was what he'd seen in the basement. Or what he *thought* he'd seen. Obviously, he didn't see his dad as part skeleton and part person. He convinced himself that the combination of fatigue and the poor basement lighting, caused his eyes to play a trick on him. All he'd really seen was his father wrapped in a blanket, sleeping on the downstairs sofa. He didn't know why his father was sleeping in the basement, but that issue didn't seem important under the circumstances.

Listening to the music coming from the record player, as well as the gentle *whooshing* in his ear, Jered finally got to work on his drawing and soon lost himself in the assignment. As he'd done so many times during his young life, he eventually was able to ignore the outside world, focusing solely on his picture. So his mother would never again have reason to be so concerned about him, he'd already decided he was done drawing skeletons. He might not even draw them next Halloween. He was done with them.

When he was about finished drawing his Thanksgiving scene, though, he noticed a skeleton had inserted itself into the picture. "Why is *that* in there?" he thought. He'd been so lost in his own little world, he couldn't even remember drawing the skeleton. The final bell rung, causing the rest of the class to jump to their feet like firemen responding to an alarm. Jered folded his picture in half, planning to throw it in the trash.

"Leave your pieces on my desk as you go out," Miss Moran instructed. "Have a nice Thanksgiving and I'll see everybody back on Monday." Jered briefly considered not turning in his drawing, but he didn't want to disobey the best teacher he'd ever had.

As the drawings piled up on her desk, Kerri realized she should have just had the students take them home. She wasn't going to grade what they created: this was just busy work. By the time she realized this, though, more than half of the class had already scurried away, so she decided to hold her tongue. She wished each of the children a happy Thanksgiving as they placed their artwork on her desk. Jered was the last one to drop off his drawing. The boy never looked like the pinnacle of health, but Miss Moran noticed his face looked unusually pale.

"You feeling okay? You look a little washed out," she said.

The boy responded with a quick shrug of his shoulders.

"Okay, then, don't eat too much turkey tomorrow!"

Through her classroom windows she watched as there was a rush of children exiting the school. Some of them were running fervently away from the school, as if there was a chance the principal would suddenly announce everyone needed to come back inside for a pop quiz. Most days there were at least a few students lagging behind, either talking to their friends or getting ready for afterschool activities. When Miss Moran looked down the halls that afternoon, they were completely empty. She stopped by a couple of classrooms and found that some teachers had left almost as quickly as their students. Tucking some papers under her arm, Kerri walked to the parking lot.

When she arrived at her apartment, she tossed the papers and her purse on the kitchen table with a sigh of relief. "Four days off!" she announced to her empty apartment.

Before she left for school that morning, she'd made sure to put a bottle of Frostie Root Beer in the refrigerator. Now she could start off the holiday right by having a bottle of her favorite pop. Kerri pried off bottle cap with a church key, then enjoyed a long, cold swallow of Frostie. After the first thirst quenching drink, she smacked her lips and said, "Ahh."

It was in this moment of bliss she noticed one of the drawings on her kitchen table. Even from several feet away, she could tell it was Jered's handiwork. She went to the table, looking down at the drawing partially covered by her purse. As he had on more than one occasion, Jered impressed Miss Moran with the detail and symmetry of his drawing.

Depicted was a large banquet table covered with dishes ready to serve. A platter with a large turkey dominated the middle of the picture. Jered had drawn the bird in surprising detail. A woman and a boy were behind the table, ready to dig in. At first, she thought this might be Jered and his mother, but they were wearing pilgrim hats with buckles in front. She moved her purse off the paper so she could see the rest of Jered's picture. Seated next to the woman and boy was a skeleton, also wearing a pilgrim hat.

Her stomach dropped. She looked at the drawing for quite some time, trying to find a hidden message in it. Apart from the skeleton, the picture was beautiful. Kerri knew a child might at times use alternative ways to communicate. Hadn't Kerri initially become fond of drawing cuddly animals because her parents insisted on having a pet-free house? The only cats, dogs, or rabbits she could caress were the ones she created on paper. That little girl figured if she drew enough small animals, her parents would finally realize their daughter desperately longed for a pet and would surprise her with a furry friend. Even as she grew older, the cuddly animals she drew were a welcome comfort. Kerri loved the ersatz pets she created.

What, then, was Jered communicating, if anything? Did this picture have meaning?

The phone ringing jostled her from her thoughts. "Hello?"

"Miss Moran, this is Madeline Stokes from Dr. Ford Freud's office. He asked me to tell you he would be honored to meet with you tomorrow at his office."

"Tomorrow? You mean Thanksgiving?"

"Yes. Dr. Freud simply considers it a typical Thursday," Madeline replied in a defeated voice. Dr. Freud made it clear to her during a lengthy rant that holidays amounted to superstitious nonsense and he expected her to be in the office alongside him on all weekdays.

"Well . . . I guess. I go to my parent's house at 11:00. Could we meet in the morning?"

"Certainly. Enter through the service door then take the elevator to room 101. We look forward to seeing you."

The receptionist hung up the phone without saying anything further, which Kerri thought was kind of rude. Kerri decided to cut her some slack, as she too would have a poor attitude if she had to work on Thanksgiving.

As she expected, Kerri found the campus deserted on Thursday morning. She parked behind the huge brick building known as Arts & Sciences Hall and made her way to the psychology department.

"I'm Kerri Moran. I have an appointment with Dr. Ford Freud."

"Oh, yes, Dr. Freud has been expecting you," Madeline said. "Dr. Freud has been talking about your father literally nonstop ever since he saw your phone message."

Kerri was perplexed. Why would the famous Dr. Ford Freud know a television repairman? Even if her father at some point fixed the doctor's TV, she doubted that they had much in common, and the likelihood that they struck up a conversation was nil. Madeline walked ahead of her, gesturing towards a door at the end of the hall.

"Dr. Freud moved into a bigger office this week, so with your visit and setting up his office, it's been quite an exciting couple of days," Madeline said.

When they arrived at a large cherry door, Madeline knocked on it while announcing

in a sing-song voice, "Dr. Freud? Miss Kerri Moran is here to see you."

A booming, baritone voice coming from inside the office replied, "Enter." The way this word was bellowed, it was four syllables long.

When door was opened, a puff of either smoke or dust wafted out of the office. When she was getting her degree, Kerri occasionally visited the offices of her professors, but they were nowhere the size and grandeur of Dr. Freud's. Conservatively, Kerri figured that she could fit four of her school's classrooms into the long rectangular office. Columns of papers and books taller than Kerri caused her to think of Roman ruins.

"Just follow the path and you'll reach his desk," Madeline informed Kerri, pointing towards a small area where the floor could be seen. "Be careful not to run into any of the stacks of Dr. Freud's papers, otherwise . . ." Madeline pantomimed an explosion by fanning out her hands and fingers.

Kerri heard a voice coming from the other side of the room, but she couldn't see the speaker. "Please come in, Miss Moran, I have been looking forward to our caucus." She began slowly and deliberately traversing the path through the columns. She couldn't help but notice that some of the papers were so old they'd turned brown and had curled up edges.

As Kerri followed the serpentine path, she called out to her unseen host, "Your secretary says you just moved in."

"Indeed. She has shared with you correct information," the voice said. "I am now, however, completely set up, organized, and ready for guests."

Kerri brushed up against one of the stacks, causing it to teeter. She instinctively held up her hands in case a waterfall of papers fell onto her, but the stack managed to right itself. When she arrived at a clearing, she was welcomed by an old man chomping on a lit cigar. His ear-to-ear smile and white beard made him look like a thinner version of Santa Claus. Kerri wouldn't have been surprised if he greeted her with a hearty, "Ho, ho, ho!"

"Whoa, whoa, whoa," Dr. Freud said. "Use care as you pass that stack of books: it can be rather temperamental."

Kerri was relieved when she arrived at an empty chair placed in front of the desk. She didn't want to make a poor first impression by causing a paper avalanche in the respected scholar's new office. She was about to sit down when the old man leaned across the desk with his hand held out. "Dr. Ford Freud at your service."

She shook his hand and replied, "Kerri Moran. It's a pleasure to meet you. Thank you for agreeing to meet with me about this unusual case."

"How could I deny your request? My understanding is that you have a young patient about whom you would like to speak. It is my honor to do so," Dr. Freud said in his typical booming voice.

"Patient?" she said. "I like to think of him as my student."

"Of course," the doctor said in a goodhearted tone. "Whatever pronoun you choose to employ is acceptable to me. Before we begin, however, please indulge me, and tell me what your father is doing these days. Is he working on something?"

Kerri wasn't sure how to respond. The learned doctor's interest in her father's repair of televisions seemed out of place.

Dr. Freud misconstrued the blank look on Kerri's face as her attempt to be coy. He assured her, "I will not share this information with anyone, Miss Moran." When she didn't reply, he added, "It has been so long since I last saw him, and I am curious if he is continuing his work in the field."

"Has your television been broken?" Kerri asked hesitantly, still not sure why the doctor was so interested in her father.

Now it was Dr. Freud who had a puzzled expression. After a few silent moments, Dr. Freud's smile once again spread across his face. "Ah, I see what we have here!"

"You do?"

Dr. Freud chuckled and said, "Your father has employed a system of code phrases to ensure that his daughter only speaks with authorized people. Is that it? What did you ask me?"

"Um, is your television broken?"

Dr. Freud clapped his hands together and laughed with approval. "Yes! And now you expect me to provide you with the correct scripted reply. You are waiting for a response such as, 'Sometimes it is the dark water that extinguishes the flames.' Something clever like that?" Kerri continued to look at the doctor blankly. "What a wonderful way of controlling the flow of information!" Dr. Freud then lowered his voice and confided, "The only problem is, I never received a communiqué advising me of the correct response. I can assure you, however, that I *am* Dr. Ford Freud, and you can speak openly with me."

Kerri had no earthly idea what to say next. She recognized that something wasn't quite right, but she was at a loss as how best to untangle the mess. As the period of silence became longer, the friendliness of Dr. Freud's facial expression began to melt away. Replacing his warm and friendly exterior was an expression of dour contempt. When the change on his face was complete, Kerri felt very small and vulnerable.

In an accusatory voice, Dr. Freud asked, "Who is your father, Miss Kerri Moran?

"My . . . my father is Ned. Ned Moran," she replied sheepishly.

Dr. Freud lifted his chin and looked down at Kerri as she nervously fidgeted in her chair. He took in a deep breath while keeping his cold eyes fixated on her. "Your father is *not* the famed Dr. Finneas Moran, is that correct?" Kerri was shaken, so she just remained silent and motionless. "You are therefore not Miss Kerri Moran, the eldest daughter of the noted neuropsychiatrist Dr. Finneas Moran, would that be true?"

She opened her mouth to speak but the professor didn't give her a chance to speak. Dr. Freud slammed both oh his fists on his desk, startling Kerri. The old doctor's face was blossoming with bright red patches brought about by his anger. He bellowed, "Nurse Stokes! Come in here right now, Nurse Stokes!"

Kerri's hands gripped the arms of the chair while Dr. Freud glared at her. The office door squeaked, and Kerri heard the receptionist's tiny voice. "Yes, Dr. Freud?"

"Come here! There is a problem!"

Kerri heard the receptionist brush up against some of the piles of papers as she followed the path to the professor's desk. As soon as she appeared from between two towers of papers, Dr. Freud launched into his cross examination of her.

"Do you know who this is?" he asked, gesturing towards Kerri. If a simple hand gesture could demonstrate scorn, Dr. Freud's definitely qualified.

The receptionist hadn't worked for Professor Freud for very long, but it didn't require a doctorate in human behavior to realize her employer was about to blow his top. When people yelled at her, Madeline's voice tended to become very high-pitched, and she spoke very quickly. "This is Miss Kerri Moran. Don't you remember? She called last week to make an appointment to see you about a child, and I asked if you were willing to meet Kerri Moran, and you said she must be the daughter of Dr. Moran, and you're always available for Dr. Moran's family, and . . ."

The only thing that kept Madeline from talking further was the open hand held up by the professor. "I didn't ask you for all of that. You have wasted my time by telling me things that have naught-all to do with the question I posed to you. Why would you do that? Hmm? Do you know how valuable my time is? My time is an extremely valuable commodity and you have just wasted some of it by not providing me a direct, concise answer to my question."

Both women saw a blue vein was becoming prominent on Dr. Freud's forehead, and his nose was now so red it looked like clown make-up. Madeline wasn't sure she could speak.

"When you informed me Miss Kerri Moran was seeking an audience with me, why would I think of anyone other than the daughter of the famed reclusive Dr. Finneas Moran?" After waiting a few seconds for a reply, the doctor continued, "You purposefully fooled me! Here I was thinking I was going to enjoy a professional summit with Dr. Moran's protégée, Miss Kerri Moran, and you give me Miss Kerri Moran, the protégée of . . . what did you say your father's name was?"

Kerri murmured, "Ned."

"Ned Moran, who is *not* someone who has written at length in the field of child development. Pray, what area of professional study does the illustrious Ned Moran claim to be an expert in?"

In a voice barely above a whisper, Kerri said, "He repairs televisions."

Dr. Freud laughed uproariously but it was a sharp laugh containing no mirth. Instead, it was filled with disdain. "You accepted an appointment with the daughter of a television repairman, not a reclusive scientific genius!"

"But . . . but I didn't tell you who Miss Moran was," Madeline said meekly. "She's just a lady who called the office for an appointment. You're the one who said she must be Dr. Moran's daughter. I don't know Dr. Moran and even if . . ."

"Now is an excellent opportunity for you to stop talking," Dr. Freud declared. "Even if I *was* mistaken, it is your job to make sure that I do not make such mistakes." Dr. Freud turned in his chair so that his back was to the two women. He let his gaze drift over the campus as he took a few deep breaths. "Miss Moran, I am sorry you had to witness this spectacle. I was led to believe you were someone else, and that is the only reason you were given an audience with me. My research and duties in the area of abnormal pediatric behavior simply do not provide me with adequate time to speak with someone who does not possess superior credentials. You will need to seek assistance from someone else."

Summoning her courage, Kerri pleaded with Dr. Freud. "But this child needs help. Something's wrong and I can't figure it out. I need an expert. I need you, not someone else."

Still looking out the window, Dr. Freud responded, "That is of no consequence to me, madam. As my headstrong friend Will used to say, beggars can't be choosers. Nurse Stokes, please see Miss Moran out."

When Kerri didn't immediately get up from her chair, Madeline made a "psst" noise and gestured for Kerri to come with her. Kerri ignored her, concentrating instead on coming up with a way to change the doctor's mind. She was convinced Jered's case required Dr. Freud's legendary expertise. If she left now, she'd be no closer to helping Jered. She owed it to him, to get the best possible doctor involved.

If you believe in the old proverb "necessity is the mother of invention," then it'll be little wonder to you that a person's creativity can be augmented during times of stress. Kerri Moran didn't graduate at the head of her class, nor was she particularly gifted at thinking on her feet. On Thanksgiving morning in Dr. Freud's office, however, she came up with a creative solution to the dire straits she was facing.

Kerri leaned back in her chair, trying to look cool and confident. She clapped her hands very slowly. In her head she was counting, "Clap, one Mississippi, two Mississippi, clap, one Mississippi, two Mississippi, clap . . ."

Dr. Freud spun his chair around to look into the eyes of the person who dared to slow-clap in his office. The young woman was now lounging in the chair with a devilish smile on her face. The woman clapped three more times before saying, "You passed the test. Well done."

Dr. Freud looked at Madeline, whose wide eyes were proof she had no idea at what was transpiring. He was disappointed Madeline wasn't already in the process of dragging her out of his office. The doctor turned his attention to the young woman who had somehow come to the erroneous conclusion that *she* was in control of the situation.

Kerri sensed she'd momentarily turned the tide in her favor, but she also recognized she needed to act quickly in order to take full advantage. "My father is a recluse, as you've stated, doctor. As you can imagine, he is very protective of his work and his family. My name is Kerri Moran. I've been sent here to get your advice about an unusual and unique child. He sent me because you are no doubt the world's greatest expert in this area." Kerri had four older brothers, so she learned at an early age how to subtly engage the male ego. "I was told by my father if you refused to get involved, this would be the indication you were the right expert for this task."

Now it was time for Dr. Freud to be dumbfounded. The doctor studied Kerri's face, using his professional skills to look for any subtle signs of deception. She responded by never averting her eyes, maintaining a steely, confident presentation. No one said anything for an entire minute, during which Dr. Freud carefully analyzed Kerri's face. Although she'd never been involved in acting, she thought her performance thus far had been impeccable. She was nevertheless anxious, not knowing if the professor would take the bait she'd set. When his frown gradually turned into a smile, she knew she'd succeeded.

"I am pleased I was able to pass the test," Dr. Freud said in a friendly manner. "I only wish I knew how to contact Dr. Moran personally and thank him for this opportunity."

Kerri understood the doctor's affable comment could have been an attempt to trip her up. She returned his smile and replied, "But, of course, you realize I can't give you that information. To do so would break my father's trust. He demands solitude."

"I completely understand," Dr. Freud said as he nodded.

Although Kerri was confident Dr. Freud was buying the story, she decided to add to the charade. "In fact, if anyone was able somehow to reach my father, he'd certainly deny that he sent his daughter on a mission to consult with another renowned physician."

Dr. Freud's expression had softened but Kerri noticed he continued to study her face while he told his assistant, "You can leave Miss Moran and me. We apparently have a young patient to discuss."

Kerri wasn't someone who was usually skilled at telling detailed and interesting stories. Once she got rolling that morning, though, she was destined to create a storytelling masterpiece. "I've developed some interesting theories about the behavior of children," she explained. "My desire was to test these theories but as I'm sure you know, it's difficult these days to get permission to test human subjects. Especially children."

Dr. Freud readily agreed. "Yes! That is true! Dr. Milgram's and Dr. Zimbardo's outlandish experiments have made it tougher on all of us!"

"Indeed, so I took a post as an elementary school teacher here in University City so I might surreptitiously test some of my theories."

"Well done," Dr. Freud said in a respectful voice. "Quite clever."

"While teaching, I happened upon a student who presented with a unique and challenging behavior issue. I don't mind admitting to you, Dr. Freud, that I found it difficult to explain. Of course, I called my father and discussed the child with him. His suggestion was I seek your input since you are such a noted authority in this field."

Dr. Freud placed his hand on his chest and said, "I am humbled by Dr. Moran's recommendation. Pray, what makes this patient so unique?"

Kerri told Dr. Freud of her artistic student and his penchant for drawing skeletons.

"This is the most recent example," she said, reaching into her purse for the Thanksgiving picture and sliding it across the desk to the doctor.

Dr. Freud's right eyebrow raised as he studied the drawing. "You say this patient has gradually become fixated on skeletons and skulls?" he asked, still scrutinizing the odd drawing.

"Yes. It's almost if he *can't* keep these images out of his drawings."

Dr. Freud remained silent for a few minutes as he considered the imagery contained in the piece. "My initial thought is time is of essence for this patient. When can I meet him?"

"What are you thinking is wrong?" Kerri asked with concern.

"I am not able to assess this patient until interviewing him. Surely you know that."

"Yes, of course I know that, but I thought maybe you could give me some ideas . . ."

"When can you present this patient to me?"

Kerri's intention was to explain the situation to Dr. Freud, listen to his opinions, and get some guidance. Having Jered meet the physician face-to-face certainly wasn't part of her plan.

"I don't know if I can bring Jered to see you. Can you just give me your thoughts without meeting with him?"

"Is this some kind of trap?" Dr. Freud said warily. "Are you trying to goad me into providing a professional opinion without conducting a proper interview?" The old doctor looked down his nose at Kerri. "Did Dr. Moran ask you to test my adherence to proper scientific procedures by asking me to give you an analysis with only partial information?"

A voice deep inside Kerri screamed, "The jig is up! Run!" The muscles in her legs tensed, ready to spirit her away out of the office. The youthful arrogance she'd received along with her college diploma stepped in to take control.

"Yes, that is exactly what I was advised by my father to do," Kerri explained confidently. "Once again, you have passed with flying colors, just as he predicted!"

The professor looked very pleased, sporting the smile of a man who is confident he always has correct answers, no matter what question is posed. "Since I am sure Dr. Moran wants this analysis right away, I will make myself available to meet with this patient tomorrow. Of course, I will undertake this as a professional courtesy to your father, and no bill for my services will be submitted to you or the patient's family. Shall we plan on a 10:00 session?"

Kerri was backed into a corner. "Yes, that would be fine." She decided the longer she spoke to Dr. Freud, the more difficulties she would likely encounter. Kerri announced, "Now I must be leaving, as I have another appointment. Thank you for your time."

Extending his hand, Dr. Freud arose from his desk. "I look forward to our next meeting."

Exhibiting the poise of a movie star, she shook his hand, then strode from the office. She walked out of the department and down the stairs with a confident gait. Once she'd reached the first floor of the building, though, she began running. Once in her car, she pulled out of the parking space so fast her tires squealed. By the time she'd reached the first traffic signal, she was sobbing. She wasn't sure whether these were tears of relief, or tears of concern for what might occur in the future. Once the tears began, it was quite some time before they stopped.

There was a part of her that knew she couldn't ever set foot again on the campus of her alma mater. Because of the intricate yarn she'd told, she couldn't risk ever running into Dr. Freud. Would he go so far to call the police to look for the daughter of Dr. Moran who'd appeared in his office, but never returned? She'd told him she was an elementary school teacher in University City, so it wouldn't be difficult to locate her. If confronted by the police she'd have to confess her story was fiction. Once Dr. Freud learned she'd pulled the wool over his eyes, could the furious professor have her prosecuted for some type of professional fraud? What would be the ramifications of such a conviction on her teaching career?

After coming this far, she couldn't abandon her effort to help the troubled boy. Dr. Freud decreed that the only means of obtaining his expert opinion was for Jered to undergo a therapy session. This was an obstacle Kerri hadn't expected, but the evaluation, diagnosis, and treatment by Dr. Freud was still the surest way to help her young student. She owed it to Jered to see this through.

CHAPTER NINETEEN

Chrissy's Misleading Horoscope

Every weekday afternoon at about 3:45, a boy riding a bicycle tossed a copy of the *University City Sentinel* near the Barstow's front door. The first thing Chrissy checked in the newspaper was the horoscope for the following day. Seeing that the stars' position in the cosmos had laid out her future was comforting to her. Even on those days when the stars foretold a difficult situation arising, the prediction always provided a window of opportunity to minimize the tribulation. For Thursday, Chrissy's horoscope advised her to be alert for hidden schemes of others. This was one of those few times the stars were way off target, and not of any assistance to her. If her horoscope had been accurate, it would have advised her it was going to be an extremely disappointing Thanksgiving.

The three members of the Barstow family weren't in synch with each other on that holiday. Each of them was following a course at odds with the other members of the family.

Rodney was usually in high spirits when Thanksgiving rolled around. He looked forward to the four-day weekend, eating until he was about to explode, and watching football on TV. This year, Rodney's mood was soured by his continued battle with the lingering effects of Monday night's headache. He couldn't remember the last time one of his headaches persisted this long, but it simply wouldn't let go.

"I can't seem to kick it," he grumbled to Chrissy when he got home Wednesday night.

Rodney thought it was a stroke of good luck that his mother-in-law wasn't going to be around for the holiday. Things at work were more tense and difficult than usual. He wasn't interested in putting on a happy face for the benefit of Chrissy and JoJo as they kibitzed incessantly about preparations for Christmas. He was looking forward to four days to recharge his batteries and hopefully ridding himself of the foul vestiges of his headache. He'd never had a headache last this long and its constant presence sapped his energy. Rodney was lethargic, longing for a cool, dark place where his nerves could settle.

Chrissy had been somber ever since learning JoJo was going to be absent on Thanksgiving. This was going to be the very first Thanksgiving Chrissy didn't spend with her mother, yet JoJo hadn't appeared to be the least bit concerned about breaking this tradition. Did JoJo even consider for one moment how her decision to fly off to be with her friends would affect Chrissy? JoJo's absence grieved Chrissy, but the fact nobody shared her disappointment caused her to be even more upset. Rodney behaved as if he wasn't the least bit disappointed. Shockingly, Jered didn't respond to the news as Chrissy anticipated.

"That's okay, I guess," Jered responded to his mother. "We can just have our own Thanksgiving. You promise she'll be here for Christmas though, right? Promise?"

Jered felt like he was walking on eggs. He knew he'd caused the fight between his parents, and he wanted to do everything possible to avoid sparking another argument. The only way he could think to achieve this was to remain as even keeled as he could. When his mother reported the bad news about JoJo, he was crushed. Despite his disappointment, he put on a brave face, telling his mother they'd be fine without her. He didn't want to make any waves, lest they grow to become a tidal wave that upset the delicate balance of the family. He remained quiet, concerned a stray word or action on his part could ignite another family crisis. Hopefully his parents would never fight again.

Chrissy yearned for the two men in her life to share in her despondency. She wanted them to join in the sadness where she dwelt. They slapped her in the face by insisting on courageously taking JoJo's absence in stride. She expected the three of them to share the sadness of JoJo's absence together as a family. Her husband and son refused to join her level of despondency. Chrissy was mourning her loss, but no one seemed to care.

Thanksgiving dinner wasn't a joyful family affair for any of them. Chrissy felt that without the vibrant presence of her mother, the three of them seemed to just be going through the motions. They ate their turkey dinner, but none of them engaged much with each other. As always, it was up to Chrissy to keep the family together, so she tried to encourage conversation as they ate. Her efforts failed. None of them seemed interested in banter. Truth was, Chrissy didn't feel like talking either. By then all she really wanted to do was to be left alone to wallow in her sadness.

After she finished washing the dishes, Chrissy noticed how quiet the house was. In the living room she found Rodney sleeping in his easy chair. His hand was covering his eyes, as if he'd fallen asleep while massaging his temples. Her son was taking a nap on his bed. If JoJo had been there, the house would have been full of conversation and laughter. It seemed to Chrissy that JoJo's absence had left them with nothing but disinterest, and this made her feel empty. Making as little noise as possible, Chrissy went downstairs. She turned on the light over Rodney's workbench and sat on the stool.

"Get yourself together, Chrissy," she said under her breath in a demanding voice. "This is just a bump in the road: nothing to be scared of. You have to be strong for your family."

Despite her brave words, Chrissy started crying. She did her best to muffle her sobs, so she didn't awaken Rodney or Jered. After her tears subsided, Chrissy stared emptily across the dimly lit basement. She wondered if there was something wrong with her darling son. She thought about her husband, trying to figure out why his mood had changed in the past few months. When she reflected on her husband and son, a skeleton always forced itself into her thoughts.

Chrissy heard stomping above her, then Rodney's angry voice. She couldn't make out what he was yelling at, but she ran up the stairs. Once she was in the kitchen, she could clearly hear Rodney yelling.

"Why would you take it down? Why?!"

When Chrissy arrived at the doorway to Jered's bedroom, she saw her son seated on the bed, his legs pulled against his chest. He looked from between his knees with frightened eyes. Rodney was gesturing towards the naked closet door.

"I . . . I . . ." was all Jered managed to say.

When Rodney noticed Chrissy's presence, he directed his ire towards her. "Did *you* do this, even though I told you *not* to?"

Despite Jered's best efforts, another fight between his parents was about to unfold in front of him. He didn't want his mother to take the brunt of his father's fury, since it had been Jered's decision to take the skeleton down. He swallowed hard, then managed to speak. "No, it was me." Jered's voice came out mousey, so he repeated himself, trying to sound more assertive. "It was me that took it down."

His father's head snapped to the right. Jered felt like he was being seared by laser beams shooting from his father's eyes. "Is that so?" Jered's father took two steps towards the bed, so that he was towering above the boy. "Do you want to go backwards? After coming this far?"

Jered had no idea what his father was talking about. He looked anxiously towards his mother for support, but she remained motionless in the doorway. He pleaded with his eyes for help, but she didn't offer any assistance. Jered was eventually able to respond to his father, but he couldn't bring himself to look into his angry face.

"I . . . I just got tired of it, ya know?" Jered explained. "Nothing big. I still like it. It'll go back up next year."

Rodney let out a short growl of frustration, which caused both Chrissy and Jered to jump. "What do you suppose should happen to little boys who don't mind their father?"

Once again Jered looked towards his mother for some kind of support, but she said and did nothing. Watching the events unfold left Chrissy bewildered and shaken. Her only conscious thought was she wanted this appalling scene to end. In her head she kept repeating the mantra: "Everything's going to be okay. This will pass. The family will be fine."

Since she desperately wanted it all to stop, Chrissy thought through force of will she could somehow quell the fierce tornado howling through her family. She remembered what JoJo told her about her duty to keep the family together even during stormy weather. She reassured herself that it was important for parents to keep a united front and not contradict each other in front of a child. When things settled down, she'd confront Rodney privately about his outburst and tell him there was absolutely no reason for him to become this angry at their son. At this moment, though, she convinced herself it was best not to undermine his authority.

Rodney raised his hand in anger, causing his son to cower. Chrissy wanted to throw herself in front of her son, but she was unable to move. Just after raising his hand, a sudden bolt of pain erupted behind Rodney's eyes, causing him to bring both his hands to his face. Rodney pushed both thumbs inward on his eyelids, trying to rub away some of the pain.

Still rubbing his eyes, Rodney mumbled in a voice Jered and his mother could barely hear, "So this is the way the two of you want it? Hm?" Without waiting for a response, he slowly left the bedroom, his palms now massaging the sides of his throbbing head. Jered and his mother remained silent and motionless as they tried to make sense of what just happened.

It was Chrissy who managed to speak first. "You know how daddy can get when one of his bad headaches comes along," Chrissy said in an apologetic voice. "Just humor your dad for now. Everything'll be fine. I'm going to help him with his headache and make sure everything is okay. You can take care of yourself if I leave, right?" Only because it was clear that it was what his mother wanted him to do, Jered slowly nodded his head. "Good boy." She left the bedroom and Jered heard her say to Rodney, "I'll get you a cool rag with ice cubes wrapped in it."

Jered was still holding his legs against his chest. He wondered what might have happened if his father hadn't been overcome with his headache. His mother hadn't come to his aid. Instead, she'd just stood there, watching the whole horrible event unfold. Why didn't she protect him? Would she have intervened if the situation got even worse? Jered felt very alone. He also couldn't help but feel ashamed. These two people had at one time been happy together, but it seemed as though Jered was ruining it for everyone. He kept replaying his mother's words. It appeared he was supposed to take care of himself. Did that mean for the rest of his life?

Skelly's voice startled Jered from his thoughts. "Okay, you do that. Jered here is just fine," Skelly said in a sarcastic tone. "You just run along—we'll be just fine here by ourselves. Ain't that right, buddy?" Despite everything that had just transpired, Jered felt a laugh building up inside his chest. The boy tried to swallow it, but it kept pushing up from his lungs. "Yep, we're just okeydokey here, Mrs. Barstow. No reason to worry about us little old cowpokes. No sirree, Bob!"

A little laugh escaped from between Jered's lips, causing him to chide, "Stop it! This is serious! Stop making me laugh!"

"Okeydokey Mr. Muskogee. No more laughing allowed. This is now officially a no-laugh zone. All laughter will be fined by the authorities."

The more Skelly rambled on the more Jered laughed. "Stop it. I'm serious."

"Yes, we've met before, Mr. Serious. You might recall my name is Skelly." Despite his best efforts, Jered continued to laugh. "Even though you're on Thanksgiving vacation, Mr. Serious, I was thinking this might be a good night to go to bed a little early. What do you think? Maybe you could close the door so we could talk in the dark until you fall asleep? I can tell you a story about one of my friends who taught me you have to rely upon yourself for protection, not somebody else."

Jered thought about the proposal for a moment, then replied, "Okay. That sounds good. Ya know, it's hard for me not to laugh when you get silly like that."

"Really? I wasn't aware of that. That's something I probably should pay attention to in the future."

Two unexpected phone calls were made to the Barstow residence later that evening.

"Really?" Rodney said incredulously to the person on the phone. "Why? Okay. I'll see you at one."

"Who was that?" Chrissy asked.

"The big boss wants me to come in tomorrow afternoon to finalize year-end reports. What an idiot! Just because he's disorganized, I have to go to work the Friday after Thanksgiving. Shouldn't that be against the law or something?"

After he plopped himself angrily into his chair, Chrissy rubbed his shoulders. "It's okay. Jered and I are just going to be out shopping the big sales tomorrow anyway. There won't be anybody home, so you're not really missing anything." JoJo taught Chrissy there'd be bumps along the road in family life, and it was imperative that the wife/mother soothe frayed nerves to usher the family unit back on track. "Besides, you'll still get to sleep-in tomorrow, and that'll be nice, right?"

Just as Chrissy hoped her husband would be distressed JoJo wouldn't be at Thanksgiving dinner, Rodney wanted his wife to mirror his displeasure at being forced to work the next day. Neither of them got the emotional response they were looking for, however.

"Yeah, I guess. It' still a crummy thing to do to someone!"

Thirty minutes later as Rodney was still grousing about going to work the following afternoon, Chrissy answered the second phone call.

"Mrs. Barstow? This is Kerri Moran, Jered's teacher."

Instantaneously Chrissy was on high alert. She glanced over to where her husband was staring blankly at the television. She pushed the phone receiver firmly against her ear to ensure no sound escaped. "Yes?" Chrissy said softly, nervously glancing towards Rodney.

"I know this might sound forward of me, but I met with a psychiatrist who believes he can help Jered."

Chrissy wasn't a risk taker, and the thought of once again going behind her husband's back made her very nervous. Against Rodney's wishes, Chrissy had taken Jered to see his pediatrician, but it had been a disaster. If Rodney found out she'd taken Jered to not one, but to two doctors, he'd flip his lid. Chrissy steadied her voice, responding with as few words as possible in order to disguise the conversation. "Okay."

"He wants to see Jered tomorrow morning at 10:00. I know this is short notice, but it was the only time he had available. He said he'd do it for free. I think it would be good for Jered to see him. Would that be something you'd like to do?"

"Yes, I understand."

From the living room, Rodney called out to his wife, "Who is it?"

"Where?" Chrissy asked, hoping to move the conversation along so it could end.

"At the University. Arts & Sciences Hall, room 101."

In a voice just above a whisper, Chrissy said, "Thank you," then used her finger to push the button in the cradle to disconnect the call. Still holding the phone to her ear, she said in a louder voice, "No, thank you. We've already made our contributions to charity this year. Thank you for your call." After laying the phone in its cradle, Chrissy walked into the living room.

"That was just another charity looking for money," she reported.

"Which one?"

Chrissy tried to think of a charity, but she couldn't think of one when put on the spot. She picked up an empty cup from the coffee table and took it to the kitchen. She hoped he'd just let his question go unanswered, but he didn't.

"Which charity was it?"

"Um, it was . . . something about feeding the needy."

"'Tis the season to get calls for money, I guess."

"Yeah," she replied, then started noisily putting away pans. She hoped the clatter would dissuade any follow up questions. It did.

Despite her horoscope usually being accurate, it failed to alert her that a solution to a problem that had been weighing on her was on its way.

As far as Jered knew, he and his mother were going downtown to fight the crowds at the after-Thanksgiving sales. Chrissy decided not to share with her son the fact their destination had changed. If Jered didn't know the truth, he wouldn't unwittingly say something to alert Rodney. When mother and son left the house that morning, Rodney was drinking coffee, still grousing about going into work that afternoon.

Chrissy kissed her husband's forehead. "You'll just be away for a few hours, then we have a whole weekend together as a family," she soothed. "We'll try to be back before you get home, but if we're not, don't worry, the busses might just be running late." Chrissy had to hedge her bets, as she had no idea how long the session with the psychiatrist would take.

When they walked to a bus stop Jered didn't recognize, he asked, "Is this the right place, Mom? We don't usually come to this stop."

"Yes, that's right, hon. Before we go shopping, we're going to go see a doctor." Chrissy did her best to hide her anxiety, but her son detected she was apprehensive.

"Again? How come?"

"He's a special kind of doctor. One who wants to talk to you about some things. Doesn't that sound like fun?"

"No, not really," the boy replied nervously.

"Could you do it for me? Like a favor? I kind of need you to do this for me."

Since he'd caused his mother such distress that week, Jered was in a giving mood. "Okay, I guess. Do you promise there won't be any shots?"

"I promise, promise!"

Jered was looking forward to perusing the shelves of toys as his mother shopped and the prospect of talking to a doctor wasn't going to be nearly as fun. He was a little disappointed but wasn't apprehensive about seeing a doctor. Everyone knows the thing to

SKELETONS ARE NOT SCARY

be afraid of with doctors was they gave shots and his mom promise promised he wouldn't see any needles.

Both Chrissy and Jered were awestruck when they stepped off the bus at the sprawling campus. Large marble and stone buildings seemed to be looking down menacingly on the two out-of-place visitors. Some of the buildings were notched at the top, making them look like castles. Chrissy noticed a gargoyle protruding from one of the buildings, its mouth ferociously agape.

"Why would anyone put such a scary thing on a building?" Chrissy thought, moving faster before her son saw the horrendous thing.

Chrissy had no idea which of the imposing buildings was Arts & Sciences Hall. "This is why I'd never want to travel," she said. "You're in a strange place with strange people. It's . . . creepy."

Jered was too busy taking in the majesty of the surroundings to reply. He felt dwarfed by the huge, shadowy monoliths covered with ivy. Even in the bright morning sunlight, the place seemed dark and foreboding.

There were a few students milling around, but Chrissy was too scared to approach one of them to get directions. Just when she'd resigned herself to the unpleasant necessity of talking to one of the students, she saw a sign pointing towards their destination. Arts & Sciences Hall was one of the tallest buildings they'd encountered that morning. The stone steps leading to the entrance reminded Chrissy of TV programs where actors climbed the proverbial courthouse steps.

A rickety elevator took them up to the psychology department. On the door to room 101 was taped a notice written in thick black magic marker: "ALL STUDENTS: DR. FORD FREUD'S CLASSES WILL MEET AT THEIR REGULAR TIMES ON FRIDAY, NOVEMBER 25."

After Chrissy opened the large, heavy door to the psychology department, she was greeted by an older woman who said, "Welcome to the psychology department. My name is Madeline Stokes. How can I help you?"

"Dr. Freud," Chrissy said in a mousy voice. "My son Jered Barstow is here to see Dr. Freud."

Madeline looked in an appointment book on her desk, then replied, "Let's see . . . Barstow . . . I don't see that you have an appointment with Dr. Freud this morning."

Chrissy thought, "This is what happens when you go to new places. If everything doesn't go just right, you're left floundering."

Jered piped in, "How many rooms are in this building?"

"That's a very good question, young man," Nurse Stokes replied.

The three of them looked at each other, expecting someone to say something. Chrissy broke the silence. "We came here by bus to see Dr. Freud. Are you sure he isn't expecting us?"

Madeline looked again at the calendar, then reported, "I'm sorry, Mrs. Barstow, I just don't see anything."

Chrissy resigned herself to the fact she and Jered made an unnecessary trip. "Okay, thank you," Chrissy said, then turned to leave. As she opened the door, she lamented to her son, "I'm sorry, hon, I thought Miss Moran had this arranged."

"Did you say Moran?" Madeline asked.

Still holding the door open, Chrissy replied, "Yes, Miss Moran is my son's teacher."

"Well, I have an appointment under the name Moran. I thought you said your name was Barstow."

"I'm Mrs. Barstow and this is my son Jered. We were told by Miss Moran to come here this morning to see Dr. Freud."

"Come right in, Mrs. Barstow. You confused me. Please take a seat and I'll let the doctor know you're here."

As she and Jered sat in the waiting area, Chrissy got a bad feeling about the whole affair. The flighty receptionist instilled no degree of confidence. A thought suddenly occurred to Chrissy: while the lady was away from her desk, Chrissy had the opportunity to escape with her son. She considered grabbing her son by the arm and running out of the building without looking back. Chrissy felt comforted when she imagined the two of them running away.

On the heels of this temporary relief were Chrissy's concerns about what might happen to them if they tried to run away. Would these people chase her down? Would they call the police to investigate? Was it a misdemeanor or felony to show up for an appointment with a doctor, then run away without providing any explanation? Chrissy didn't feel good about staying but was too scared to run away.

If her son's candy skull was asked about Chrissy's gut feeling, he may have advised, "A golden opportunity is seldom labeled as such."

CHAPTER TWENTY

Dr. Freud's Analysis

When you're arguably the smartest man in the world, there's rarely an opportunity to be nervous. What is there ever to be anxious about when you know more than anyone else? It was therefore unusual for the famous Dr. Ford Freud to be so tense. He hadn't eaten or slept for two days. Once the appointment with Dr. Moran's daughter was scheduled during the phone call Wednesday afternoon, Dr. Freud sequestered himself in his office to review materials he might need for the meeting. After the meeting Thursday morning, he again remained in his office, reviewing more textbooks and journals in preparation for possibly the most important patient in his career. Whenever he felt his energy flagging over the past 48 hours, the professor revived himself with a large dose of strong black coffee.

If famed psychologist Dr. Moran was sending a child to him for evaluation, one of two things must have been true. One possibility was Dr. Moran found this patient to be particularly interesting and wanted to see if Dr. Freud settled on the same diagnosis he'd reached. The other more intriguing possibility was that Dr. Moran was stumped and needed Dr. Freud's learned insights in order to solve the mystery. One of the challenges of being the zenith of knowledge is there are few opportunities to collaborate with peers who have achieved a similar level of expertise. When you're a shining paragon, everyone comes to you to solve their problems, but you're almost never called into a situation wherein you'll work alongside your intellectual equivalent.

Dr. Freud considered attempting to reach Dr. Moran by telephone to thank him for the opportunity to evaluate the patient. but decided to wait until after he'd reached his conclusions. He didn't want any stray comment by Dr. Moran to taint his analysis. There would be time enough to thank Dr. Moran once Dr. Freud had successfully diagnosed the child.

"Dr. Freud?" Madeline asked from the doorway. "Your nine o'clock patient is here."

"Do you want to try that again?" Dr. Freud replied curtly. Madeline didn't know what to say. "It is currently 9:58 AM, thus . . ."

"Oh, I mean your ten o'clock appointment is here."

"Splendid. Send him and his mother in."

"His mother isn't here. He's accompanied by a woman whose name I think is Moran."

"Curious! That's not what we agreed to, but it will be acceptable. I have already met with Miss Moran, so just send in the patient if you please."

While Nurse Stokes collected the young patient, Dr. Freud lit the stub of a cigar he'd been periodically enjoying since four o'clock that morning.

"Just weave your way through the stacks of papers until you get to the doctor's desk," he heard Madeline say from the doorway.

After the office door was closed, Dr. Freud heard a boy's voice. "There sure is a lot of paper in here. What is all this?"

"Pray, stop ogling my important papers and follow the path to me, my young patient," Dr. Freud ordered.

A boy with wonder spread across his full moon face eventually appeared from amongst the columns. "What are all these papers about?"

"We don't have time for that discussion. Please take a seat so we can begin without further delay."

Jered had been taught by his parents, and especially his father, to always follow the orders of authority, so he dutifully took a seat in front of the doctor's desk.

"As I am sure you already know, I am Dr. Ford Freud. You have been sent to me by Dr. Moran for further evaluation, understood?"

"I don't know a Dr. Moran. The only Moran I know is Miss Moran: she's my teacher. My name's Jered."

Dr. Freud thought for a moment, then reached an epiphany. He nodded his head as his inner voice commented, "Dr. Moran is very crafty. He apparently does not identify himself as a physician, thus encouraging patients to share more information. This is an interesting tactic I need to explore with future patients."

Dr. Freud smiled, then asked in a friendly voice, "Enlighten me as to what psychological testing or analysis you have already undergone."

Jered wasn't sure what the old man was referring to. He scrunched up his face into a look of confusion and replied, "Um, I don't know."

"While I am certain you do not know the official names given to the tests, perhaps you can explain what took place during your previous sessions with the other physician. You remember, the one in Texas."

"I've never been to Texas, Mister."

"Doctor, if you please."

"I've never been to Texas, *Dr. Ifyouplease.*"

It appeared that this patient was going to try Dr. Freud's limited amount of patience right off the bat. Dr. Freud felt the muscles in his jaw clench, and he became aware he was grinding his teeth. What caused his jaw to relax was a sudden recognition of what Dr. Moran would have told the patient. "Yes, of course, Master Jered. You are unable to tell me about the testing because to do so would be a breach of your confidential physician-patient relationship with Dr.

Moran. Is that the reason you are unable to answer my inquiry?" Dr. Freud smiled as he nodded his head, which caused Jered to nod his head as well. "Excellent! Dr. Moran would be very pleased that you did not share that information with me." Dr. Freud leaned across the desk a little and spoke to Jered softly. "You can be assured I shall not ask you any further questions about your previous evaluation and treatment."

The boy wasn't a hundred percent sure what was happening, so he just continued nodding at the doctor, as this seemed to satisfy him. Dr. Freud leaned back in his chair and said, "Let's begin at the beginning, shall we? I'd like to perform a relaxation exercise for me. Close your eyes and clear your mind. I want you to relax, thinking of nothing. Can you do that for me?"

"Sure. I do this with my dad before I go to bed," Jered said, relieved the doctor was at last talking about something he understood.

As instructed, Jered closed his eyes and began taking deep breaths. "That's very good, Master Jered. You have relaxed your body. Now relax your brain." After Dr. Freud noticed the boy's respirations had become deeper and less frequent, he spoke to him in a very quiet, soothing voice. "Tell me about your oldest memory. What was the first experience in your young life you can remember?"

For most people, answering this question would require at least a little thought. In Jered Barstow's case, the answer was readily available. It was something that he'd thought about quite a bit during his short life. "I don't know exactly how old I was, but it was definitely before I started kindergarten. Maybe I was three or four years old, I'm not really sure," Jered replied.

"Currently you are eight years old, correct?"

"Eight and a half. What I remember was that we were getting a family picture taken at K-Mart. We were waiting in line, and there was lots of other people waiting to get their picture taken. Seeing all those kids with their parents made me think about how little I looked like my parents. I got very light, blonde hair, but my dad's and mom's is black. Even though almost all the pictures in our photo album aren't in color, it looks like everyone in my family had very dark hair. No one has light hair like I got. My oldest memory was feeling something wasn't quite right.

"How recessive genes operate is difficult to explain to a child such as yourself with limited exposure to the intricacies of genetics. Let me assure you, though, that a child may look different than his parents due to the way the cells from the mother and father combine."

"Yeah, we learned in school about how pea plants can have different colored peas." Dr. Freud's right eyebrow lifted when he heard Jered say this. "But my hair's not the only thing," Jered continued. "I started noticing that my parents just seem different than me in a lot of ways. The way they talk, how their faces look, and just . . . well . . . they're different. I love my mom and dad a lot, but I don't know for sure I'm their real son."

"Do you know what adoption is?"

"Yeah. There was this girl in my kindergarten and first grade classes who was born in China. She was adopted by a mom and dad here in University City. One time I asked my Mom if I was adopted, and she said 'No.' She said I grew inside her tummy and I was born at University Hospital. She showed me pictures of her while I was inside her body; she looks really fat. There's even a picture of my Mom holding me in the hospital."

"So, if you're not adopted, why do you think you're so different than your parents?"

"I . . . I just feel it. Deep down like. I just feel it somewhere inside my body they might not be my real parents. It's kinda like when you feel inside that you're hungry. I just feel a certain way inside me." Dr. Freud remained silent, hoping his young patient would continue down this path of inquiry. He knew a child may try to distance himself from other family members as a means of dealing with behavior problems.

His young patient was trying to change the focus of the session. Dr. Freud planned to address the boy's morbid fixation on skeletons, but the patient was introducing aspects of Foundling Fantasy Syndrome. Experienced practitioners such as Dr. Ford Freud know that they must remain on task and not be led astray by what the patient wants to talk about. Dr. Freud was determined to keep the session focused on the underlying concern.

"My understanding is that you consider yourself quite an accomplished creator of visual artwork, is that accurate?" Dr. Freud asked, studying the drawing provided by Kerri Moran.

Once again, the doctor spoke in a way that almost sounded like a foreign language to Jered. The boy tried to translate what he said, then asked, "Are you asking me if I like to draw?"

"That is precisely what I asked you," Dr. Freud sniffed indignantly. "Have you spent more of your time drawing than attending to your studies in language arts and grammar?"

As he had before, it seemed to Jered that the best thing to do was to simply agree with the doctor. "Yeah, I guess so. If you say so."

"I say many things and I can assure you that everything I say is most definitely *so*." Without looking up from Jered's picture, Dr. Freud grinned at his clever wordplay. "My understanding is that you're quite an artist, is that accurate?" Dr. Freud cooed in a velvety smooth voice.

"Yeah, I really like drawing pictures," Jered responded eagerly. "And I'm good at it."

"So I hear. I am a lover of fine art. Would you mind drawing a picture for me?"

"I guess, but I don't have nothing to draw with."

Dr. Freud gestured towards a cardboard box sitting on the edge of his desk. "That box will contain everything that you require."

Jered slid the box towards him and found a large collection of crayons and paper in it. Dr. Freud moved some of the piles of papers from his desk to the floor so that there was a small area in front of Jered that was clear. When Dr. Freud pushed aside some of the piles, there was a puff of dust and cigar ash.

"Okay, so what do you want me to draw for you? I can draw cars really good."

"*Well.* You can draw *well*," Dr. Freud corrected.

"I'm not sure what you mean. Are you talking about a wishing well? You want a picture of a well where you throw pennies to get a wish to come true?"

"If you listen carefully, I will clearly tell you what I want you to draw." Jered became silent in response to the doctor's sharp rebuke. Dr. Freud tried to reopen the path of communication with his patient by attempting to chuckle goodheartedly. "What I meant to say is I would appreciate it if you would draw me a picture of you. You as a tree."

"A what?"

"Draw a picture of yourself, but as if you were a tree."

Jered felt a sense of pride that the doctor asked him to draw a picture, but he was also a little nervous. He'd been put on the spot and wanted to create a good drawing for the old man. Jered considered the request, then said, "I don't think I can do that."

"I was told you were a good artist."

"I am, but it doesn't make sense. I'm a boy, not a tree."

"That's the challenge, Master Jered. I want you to show me how you'd look if you were actually a tree."

As most children do, Jered had drawn plenty of funny and silly things, but Jered was hesitant to step into the world of make-believe with a doctor. "I can't draw something like that. Can I draw something else?"

Dr. Freud wrote in his notebook, "Patient refuses to engage in the Tree-Self Drawing Test."

"I'm sorry; I just don't get it," Jered added.

"Let us proceed to another task. Would you be willing to draw me a picture of yourself?"

"Okay. Do you want me to be doing something in the picture?"

"Whatever you choose. I do not wish to impose myself on your artistic ability."

On the desk Jered lined up the crayons from dark to light colors. He began drawing, making use of several different colors, all under the watchful gaze of Dr. Freud. During the entire time Jered was drawing, Dr. Freud was evaluating him. What was his facial expression when he was drawing? *Intensity and focus.* What expression did he draw on his face? *He was smiling pleasantly.* Did the patient draw any kind of background? *No, just himself.*

"Next I want you to draw a picture of your best friend if he was some kind of animal." Jered's face was again confused. "Is that something you can draw, oh great artist of University City?" When Jered didn't answer, the doctor raised his voice a bit to get the patient's attention. "Well? What is the reason for this delay? A drawing of your best friend as an animal, if you please."

Jered averted his eyes from the doctor, mumbling softly, "I . . . I don't really think I have a best friend. There's a couple kids I might play with every once in a while, but they're not a real best friend."

"Everyone has a best friend," Dr. Freud scoffed. "First you won't draw yourself as a tree, and now you hand me yet another refusal?"

"No, I'll draw stuff for you, it's just that . . ."

"Every child has someone they confide in. Sometimes a child's best friend can be a family member, instead of another child. Who is it that *you* go to for advice? Who do you share stories with?"

The first person to pop into Jered's head was JoJo, but she was his grandma, not really a best friend. Jered loved her dearly, but she didn't seem to fit into the description of a best friend. He was about to tell the old man there was no one in his life who fit the description of a best friend, then asked, "Can I just draw my best friend? Ya know, as he really is, not an animal?"

"At this point I am willing to accept your terms. Please do so. Draw your best friend on another piece of paper."

Dr. Freud looked over his glasses as the boy began drawing. After a few minutes, Dr. Freud said, "You are drawing a picture of your best friend, is that correct?"

Jered didn't look up. "Yeah, you said to draw him as he really is."

After another minute or so, Jered said, "Almost done."

Dr. Freud was incredulous. "Really? Almost done?"

With a broad look of satisfaction, Jered held up his drawing so the doctor could see it. Dr. Freud looked at the picture, then his patient, back to the drawing, and then back to his patient in rapid succession. After a momentary silence, the doctor asked, "What is this supposed to be?"

Proudly, Jered declared, "This is my best friend, Skelly."

Dr. Freud gazed at his patient, trying to determine whether he was the butt of an elaborate practical joke. Had Dr. Moran sent this patient to him as a prank? He scanned his office for any hidden cameras which may have been placed by Allen Funt for the *Candid Camera* television program, but Dr. Freud didn't detect any. Returning his attention to Jered, the physician said, "This looks like a skull."

Still smiling, Jered said, "Thanks. This is my friend Skelly. He's a skull."

Dr. Freud stared at Jered with a mixture of puzzlement and concern. Plenty of psychopathic patients had been evaluated by Dr. Freud. As one of the world's pre-eminent consulting physicians, Dr. Freud had been summoned to evaluate prison inmates to determine the reasons they committed horrific crimes. He'd looked into the eyes of maniacs and seen nothing but chaos. Behind the eyes of murderers, he'd seen unbridled rage. Was this patient a maniac or a budding criminal?

Dr. Freud employed all his skills of perception as he evaluated the young patient. Was the boy trying to manipulate the doctor by claiming his best friend was a skull? If not, why would the patient use such inappropriate and shocking imagery? The professor's bushy gray eyebrows drew together as he tried to visually dissect the mind of his patient. Despite these efforts, he was having difficulty unveiling the hidden reason for the boy's ghoulish fixation. For some reason, the professor sensed his thinking was not as sharp as it usually was.

Still searching for a chink in the boy's armor, Dr. Freud probed further. "Do you understand what a best friend is, Master Jered?"

"Sure, I guess so," the boy said casually, not recognizing the trained physician was actively trying to deconstruct the boy's actions and words. "Kinda like you said: a friend you share stories with. And get ideas from, like advice and stuff."

After a prolonged silence during which the world-renowned practitioner of the behavioral arts continued to scrutinize his patient, Dr. Freud asked, "Do you actually believe a human skull is your best friend?"

Without hesitation, Jered replied, "Sure, I think so. He sometimes helps me with things."

Dr. Freud's analytic brain tumbled to a rational explanation for what the boy was saying. "Ah, I think I may understand. Are you referring to the skull inside your body? Is Skelly the name you have given to your own skull: the part of the body which protects your brain?"

"Huh, uh," Jered said, shaking his head. "Skelly isn't inside my head."

"Then where, pray tell, is Skelly?"

"He's sitting on the little table next to my bed."

"Are you sure?"

"Yeah, that's where he stays."

"How can you be so sure that the talking skull is there if you are here with me?"

Jered looked at the physician incredulously, a bit surprised being asked a question the boy thought was downright absurd. "Because that's where I left him."

"And how long has he remained on that table?"

"Ever since JoJo gave him to me."

Dr. Freud jotted a short note, then asked, "Who is JoJo? Is that the name you have given to another skull or piece of a skeleton? Is JoJo a talking ribcage, perhaps?"

"No, JoJo is my grandma," Jered giggled.

"Is your grandma a skeleton as well?"

Jered laughed. "No, silly, she's my grandma. A real grandma."

"Ah, so there is a difference in your mind between what is real. and what is make believe. Is that what you are telling me, Master Jered?"

The boy thought for a few seconds and then agreed. "Sure. Everyone knows that there are things that're make-believe, then there are things that're real."

"Give me examples of things that only exist in the make-believe world."

"Well, I guess, lots and lots of things. Scooby-Doo. Bugs Bunny. Monsters."

"Monsters, you say? What kind of monsters are you referring to?"

"Frankenstein is a monster, but he isn't real. Godzilla isn't." Jered thought for a moment, then added to the list. "Dracula isn't. A monster in your nightmare ain't, I mean isn't real. My dad says there's no such thing as monsters that hide under your bed, in your closet, or in dark basements."

"Ah, so you recognize that monsters do not hide under your bed, is that correct?" Dr. Freud asked, making a mental note that this patient may be smarter than another young patient he'd recently evaluated.

"I guess all I can say is I've never known anyone who had a monster living under their bed. I make sure to jump to my bed, so I'm not scared of a monster under my bed."

"And there is no reason you should be afraid of a monster under your bed." Dr. Freud looked as though he was pleased with Jered's last answer and jotted a note. "Let us talk some more about things you think are real, as opposed to those that you know are made up. You told me your grandmother is real: what else is real?"

Jered was momentarily stumped at the question because the list of real things was so enormous. "Well, I guess everything that's around us is real. Everything that's not pretend."

"Such as?"

"You. Me." Jered looked around the room, listing things he saw. "This desk. This building. My clothes. My shoes. These books all around us. All these papers. You know, everything. These are all real."

"Skelly?"

"Yeah, stuff like that. Skelly, my Mom, my Dad, our house: stuff like that."

"Your friend Skelly is definitely real, is that what you are claiming?"

Without hesitation, Jered responded, "Of course. I can hold him in my hands if I want to. All I have to do is pick him up. I could lick him if I wanted."

Dr. Freud looked appalled. "You mean with your tongue?"

"Sure. I could eat Skelly if I wanted, but I'll never do it. I don't want him to go away."

"You have the ability to eat a skull?"

"Sure, if I wanted to."

Just about the time Dr. Freud had the patient figured out, the ground beneath him seemed to shift. The fog in the professor's head seemed to be getting worse as the interview continued. "When it comes down to what is real, you recognize that skeletons are scary, right? You realize you *should* be afraid of skeletons and skulls?"

"I used to be scared of them. My mom's afraid of lots of things and that made me scared of stuff like skeletons, too. But my dad taught me skeletons don't gotta be scary. Did ya know some skeletons can help you, even talk to you?"

Dr. Freud's eyes narrowed as he tried assembling the curious puzzle which had been presented to him. "Help me understand this situation. Hold up the picture of you next to the one of the skull and give me an example of the type of conversation you might have with it."

Jered held the two pictures, moving them as each spoke. "Hi, Skelly. Hi, Jered. What's going on? Oh, not much. Can you help me figure something out? Sure, what is it? I want to make sure I don't make my parents fight again. Okay, well, my mean old Uncle Ed used to tell me that . . . um . . . a butterfly won't flap its wings if the farmer's cow isn't standing in the rain. What does that mean? It just means that . . . sorta like . . ." Jered couldn't think of what next to say, so he put the pictures down. "Kinda like that sorta stuff."

Watching the impromptu puppet show, Dr. Freud felt a bit light-headed. He squeezed then opened his eyes a few times to clear the fog from his mind, then asked, "So, you were once afraid of skeletons and now they actively participate in your life? Is that what you are suggesting?"

"I guess, yeah. I'm not as scared of some things no more. My teacher helped me not to be afraid of bullies or things I'd never done before. My dad's taught me not be afraid of skeletons. He also taught me how to use my imagination, so it feels like you're kinda flying."

As he often did when deep in thought, Dr. Freud clasped his hands together and placed them under his nose so it appeared he was praying. His high back leather desk chair emitted a long squeak as Dr. Freud leaned backward. Although the old man's eyes were open, Jered got the sense Dr. Freud wasn't actually looking at anything in the room. Instead, he appeared to be looking through the walls of the office, towards something very far away. The boy was concerned when he saw the color gradually dissipate from the old man's face, leaving a cold, stone golem. The doctor remained frozen in this position for minutes, causing Jered to become a little scared.

Hesitatingly, Jered asked, "Dr. *Ifyouplease*? Hello? Are you okay?"

The renowned scholar seated across the desk from Jered didn't respond. His analytical mind was churning through a myriad of thoughts. The reclusive genius Dr. Moran had sent him a very unusual patient, and the breadth of Dr. Freud's abilities were being tested. Dr. Freud's concentration was so intense he became profoundly lightheaded. His entire body felt light as a feather. Eventually he wasn't in his office any longer: he was floating in an ocean of paper. Dogpaddling in pages torn from books and endless sheets of his handwritten notes, Dr. Freud randomly grabbed pieces of paper, looking for the one that held the answer to this patient's problems. When his head sunk below the waves of papers, Dr. Freud held his breath, then pushed himself back to the surface.

As he bobbed up and down the increasingly large swells in the paper ocean, the doctor heard a voice. At first it sounded like nothing more than the cry of a seagull but then he could make out the words, "You don't look so good. Are you okay?"

The seagull's question caused the doctor to reply plaintively, "You have no idea how difficult it is to live in a world surrounded by insane people."

In response, the bird said, "Huh?"

Dr. Freud didn't explain himself any further to the seagull, and just let the waves of paper carry him up and then down in the turbulent ocean. There was no danger of drowning. Somehow, he knew he could safely swim all day in the paper ocean. "If I am always taking care of others, I do not have the opportunity to pay attention to the illnesses that are ravaging me." he said.

In the midst of this storm, the doctor heard a young boy's voice: "I don't understand."

The old doctor suddenly startled, as if he'd awoken after momentarily dozing off. The doctor's expression was at first one of confusion. Jered saw him blink his eyes several times, after which the old man looked embarrassed.

"Are you okay?" Jered asked tentatively.

There was still fog in Dr. Freud's head, but it wasn't quite as thick. He remembered something about an ocean and a seagull, but he wasn't yet clear what happened. Gathering some of the papers on his desk and arranging them into a neat pile, Dr. Freud tried to sound offended. "Of course I am, Master Jered. Why would you think otherwise?"

"Well, you seemed to kinda get spaced out for a little bit and . . ." Jered replied, his answer trailing off when the doctor's eyes suddenly widened, and he intensely glared at the boy.

Dr. Freud was concerned what he might have inadvertently disclosed if he had some kind of lapse in his consciousness. "Did I say something? What did I say?" Seeing the boy was frightened, the psychiatrist managed to soften his voice. "Did you hear me say anything?"

"Um, it was something about the world being filled with insane people."

"That's it? Nothing more?" Jered shook his head, and Dr. Freud was relieved. The professor knew the unconscious mind is a pit that descends all the way to insanity. If the mouth gives the unconscious mind a voice, horrific things meant to be kept in darkness can be let loose. He'd apparently made it through this bizarre episode without unintentionally sharing the thoughts best kept under wraps. With that pitfall averted, the doctor focused himself on what had just happened to him. Dr. Freud peered over his glasses at the boy. "Did you just do something to me? Something to my thoughts?"

"Like what?" the confused boy asked.

"How about *you* tell *me*?"

"You're scaring me, mister."

"Doctor."

"What just happened to you? Did you fall asleep? Were you talking in your sleep?" Jered asked, watching the old doctor carefully in case there was another rapid change in his demeanor.

Dr. Freud continued to stare at Jered, as he struggled to clear his head. "Nothing. Nothing at all," the doctor said in a nonchalant tone. "I sometimes become so engrossed in my thoughts it overcomes me." When his patient continued to look at him warily, Dr. Freud stated, "That interlude was merely another test I have administered to you. The objective of that test was to determine if you were paying attention. You apparently *were* paying attention, which I applaud. At times I introduce such elements to make the session something more than a mere exercise of joyless analysis. How did this make *you* feel?"

Once again, Jered thought it sounded almost as if the doctor was speaking a foreign language. The only thing he understood was the doctor's last question, so Jered answered it. "Um, I guess I'd say . . . surprised. You just were kinda out of it. Did you fall asleep?"

Dr. Freud's retort was loud and pointed. "Certainly not! What an outlandish allegation for a patient to make! I was in the throes of deep introspection and analysis, which you are too young to fully appreciate."

"Okay, okay, I guess you didn't."

"Precisely! Now you can take your leave. I do not need anything further from you, so this session is now completed." Dr. Freud pushed the intercom button. "Nurse Stokes, please bring Miss Moran into the office to collect the patient."

"I'm sorry, Dr. Freud, I don't think Miss Moran is here."

"Then who is out there with you?"

"Let me ask." There was a short pause, then Nurse Stokes replied, "This woman is apparently the patient's mother."

Exasperated, Dr. Freud growled, "Just send her in to collect the patient right away!"

There was a long awkward silence while doctor and patient waited for Jered's mother to arrive. All the while, Jered felt as though the old man's eyes were still burning holes into him. Even during this silent interval, Dr. Freud's analytical mind was processing the information he'd collected. He'd momentarily lost control of his patient during this session and he'd have to determine why.

"Hello," Chrissy said in a mousy voice, "I'm here to pick up Jered."

The doctor's thoughts were still monopolized with his ongoing analysis, so he just silently brushed the back of his hand in Chrissy's direction.

"Do I need a prescription or something, doctor?" Chrissy asked hesitatingly.

The learned doctor remained totally immersed in his thoughts and didn't reply. When Chrissy and Jered returned to the waiting area, she asked Nurse Stokes when she'd know of the doctor's diagnosis.

"We will call you when the doctor is ready to share his conclusions with you. I can't tell you how long it will take. Thank you for stopping by, Mrs. Moran."

Chrissy was about to correct the doctor's assistant, then decided to just leave. As they walked to the bus stop, Chrissy gently inquired about what had occurred. "What went on in there?"

Jered was unimpressed with the experience. For the most part, the whole session with Dr. Freud was a jumble of questions and comments the boy couldn't make heads or tails of, so he brushed them off. "We just talked. Oh, and then I drew a couple pictures for him."

"What did you draw?"

"A picture of me, then a picture of the candy skull JoJo brought me."

Chrissy's eyes widened. "What did the doctor say about the skull?"

"Not much, just that he heard I was a good drawer. Where are we gonna go shopping?"

"Are you sure he didn't say anything else about the skull?" Chrissy pressed.

"Naw, I think he's a little sick, like the flu or something, because he didn't look very good. I thought he might've fallen asleep, but he didn't. Can we find a bathroom at the first store we go to?"

"Store?"

"You said we could go look at toys after we stopped here to see *Dr. Ifyouplease*. We're still going, right?"

"Sure. Yes, of course, honey."

During the bus ride into downtown University City, young Jered's thoughts were full of anticipation, wondering what new toys he might see. The unusual meeting with the unusual old man quickly became an afterthought. On the other hand, Chrissy could think of nothing except what the doctor might ultimately tell her about her son.

CHAPTER TWENTY-ONE

Dr. Freud's Lecture

On an episode of *The Rockford Files*, James Garner informed viewers in his sly, devil-may-care voice that he didn't "suffer fools gladly." Although he wasn't completely sure, Rodney thought Jim Rockford wasn't the first who used this phrase. After giving it some thought, he concluded John Lennon coined the phrase around the time The Beatles broke up. Whether it was Rockford or Lennon who came up with this saying, Rodney was growing increasingly weary of the fools at his job. Especially his boss: King Fool. Being forced to work on a day he was supposed to be lounging at home put Rodney in a very foul mood.

"I'm the only one here?" Rodney asked incredulously, holding out his arms to emphasize all the desks were empty.

"Yeah, I just needed a summary on your projects." King Fool could hardly look Rodney in the face as he spoke. Rodney knew his boss must have done something stupid, and now it was up to his star employee to bail him out of a mess. "What I need to get a handle on," his boss explained, "is where you stand on the various projects you've been assigned to. If you've just done a little bit or you haven't had a chance to work on some of them at all yet, that's fine, I just need to get a comprehensive review of where you're at on everything."

"It'll take me a little bit of time to do all that," Rodney said with a hint of frustration.

"Well, I figured the phone won't be ringing today and there's nobody else around, so we'd be able to get a handle on this faster."

Rodney sat at his desk and begrudgingly started compiling the information per King Fool's edict. Despite getting some extra sleep, he was still wrestling with the vestiges of the headache that had persisted since Monday night, which caused his left eye to periodically twitch. "Why are you still hassling me?" he asked the headache under his breath. Rodney wished the headache would either come to a full boil or just go away once and for all.

While he waited for the Xerox machine to warm up, Rodney let his mind wander. Although he'd never written it down on paper, Rodney kept a running list of the burdens he bore. Number one on the list was being required to suffer the fools at his office. His teachers had preached that having a high school diploma would open doors in the real world. While this ended up being partially true, Rodney learned these doors usually opened on tedious jobs without much chance of advancing to the real money. Unlike the self-employed private eye Jim Rockford, Rodney was forced to suffer the fools who surrounded him at work. At least for the time being. Until things changed. Until Jered changed.

For reasons unknown to Rodney, he seemed to often be at odds with his boss. When these conflicts arose, Rodney did his best to suffer the fool, then found an empty bathroom stall where he could focus on calming his nerves. Inner peace was usually restored when Rodney fantasized about King Fool getting his just desserts. In his imagination, Rodney soared through the night sky until he was drawn into his boss' house. After whispering suggestions into the ear of his boss, Rodney watched as King Fool went on a crime spree. Most times his boss was captured and placed in a cold prison cell to rot for the rest of his life. Other times the police had no choice but to fire their service revolvers, causing the criminal to fall to the ground in a heap. Rodney vacillated as to which ending he liked best.

Going to the downtown department stores wasn't appealing to Chrissy, but Jered wanted to go. Besides, taking Jered to a few stores would permit Chrissy to truthfully tell her husband that they went shopping that morning. Traversing the swarms of shoppers was exhausting and all she could think about was the psychiatrist. Chrissy's heart wasn't into it, so she decided to cut the shopping trip short after just an hour. On the bus ride home, Chrissy was so tense she could feel her neck muscles become hard as a rock. She'd thought taking Jered to the psychiatrist would calm her and give her peace of mind, but it seemed to have had the opposite effect. Her imagination kept coming up with horrific scenarios about what the doctor might conclude. Chrissy was pleased that Jered appeared relaxed, chattering excitedly about toys he'd seen at the department store.

During the entire bus ride home, Jered was thinking about Christmas and what toys he might receive. The earlier conversation with Dr. Freud was so confusing to the boy, he didn't even think about it. Instead, he thought of how his Major Matt Mason's left arm would no longer bend and how much he hoped a new one would be under the tree. Special art paper like the kind Miss Moran had him use during their lessons was also going to be high on his wish list.

Later that afternoon, Jered asked, "I'm gonna ride my bike, is that okay?"

"Sure, just wear something warm on your head: it's pretty nippy out there."

Once Jered was gone, Chrissy sat at the kitchen table, staring blankly through the window as she second guessed herself. Had she and Miss Moran detected the beginnings of an emotional problem or was the whole affair nothing to be concerned about? What she hoped the doctor was going to tell her was that this was all a natural part of an imaginative child's development and nothing further needed to be done. However, the fact that Dr. Freud didn't tell her everything was fine immediately after he finished talking to Jered led Chrissy to worry that something was indeed wrong.

One moment she was hopeful and the next she was pessimistic. After batting these thoughts back and forth for a while, Chrissy abruptly stood up and put on her apron. She resolved that she needed to keep busy, otherwise time was going to drag. "Besides," she announced to the empty kitchen, "I've got a family to keep together!"

When Chrissy was growing up, her mother was fond of saying, "There's always something in a house that needs cleaning." Chrissy hoped doing some housework would keep her mind occupied. Although she went through the motions of cleaning her small house, she wasn't paying much attention to what she was doing. It was almost like she was a robot, mindlessly going through the chores she'd been programmed to complete. As Chrissy dusted, she was able to forget about Dr. Freud for a minute, but then her concerns about his final analysis would kick down the door and barge back into her conscious mind. What conclusions would he reach? How long will it take before her little boy is back to normal?

She was so preoccupied with these thoughts that she was careless with the dust cloth, accidentally knocking over one of her figurines. The small glass statue of a little boy holding a flower had been a gift from her father when she was very young. For most of her life, Chrissy treasured the glass boy who shyly held a flower out to her. There were plenty of times prior to meeting Rodney when she wondered if this was the only boy who'd ever offer her a flower. As soon as the little boy started to fall, Chrissy snapped out of her daydream, reaching out to snatch it out of the air. Gravity was too fast for Chrissy and shards of the boy scattered when it hit the hardwood floor.

Chrissy looked down in horror at the destroyed figurine. She dropped to her knees and gathered some of the larger fragments, but it was obvious there was no possibility of repairing the flower-toting boy. A jagged crack appeared in Chrissy's brave veneer and she wanted to cry. There was something deep inside her that suggested weeping over a cheap dime store bauble was an affront to the real world concerns she was currently dealing with. She did her best to stifle her sobs as she solemnly retrieved a broom and dustpan to clean up the mess. Lovingly sweeping up the remnants of the boy, she gently laid the broken pieces to rest in a paper grocery bag. One of the large pieces made a sickening thud when it hit the bottom of the bag.

Once the solemn duty was completed, Chrissy took the grocery bag from room to room and emptied all the wastebaskets. When she leaned over to grab the small wastebasket in Jered's bedroom, she caught sight of the grinning skull on his nightstand. It was clear the skull was laughing at her and mocking the fact that she'd accidentally broken the statue of the little boy. She turned her head away in disgust. Chrissy sensed the grinning skull felt victorious now that her cherished glass figurine was destroyed. After emptying the wastebasket, Chrissy managed to bring herself to once again look at the skull. Glowering at the terrible thing, she thought of how it was unfair the precious little boy was in a million pieces, but the scary skull was intact and permitted to mock her.

She frowned in disgust at the skull, then noticed she still had the dust cloth tucked into her apron. A cunning thought flashed in her mind. Chrissy looked around the room, guiltily checking if the coast was clear as she approached Jered's nightstand. She carefully and slowly dusted the nightstand, making sure that the dust cloth was touching the skull. With a sudden flourish, she whipped the rag away, causing the skull to slide off the nightstand. Just before the candy skull shattered on the floor, Chrissy thought she heard a faint voice say, "Wait!" She later concluded she hadn't heard anything; her imagination had just got the best of her.

Wearing the satisfied smile of a victorious prizefighter, Chrissy was pleased to see that JoJo's awful present was obliterated. The corn syrup holding the sugar together was dry and brittle, making it no match for the violent collision on the hardwood floor. If one hadn't seen it prior to its fall, there'd been no way of knowing that it had been until recently molded into the shape of a skull. Even the larger shards of sugar provided no clue as to what it had been. In stark contrast to the care she used in sweeping up the pieces of the glass boy, Chrissy unceremoniously swept up the pieces of sugar, and dropped them into the bag.

"I'm so sorry, honey," Chrissy said, trying to sound apologetic. "I came in your room and found it shattered on the floor. A gust of wind must've blown it off the nightstand." After rehearsing her lines a few times, Chrissy thought she'd been able to say them with an adequate amount of regret in her voice. "No, I'm sorry, it broke all up and there was nothing left but little clumps of sugar. It just disintegrated when it hit the floor." Chrissy was so focused on reciting her lines, she was startled when the phone rang. She ran to the telephone while carrying the bag.

"Dr. Ford Freud would like to inform you that you need to attend his lecture later this afternoon," the receptionist said in a stilted and formal voice. "He wanted me to inform you he will include his analysis of your son as a case study during his presentation to the students."

Even after spending so much time wondering what the doctor's conclusions would be, Chrissy was taken a little off guard by the phone call. "Today? But we only have one car. What time will I need to be there?"

"The lecture begins at 4:30 in the main lecture hall located in Arts & Sciences Hall." In a friendlier voice, the receptionist added, "He doesn't like it when students or observers arrive late, so do yourself a favor and be on time."

As she hung up the phone, Chrissy heard the rumbling engine of the garbage truck approaching. She ran out to the patio, dropped the grocery bag into their metal trash can, then rushed the can to the curb.

"That was close!" the man holding onto the back of the garbage truck said. "You almost missed us!"

"Yeah, I plum-near forgot there was trash pick-up today," Chrissy replied, watching as the can was emptied into the maw of the truck.

"A lot of people forgot or they're still out of town." As he handed the empty can back to her, he said, "Enjoy the rest of your holiday weekend."

She checked the street in both directions but didn't see Jered. It was nearly 3:30 and she'd need to get to the bus stop soon if she was going to make it to the university on time. Unless he lost track of time, she was sure he'd be home soon. One of the TV stations showed cartoons every weekday from 3:30 until the 5:00 local news. For kids, this was must-see TV: a half hour of Looney Tunes, followed by Tom & Jerry, and finally The Flintstones.

As she waited in the house for her son, Chrissy began to experience conflicting emotions. She wanted to hear what the doctor had to say but at the same time she was fearful of finding out what he'd concluded. At 3:30, Jered rushed through the front door, dumped his coat onto the living room floor, and plopped himself in front of the television. Chrissy took a moment to enjoy the sight of her son sitting on the floor watching TV, his rosy nose and cheeks glowing from the brisk November air.

Jered noticed his mother was looking at him. "What? Is something wrong?"

"Everything's fine," Chrissy reassured her son. "I was just noticing how red your face is. Was it cold out there?"

Without taking his eyes from the TV, he replied, "Naw, just a little."

While Jered was engrossed in a Wagnerian opera starring Bugs Bunny and Elmer Fudd, his mother said she needed to run an errand.

"Can I go with you?" Jered asked.

His mother hesitated, then said, "No, it's probably best if you didn't. I just have some boring stuff to do. Besides, I have to take the bus to get there, and I don't want to pay for two fares. Will you be alright if I leave you for a while by yourself?"

Jered shrugged his shoulders. "Sure, I can take care of myself until Dad gets home. No big whoop."

There was a part of Chrissy that hoped her son would beg her to stay. If Jered objected, she'd have a good reason not to go to the university. She was getting increasingly apprehensive about making her way back there and attending her first college lecture. On the other hand, if she didn't go, she might never find out if her son had a problem. "Are you sure? You'll be in the house all by yourself. Don't you think you'll get scared?"

Jered could tell his mother was nervous about leaving him alone and tried to reassure her. "It's okay, Mom, I'm not a scaredy-cat no more."

"I put some clothes on your bed; will you put them away before I get home?"

"Sure, Mom," the boy said absently, his attention still fixed on the TV.

Chrissy's hesitant smile contained both admiration for her brave son and a mother's intuition that something wasn't quite right. Why did she feel she was somehow leaving her son in danger? "You won't turn on the stove or oven, right?"

"I know the rules, Mom. I won't use anything that I have to plug in or that is hot."

"And you won't answer the door if a stranger comes? You won't have any friends over to the house while you're alone?"

Jered assured his mother he'd do none of these things. Although it didn't happen often, this wasn't the first time being left at home by himself for a few hours. "I know what to do," he assured his mother. "Don't worry. I'm a big boy."

Finally satisfied, Chrissy kissed the top of her son's head. "You're such a brave little boy; much braver than I am."

What Jered said next surprised both of them. With his eyes still on the TV, words popped into Jered's head. These words simply rolled off his tongue and were in the air before Jered realized what on earth he was saying. "Maybe being brave isn't always such a good thing," the boy said in a dreamy voice. "Maybe we *should* be afraid of more things. If we're not scared of them, maybe they'll hurt us."

Chrissy was taken aback by what her young son said. "What do you mean by that, honey? Are you alright?" she asked with concern.

Jered shook his head as if he was banishing an unpleasant memory from his mind. "What? I don't know where that came from. That was dumb." He shook his head once again, adding, "Don't worry, Mom, I'm fine."

She watched him for a little while longer. When he laughed at the cartoon, she was confident there was nothing wrong. "Okay, well, there's leftover casserole in the fridge. You and your dad can have that for supper. I'm not sure how long this will take, because I have to switch busses a couple of times."

"I'll see you when you get back, Mom," he said. When Jered noticed his mother was still looking at him pensively, he added, "I'll be fine."

As she collected her purse and coat, part of her wanted to just sit down next to Jered and watch cartoons with him. The possibility of Dr. Freud relieving her fears was too strong, though.

It took the entire afternoon for Rodney to finish the reports King Fool wanted. Just as Rodney was about to leave, his boss dropped a bombshell. Despite the fact he hated his job, Rodney was nevertheless infuriated when he was fired.

"How can you do this to me?!" Rodney fumed, waving his arms angrily. "This isn't fair!"

His boss did his best to handle the firing in a professional manner. "Clean out your desk. I did you a favor by doing this today, so you could leave without everyone watching."

"A favor? Are you kidding me?" Rodney yelled at his boss.

Rodney stomped out of his boss' office as he continued to shout. The ranting was so loud his boss resorted to ordering Rodney to vacate the premises. "We'll have someone deliver your personal effects to your home. You just need to leave."

Rodney stormed out of the office building, all the while yelling a long list of reasons why he shouldn't have been fired. It was galling: even though he'd done his best to suffer the fools at work, the numbskulls had fired him anyway.

"That's gratitude for ya," Rodney grumbled.

On the walk to his car, the left side of his head started to throb. Sometimes people say that they're so angry they can't see straight, but in Rodney's case this was actually true. When he pulled out of the parking lot, the pressure behind his left eye made it difficult to see through it. It didn't take long for the pain to spread to his right eye. Even the dim glow from the November sunset was enough to accost his light sensitive eyes. Rodney donned sunglasses to shield him from the painful light, but they afforded very little relief. As the pain intensified, Rodney began seeing flashes of colorful lights. The only thing that took his mind off the headache was daydreaming about what he'd like to do the man who just fired him.

"If I could control my Way-Outs," he thought wistfully, "I could give King Fool what he deserves." Alas, Rodney didn't have such ability. It wasn't long before he was so enraged that his forehead felt warm to the touch. If the stars aligned and Rodney took a trip that night, he figured the random person he visited was going to be the unluckiest sap in the world.

By the time Rodney pulled into the driveway, the late November sky was dark. The time spent sitting in traffic gave Rodney an opportunity to sort out a few things. There was no way he was going to tell Chrissy he got fired while he was fighting one of his headaches. Nothing would be harmed if he waited until Monday to tell her the bad news. Further, he knew the likelihood of experiencing a Way-Out was high, especially since he didn't have one after the argument with Chrissy. If he went on a Way-Out, the headache would go away, and he could think a little clearer.

Between the end of *Looney Tunes* and the beginning of *The Flintstones*, Jered had an unsettling thought. Would his father still be mad at him when he got home from work? Had the proverbial hatchet been buried, or was his dad going to resume the argument where he left off the previous night? His dad had never before shown such anger, so the boy didn't know what to expect. Jered wondered if he should have asked his mother not to leave. To keep his mind off this, Jered stayed focused on the cartoons.

Just as *The Flintstones* finished, Jered heard his father's car rumble into the driveway. Jered decided he'd just pretend nothing had happened on Thursday night and see how his father responded. Fred Flintstone often got into shouting matches with Wilma and

Barney, yet they were on friendly terms just a few minutes later. Hopefully, this was how it would be with his dad.

Rodney turned off the car and closed his eyes. He rolled down his window and took several deep breaths of the biting November air as he tried to compose himself. The painful chaos was rampaging full tilt inside his head. It was severe enough that Rodney wondered if he'd be able to eat any supper. Unless the headache abated at least a bit, he might have to change clothes and descend directly to the cool dark basement. He took a few more deep breaths and tried to be calm. Just about the time he was able to relax a little, he'd remember he was now unemployed, which caused his anger to rise. When he thought about King Fool, his pain surged.

"Suck it up," he told himself as he finally got out of the car.

When Rodney walked through the front door, his son was seated on the couch with his hands folded in his lap. Rodney wondered why Jered was posing for the magazine cover of *Obedient Child Monthly*. Jered tried to sound as if nothing horrible had occurred the night before. "Hi, Dad."

"Hi, son," Rodney replied with a touch of wariness in his voice. Jered remained seated, smiling at his father. Rodney glanced into the kitchen but didn't see Chrissy. Usually she was eager to regale him with news of her day as soon as he set foot in the house. "Where's your mother?"

"She had to run an important errand. Said there's leftovers in the fridge," Jered replied.

Without removing his coat, Rodney dropped himself down into his easy chair, letting out a sigh of relief. "What a day," he lamented.

"I'm not supposed to use the oven when Mom's gone, so the casserole is still in the fridge."

After resting for a little bit, Rodney said, "I'm not hungry, are you?"

SKELETONS ARE NOT SCARY

Jered noticed his father was quite pale and he had his head low-ered a bit as if the living room lights were bothering him. The boy knew these were telltale signs his father was battling a headache. "Nah, I can wait if you want. Whatever you want to do."

Rodney leaned his head back, closed his eyes, and replied, "Good. Good." Rodney tried to get a handle on the headache and his anger. Just as soon as he thought he was making progress on one, the other would intensify. He didn't know how long he engaged in this struggle but when he opened his eyes, Jered was now lying on the living room floor drawing a picture.

"Whatcha drawing, buckaroo?"

Jered held up his incomplete work. "See these guys? They're flying around like they're Space Ghost. But they're not actually superheroes; they're just guys who can fly. These other guys down here on the ground are using flashlights so they can find this mon-ster hiding inside the house. It's like a big octopus and has a tentacle that's reaching out to grab the flashlight guy."

Through the pain, Rodney latched onto something in Jered's description. "You say they're guys who can fly but they're not superheroes?"

"Yeah, the flying guys don't see the monster, so they're just flying around waiting to . . ."

Inside Rodney's head, events that occurred over the past several weeks began to arrange themselves into a pattern. Jered's sensation of flying on Halloween, the exercises they conducted every night, and Jered imagining men who could fly, all combined to create an intriguing scenario. Could his sudden firing be a blessing in disguise? Was this an opportunity to awaken all his son's abilities?

"You liked the skeleton costume I made you, right?"

"Sure, Dad, it's neato."

"You're not afraid of skeletons anymore, are you?" Rodney was deep in thought, so the questions he asked were in a distant voice.

Jered giggled. "No, Dad. Skeletons aren't scary. They're cool. I like skeletons. And skulls. They're fun to draw but I'm not gonna draw them for a while." Jered cautiously approached the issue that had ignited his father's anger the previous night. "I thought I'd take the one down from my closet, you know, just for a while, I guess."

"Yeah, I'm sorry I yelled at you last night. I just wasn't feeling very well. I shouldn't have flown off the handle like that. Can you forgive me?"

Jered was both relieved and pleased his father was willing to put the whole incident behind them. "It's okay, Dad. I know how you get when the bad headaches come."

Rodney's eyes studied his son. Did Jered just intimate he'd seen his father as a skeleton? No, that's not what the boy meant. Rodney thought of the old proverb: when one door closes, another one opens. Rodney decided it was time for them to courageously walk through that second door. Rodney slapped his thigh with his hand.

"Say, I know something we can do that's fun! I know it's not bedtime yet, but wouldn't it be fun to do our Way-Out exercises?" Rodney suggested. "I've had a rough day at work, and I could use a nice break."

"Okay, Dad, sure." Jered enjoyed their Way-Out exercises. It was nice to have one-on-one time with his dad and Jered always felt pleasantly relaxed afterwards.

"If we let our minds relax tonight, I think we can go on a real journey."

Hearing the phrase "a real journey" caused Jered's eyes to widen. He thought this had to be the kind of thing Skelly told him about. Per Skelly's instructions, Jered needed to make a stop at his bedroom to talk to his friend before doing anything further.

"When did you want to do it, Dad?"

"How about right now? No time like the present, as the old saying goes. Let's go to the basement: it'll be darker and quieter so we can really focus our thoughts," Rodney said eagerly.

Jered needed time to consult with Skelly, so he said, "Okay, but Mom wanted me to put some stuff away in my bedroom, so I should do that first."

"Sure. Just come downstairs when you're ready."

The second trip to the university wasn't much easier than the one earlier that same day. It required changing busses and venturing into areas of University City that were unfamiliar to Chrissy. Strange surroundings always evoked anxiety in Chrissy and Dr. Freud's cryptic invitation only heightened her apprehension. She tried to steady herself by clutching her pocketbook tightly to her chest. Multiple times she anxiously checked her watch, but there was nothing she could do to make the bus go any faster. She bolted off the bus as soon as it stopped and ran across campus.

Dr. Freud's lecture had just begun when the lecture room door squeaked open. Once she softly closed the door behind her, Chrissy was taken aback to see all the students had turned their heads to stare at her. She opened her mouth to apologize for her noisy entry, but she was too mortified to say anything, so she just stood there with her mouth agape.

"Thank you for attending," Dr. Freud said, "even if you are a bit tardy." The professor pulled the pocket watch from his vest pocket and looked down at it. "Please take a seat and we shall continue despite the interruption you have imposed on us."

The students turned their attention back to Dr. Freud, some of them casting a final look of derision towards Chrissy. Despite Dr. Freud's direction, Chrissy remained standing in front of the door, too shy to venture into the classroom full of strangers to look for an open seat.

"As I was saying, fear is an interesting psychological phenomenon," Dr. Freud explained to his class. "Adults often chide their children when they express fear. Overbearing fathers warn their sons not to become a *fraidy-cat*. The question arises: is this good parenting or is it potentially dangerous?"

Dr. Freud stepped from behind the podium, pacing slowly in front of the class with his head bowed in thought. "While evaluating a particularly challenging patient recently, I was led to consider in greater detail how and why adults train children *not* to be scared. For a moment let us consider the life of a Neanderthal Man. If he feared unusual things, he likely had a better likelihood of survival than those who were brave or reckless. One would be more likely to live another day if one was scared when seeing a new animal. While this animal might be food, it could just as likely be deadly. Thus, we can reach the conclusion that fear can be an excellent emotional response.

"This being so, logic dictates that we, the descendants of these wary Neanderthals, should likewise approach life with an abiding sense of trepidation, especially regarding new stimuli. If this is true, why then do parents insist on their children being foolishly brave?" Dr. Freud looked up, surveying his audience, but no one raised their hand.

Returning to his thoughtful pacing, the professor continued, "There are actually a number of reasons for this. First, children are taught to be unafraid primarily because this fits in well with the parents' desires. If a child is afraid, this becomes an indictment of the parents' efforts to provide a safe, loving household. In the eyes of parents, there simply is no reason for their child to be scared, since a safe home has been provided by the parents. If the child nevertheless is afraid, this indicates to parents that they have failed in some way to create a safe environment.

"Second, the fear shown by the child is a stark reminder to the adult there is much in the world they cannot control. Fear is an emotion we as adults attempt to keep out of our lives entirely. Although adults may occasionally seek to embrace fright as a recreational interlude, such as willingly boarding a rollercoaster, they for the most part seek to make their everyday lives fear-proof." Students jotted notes, and many were nodding their heads.

"If we as adults are experiencing panic or anxiety, it is because we sense that we have somehow lost control. If those around us are fearful, even if they are just children, this can lead us to likewise become apprehensive. By teaching children not to be afraid, parents create an environment more in line with the adult world. We then come full circle and ask again whether this is helpful, or is it potentially damaging to the child's developing brain?"

A student in the front row confidently raised her hand. Since Dr. Freud was still deep in thought and looking at the floor, he didn't realize this until she delicately cleared her throat.

"Ah, as usual, Miss Granger has a thought on this matter. My question was merely hypothetical but since you are so intent on expounding on this issue, please proceed."

"It's appropriate because if the child is taught to be afraid of everything, he won't be able to adequately function," the student suggested.

Dr. Freud smiled, then returned to slowly pacing with his head bent. "While I am tempted to applaud your eagerness, I am disappointed by your lack of insight. There is much more to this issue. As our society has developed, additional factors have been introduced which makes this conundrum even more difficult to grasp.

"For example, our modern society has fostered an unfortunate situation wherein children are bombarded with conflicting and confusing cues as to when they should be scared. During the sense-less holiday of Halloween, children are encouraged to be fearful of things which do not exist. Society relishes in making children afraid of vampires, ghouls, witches, and monsters. How many of you were concerned at some point during your childhood that a monster was lurking under your bed?" Nearly all the students raised a hand. "Precisely. What have you learned this semester about monsters?"

In unison, the students repeated the axiom Dr. Freud had taught them. "The only real monster is the human brain."

"Precisely! Once you realize everything horrible actually exists in your mind, you will stop checking under your bed for monsters. If children expend their energy being afraid of fictional threats, they are less likely to be wary of true dangers. Parents have unwittingly sensitized their children to adopt absurd, irrational fears. It would appear as though All Hallow's Eve is nothing but a maniac's devious plan to make sure children are focused on make-believe monsters, as opposed to actual dangers lurking in the darkness.

"If we desire to have a holiday during which fears are empha-sized to our children, my suggestion is we remove all instances of fictional horrors such as mummies, blood-sucking bats, and ghosts. Instead, we would want to use this holiday to sensitize children to actual dangers such as kidnappers, Staph infections, bicycles, and litigation, as these are *real* threats to them."

Chrissy had difficulty following everything the doctor was saying. Was it good or bad for a child to be taught fear of the unknown? In her head, Chrissy timidly said, "I can't help it if I'm scared; there's just so many things that can hurt you."

"Another more subtle effect of Halloween is it desensitizes children to actual threats. Take for example, the widespread use of skeletons and skulls in October." Dr. Freud met Chrissy's eyes from across the room, and she could feel his intensity. "During this season, skeletons are depicted as cartoons and everyone knows you do not have to be afraid of cartoons!" Some of the students tittered, which caused Dr. Freud to flash an appreciative smile. "They are inundated with images of skulls as part of Halloween, which makes them less afraid of these symbols. The problem with these seemingly innocuous decorations is the image of skeletons and particularly skulls, is that they're something a child *should* be afraid of."

Chrissy's emotions volleyed back and forth during Dr. Freud's lecture. What initially seemed to be an indictment on her parenting skills now appeared to be the prudent course. Was the noted professor saying she was right or wrong to oppose her husband's efforts to expose Jered to skeletons?

"The skull is something that for children, as well as adults, should trigger concern and trepidation. What is on the warning labels of poisons? A skull. On warning signs directing us to avoid areas of danger, we likewise see the depiction of a skull. Why, then, would we encourage children to become accustomed to these images? Once these symbols become commonplace, the child becomes desensitized to them. The child is therefore less likely to experience the apprehension such ominous symbols should trigger. While dangerous monsters do not exist, skeletons are *very* real. If we do not feel anxiety when confronted by a skull, we are at risk for inadvertently drinking poison. My thesis, therefore, is that it is the failure of parents to establish what should be feared from what should not which endangers a child."

Chrissy thought, "Then what should a mother do?!" She was surprised to see the students all turn to her. Had she inadvertently spoken this thought? Apparently, she had.

"Yes, what should be done? This is an appropriately pragmatic question. My conclusion on this point may be vexing to parents." Dr. Freud paused so his students could prepare themselves to receive the wisdom he was about to impart. "The problem is a child's mind is unstructured and chaotic. Despite appropriate guidance from parents, a certain number of children will veer off course.

"When I am confronted with children who exhibit abnormal behavior, I am tasked with answering the question 'Why did this abnormal behavior arise?' I analyze the patient and dig through his mind looking for the explanation like an archeologist trying to discover a buried artifact. With regards to the patient I recently evaluated, the only possible conclusion was that this child was destined to be abnormal. He was unfortunately born with a condition which interfered with his ability to appropriately receive stimuli and respond in a socially accepted manner. The intricate network of neurons in his brain is somehow different than others. Somewhere in his development both before and after his birth, his brain developed abnormally, which provided him the ability to enter a world unknown to the rest of us. It is a world of pathological behavior. Regardless of parental guidance, this patient was going to be a unique outlier whose bizarre behavior cannot be explained other than to conclude he was destined to be this way."

A murmur arose from the students, causing the learned doctor to raise his hand.

"Luckily, the chance of a child having such an unusual ability is infinitesimal. All of our research and efforts are not rendered void simply because this rare biological aberration has arisen from the populace."

A gush of panic flowed through Chrissy. What she heard was Jered had a rare illness. The doctor said Halloween and skeletons had made her little boy's illness even worse! Chrissy desperately needed to go home and cradle her son in arms, but she was momentarily too afraid to move. If she stepped backwards to open the door, everyone would once again look at her. As much as she wanted to rush out of the room and sprint to the bus stop, she couldn't bear the thought of Dr. Freud and the entire classroom showering her with more hateful stares. While he continued to lecture about how children deal with fear, Chrissy wasn't listening. All her thoughts were on her son and how she'd make sure he wasn't exposed to anything frightening again, so he could get better.

As soon as Dr. Freud dismissed his class twenty minutes later, Chrissy sprinted out of the classroom, running as fast as she could towards the bus stop. She called out to a bus that was pulling away just as she arrived, but it didn't stop. The fifteen minutes she waited for the next bus to arrive seemed like hours to her. She spent this time convincing herself that a fifteen-minute delay wouldn't make any difference.

CHAPTER TWENTY-TWO

The Way-Out

Jered did just as his friend instructed. Skelly told Jered to come talk to him if his father mentioned anything about an unusual trip. The boy was anxious to find out what his friend had to say. Since coming home from riding his bike that afternoon, Jered hadn't needed to go into his bedroom. Standing in the doorway, he saw the small stack of clothes his mom left on his bed. As he entered his bedroom, Jered sensed something was wrong. Something was missing. *He* was missing. There was nothing on the nightstand. The boy ran to the other side of his bed, certain he'd find Skelly broken and lying on the floor. When there was nothing on the floor, Jered felt both relief and concern. Jered frantically looked under the bed, in his closet, and in his four dresser drawers, but the candy skull was missing.

"Where'd he go?" Jered desperately asked the empty room.

He was certain Skelly was sitting on his nightstand when he'd last been in the bedroom that morning. He'd even told creepy *Dr. Ifyouplease* he was sure Skelly was on the nightstand. Did the doctor somehow have something to do with Skelly's disappearance? That didn't seem possible. Skelly had some special skills, but Jered didn't believe that walking around was one of them. At least as far as he knew. The skull should've been just fine, as there wasn't anyone else in the house during the day other than . . .

Jered thought about how much his mother hated skeletons. He looked in each of the upstairs wastebaskets and when he found nothing, he went outside to check the garbage can. It was completely empty.

"Mom, have you seen my . . ." he yelled from the kitchen before stopping in mid-sentence.

"What?" his father called out from the basement.

"Um, have you seen my candy skull? It sits on the table next to my bed." Although it was unlikely his dad knew anything about the missing skull, it didn't hurt to ask.

"I haven't seen it since JoJo gave it to you."

Jered ran back to his bedroom to search again. Fueled by escalating concern for his friend, Jered was bold enough to go into his parents' bedroom to look for the skull. When all these efforts were fruitless, the boy was left with the unsatisfying conclusion that Skelly quite simply wasn't in the house. It was as though the skull had simply disappeared.

A horrible thought popped into his head. In his imagination, he saw his mother tossing Skelly into the garbage can. Jered shuddered when he visualized Skelly being unceremoniously dumped into a garbage truck, then cast onto a heap of trash at the landfill. Was Skelly right now perched on a pile of coffee grounds and wet newspapers, calling out to his friend for help? This thought made Jered's chest hurt and was too sickening to dwell upon. Sure, his mother had taken down the skeleton from his closet but throwing away the candy skull was such an immense breach of trust it was difficult to even consider.

Jered just barely heard his father call to him from the basement. "Are you about ready, buckaroo?"

"Just a sec, Dad," Jered shouted.

There was nowhere else to look. He'd ask his mother about the skull once she got home, but Jered had a sinking suspicion she'd done something with it. Maybe she hid it from him as a practical joke. Although she'd never done such a thing in the past, it was at least possible. Jered resigned himself to moving ahead without knowing what Skelly wanted to tell him.

Jered tried to convince himself that not hearing Skelly's advice wasn't a big deal. "He'd probably just tell me a silly story about one of his friends who told him a proverb." Jered didn't believe this, though. He was sure Skelly had something important to tell him.

While waiting impatiently for the next bus to arrive, Chrissy saw a pay phone about a block away. After she checked to make sure a bus wasn't approaching, she sprinted to the pay phone. Her hand was shaking as she inserted a dime into the slot. She listened to their home phone ring repeatedly, but no one picked up. Eventually a recorded voice advised her that the party she was trying to reach wasn't answering their phone, so she should try another time.

Jered walked down the wood steps that led to the basement.

"Don't turn on the other lights," his father instructed.

The only light was coming from the single fluorescent tube that hung over his dad's workbench, and it provided only a weak amount of bluish light. The glass tube flickered and crackled, as if there was a moth inside trying to escape. Seated on the concrete floor at the edge of the shop light's reach, Jered's father welcomed his son with a bright voice. "Come on, son, we can sit here. It's a little cold but it's nice and quiet."

Jered sat cross legged on the floor across from his father, still thinking about what Skelly might have told him.

"I'm so proud of you, son. This is a big step for you. And for me. Are you ready?"

"I'll try, Dad."

"Good boy." In a hypnotic voice, Rodney said, "Just like we've done before, we want to clear out all the thoughts. Close your eyes. Pretend your mind is a big chalkboard with writing all over it. Can you see it?" Jered nodded. Over the past few weeks, Jered had become pretty good at his father's relaxation exercises. "I want you to take an eraser and wipe all those thoughts away. Do that now. Wipe away everything you're thinking about so the only thing in your mind is a blank chalkboard. Deep breaths. That's it . . . don't think about anything. Your mind is wiped clear.'

Jered discovered that erasing his thoughts was more difficult on this occasion. His concern about Skelly kept interrupting the boy's efforts to shove all his thoughts to the side. About the time Jered felt as though he was close to wiping off the chalkboard, "Where is Skelly?" would suddenly appear. When Jered buffed these words away with his eraser, they'd appear again on another part of the chalkboard.

"Are you there? Have you cleared your mind of thoughts? Is the chalkboard blank?"

"Yes," Jered replied, trying not to betray the fact he was lying. Despite Jered's efforts to wipe it clean, the long chalkboard he visualized in his mind wasn't blank. Written in chalk were such things as, "Where'd Skelly go?" and, "What did he need to tell me?" To Jered's relief, his father didn't realize he was fibbing.

"Good. I knew you could do it. Now that your mind is clear, we can move forward." Instead of taking Jered through another set of relaxation exercises, Rodney decided to try another way to awaken his powers. With his son's conscious mind open, Rodney for the first time tried to draw out his abilities by triggering his anger. "This

SKELETONS ARE NOT SCARY

time, buckaroo, I want you to think of something or someone who really makes you mad. I'm talking about really super mad."

Jered thought for a few moments, then said, "I can't really think of anything."

"Come on, surely there's something that makes you very mad. Is there someone who teases you at school? Someone who punches you during recess?"

Once again, Jered thought about it, but didn't come up with anything that fit his father's description. "Sometimes kids make fun of me cuz I can't hear right, I guess."

Maintaining his soothing tone, Rodney said, "Yes, that's good. That probably makes you really mad, doesn't it?"

"Not really," Jered replied truthfully. "You and Mom told me not to pay attention to people who say mean things."

Rodney opened one of his eyes so he could take a peek at Jered. His son's eyes were closed, and it was obvious from his expression he was genuinely trying to follow the instructions. Rodney thought, "How does that old saying go? Hoisted on my own petard?"

Just as Rodney thought the exercise had hit a roadblock, Jered offered, "This boy called Eddie sometimes makes fun of me 'cuz of the pictures I draw."

"That must make you mad, I bet."

"No, Miss Moran kinda taught me about what to say when people are mean like that. One day, him and two other boys were making fun of me and I . . ."

Rodney cut off his son. "Okay, okay. Let's go back to our regular relaxation game and forget about things that make you mad. Start off again by clearing your mind. Think of your brain as a big Etch-A-Sketch. Got it? Now shake it until it's blank."

Despite doing just as his father instructed, all the questions about Skelly that had been on the chalkboard were now scrawled in jagged letters across the Etch-A-Sketch. As he'd done before,

Rodney guided his son through an exercise to relax both his mind and body. Gradually, Jered felt the tension in his neck and shoulders loosen. While he was guiding Jered, Rodney was performing his own meditation. Rodney was trying to ignite his special power by recalling every aspect of his firing. He visualized King Fool's face as he told Rodney he was fired. As his anger rose, his muscles tensed to the point they were uncomfortable. Jered, on the other hand, was becoming increasingly relaxed.

In a soft voice that hid the anger he was stoking inside of himself, Rodney asked, "Can you picture yourself flying through the sky? Try it. Feel yourself lift up."

The boy was in a pleasant state of calmness and relaxation, his mind feeling light as a feather. In a dreamy voice, Jered replied, "I feel . . . light. I feel . . . relaxed."

"Good. Now let yourself float up like a balloon. You don't have a care in the world. Can you feel yourself being drawn upward?"

Despite being very relaxed, Jered didn't quite feel like he was on the verge of floating off the floor. He closed his eyes even tighter, concentrating very hard, but nothing happened. "I'm sorry, Dad, I don't think I can do it," he said in an embarrassed voice. "I'm trying real hard, but I just can't seem to lift up."

Jered opened his eyes to look at his father and was surprised to see his facial expression wasn't one of peacefulness. When his father exhaled through his nose, it sounded like an angry, snorting bull. The corners of his mouth were pulled down, making him look like that same angry bull. Jered had never seen his father's face twisted in such a horrible expression, even when he'd been so mad at Jered the night before.

"Dad . . . are you okay?" Jered asked with trepidation in his voice.

Rodney had successfully pumped himself up into an angry lather. When he opened his eyes and saw his son's frightened face, he suddenly realized what he must look like. He did his best to relax the muscles in his face and smile casually, but to Jered he still looked strange.

Despite pulsing with adrenaline, Rodney spoke to his son as calmly as he could. "It's okay, son. It's okay you're having problems. This is a hard thing to do. That's why we've been practicing. Don't give up quite yet, though. Try hard." Yes, his father was saying things to make him feel better, but Jered could tell his dad was disappointed the boy had failed.

In the midst of these efforts, Rodney became aware of just how severely his headache had become. By stoking his anger, he'd also poured gasoline on the wildfire of pain raging in his head. Rodney wasn't sure what to try next, but he wasn't yet willing to give up on the experiment. This was a unique opportunity when all the proverbial planets appeared to be in alignment. Jered's abilities were blossoming, and the rage Rodney felt towards his ex-employer would surely act as rocket fuel. All he had to do was manage to get his son free of the material world's gravitational pull. Once he'd pulled free, Jered could soar into the realm only the two of them could navigate.

"Rocket fuel," Rodney murmured under his breath.

Rodney envisioned a rocket sitting on a launch pad. It was a huge white Saturn rocket ready to blast off to the moon. He imagined his son as a brave but hesitant astronaut seated in the nose cone of the rocket. What Jered needed was a mighty thrust into the sky so he could escape earth's atmosphere. If there was enough power at hand, the pioneering astronaut would be jettisoned all the way to the moon. And to glory.

Reaching out to his son, Rodney said, "Take my hands. I'm gonna help you break free. Ever since I was your age, I've taken trips to a special place, and now I want to help you go there. If we work together as a team, we can make it!"

The boy was relieved to see much of the anger wash out of his father's face and was excited at the exotic place he was alluding to. "What kind of place? Like an island? Hawaii?"

"Even better. It's a wonderful place but you need to work with me so we can get there together. I'm going to help you by giving a hard push, just like when I taught you to ride a bike, do you remember?"

"Sure, Dad, I remember. Tell me what to do."

Jered was excited to be given another chance. He wanted to please his father and go this wonderful place. The boy's small hands were swallowed up in his father's. Jered's hands were squeezed firmly but not so much that it was painful. He felt safe and smiled at his dad.

"That's it, we can do this together. Now close your eyes again and keep them closed. Breathe deeply and wipe clean the chalkboard in your mind." Jered did as he was told and was pleased the chalkboard remained blank after he erased it. He heard his father's breathing increase, but Jered didn't open his eyes. His father's hands gradually became uncomfortably hot and damp. As the minutes passed, Jered felt as though he was sitting under the glare of a hot August sun. Beads of sweat started to form on the boy's forehead.

When his father gave additional instructions, it almost sounded as if he was gasping for air. "Picture yourself rising up, son. You're light as a hot air balloon. The floor couldn't keep you from floating up even if it wanted to. Concentrate. See yourself floating up in your mind so that it comes true."

The boy's eyes were closed tightly as he focused on the picture he'd created in his imagination. A boy wearing a black tuxedo holding the strings of a large bunch of helium balloons was floating a few feet off the ground. The boy landed, then handed the strings to Jered. Even though Jered did his best to visualize the balloons slowly pulling him upward, he could still feel the cold basement floor. Jered concentrated so intensely for so long, his temples began to hurt. Although he'd had a few headaches during his short life, none of them were as intense as this pain. It was as though the sides of his head were being pushed inward.

"My head hurts," Jered complained in a dreamy voice.

Between gasps his father assured him, "That's okay; that's just part of it. The pain will go away. Just keep thinking as hard as you can."

Jered thought he could just barely hear a telephone ringing in the distance, but it eventually stopped.

"Stay focused, son."

Jered did as he was told, even though it felt like a vise was squeezing his head.

Rodney's voice was full of hope. "We can get there! Just keep concentrating!"

Although he kept his eyes shut and was thinking as hard as he could about floating up into the air, Jered was losing faith he'd ever be able to do it. The large fleshy hands which enveloped his own turned from hot and sweaty to ice cold. Jered's hands felt as though they'd been plunged into a snow drift.

As he continued to picture himself floating into the air, the beads of sweat on his face turned into ice crystals. The sweat on their hands also froze. Wherever the sweat froze, it felt like small needles were jabbing him. When Jered opened his eyes to see if ice was actually forming on their hands, his eyes were accosted by the dim shop light. It felt as though Jered was staring directly into a powerful spotlight and pain seared all the way to the back of his head. He quickly shut his eyes even tighter.

Rodney struggled to boost them from the bounds of the mundane world. A few times he felt himself rise from the ground, but his son did not budge. It seemed that the harder he pulled on his son's arms, the stronger Jered's connection to the ground became.

The boy didn't feel anything except his arms were now up in the air. A fervent yank on Jered's arms caused a tearing sensation to rip through one of Rodney's shoulders. There were times Rodney wanted to cry out in pain, but he managed to remain silent and focused. Letting out a howl of pain would surely frighten the boy and likely cause Rodney's job to become even harder. As he floated higher and strained to pull his son along with him, Rodney existed in two different worlds at the same time. His skin, soft tissue, and muscles all felt as though they were being torn apart. He didn't know how long he could keep it up.

Jered didn't slowly float upward. Instead, he was suddenly jerked off the cool basement floor. His arms were raised above his head, as though he was being dragged by his hands by a speeding car. Jered couldn't help himself: he had to open his eyes. Once he did, he discovered they were no longer in the basement.

With his father's hands still tightly holding onto his, Jered was awestruck as they slowly glided in a circular orbit just above the tallest trees. He looked down on the houses and the streetlights. At first his eyes watered because of the cold nighttime breeze but they quickly acclimated. Jered's legs fluttered behind him like a kite's tail. Just as his dad promised, Jered was flying. True, he wasn't flying on his own; he was being towed along by his father, but that didn't matter.

This was the greatest moment in Rodney's life; the wondrous culmination of his hopes and dreams. Amid the agony of being gradually torn apart, Rodney had suddenly felt his son's attachment to the mundane world snap. No longer tethered, Rodney felt the two of them effortlessly ascend. When he opened his eyes to find he and his son floating in the night sky, he swelled with emotions. The proud father let loose an elated laugh while his eyes pooled with tears of joy. He had the urge to let go of his son's hands and give him a big loving bear hug, but something inside him warned it would be best to keep a safe grip on Jered, at least for the time being. Rodney concentrated on maintaining their current position in the sky. In addition to giving his son a chance to get accustomed to this new experience, Rodney needed a few minutes to recover.

Jered's mother taught him if he ever wanted to wake up from a dream, all he needed to do was pinch himself and he'd wake up. If he had control of his hands, Jered would have pinched himself to make sure this wasn't gliding in an elaborate and very realistic dream. There were instances when Jered's wide-eyed wonderment briefly drifted into uneasiness as they circled but being safely in his father's grip comforted the boy.

Rodney concentrated on the two of them rising to a higher altitude. Nothing happened right away but eventually they started to float higher into the night sky. As they ascended, Rodney smiled in satisfaction when he heard Jered marvel, "Wowwwww." It appeared Rodney had indeed become the world's utmost Little League Dad. He was confident, though, that the amount of pride and joy he was feeling would easily dwarf the emotions a father felt if his son hit a game winning home run in the World Series!

While he enjoyed the moment, Rodney reminded himself they still had a lot of work to do. It would take time and effort for Jered to refine his abilities. Luckily, the boy was going to have something Rodney never had: a trusted mentor. He was going to be there every step of the way, assisting Jered as he honed his amazing preternatural abilities. He looked back at his son again, smiling with satisfaction, then pulled Jered so they were eye-to-eye.

"Isn't this amazing, buckaroo? We did it, son!" Rodney proclaimed with a voice chock-full of happiness and pride. "Or maybe I should say *you* did it!"

Although it was exhilarating to fly alongside his jubilant father, Jered couldn't help but feeling a little unnerved once they'd climbed to a height that permitted them to look down on the entire neighborhood. He felt a tickle in his stomach as the houses became smaller and smaller. He'd been on Ferris Wheels and a roller coaster, so Jered recognized the tingly feeling in his stomach caused by quickly going up or down. Everything was happening so fast, the boy still wondered if this was only occurring in his imagination. Was this really happening? The sharp, cool air pricking his face and arms as they soared certainly felt real.

"Just . . . what is all this?" Jered thought. His young brain, however, couldn't offer a comforting explanation. He'd never heard of anything like this happening, not even on television. No one at school ever mentioned taking a journey into the sky with a parent.

Feeling his son's hands begin to writhe inside his grasp, Rodney understood the anxiety his son was experiencing. "It's okay. Everything is fine. You're with me. I've been here before and I'll show you how it all works," Rodney soothed. He smiled at his son, remembering how terrifying his initial episodes had been when he was young. "Look at me, Jered." When his son obeyed, he smiled and promised, "I'm not going to let anything bad happen to you. There's no reason for you to be afraid. There's no scaredy-cats allowed here."

His father's assurances helped relieve Jered's misgivings. He noticed the headache he'd started to feel in the basement was now gone. The boy scanned the area. Now when he looked straight down, he no longer felt the roller coaster tingle in his stomach. Effortlessly floating in the darkness with his father, Jered felt an increasing sense of contentment. With eyes wide and full of wonder, Jered looked over the nightscape, all the way to the vanishing horizon.

"Isn't this amazing?" his father asked.

It took a moment for Jered to reply. When he did, it was hesitant and uncoordinated, like the first steps he took as a toddler. "Yeah . . . I . . . what . . . what is all this?"

"It's a place only *we* can get to. We'll have time to talk more once we get home. I'll tell you about all of things I've done here. Right now, though, we only have a little bit of time to explore. So, let's go; sound good?"

In an unsteady voice, Jered replied, "Sure . . . Dad." At that moment Jered was actually sure of very little.

"I've got so much to show you in a short time," Rodney said excitedly. "Come on, let's see if we can find someone to visit."

Still holding his son with both hands, Rodney imagined slowly turning the dial on a radio, trying to find a strong signal he could latch onto. He cleared his mind until he could see the innumerable radio waves passing through the air. While he searched, Rodney let the two of them be carried on the breeze like two autumn leaves.

Jered watched curiously as his father lifted his head, appearing as if he was trying to detect a faint odor in the air. After this continued for several minutes, Jered asked, "What are you doing, Dad?"

"Shhh, just listen. Can you hear what's in the air?"

At first, Jered had no idea what his father was talking about. After listening to the breeze for a while, Jered noticed a vague humming sound, as if a swarm of noisy mosquitoes was buzzing around his ears. With confusion on his face, Jered looked at his father.

"Yeah, you're starting to pick up the signals, aren't you? Listen carefully. They're like invisible radio waves in the air, but what you hear is people thinking. The angrier they are, the easier it is to figure out what's being said inside their heads. Get it? We're surrounded by thin strands of thought. Of emotions. Try to pick out what's being said in them."

Jered pictured himself in his parents' car, slowly turning the knob on the radio to find a strong signal. Sometimes all he heard was static, then just a few words, and finally he'd stumble upon a broadcast. Jered heard a distant voice, ". . . ever again I'll give him the what's for with my fist!" Jered snapped his head towards his father with eyes full of amazement. Rodney nodded his head with a proud expression of a father whose son just hit his first base hit.

"You heard one, didn't you?" Rodney remarked with satisfaction.

Typically, it took several minutes of listening to static and far away phantom voices before locking onto a target, and this night was no different. Rodney listened intently for a certain kind of voice; one filled with anger and impending rage. He was searching for a voice teeming with raw emotion emanating from someone who might be susceptible to Rodney's gentle persuasions.

"I never know where I'll eventually end up," Rodney explained as he looked lovingly at his son. "With practice, someday you'll be able to control exactly where you land."

"But . . . but . . ." Jered had a thousand questions; he didn't know which one to ask first.

Rodney interrupted his son, as this wasn't the time to answer the little boy's questions. "Out here everything is possible, son! No limits! You'll be the king of the universe out here!"

Jered wondered what his father meant. Did that mean he could have any toy he wanted? If everything was possible, could he become a superhero, flying through the sky to defeat bad guys? "Dad, I don't . . ."

"Shhh. Be quiet for a little bit. I need to listen."

While trolling the stream of thoughts, Rodney could just barely make out someone's menacing growl through the static. "You better not . . . I'm not kidding!" Rodney was drawn slowly towards the faint transmission. "You . . . you . . . you don't . . ." Rodney was pulled faster towards the source of the broadcast. He and Jered maintained a steady course when the signal was strong but circled in a holding pattern if the broadcast became weaker.

Listening to the random thoughts of others was somewhat unnerving for Jered. He felt as though he might be doing something wrong and was listening to things that were supposed to be private.

SKELETONS ARE NOT SCARY

The satisfied expression on his father's face, however, indicated everything was fine.

As Rodney was pulled closer to the source, he often became impatient. While still focusing on the radio wave, Rodney sent out his own communication: "Talk to me! Where are you? Help me find you." He had no idea if this made any difference, but sending these orders through the stratosphere made Rodney feel a little more in charge.

The next statement Rodney heard was so clear and loud, it was if a man right next to him, shouting into his ear. "He can't do this to me! To me!"

"We've got a live one!" Rodney declared joyously. "Here we go!"

Father and son were violently jerked downward. The suddenness of their dive ripped Jered's right hand out of his father's grip. Rodney reached out to regain his hold on Jered's hand but failed, which led him to squeeze his son's left hand even tighter. Their speedy descent elated Rodney but scared Jered. Instinctively, the boy stuck his legs straight out in front of him, trying to dig in his heels, but there was nothing to push his feet against. Something was reeling them in. The lights on the ground became larger and clearer.

Jered closed his eyes and wished for their plunge to end. His wish was granted. Their descent came to a sudden stop. He and his father tumbled awkwardly on the ground after they landed. His father's death grip on Jered's left hand wasn't loosened by the impact and the two of them somersaulted awkwardly a few times.

"You okay, son?" Rodney asked.

Seemingly unfazed by the sudden crash landing, Jered said, "Yeah, I'm okay, Dad." At first Jered thought they'd landed in a large cave, with dark walls that extended high above them. The only light came from images projected against one of the walls. The boy wondered if they'd been dropped into the world's largest drive-in theater.

Years of Way-Outs had honed Rodney's abilities so he could look directly through the eyes of those he visited. If Rodney wanted to look in a certain direction, he could usually move the person's eyes to accommodate his wishes. He'd become accustomed to entering the person and taking full control. Tonight, however, the perspective was much less exciting. Instead of looking through the person's eyes as if they were his own, Rodney was relegated to be a spectator.

"Probably because it's his first trip," Rodney surmised.

Father and son saw what the person was seeing projected on the wall. The boy glanced around them and wondered where all the cars were. If this was indeed a drive-in theater, there should be carloads of people watching the movie through their windshields.

"Where . . . where . . . ?" Jered asked meekly.

Displayed on the wall was a living room. From the looks of the furniture and décor, Rodney thought they were likely in a different country. Even though it was a one in a billion chance, Rodney hoped against hope they'd be drawn to King Fool. Instead, he saw a heavyset man speaking in a language Rodney didn't recognize. In Rodney's head, the words were instantly translated into English: "I deserved it! It's not right he got it, and I didn't!"

"Can you understand what that man is saying, son?"

"Kind of," Jered replied. "At first it sounds weird but then it's like someone repeats it so I can understand. How's that happening?"

"We've travelled into someone's consciousness. Do you understand what that means?" Jered shook his head. "We're inside his thoughts. Pretty neat, huh?"

Jered's young brain struggled to make sense of this bizarre situation. He tried not to be too scared, reminding himself that his father would never put him in danger. "Do other fathers do this with their sons?" he asked.

SKELETONS ARE NOT SCARY

Rodney laughed goodheartedly at his son's innocence. "No, I'm certain we're the only ones who can do this! Are you doing okay so far?"

Although this experience was at times exhilarating, Jered couldn't help being frightened at the whole spectacle. It was obvious this was something his father wanted him to eagerly embrace. The greatest man he knew, his father, encouraged him to keep his fears under control. The boy was concerned if he expressed feeling any degree of fear, his dad would conclude he was a scaredy-cat and never again take him on such a wondrous trip. Jered suppressed his misgivings and nodded, hoping to reassure his father he was a big boy and was fine. His young face, though, was covered with uncertainty.

"I can understand why the cat's got your tongue," Rodney chuckled. "This is a lot for a young man to take in. Can you imagine what I had to go through when I was your age? I made these trips on my own, without anyone helping me!"

Standing in the cave/drive-in theater, Jered's head was abuzz with thoughts and questions. A picture of Skelly flashed in Jered's mind. Did Skelly know this was going to happen? Was Skelly warning Jered of this? The boy's imagination inserted itself into the conversation. Was this another realm of the universe where dragons dwelt? Or unicorns? Or his *real* parents?

"Now comes the really fun part," his father said, a sly grin appearing on his face. His father shouted, "Who does he think he is? Huh? Someone's cruising for a bruising, don't you think?"

Jered was surprised his dad was yelling, as it seemed as though this might be a place where you needed to be quiet, like a library. His father's voice bounced off the cave and echoed back to them. There must've been speakers hidden in the cave because a whispered voice devoid of emotion replied, "No." The calm voice echoed inside the cave, just like his dad's.

"Aw, come on, you can do it. Tell me, what did that guy get that we didn't? Hm?" Rodney cajoled.

Once again, the hidden speakers filled the cave with a soft, unemotional reply. "Big ole' Tony got the job and I didn't."

Jered was befuddled. He looked at his father, then the screen, and back to his father, trying to somehow make sense of this odd conversation. His dad's voice became bolder. "Tony got that job by *cheating* you out of it. You deserved that job. Don't you think you should give Tony what's coming to him? Hm? Tony needs to be taught a lesson about what happens when people cross you. Sounds like he's cruisin' for a bruisin'!" He waved his free hand when he spoke, as if trying to whip his audience into a lather.

In the same expressionless tone, the voice said, "Yes, Tony needs to be taught a lesson. A very harsh lesson."

Rodney looked at his son to make sure Jered was paying attention. His son was looking up at him with saucer eyes full of confusion. He whispered to Jered, "After doing this, you'll feel like a million bucks! When we get back home, you'll feel the best you ever have in your life!" Jered was unable to respond in any way.

Rodney shouted, "Yes, a firm lesson no one will ever forget. That's what Tony needs!"

What his father said combined with the tone of his voice rattled Jered. He felt just as if his father was yelling at *him*. His arms and legs started to shiver uncontrollably. Realizing his father would be able to feel the tremors as they travelled down his arms, Jered tried to will them to stop. All that focusing on the shivers did was to make them more intense. Out of the corner of both eyes Jered saw flashes of bright light, as if dozens of flash bulbs were going off. When he turned his head to see where the brilliant flashes were coming from, he couldn't see anything.

The boy didn't know what was happening, but he certainly knew he didn't like it. In unison the calm voice and his father began to snicker, which just made it even more unsettling. What was shown on the screen changed; two adult hands were slowly flexing its fingers, as if getting them ready. All the while, the laughing continued. It didn't sound to Jered like a happy laugh; it sounded menacing.

The boy's response to the events unfolding around him came from deep inside him. Something just wasn't right. Jered couldn't bear to watch any longer, so he turned his head away from the movie. Jered's only conscious thought was he wanted it to stop. Whatever all this was, he was done with it. All he wanted was to just go back home. In his imagination, he pictured being jettisoned out of the cave, then flying through the night sky back to his house. He imagined sitting on the cool cement floor across from his dad. Jered felt his body nudge upward just a bit, so that he was standing on his tip toes. This movement encouraged him to concentrate even harder. Pretty soon his shoes were a few inches above the ground. The hope of escape energized Jered.

"Where are you going?" his father asked harshly, yanking his son back down by his left hand. "This is what we've been waiting for all these years!" The sudden wrench of his arm interrupted Jered's thoughts. Jered looked at his father with terrified eyes that were pleading for it all to end. When Rodney saw the panic in his son's face, he tried to console his son. "There's nothing to be afraid of. No reason for you to be a scaredy-cat."

Rodney's attempt to calm Jered had no effect. Just as his mother had done on many occasions, Jered had securely locked himself into a state of fear. In this condition, Rodney knew no amount of cajoling would break the spell. A different tact would be needed to break through the fear and bring Jered back to his senses. Rodney's expression switched from kindness to indignation. "You'll stay here with me!" Rodney barked like a drill sergeant while intensely glaring at Jered. "Do as I say!"

His father's outraged face and despotic commands only succeeded in intensifying the boy's fear. To escape his father's blazing stare, Jered turned his head and closed his eyes. Frightened tears were beginning to well up in his eyes as he again pictured himself flying home. Jered tried to wrench his hand out of his father's huge vise hand, to no end.

"You're not going anywhere! You have to stay here!"

Jered's fear became so profound it turned into panic. He squeezed his eyes shut even harder while concentrating with nearly hysterical fervor on his desire to go home. An impassioned series of snapshots flashed into the boy's mind. Their house. His bedroom. His mother. Skelly. By focusing all his attention on images of home, Jered drowned out his father's voice.

With a sudden jolt, Jered shot off the ground. Hovering a foot above the ground, Jered's left arm felt as though it was going to be pulled out of its socket. As Jered winced in pain, his hand pulled free of his father's grip. The boy slowly continued to rise until his father managed to grab his ankle.

His father's thunderous voice exclaimed, "No! Stay here!"

The tight hold on Jered's skinny ankle felt as though rope had been cinched securely around it. After a brief pause, Jered slowly began drifting upward. Jered looked up and saw he still had a long way to go before reaching the cave's ceiling. His foot, ankle, and lower leg were screaming with pain. Gazing down on the hand firmly encircling his ankle, he wondered if a foot could be pulled so hard it broke off. In the limited light, it looked to Jered as if the arm that was straining to pull him back down had become stretched unnaturally long, as if it was a rubber band. Jered's rise once again stopped and this time he was pulled downward. The long rubber band arm gradually shortened as his father reeled Jered back down.

Hovering just a few feet above his father, Jered looked into his contorted face and pleaded, "Dad, I don't want to be here! I'm scared! Please! Let's get out of here!"

"Don't be afraid! This is what you're destined to do, son! You don't have to be scared just because you've never done this before."

Now even more desperate to escape the awful cave, Jered thought of himself as a rocket being launched towards home. Not only could Jered see the huge boosters pushing the rocket up, he could hear their thunderous roar. Once he was engrossed in these images, Jered started to edge upward, causing his father's arm to again stretch to an unnatural length. While still holding fast onto Jered's ankle with his rubber band arm, his dad screamed. It was an agonizing shriek, as if his father had been badly injured.

"Dad, are you okay?" When his father didn't immediately reply, Jered tried to encourage him. "Come on! Come with me! Let's go home! We gotta leave!"

His father was breathing heavily but managed to say between his labored gulps of air, "Stop fighting! Don't ruin this for me!"

Jered wondered how long the rubber band would stretch before it broke. If his dad would just abandon his efforts to stay in the cave, they could escape together. "I'm not fighting you! I just wanna go home! I don't wanna be in this scary place!" he pleaded desperately.

In his imagination, Jered pictured them hand-in-hand, flying back to their basement. Once they were safely home, he and his dad could laugh about their bizarre adventure. "Fly home! Fly home!" Jered kept repeating to himself.

As his dad's arm got longer, its downward pull on Jered's ankle became weaker. By the time Jered reached the cave's ceiling, he was moving steadily upward. In quick succession, Jered slid out of the cave, into the man's living room, through the top of the house, and finally into the crisp night air. Even though Jered was in the air, his father still had a strong grip on his ankle. Even though he couldn't see but a portion of his father's arm, he pleaded to him, "Come on, Dad! We're almost there!"

First the head, then the torso of his father was gradually drawn out of the house. His father's entire body was stretched as if it was taffy, causing his father's face to have a long sorrowful grimace. A steady downward pull was still being applied to Jered's ankle. As he inched ever higher into the nighttime sky, his father was stretched even further.

"That's it, Dad! Forget the cave! Come with me!"

Jered heard the unmistakable cracking sound of glass that was beginning to fracture. The strong hand wrapped around his ankle had tendril-like fissures forming on it.

"Jered! Help me!" his father cried. "Use your power! I'm losing my grip!"

"I don't understand!" Jered yelled helplessly. "What can *I* do?"

As his father once again cried out in pain, the hand gripping his ankle shattered into a hundred small pieces as if it were a glass figurine. Or a candy skull. A massive explosion of sound enveloped Jered, as if a hundred mirrors were all shattered simultaneously.

"Dad!" the boy cried out, as he watched his father's body blow apart into thousands of jagged pieces of glass. As the shards floated away from each other, each of them shattered as well, until there was just dust floating beneath Jered. When the particles of dust fractured, nothing was left.

Before he had time to completely appreciate what he'd just witnessed, he was racing through the sky. The sudden acceleration took his breath away. As he sliced through the night sky at break-neck speed, Jered couldn't catch his breath. The lights below flew past him in a blur.

"How long can I make it without taking another breath?" Jered thought.

After shooting through the sky for who knows how long, Jered came to a sudden stop. The abrupt deceleration caused his upper body to fold forward and when he straightened his back, he was happy to discover his lungs were working again. It took Jered a little bit of time to clear his spinning head but after surveying the area, he eventually realized he was floating several yards above the roof of his house. After he hovered for a short time, Jered closed his eyes and focused on finishing the trip back home. He remembered how the cold cement floor felt as he sat on it with his dad and tried to visualize himself back in the basement. Despite thinking very hard, nothing seemed to happen, and he just remained dangling in the air.

Chrissy was already crying out her son's name as she was fumbling with the key to the front door. It didn't take long for Chrissy to check the main floor: each of the rooms was empty. While in the kitchen, she noticed a faint light coming from the basement.

"Jered! Jered!" she shouted, stumbling clumsily down the stairs. She caught her toe on the second to last step, causing her to spill onto the floor. Both her hands slapped down hard on the cement floor, causing jagged bolts of pain to shoot through her wrists up into her forearms. "Jered!" she cried through the pain.

The work light dangling above Rodney's workbench was on, illuminating only a small portion of the cinder block basement. If she hadn't been so shaken, she would have flipped the light switch. Instead, she squinted her eyes as she scanned the shadowy basement. When she saw the basement was empty, she screamed in desperation, "Jered! Rodney!"

It was only because the lighting was so poor that Chrissy saw a faint glimmer swirling on the floor to her left. Through the darkness, she was able to just barely detect a small whirlpool of dim hazy lights on the floor. As soon as she saw the uncanny swirling lights, her heart began to beat even faster. Just as it had on so many other situations when Chrissy was frightened, an uncomfortable sweat quickly formed on the back of her neck. Despite this fear, something drew her towards the lights. For reasons she'd never be able to determine in the years that followed, the odd flashes of light somehow filled her with hope. She approached cautiously, the whirlpool of odd lights no larger than a car tire.

When she was just a few steps away, the colorful whirlpool abruptly vanished. Chrissy felt her stomach drop when the lights disappeared. She stopped in her tracks, wondering if she'd somehow caused the whirlpool to go away. Although she didn't know what the lights were, her maternal intuition told her the small whirlpool was important. Important for Jered.

The scared little girl inside Chrissy warned her to stay away from the area but she didn't listen to that voice. Chrissy did her best to ignore her fear and moved so she was kneeling near the area where the swirling lights had momentarily appeared. She spread her hands over the floor, like she was pushing wrinkles from a newly laundered bed sheet. Chrissy moved her hands slowly around the perimeter of where the whirlpool had just been, as if she was searching for a secret switch.

"Where did you go?" she uttered under her breath. "What are you? Please come back."

She gasped when the twinkling lights appeared again, spinning like a colorful little dust devil on the basement floor. Chrissy heard her pulse thudding in her ears, so she took a deep breath and tried to steady herself. With a trembling hand, she reached towards the whirlpool. There was a painful snap of static electricity that pricked her fingertips, causing her to abruptly pull her hand back.

When the shock of the pain faded, she once again reached out cautiously. Another electric shock nipped her fingers, but she kept

SKELETONS ARE NOT SCARY

moving her hand forward. When her fingertips touched the light, it felt as though she'd immersed them in ice cold water. Startled by the uncomfortable cold, she once again yanked her hand away. She hesitated to reach again towards the swirling menagerie and touch the cold fluid. Chrissy squinted her eyes, peering into the void. She felt as though she was looking down into a deep well, trying to see if her husband and son had fallen in.

"Jered? Rodney?" she asked warily. "Jered are you there, honey?"

Seemingly in response to her voice, the tiny lights spun faster, then brightened just a bit. Encouraged by this response, she kept saying her son's name. The lights once again pulsed with more brightness and vivid color, but then suddenly went out.

"No. No!" Chrissy called out to her son again, in a voice every parent would use to beckon their child away from danger. "Jered. Come to mommy."

The whirlpool of lights dimmed, became brighter, and then faded away several times as Chrissy was calling out to her son. Deep in the abyss of the well, she thought she could just barely make out her son's face looking up at her.

"Yes! Jered! Mommy's here!" she shouted joyously, her hands held just above the whirlpool as she gestured for him to come to her.

It was as if her son was swimming in black coffee. Chrissy could only manage to get periodic glimpses of his face through the dark water. Jered was looking up at her with a full moon face and it looked to her that he was confused. She wasn't sure how far away he was. One moment he looked as though he was just a few feet below the surface and the next he appeared much deeper. Gray fog at times floated between her and Jered, causing her view to be further compromised.

"Can you come the rest of the way?" Chrissy asked. "You're almost here. Swim towards mommy! Reach out! You can do it! Don't be afraid! Just come this way a little further." She looked down on her son with a wide, encouraging smile. When Jered's facial expression didn't change, Chrissy switched to pleading with her son. "Please, Jered. Mommy's waiting. Please come a little further."

Jered thought he saw his mother's face materialize out of the darkness. Her mouth was moving and he heard her voice, but the words were distorted so much he couldn't understand her. It was like being at the bottom of a swimming pool and trying to decipher what was being said at the surface. From her facial expression and gesticulations, it was clear she was encouraging him to come towards her. Jered reckoned they were separated by maybe five car lengths.

His mother's voice got louder, and her gestures became more emphatic. He was about to reach towards her, but he hesitated when voices in his head started asking difficult questions. Why hadn't she told Jered of his father's plans? Why hadn't she stepped in to protect him from his enraged father last night? Unless she played a part in this scheme, wouldn't she have intervened to shield Jered from harm? Overwhelming these concerns was another voice sounding a lot like Skelly's that said, "Maybe she knew as little as you did."

Jered reached out towards his mother. The night air felt heavy, as if he was in water. He focused his attention on moving nearer to her. Jered thought of being in a swimming pool and began churning his arms in her direction. When the distance between them didn't appear to lessen, he kicked his feet to help propel him forward. He pictured himself as a fish so strong it could swim against the current, and he saw his mother's face get larger as he approached.

The sound of someone playing a snare drum erupted from behind him, causing Jered to look over his shoulder. In the distance, he saw a circular area that was turning clockwise. As best he could tell, it looked like a whirlpool filled with water that was even darker than the rest of the night sky. As the whirlpool churned, the *ratta-tat-tat* of the unseen snare drum continued. Jered looked around him, expecting to see soldiers in formation marching to the sound of the drum's cadence, but there was none. As the drumming gradually got faster, Jered saw the undulating black circle begin to spin faster. Although at first it was very subtle, Jered felt himself being pulled downward.

Chrissy heard a steady stream of static coming from the well. It sounded like a TV that wasn't tuned to a station. "Can you still hear me, honey?" she called out, doing her best to keep the fear out of her voice. What she figured Jered needed to hear was encouragement, not panic.

Jered was close enough to see his mother's desperate face. He kept looking ahead as he moved his arms faster and focused his thoughts on bridging the gap between them.

"That's it! You're doing it!" Chrissy exclaimed, clapping her hands. "Keep going!" Through the fog and water, she wasn't certain how far away he was, but clearly he was closer.

The speed of the drumming continued to increase. Despite the persistent pull towards the swirling darkness, Jered was managing to inch closer to his mother. Her son was close enough she could see his sparkling blue eyes through the dark water and fog. She thrusted her arms towards him, but the sharp static shock caused her to pull them back. Summoning her courage, she plunged both arms into the well. The fluid was cold and felt more like thick oil than water, causing her to feel nauseous.

The boy was getting tired. This was the longest he'd ever swam, and the gentle pull backwards was becoming more insistent. Two hands appeared through the darkness. They were tantalizingly close, and this gave him a surge of energy.

When the fingertips of their right hands brushed against each other, both curled their fingers, hoping to snare the other's hand.

"You're almost there!" Chrissy cried out, her arms and hands so cold they were throbbing with agonizing pain. They were close enough that Chrissy could hear Jered's breathing and he could understand what she was saying.

Just as he again reached out and brushed his mother's hand, something astounding occurred. At first Jered thought the steady drumming had simply become louder but then realized he was hearing the cadence through *both* of his ears. The boy pulled his hand back and touched his ear. It was still deformed, but for the first time he could hear clearly through it. The drumming was the most wonderful thing he'd ever heard. It was full of texture and depth. His young brain for the first time integrated what both ears heard into one glorious stereo sound.

"Has everyone been hearing things that sounded this big? This . . . full?" Jered thought.

He had no idea what he'd been missing until the moment he experienced complete sound for the first time. Jered's heart started beating in time with the drum. *Ratta-tat-tat.*

"Is this what Dad meant when he said this was a special place? Could anything happen here?" Jered wondered as he was pulled slowly backwards.

When he glanced over his shoulder at the whirlpool, it now looked as though he was looking through a colorful kaleidoscope. Gleaming red, orange, and yellow lights spun slowly inside the dark circle, like a hundred birthday candles. The sight invoked memories of all the birthday candles he'd blown out, and the same wish he made every year. Unfulfilled wish.

When her son's fingertips touched Chrissy's a second time, it felt like fluffy cotton balls brushing across her fingertips. Just as she felt the soft cotton touch her fingertips, it was gone. She tried to push her arms deeper into the pool, but the dark water wouldn't let her. Elbow deep in the water, she cried, "Come on, honey! Don't be scared: you're almost there!"

Her son looked serene and replied, "I'm not scared, Mom."

When she heard him speak, Chrissy was boosted by a surge of energy. "Right! Yes! You don't have to be afraid! Just come closer!"

In a calm, matter-of-fact voice, Jered replied, "I don't think . . . I'm allowed."

The thought of losing her son now that he was so close caused her to scream down the well. "No! Don't even say that! Just come a little closer! You can do it! Don't be afraid!"

When Jered looked up at her, he had a satisfied smile on his face. In a gentle and serene voice, he said, "I'm not scared, Mom. Don't worry about me. I've never done this before, but that doesn't mean I can't do it. It's like you said: I'm a big boy. I can take care of myself."

Fog once again obscured her view as he slowly retreated into the darkness. What Jered said next puzzled Chrissy for the remainder of her days. It was so strange that as the years passed, she began to doubt that he'd ever said, "Hopefully I'll find my parents here."

When she lost sight of him, she pleaded, "Wait. Wait! Jered!"

Shortly after Jered faded from view, the lights spinning in a circle on the floor dimmed, then went out, leaving Chrissy in a dark basement with nothing but the dim light from Rodney's workbench. Chrissy slapped the floor with her hands, calling out to her son over and over again. "Jered! Jered!" While repeatedly striking the floor, there was a loud snap from her left wrist, but she paid no attention. "Jered! Please, Jered! Come back!"

After pleading and sobbing for quite some time, Chrissy gently made circles on the floor with her hands, desperately trying somehow to coax the swirling pool to reappear. No matter what she did, only a plain gray floor stared up at her. She didn't know how long she remained lying on the floor. At some point she rested her cheek on the cold concrete, trying in vain to detect any miniscule amount of swirling movement just above the floor.

The despondent young mother remained in that position as a pool of her tears collected on the floor. The cheek lying on the concrete became soaked with her tears, leaving her face wet and cold. "Please, Jered. Don't leave me alone. I'll be so scared. Don't leave me."

After he saw his mother fade away, Jered was drawn downward. He floated into the kaleidoscope of lights. The drumming stopped, replaced with gentle tinkling noises like a wind chime makes. It seemed the sounds were coming from the lights.

His fingers and toes were the first places the boy felt a strong tingling sensation. When the tingling started, Jered again heard what sounded like fracturing glass, but this time it was a full, vibrant noise.

Jered felt a tingling sensation on his knuckles as if an insect was crawling on them. Holding up his hand, he saw himself slowly melting away. Jered wasn't the least bit frightened. He felt an abiding sense of contentment as he watched in curious wonder the skin and tissue of his arm gently willow away. A vivid memory popped into his head when he ate cotton candy at the Independence Day parade. The little boy thought fondly of how the freshly spun puff of sweet cotton candy simply melted away on his tongue. Jered mused that he was the pink wispy confection that was slowly becoming nothing.

When the skin and muscles dissolved, Jered saw his skeleton. As he looked at his bones, Jered thought that the people who'd created his glow-in-the-dark skeleton had done a pretty good job of drawing how the human skeleton looked in real life. Once the bones were nearly washed away and they were paper thin, he could see through them to the twinkling lights.

Before the last of the little boy with a talent for drawing melted away, he thought, "I hope my *real* parents will be able to find me here."

The essence of Jered was nothing more than a bead of ink dropped into a huge ocean. The splash it created existed for just a moment, then faded away.

For the following month, Chrissy spent most her time in the basement. She was often found by JoJo with her body curled around the portion of the cold cement floor where she'd last caught a glimpse of Jered. In the blink of an eye, her white knight and young prince were gone. Cruel Fate had inexplicably decided to take them away from her. The police set up roadblocks looking for the father who'd abruptly run off with his son, but Chrissy knew these efforts would fail. She didn't know where they'd gone, but she knew it was certainly beyond law enforcement's jurisdiction.

She didn't know how, but Chrissy remained convinced for the rest of her life that the scary skeletons were somehow to blame.

CHAPTER TWENTY-THREE

Seth

For some reason, eight-year-old Seth had a nagging suspicion that the people who were raising him might not really be his parents. Something just didn't feel right. It was like trying to fit a round peg into a square hole. Seth and his parents for the most part remained emotionally distant from each other. They seemed to him to be nothing but casually interested caretakers who expected Seth to entertain himself. Seth daydreamed about the possibility his *real* parents were out there somewhere. The boy envisioned his real parents being much more appreciative as to how clever and special he was.

Seeing other kids act nicey-nicey and lovey-dovey with their parents disgusted him. Anger began to boil inside of him when he saw children being joyfully embraced by parents. Why should *they* have such a close relationship with their parents, when Seth didn't even know where his parents were? When he saw kids running happily into the arms of parents after a school function or ball game, Seth secretly wished they'd fall and hurt themselves. It would be fun to watch the adults become frantic when their little angel had a bloody nose. Ha!

At times it appeared his custodial parents shared in his suspicion there'd somehow been an error in the newborn nursery. His "father" was fond using the phrase "No son of mine is going to . . ." Seth interpreted this to mean the man had a deep-seated hunch he possibly wasn't raising his true son. His "mother" told Seth innumerable times, "If you're ever going to be an upstanding member of the family, you need to . . ." Again, it seemed to Seth this was a veiled admission of her misgivings.

On top of everything, these people were always punishing him because of things Seth did or failed to do. It appeared to Seth that no matter what he did, he was in trouble. Maybe that was because they believed Seth didn't behave exactly as their *real* son would have.

When Seth became very angry, his head would throb, and he saw bright sparkles of light with each heartbeat. A few times Seth got so angry at them he yelled, "I don't think you're even my real parents, so you can't make me do anything!"

This prompted his father to bellow, "No son of mine . . . ," which kind of proved Seth's point.

Shortly after his eighth birthday, Seth was grounded. While his friends were enjoying a warm spring afternoon playing football, all Seth could do was watch them enviously from his bedroom window. One of the boy's yellow lab joined the fun, chasing the boys through the neighbor's back yard when one of them ran with the football.

Everyone was having a wonderful time. Except Seth. The more fun they had, the angrier Seth became. All he could do was seethe as he massaged the sides of his pounding head with his fingers. Why should they have so much fun? It wasn't fair. Seth wished a cloud would open and a sudden downpour would soak the boys until they were cold and miserable. Wouldn't that be keen? Of course, no rain came.

Seth wondered what else could bring the fun to an end. If one of the kids got hurt, everyone would probably go home. Standing at his bedroom window, he closed his eyes and smiled deviously as he contemplated what kind of injury would accomplish this. As he daydreamed, he heard the playful bark of the dog playing with the boys. This sound prompted Seth to focus his thoughts on the big yellow lab happily cavorting amongst the boys. It wasn't easy to

SKELETONS ARE NOT SCARY

do. The harder Seth concentrated, the more painful his headache became. He had to hold onto the windowsill for support.

"Bite! Bite!" Seth screamed in his head. He fantasized about somehow travelling from his bedroom to the dog's brain. In his imagination he pictured himself standing in front of a control panel covered with lots of buttons, switches, and blinking lights. Randomly he pushed some of the buttons, hoping to gain control over the dog. As he was doing this, he continued to shout in his head, "Bite! Bite!" Even with his eyes closed, Seth could feel the room spinning.

Seth opened his eyes when he heard one of the boys scream. One of the football players was cradling a bloody hand. Feeling lightheaded and nauseous, Seth sat down on his bed. Just keeping his eyes open was a struggle because the daylight was causing daggers of pain to plunge into his head. The pain quickly became so severe he couldn't look out the window any longer. Seth closed his eyes and laid down on the bed, covering his head with his pillow. Seth had had plenty of headaches during his short life, but nothing nearly severe as this one. Even though he was incapacitated by the pain, the boy was able to think about what had just happened.

"Did I just do that?" Seth thought to himself. "Did I make that dog bite? Could I do it again, or is this a one-time thing? Does it only work on dogs or can I somehow do the same with people?"

Well, there was only one way to find out for sure.

CHAPTER TWENTY-FOUR

Miss Kerri Moran 1982

A well-known saying is: another day, another dollar.

A less well-known saying is: another school year, another new set of problems.

After pulling into the parking lot, Miss Kerri Moran turned off the ignition but remained in the driver's seat. She stared blankly at the back of the elementary school, which was comprised of red, gray, and black bricks. There was no pattern to the bricks. It was all random.

How many times had she pulled into this parking lot and seen this same brick wall? She'd taught at the same school since graduating from college five years earlier, so she could probably calculate the exact number if she had the time or inclination to do so. Kerri had neither. She sighed at the thought of all the duties she was saddled with each new school year.

First on the agenda would be learning the names of her students. How many pupils had she taught? When she got out of college, she naively believed she'd always remember the names of all the students she'd ever taught. Now thinking back on it, she couldn't remember a quarter of the names of her first group of students and that was just five years ago. She, of course, would always remember one of them. She felt a girdle cinch around her chest and squeeze out some of her breath when she thought of Jered Barstow.

The grizzled veteran teachers told her during that first year she shouldn't become attached to her students. "They're only going to be with you for a year, then they're gone forever. Out of sight, out of mind," one of the older teachers advised. "If you get too attached to them, you'll burn yourself out quicker than a wad of newspaper thrown into a roaring fire."

Kerri hadn't listened. To the contrary, she vowed to be the teacher who'd be a significant influence on every student assigned to her. She'd tried so hard to be the ever-vigilant shepherd who'd protect her young lambs and guide them to pastures of success and happiness. But she failed. Horribly. One of the lambs somehow wandered away and was lost forever. Kerri had a little lamb, but she fell down on the job, so the lamb paid the ultimate price. And everywhere that Kerri went, her crushing guilt was sure to go.

She couldn't help but believe she'd somehow played a part in Jered's disappearance. Although she thought about it for countless hours, Kerri couldn't pinpoint exactly what she could've done to intervene and stop the tragedy from happening. This realization should have provided some solace, but it only intensified her guilt. Five years later it still gnawed at her heart.

Simply as a means of survival, she vowed thereafter she wouldn't . . . she *couldn't* get attached to the children. They were just livestock travelling along a processing line. She had a job to do, she did it, and then the little ones moved on to the next processing point. They'd be processed by another teacher, then passed along to the next, and so on.

She understood if she didn't construct a protective enclosure around her heart made up of red, gray, and black bricks, there'd eventually be nothing left of her except an empty husk. Each autumn she wrote the names of her children on an Etch-A-Sketch in her brain. As soon as the last day of school was over, she turned it over and shook it.

IN THE CIRCUIT COURT OF
UNIVERSITY CITY

Dr. Ford Freud,
Plaintiff, a Renowned
Individual,

vs.

J. A. Ford,
Defendant, an Individual
of Ill Repute.

PETITION FOR AWARD OF DAMAGES

Dr. Ford Freud (hereinafter referred to as Plaintiff) brings this legal cause of action against J. A. Ford (hereinafter referred to as Defendant) for slander, libel, slibel©, general torting, and the wrongful publishing of scandalous material, all of which has caused significant and irreparable damage to Plaintiff's heretofore pristine reputation.

STATEMENT OF THIS COURT'S JURISDICTION OVER THIS DISPUTE

The Court has legal jurisdiction over this legal dispute, as evidenced by previous cases this Court has accepted for adjudication. Such cases this Court has previously accepted jurisdiction over include, but are not limited to the following:

Buckeye Pride of Columbus Industries v. Grimes *(criminal mischief and constitutional rights).* Defendant's violent, and repeated acts of defacing Plaintiff's promotional vehicle known as "The Buckeye Pride Buggy" constitutes a crime, and the conviction for committing said crime did not infringe on Defendant's right to free speech, thus Defendant's indefinite incarceration at OSU [Ohio Stockade Utility] was appropriate.

State v. Sisters of Aurora *(admissibility of evidence at trial).* DNA is generally unobtainable from ethereal, or make-believe persons, thus DNA evidence cannot be used to prove the existence of such shadowy characters allegedly haunting the basement of Defendant's home, and any alleged DNA evidence purporting to do so is quite absurd, making it therefore inadmissible at trial pursuant to the legal canon *Sillius Non Admissiblius.*

In re: Living in Paradise, Inc. *(trademark & copyright law).* Defendant's attempt to incorporate and copyright the catchphrase "Ca-Caw" into its marketing materials was deemed inappropriate inasmuch as crows, ravens, and rooks have used the utterance "Ca-Caw" since time immemorial, thus precluding Defendant's attempt to gain exclusive rights to this phrase.

City of Shakopee v. Wegener *(land use restriction litigation).* Homeowner failed to remove Halloween decorations (including scary skeletons) in a timely manner. Defendant's attempt to remedy this situation by placing tinsel, and garland on the skeletons did not adequately transform eerie and macabre Halloween decorations into festive adornments appropriate for Christmas, thus homeowner was properly ordered to remove all instruments of fear/scariness from his property.

PLAINTIFF'S DEMAND FOR LEGAL REMEDIES

WHEREAS Defendant agreed to write books which highlighted the greatness of Plaintiff to the general public, and

WHEREAS Defendant failed to write any such books, having managed by deceit to convince a reputable publisher of impeccable reputation (Mascot Books) to print, and distribute three utterly absurd, untrue, and generally farcical stories not based in fact, and apparently nothing more than bizarre tales he made up in his pathological, warped imagination, and

WHEREAS Defendant had the audacity to write these three stories in such a way to make Plaintiff look unprofessional, and unskilled in his WHEREAS occupation, and

WHEREAS in Book #1, it was suggested the patient now exists in the dreams of other children; in Book #2 it was suggested the patient was spirited away by a monster; in Book #3 it was suggested the patient now has some kind of ethereal existence, and

WHEREAS Plaintiff has been damaged, injured, maimed, filleted, tortured, subjected to public evisceration, humiliated, broken out in an itchy red rash, lost sleep, lost the pleasure in life to which we are all entitled, and otherwise had his entire body, mind and soul as a whole damaged by Defendant, and

WHEREAS, for all of the reasons set forth in this properly, and skillfully drafted legal document, as well as additional charges which Plaintiff's counsel will come up with prior to trial, Plaintiff must pray to this honorable Court for an award of damages to Plaintiff in excess of one kajillion dollars, in an amount this Court deems proper, and just under these circumstances.

FURTHER, FURTHERAS, and WHEREAS, Plaintiff will be damaged by people reading these scandalous publications, Plaintiff seeks an order from this Court requiring that all copies of "The

Fordian Trilogy" be confiscated, and set on fire in a public square, courthouse parking facility, or public library so that no further persons will read any of these three horrific books.

CONCLUSION AND SUMMARY

Legal Counsel Further Sayeth Naught, as this is the true end to this sordid matter, and there is nothing, naught, null set, zero, and otherwise nada further left to say.

MALUS "LEX" LITIGO, ESQ.
Malus Lex Litigo, Esq.
Greecey & DeTestable, Attorneys at Law
10 Main Street, Suite 101
University City

ABOUT THE AUTHORS

DR. FORD FREUD, M.D., PhD., O.O.P.S., Civil Plaintiff

Amongst Dr. Freud's many endeavors is his desire for all children to be trained in his program of intensive pediatric psychiatry. The hope is that by doing so, children will stop exhibiting pathologic behaviors such as creating imaginary friends, performing boring and pointless Show-and-Tell presenta-

tions, and all activities premised on, "Let's pretend that..." Dr. Freud travels the globe, giving lectures so that others may be enlightened by his discoveries.

J. A. FORD, Uncivil Defendant

Amongst Mr. Ford's many endeavors is his desire to find out whether a scary skeleton is lurking inside his body. The hope of Mr. Ford is that if a skeleton is indeed concealed therein, it will not escape its corporal confines and try to choke him while he sleeps. Mr. Ford travels throughout the tri-county area, searching for an open-faced roast beef sandwich capable of bringing enough fleeting joy to momentarily silence the cacophony of voices constantly bickering inside his head.

ACKNOWLEDGMENTS

Once again, I want to thank my Beta readers for their invaluable input. The final product is due in part to their willingness to share their thoughts and be frank with their opinions. I am indebted to Craig Grimes, Bryant Paradis, Dawn Ford, and Rosetta Ford.

Thanks to my partners at Mascot Books. I am grateful for the work done by Claire Pask (editor), Matt Gonsalves (art and layout), and Naren Aryal (the big boss).

I also want to thank all of you who have shared this journey with me. At book signings and conventions, I have met a slew of people who accepted my invitation to take a stroll down a dark and tortuous path. I am humbled by your willingness to read my twisted stories.

Thanks to Paul Wegener for reprising his role as Dr. Freud for the author page photo.

My hope is that Mr. Poe would approve of all this.